D1472059

# O'Banion's Gift

Michael O'Rourke

*To Pat Flynn —*
*Best wishes!*
*Michael O'Rourke*
*6/07*

St. John's Publishing Company, Inc.

Opening Capone quote, see *The Gonif*, Morris Rudensky and Don Riley (Blue Earth, Minnesota, Piper Co., 1970), and *Capone: The Man and the Era*, Lawrence Bergreen (Simon & Schuster, 1994).

Copyright © 2003, Michael O'Rourke

First Edition

ISBN: 0-9744777-0-2

Published by: St. John's Publishing Company, Inc. in association with Chicago-Wetherby Press, 27 N. Wacker Drive, Suite 404, Chicago, IL 60606 (Wetherbook@aol.com).

Jacket design and photography by Peter Beck (www.peter@peterbeck.com)

Pre-press book production by North Star Press of St. Cloud, Inc.

Printed in Canada by Friesens.

For Tuny, always.

"We saw the world so differently, Gus and I. When at a party together, early on, the hostess made reference to the James brothers. My mind turned immediately to William and Henry, his to Frank and Jesse. I should have known then that our association would be troubled."

Riley McReynolds

"Those silly Irish bastards. They have more guts than sense. If we'd only hooked up, I could have been president."

Alphonse Capone

# 1

---

A LAVISH AFTERNOON SUN streamed through the windows of the den, making it hard to see the television screen clearly. Riley McReynolds moved his chair a few inches to the right and felt a searing pain in his upper back, the result of a recent injury. He gave out a small yelp, causing Tuffy, the family terrier, to jump from his lap.

The oversized TV peered out from its spot at the center of an oaken bookcase which covered a full wall of the room; it was surrounded by volumes chosen more for their decorative bindings than for their contents. On the top shelf was a row of artist's drawings depicting Riley in various courtroom scenes, rendered during high-profile criminal trials—robbery, kidnapping, murder—in which he had been the prosecuting attorney. Cameras weren't permitted in Minnesota courtrooms, then or now, and while he liked seeing his image on the six o'clock news, especially early in his career when he was on fire with righteousness, he never thought the artists had done him justice. He was sure he was better looking, and thinner, than the almost cartoonish figure at the center of these hurried drawings. On other days, though, depending on his mood and level of self-esteem, he seemed heroic in those portraits. But on days like today, when he dragged in body and in spirit, he avoided eye contact with his younger self, for he knew that the sight of those chalky, pastel images would land like a bad yearbook photo.

He sat deep in a heavily cushioned chair covered in a lively plaid fabric. The chair stood less than six feet from the bookcase and was flanked by a small cabinet on which sat a telephone and accompanying caller-ID, that morning's newspaper, and a doctor's brochure illustrating exercises for the upper back. Inside the cabinet were essential articles like writing instruments, legal pads, paperclips, Post-it Notes, his electric razor, and a box of Milky Ways.

While loosely palming the channel changer in his right hand, he watched the last scene of an *Andy Griffith Show* rerun in which Barney Fife was using a reconditioned motorcycle, with an attached sidecar, as a traffic control vehicle for the Mayberry Police Department. As always, the sun was shining in Mayberry and no one was being deliberately mean to anybody else. At times like this, Riley loved these old reruns; they seemed to pick him up and convey him to another place, timeless and safe, far from the ugly divorce case he was handling under protest—a case in which he'd much rather be on the other side.

It was true that he had faced that same problem at other times in his quarter-century as a lawyer, but for some reason this time was the worst. As a prosecutor, and briefly as a defense lawyer, he had dealt with crimes involving every known species of cruelty and barbarism. But for some reason those cases hadn't produced in him the peculiar stress he was experiencing in the Tanzdahl divorce case. He thought about how much he'd rather be in Barney Fife's sidecar.

When the program ended, he surfed the cable menu, bouncing from channel to channel. This produced a scolding from his wife, Betsy. She turned to him and said, "You are such an ass."

Betsy rarely gave herself over to this kind of language, no matter what the provocation. His hypochondria sometimes got to her, all those imaginary illnesses that seemed to befall him during times of stress, diseases ranging from cancer and hepatitis to brain tumors and kidney failure. But as irritating as his health complaints could be, she had grown accustomed to them over the years. But his compulsive channel changing was something else altogether.

Riley watched the lines around her eyes tighten as she glared at him across the den, holding her hand, palm up, in his direction. It was a look that promised terrible consequences if he didn't stop what he was doing. Chastened, he handed her the clicker in the style of a defeated general relinquishing his sword.

Even when in a snit, Betsy was as pretty to him as the high-school cheerleader she had once been. They had passed through childhood and adolescence together; he had even been there when her braces came off. They were just childhood companions, buddies, in the early years, but then at age fourteen she grew these adorable little breasts. And her legs, which he had previously taken no notice of, grew long and straight and led upward to a perfectly shaped fanny that swayed magically when she walked. The sight of all that new equipment caused a tingling sensation in places he had hardly known existed. Suddenly no longer the neighborhood kid with whom he climbed trees, built forts, and read comic books, she took on a strange, mythical power, sort of like the girl who had played Helen of Troy in the movie they had seen at the Radio City Theatre in third grade.

In the twenty-eight years they had been married, channel surfing—or "clicker abuse" as she called it—was about the only thing that put them at serious odds. It had become more of a problem recently, since he left his position as an executive at the old-line Lindbergh Life & Casualty Company over a cover-up by a greedy and dishonest CEO. Feeling he should take a rest and horse around for a while before jumping back into the working world, Riley spent most of his time at home, watching TV and following Betsy around in her daily routine, offering advice on all aspects of modern housekeeping. She was a good sport about all that, but when he started traipsing after her to the supermarket, reading aloud the carcinogenic properties of the items she was putting in the shopping cart, she had had enough.

So he succumbed to a long-standing offer from Cosgrove & Levi and returned to the law. His present roster of clients consisted mostly of healthcare executives who had become lost in the Byzantine labyrinth of federal regulations so broadly drawn that, along with the real criminals, they often swept the merely negligent or confused into their net. This was a gentlemanly, white-collar form of criminal law, a welcome contrast to the chaos and violence of the urban criminal courts, and even a nice change from his brief foray into big business at The Lindbergh, where some of the senior executives, though better dressed, were hardly more law abiding than those he used to encounter on the felony arraignment calendar.

Crunching his aching back deeper into the chair, he let out another small cry of pain. He was sitting at a leftward tilt, the only configuration that provided even a small measure of comfort. Two days before, he had strung a seventy-five-pound punching bag from the basement ceiling to relieve the mounting tension of the Tanzdahl case. He put on a pair of gloves and danced around the bag, ducking and weaving, throwing jabs, hooks and roundhouses at a target that didn't hit back. Boxing had been a part of growing up in his family of four boys and a father who had once been a semi-professional fighter. The basement "heavy bag" in their large Kenwood home had been a release valve for much of the testosterone that otherwise would have been expended outside the home. So it seemed natural for Riley, at this stressful time, to resort to a release valve learned as a boy.

But he had given no thought to the strain that that kind of workout places on a body in its late forties. In consequence, a disc high in his back was seriously destabilized. The initial pain was sharp but tolerable and gave no hint of what was to follow. But by eleven o'clock that night he could hardly move without excruciating pain. A midnight visit to the emergency room confirmed a partial herniation. A two-hour soak in a scalding hot bath, combined with a chunky orange pain pill ordered up by the doctor temporarily dulled the most frightening sensations. Now he was in a state that might best be described as ordinary agony.

Betsy was unmoved. "Yes, darling," she said, rolling her eyes as she left the room.

"Where are you going?" he whined as the phone next to his chair started to ring. In a stiff, Boris Karloff-like motion, he turned to his right and picked up the receiver without looking at the caller-ID. "Hello," he said in a voice tinged with self-pity.

"Good morning, Mr. McReynolds," replied an officious female voice. "Please hold for Mr. Tanzdahl."

*Oh perfect*, he thought. He wanted to hang up, but that wouldn't be a good idea here. Gus Tanzdahl was the largest and most profitable account at Cosgrove & Levi. So, instead of hanging up, Riley reached for his electric razor, and turned it on close to the receiver. Then, with a raised voice, he said, "Sorry, we've got a bad connection." After a short interval, he disconnected and left the phone off the hook.

The Tanzdahl divorce file was not something Riley had sought. In fact, the assignment violated the deal he had made with the firm. When first negotiating a partnership, he had been assured by Ladge Wilkaster, the managing partner, that he could structure his practice any way he wanted. Business crime, corporate investigations, tax evasion, no problem. Those clients were all welcome, for there were few areas of practice more lucrative than the point where big business intersected the criminal law. Haughty, arrogant executives who scared secretaries, middle managers, and caddies nearly senseless—men who from the safety of their board rooms and country clubs used war metaphors about "taking no prisoners" and "cutting their nuts off"—went suddenly leaky with terror at the prospect of a member of the underclass having his way with them in an eight-by-ten prison cell. By the time these golf course warriors got to Riley's office, the martial metaphors and cocky arrogance had given way to a sphincter-quivering docility. They couldn't wait to write big checks to Cosgrove & Levi for the services of the former ace prosecutor Riley McReynolds. And the fees came up front. In cash.

But in spite of the managing partner's assurances that he could choose his own clients, it wasn't ninety days before Ladge Wilkaster and two other members of the firm's management committee showed up in Riley's office and explained why an exception to the deal had become necessary. It seemed that a divorce file had been opened involving the firm's most important client, Gus Tanzdahl, the CEO of Tanzdahl Industries, which accounted for a whopping thirty-seven percent of Cosgrove & Levi's gross revenues and nearly fifty percent of its net profits.

"But I don't do domestic work," Riley had protested. "I haven't handled a divorce case since my legal-aid days twenty-five years ago. And the only family cases I handled at the prosecutor's office were parental rights terminations . . . you know, cases where the state had to separate children from junkies and psychopaths." He looked around at the committee members. "Those were criminal cases, gentlemen, conducted in an entirely different manner. Gus Tanzdahl needs a domestic relations lawyer."

Ladge Wilkaster had leaned forward in his chair and, with great earnestness, pointed a finger in Riley's direction the way people do when they think they're about to say something really important. "And he *shall* have a family lawyer, Riley. Sara Hall, our brightest young associate and the author of sixteen published articles on matrimonial law, has been assigned to the case. But in this instance she will be second-chairing the veteran Riley McReynolds, who just happens to be a personal friend of most of the judges in this district, including the current chief judge of the family court."

Ladge arched his eyebrows in triumph. The other two partners—desk lawyers who had never seen the inside of a courtroom and who Riley wouldn't trust to handle a traffic ticket—nodded their agreement.

Riley folded his hands on the desk and looked across at Ladge Wilkaster. "Let me tell you something else that bears on this subject, Ladge. I know Gus Tanzdahl. I've known him, on and off, for thirty-five years. Trust me, I'm not the guy for this case." He then paused briefly and looked out the window, tilting his head reflectively. "I know people . . . good people . . . who think that Gus is the biggest prick in the state. Maybe in the whole world."

And, indeed, Riley did know Gus well enough to dread the prospect of representing him, especially in an emotion-charged divorce case with a young child involved. They had first met in college, before Gus grew rich and powerful as the result of a software patent he had acquired under less than honest circumstances. That was when Gus was just a short, fat kid with a bad complexion and a reputation for being the biggest bullshitter on campus. His ceaseless strivings to join the in-crowd had made him the object of fun and ridicule, and even an occasional roughing up.

Unlike most of his peers, Riley had put Gus's behavior down to a deep insecurity resulting from an emotionally deprived childhood that included a violent father and an alcoholic mother. On more than one occasion, he had saved Gus from episodes of bullying at the hands of thoughtless frat boys having wicked fun at his expense.

Upon graduation, Gus became a spectacularly successful aluminum siding salesman, then a high ticket, if somewhat pedestrian, career for an enterprising young man. In 1975 he married his first wife, the frumpy daughter of a large and conventional St. Paul family. Three children were born of that union before it degenerated into a series of nasty recriminations and accusations of infidelity against Gus.

With the acquisition of the software patent, Gus's already sizeable net worth grew exponentially. When he reached $25,000,000, his ego broke the bonds of earth and soared to heights rarely seen in these parts. With the status that attaches itself to great wealth came an assortment of counterfeit friends and camp followers who provided Gus with the validation he had so long sought. He even bought a stretch limousine and hired a driver and bodyguard. No one had ever accused Gus of good taste, but this went beyond everyone's worst expectations and prompted Riley, at the time, to explain to Gus that in Minnesota limousines were used only by pimps, rock stars, and prom-bound high school seniors in white tuxedos.

But Gus was not one to take advice. With his fortune assured and his first wife safely discarded, he married his present wife, Ellen, whom he met during a round of golf at a country club where she was employed as a waitress and lifeguard. At the time of their marriage Ellen was a luscious twenty-one-year old with an eighth-grade education and a starry-eyed infatuation for the short, heavy-set man in the polyester golfing ensemble. That he was loud, obnoxious, and nearly twice her age, did nothing to lessen her ardor.

In the initial phases of that marriage, Ellen had been like a breath of spring to Gus's middle-age vanity, providing adulation and a body that fired his aging loins. But as infatuation waned and she became the mother of a screaming infant, the social awkwardness and Valley Girl bad grammar that had once so enchanted him became acutely embarrassing. She didn't fit in with the old-line business interests he was trying to cultivate, not to mention the sophisticated wives of the industrial barons whose social set he longed to join. Her plebeian idiosyncrasies, once thought girlishly charming, came to be viewed as cheap and common, and a more than adequate pretext for her banishment.

Besides, Gus's romantic yearnings had attached themselves to a replacement—one with a congenital spot on the
social register. Trudi Hansdale's family was part of the landed gentry in the area, striking a welcome contrast to Gus's
family of origin, which, socially speaking, was just a notch or
two above the Clampetts.

So it was time for Gus to set aside his embarrassing young
wife and four-year-old son with a minimum of scandal and
disruption. And what better place to turn for assistance in
that delicate task than the offices of his principal outside law
firm, Cosgrove & Levi, and their influential new partner, his
old schoolmate Riley McReynolds.

"And what's more," Riley had protested to Ladge Wilkaster
in that fateful meeting, "I've got a keen eye for crooked activity, and it wouldn't surprise me if Gus is dirty in some of his
dealings. That would put the firm in a bad spot, Ladge. As a
director of his company, you should know that. You could run
into professional conflicts yourself."

Riley thought that would put an end to the matter, get him
cleanly off the hook. But Ladge Wilkaster just smiled indul-
gently. "None of that matters, Riley. Gus specifically asked
for you. He said he's known and admired you for years, and
that you two have been good friends going all the way back
to college." Ladge then winked and again pointed at Riley.
"You may not think much of him, but he likes you a lot. When
I told him you weren't handling any domestic cases, he said
that there was nothing more to talk about, that he wouldn't
take no for an answer."

Wilkaster stood up, straightened his shoulders, and
squinted earnestly. "Gus will move the whole damn account
if we turn him down on this. And let me remind you that his
fiancée, Trudi Hansdale, is a first cousin of Bayard Van
Studdiford, our second largest client account. If Gus walks—
and especially if he takes Van Studdiford with him—this
firm will implode, cease to exist. The good lawyers would
land on their feet, of course. But our ordinary employees,

two-hundred of them—small people who need the work—would be out on the street."

With the skill of a salesman who knew how to go for the soft spots, Wilkaster then went in for the close. He leaned on Riley's desk, lowering himself to eye-level. "I hope your sensibilities about which clients are worthy of your representation are not so refined that you'd be willing to put a bunch of low-level employees out on the street."

One of the other members of the management committee looked ruefully down at the floor and said in a suspiciously rehearsed tone, "That's a bit of cheap shot, Ladge. We all know that Riley would be the last guy in the world to put the firm's little folk at risk."

The third committee member, an investment lawyer with inherited wealth, a man who wouldn't give the time of day to little folk of any description, quietly nodded his agreement.

Riley felt himself falling for the pitch—or at least cornered by its logic. Gus was just the kind of guy to exact a terrible revenge on Cosgrove & Levi should his demand not be met. And if he pulled his accounts, the firm—which had unwisely wed its survival to the Tanzdahl relationship—would crater. This was just the kind of petty retribution for which Gus was famous.

So, in spite of his reservations about Gus Tanzdahl and getting involved in an ugly domestic case, there was no way out of this assignment short of resigning from the firm. And that would have cost him a fortune in the form of a forfeited capital account, an account in which he had just invested most of his family's life savings. For many years, Betsy had put up with the financial privations attached to public service, but she was glad when it was over. It was time to make some real money to provide for college tuition and a more comfortable life for the family. When Riley bid farewell to The Lindbergh Life & Casualty Company and its corrupt CEO, leaving behind the prospect of substantial wealth, she was disappointed but understanding. Now they had invested the family's resources in an old-line law firm from which separation would spell near-bankruptcy. That she would not understand.

Anyway, apart from Betsy's feelings, he was not prepared to go that far. Being high-minded was a wonderful thing—but not at this price. He told himself that he was acting out of concern for the firm's ordinary employees by acceding to Gus Tanzdahl's demand, but when all was said and done, he knew it was more about the money.

The assignment made, that very afternoon he was summoned to appear at the world headquarters of Tanzdahl Industries, where Gus and his senior executives were housed in regal splendor. The corporate headquarters of Tanzdahl Industries rose twelve stories from a wooded site near Lake Minnetonka. Riley and Sara Hall, the eager, attractive and highly trained thirty-one-year-old family lawyer assigned to assist on the case, sat in the waiting area of the executive floor for twenty minutes beyond the time set for their meeting with Gus. Riley passed the time surveying the expensive art works hanging on the walls of the two-story reception room, smiling to himself over Gus's waiting game. It didn't matter how long a time-keeping lawyer was kept waiting; the meter just kept spinning at $400 an hour. The last laugh always went to the attorney.

As he sat admiring the receptionist—a young woman of arresting good looks and seductive smile—an older woman of rigid bearing appeared in the doorway and wordlessly signaled for Riley and Sara to follow her.

The offices in the building were expensively appointed in the modern corporate style, but Gus Tanzdahl's suite was in a class by itself. Occupying a full wing of the top floor, it consisted of a series of chambers of varying sizes, including a billiard room, a fully equipped workout space, a sauna, two conference rooms, individual offices for Gus's bodyguards (known in corporate parlance as "executive protectors"), and a series of connected offices over which his executive assistant—a middle-aged, conservatively dressed woman—reigned supreme.

The assistant met them at the end of the long hallway, standing before a set of heavy double doors leading to Gus's personal office. She swung open the doors and gestured for them to enter.

The office was a long, broad expanse, heavily carpeted in dark maroon and flanked on its borders by arches and pillars which seemed, even to Riley's unschooled eye, to be incompatible with the building's overall motif. The air was thick with cigar smoke. At the end of the room sat a giant desk behind which Gus was enthroned in a high-backed leather chair. The desk stood on a raised platform, making Gus appear, in the style of J. Edgar Hoover, to be two or three inches taller than his five-foot-six height.

As Gus continued talking into one of the three color-coded phones stationed on his desk, he gestured for his guests to be seated in the chairs facing him. The chairs were deeply cushioned, causing the visitor to sink a little. At just over six feet, Riley was now roughly eye-to-eye with his vertically challenged client. As he set his briefcase on the adjoining table Riley was reminded of how large a part Gus's small stature had always played in his behavior and need to dominate. That probably amounted to "sizeism," the latest "ism" denounced by the speech fascists, but he didn't much care. Nevertheless, he silently vowed to steer clear of the topic, for Tanzdahl Industries was rumored to have fired a company employee overheard remarking that Gus was short enough to play an extra in *Snow White*.

While waiting for Gus to complete his phone call, Riley scanned the large, overdecorated room. One wall was covered by an enormous mahogany breakfront with shelves stocked with books of varying sizes and a series of plaques awarded to Gus over the years in exchange for charitable contributions made by the company foundation. His eyes came to rest on an empty space in the middle shelf. He could tell that the recently vacated space had once held pictures of Gus's wife Ellen and their four-year-old son Josh. There was a ghostly feel to that once-honored spot, now lonely and abandoned. In spite of the shallowness of the Tanzdahl marriage, the sight produced in Riley a small rush of sadness.

Behind Gus's desk, illuminated by an attached light, hung a portrait of the Tanzdahl executive jet. A sleek and elegant Gulfstream V, it had cost the company's shareholders thirty-five million dollars, maybe more. In this day and age, no self-respecting corporate chieftain could be without a private jet, which in the loathsome calculus of corporate America had replaced expensive automobiles as the metaphorical proxy for executive manhood.

On the wall opposite the desk was a large glass panel that Riley initially took to be an over-sized aquarium but on closer inspection turned out to be one side of a swimming pool that had been built into the roof of the building. This peculiar sight brought to mind a story that had circulated a couple of years earlier about Gus having naked women swim in a rooftop pool while he and his entourage admired their kicks and strokes from the comfort of his office. Riley felt a small rush of guilty prurience as he wondered if the knockout receptionist at the front desk was among Gus's aquatic delights.

Gus was now chuckling lustily into the blue phone with Trudi Hansdale, the society woman who, upon completion of his divorce, was slated to become the third Mrs. Tanzdahl. Trudi, too, had been at school with Gus and Riley, but in those days she wouldn't have so much as looked at the likes of Gus Tanzdahl.

When the call light began blinking on the adjacent red phone, without breaking stride Gus picked it up with his other hand and, pressing the mouthpiece of the blue phone against his shirt, began cursing violently at some hapless Tanzdahl manager over the terms of a contract renewal. While the manager abjectly pleaded his case, Gus returned to the blue phone and recommenced a lewd and whispered dialogue with Trudi, heavy on sexual references and low, salacious laughter. Just as suddenly he returned to the red phone and again started screaming obscenities at the manager.

In the midst of this performance he looked up at Riley and winked.

Though he wasn't prepared to conclude that Gus had orchestrated this exercise solely for his benefit, Riley also didn't consider the timing to be pure coincidence. He and Sara could have been kept waiting in the lobby a few minutes more while these phone calls were concluded, but that would have deprived Gus of his chance to strut his stuff for an audience he had long wanted to impress. It was vintage Gus. And it had the added benefit of signaling that he, rather than Riley, would call the shots in the divorce case.

Gus finally concluded his phone call. "Riley, you dog, how the hell are you?" he shouted as he reached across the large mahogany desk and grabbed Riley's hand.

Sara Hall rose from her chair and extended her hand toward Gus, which he seemed more to fondle than shake as he looked her up and down. "Whoa, I bet the boys at the firm love you," he said.

Riley looked down in embarrassment. Sara just smiled, accentuating her rather attractive dimples. She issued no reprimand, verbal or otherwise. She knew the importance of the Tanzdahl Industries account to the firm and seemed to welcome the chance to strike a rapport with the company's CEO. Overlooking a little coarseness was a small price to pay for the career advancement she might experience if Gus's favor were to fall upon her.

Gus then returned to his seat and punched the intercom. "Tell Harv to come over," he said to his secretary, leaning into the small box.

Presently, a short, heavy-set man with a large, pale face and a pointy hairline scurried into the room, making a shallow bow in Gus's direction. He was formally dressed in coat and bow tie. A brief introduction established that Harvey Aingren was Gus's "chief of staff."

At Gus's signal the group took seats around a large circular table in a corner of the room close to the sunken swimming pool. It occured to Riley that if the glass panel were to break, they'd all be drowned. Gus started in on his evaluation of the divorce case. According to him, this "ungrateful tramp Ellen" had conned him into marrying her nine years earlier, and in spite of having assured him orally that she would renounce any share of his wealth in the event of a split up, she was now demanding half his net worth, none of which she had any part in creating. "She's just a greedy little bitch who's trying to rip me off," he said, turning to Harvey for confirmation.

"You got that right, Gus," said Harvey as he wiped beads of perspiration from his forehead.

Gus then leaned forward in his seat, his arms crossed on the table before him. His expression seemed to soften. "Of course, I'm willing to provide her with a generous allowance, maybe five thousand a month, and she can keep the car and the jewelry I gave her. And she can stay in the house until the kid is eighteen. I mean, I'm not an unreasonable man."

Presumably the "kid" Gus was referring to—the issue of his loins—had a name, but either Gus didn't remember it or found its recitation distasteful.

Riley looked down at his notes, trying not to betray his feelings. Sara shifted in her seat, straightened her short skirt, and nodded in Gus's direction.

Harvey Aingren stared admiringly at Gus. "You've been more than generous with her, Gus. There's no doubt about that."

Riley knew that no matter how bad the present wife might be, no matter how much damaging evidence they might be able to marshal against her, in the absence of an enforceable prenuptial agreement she was basically entitled to half of the assets accumulated during the marriage. Tanzdahl Industries—in which Gus personally owned eighteen percent of the common stock—had undergone spectacular growth over the last several years. And because the company was publicly traded, the market value of that stock was as accessible as the morning newspaper. At the opening of the market that day, for example, Gus's interest was valued at fifty million dollars, a number sharply in excess of the ten-million-dollar valuation appearing on the sworn financial statements he had prepared at around the time of his marriage to Ellen.

Riley took a deep breath and looked across the table. "Gus, let me give you some bad news. You're about to lose almost half of your net worth, plus being assigned a long-term child support obligation that will be substantial. The law establishes certain presumptions, and one of them is that assets acquired during a marriage, other than by gift or inheritance, will be split evenly when the marriage is dissolved."

Gus leaped from his chair and came tearing around to Riley's side of the table. Harvey lifted his legs to clear a path. Riley sat calmly with his notes resting on his lap, his eyes focused straight ahead. These sorts of client histrionics were more tiresome than upsetting, something to be endured.

Gus stopped just short of reaching Riley. He glared down at him. "That bitch never lifted a finger to help this company. All she ever did was sit in the sun and go to the beauty shop and yoga classes and psychotherapy and talk on the phone to her half-witted sister in Des Moines. She didn't even act as a hostess for company entertainment because she was too dumb to be of any use to me. And then when she got bored, she stopped taking her birth control pills and got knocked up so she could get her hooks into me for a lifetime." He now looked over at Harvey. "It was sex under false pretenses, that's what it was. And then she refused to get an abortion when I told her to. That proves her bad faith."

Harvey nodded, sharing his boss's outrage. "You got that right, Gus," he snorted.

Sara stared up at Gus but said nothing.

Riley didn't move from his seat or even look up. He just focused his gaze on Gus's empty chair. When Gus stopped shouting, Riley calmly started up where he had left off. "Anyway, Gus, maybe the law shouldn't be as it is, but we have to take it as we find it. And the issue of her not making a contribution to the success of the company will have very little effect on the outcome. The law generally assumes that a spouse who stays at home is a supporting partner in the family and is, therefore, entitled to one-half of the fruits of any financial gains during the marriage."

Gus looked over at Sara, who timidly nodded agreement with Riley's analysis. She could hardly do otherwise; it was she who had briefed Riley on the law as they drove to the meeting.

Gus leaned back on the front edge of the table, knocking off a bookend and causing a row of ornate volumes to spill to the floor. Harvey scurried to pick them up.

Gus looked down at Riley. "What if Ellen agrees to take less, like the exact amount I'm offering? Will the court approve that?"

Riley and Sara both nodded affirmatively. Riley then said, "But who in her right mind would walk away from the kind of money we're talking about here?"

"She might," said Gus with a devious smile. He shifted his eyes to Harvey, who smiled back. "Ellen was a bit of a tramp when she was younger. I mean a real slut. And I don't think she'd like to have her past come out in court." Again he looked over at Harvey. "What do you think, Harv?"

Harvey's eyes widened theatrically. "Nooo, I don't believe she would."

Riley looked back and forth between Gus and Harvey. "I wouldn't get my hopes up on that account, either. This is a no-fault divorce state."

"That's right," interjected Sara. "She could have been working the Shriners Convention last week, and it wouldn't affect the property distribution."

Riley winced. *The Shriners convention?*

Gus turned to Sara and smiled admiringly. "I think I'm going to like your style," he said. "But what I'm saying is that even though 'working the Shriners Convention' wouldn't

17

matter in and of itself, it would mean that she's not a very fit mother, wouldn't it?"

Riley now saw what he was up to. It was not uncommon for wealthy husbands to contest child custody for the sole purpose of scaring the mother into renouncing her full share of the marital estate. And the younger the child, the more often the strategy worked. In this case, if Gus were correct about Ellen having had a racy past, there would be legitimate grounds to have it out with her on the custody issue. A wave of nausea passed through him. This was why he hated divorce cases.

"But, Gus," he finally said, "You don't seem to care much about the child . . . and we've had no instructions up to this time to contest custody."

Gus ignored the question. "That kid is everything to Ellen. She'll fold like a house of cards as soon as she finds out that the social worker evaluating custody just might get certain information about her past."

Riley's eyes narrowed. "But a child can't—or shouldn't—be used for financial leverage in a divorce."

Gus looked away, walked over to the window, and gazed down on the elaborate gardens surrounding the Tanzdahl headquarters building. His expression turned solemn, and he seemed almost to be blinking back tears. "No, no, I don't mean that. Don't get me wrong, Riley, I'm a good father. I love my son with all my heart . . . and I feel an obligation to see that he doesn't end up with a whore and a junkie as his custodial parent." His face was now a mask of fatherly tenderness.

Harvey nodded at Gus and then turned to Riley. "Gus is right, Riley. He's a hell of a good father. He loves all his kids."

The whole scene was so staged that Riley half expected someone to cue up an orchestra.

Returning to his desk, Gus began opening the morning mail. Without looking up, he said casually, "You put in a demand for custody, Riley. Those are my instructions. Never mind about the rest of it."

\* \* \*

SINCE THAT INITIAL meeting, things had only gotten worse—round-the-clock phone calls, unreasonable demands, unfair criticisms, manic displays of temper, and always the scent of dishonesty, both in the information Gus was supplying and in the agenda he was trying to advance. Among the many crimes he was now accusing his wife of were "prostitution," "drug dealing," and the most explosive, "lewd conduct involving a minor." Not one of these charges had been raised before Ellen Tanzdahl's share of the estate had been calculated, making Gus's purported shock over her unfitness as a mother more than a little suspect. Nevertheless, the claims would have to be checked out, one by one, through the firm's investigators.

Repeated attempts to withdraw from the case, using every excuse Riley could concoct, had been met with flat-out refusals from both Gus and Ladge. And despite Sara Hall being the family law expert, Gus pretty much refused to deal with her directly, treating her gender and relative youth as disabilities.

For a guy who liked just about everyone, Riley was coming uncomfortably close to hating Gus Tanzdahl. The tension and stress mounted fast, eating at him like a toxic chemical. And, as at other times of life when stress had been laid upon him in such large portions, he turned not to ordinary escapes like golf or booze or meditation or tranquilizers, but rather to TV reruns, old movies, and historical documentaries. They seemed to pick him up and deliver him to another time and place, to a world of black and white, of unshaded right and wrong. Just moments before he would have stepped through the television set—right into the Village of Mayberry—if it was possible. He especially loved the historical documentaries, those precious bits of archival footage in which real human beings, most now dead, moved about the screen to the beat of matters no longer important.

According to his mother, this taste for the past, this odd, ethereal approach to life, was the product of an undisciplined imagination, plain and simple. She had scolded him as a child for his daydreaming and lack of attention to important things like school lessons and summer jobs. At least once a year in grade school his mother and father would sit in the principal's office, with a gaunt Sister St. Lillian stationed between them. From his chair on the other side of the table, they looked like a senate investigating committee. They wondered aloud why a boy with such a fine mind could fluctuate so wildly in his school work, one marking period getting all "A's," the next all "D's." In fourth grade, they thought the problem might be a crush he had on Sister St. Joan, the young novice from Winona. But the pattern continued into fifth grade, when his teacher weighed 240 pounds and had a long black hair growing out of a mole on her chin. Not the stuff of boyhood crushes.

These parent-teacher conclaves never bothered him. He adored his parents and was as interested in his own oddities as they were. He even liked Sr. St. Lillian, and he was about the only kid in the school who did.

"It's because I'm searching," he said to them in second grade, though his views had not been sought and he didn't know exactly what "searching" meant. It was the best he could come up with to describe what seemed to be a small empty space in his heart, a space that was at least temporarily filled by his mental wanderings.

By the time he and Betsy were in college, she had found common cause with his parents, warning that if he didn't get his feet on the ground, she'd take the fanny he so admired and find some other boy to grow old with. But those were idle threats, and he knew it. And she knew he knew it. The two of them had been almost a single unit their whole lives, hardly knowing where one started and the other left off.

Riley checked to be sure that Betsy was out of hearing range before he clicked over to the History Channel for an afternoon documentary, a long historical account of the rise and fall of Al Capone, the infamous rackets king of Chicago in the 1920s, the most famous of all American gangsters. He had been looking forward to today's offering all week.

The well-dressed, thuggish men caught on the scratchy celluloid of the documentary moved about the screen in short, choppy motions, alive again in 1996 in his suburban den. Chemicals in his brain began firing at the sight. He twitched a little as he felt the presence of the figures on the screen through the silent membrane of the ancient film. It was a wonderful escape, a doorway to another world. He momentarily forgot all about the pain in his back and about Gus Tanzdahl.

The sounds of a neighbor's lawn mower mixed discordantly with machine gun bullets exploding from the TV as the documentary told of the rise of the Capone Mob and the brutality with which it eliminated rival gangsters. This was somewhat familiar territory. His father had been fascinated by the Capone saga when Riley was growing up, following everything relating to the dashing and dangerous Chicago Mob. But Riley was just a child at the time, and crime was adult business, much like the atomic bomb and communists in the State Department were adult business.

His father would have loved this documentary, Riley mused, for it told in considerable detail the story of the early Chicago prohibition experience. About how Capone had formed strategic alliances with other gangs, trying to keep peace long enough for all the players to make a reasonable profit. About how he and his peace-loving partner Johnny Torrio just couldn't get their rivals to be nice—men like the Sicilian Genna brothers and the hot-headed Irishman, Dion O'Banion, the powerful and mischievous Northsider who was the model upon which Hollywood based its most enduring gangster portrayals, ranging from James Cagney playing Tommy Powers in *Public Enemy* to Robert Shaw playing Doyle Lonergan in *The Sting*. It was said that, in preparation for his part in *Public Enemy*, Jimmy Cagney spent hours before the mirror replicating O'Banion's movements and speech patterns.

According to the documentary, Dion "Deanie" O'Banion was a study in contrasts, on the one hand a devoutly religious former choir boy who tended lovingly to tulips and roses in his florist shop on North State Street, a light tenor who crooned out sentimental Irish ballads so sweet and moving that even his gangster confederates teared over, and a man of enormous personal generosity who distributed food and money to the widows and orphans of Chicago's North Side. But he was also the ruthless gang chieftain who had bootlegged, hijacked, extorted and murdered his way to the top rungs of the Chicago rackets.

O'Banion's boyish face appeared on the screen, bringing to mind the sweet countenance of so many of the career criminals Riley had prosecuted over the years. Often little more than teenagers, they projected that peculiar blend of mama's boy and social rebel that formed the signature of the criminal sociopath. For all their charm, to a man they possessed a finely distilled rage that with the thinnest provocation could break through a warm and sentimental exterior into a murderous rage. Such was the case with O'Banion. You could see it in his soft, smiling face, the face of an angel that could turn killer in an awful instant.

According to the documentary, it was inevitable that O'Banion and Capone would one day enter into a death match, and so they did. The precipitating event was a dispute over the loss of a North Side brewery they jointly controlled, a dispute in which O'Banion was the initial winner when he suckered Capone and Torrio into cashing out his investment just before the brewery was seized in a prohibition raid of which he had received advance notice. Capone was hurt and disappointed by this betrayal and gave expression to those feelings by sending a team of hit men over to Schofield's flower shop, where they put six bullets into Deanie.

Just at that moment in the documentary, the phone rang again. Irritated, he turned and checked the Caller ID: "Tanzdahl Industries— Executive Offices."

His heart sank and his knee bounced nervously as he considered whether to do his duty and talk to Gus Tanzdahl or
to keep his head in 1920s Chicago. He really didn't want to
talk about the divorce now—not now when Dion O'Banion
lay dead on the floor of his flower shop.

So he let the call roll to voice mail and returned to the TV,
where Deanie's casket was being borne by his grieving lieutenants to its last resting place at Mt. Carmel Cemetery, not
far from some of the guys he had personally knocked off.
Deanie's widow and father led the procession. Flanking the
casket on both sides, moving in choppy motions on the gauzy,
blistered film, were some of Chicago's most flamboyant hoods,
each a devoted acolyte of the departed florist: Louis "Two
Gun" Altiere, Vincent "Schemer" Drucci, Dapper Dan
McCarthy, Maxie Eisen, and two of the most feared trigger
men in the history of organized crime, Earl "Hymie" Weiss
and George "Bugs" Moran.

In the second row, wearing a suitably mournful expression,
stood Big Al Capone himself, flanked on four sides by bodyguards. He was doing his best to ignore the murdering stares
of Weiss and Moran, launched at him across the open grave
of their fallen leader. Despite nerves of steel, Capone looked
scared that day, for it was said that Hymie Weiss was the
only man in Chicago he actually feared.

Riley leaned forward in his seat to get a better view of the
screen. To capture the moment he pressed the "record" button
on the VCR. As his gaze traveled along the front row of mourners, his eyes fell upon a strikingly beautiful young woman—a
girl really—leaning unsteadily on the arm of an older man. She
had long dark hair and pale skin, and she was plainly grief-
stricken. And she was young—but how young he couldn't tell.
Mid to late teens, he guessed. Poised between youth and that
moment when a girl ripens into a beautiful woman.

His pulse picked up speed as he studied her face. She was
staring sadly down at the casket. This was a man for whom
she had obviously cared deeply. Riley pulled his chair closer

to the TV, coming to rest just a few steps from the screen. At that moment, the girl took her eyes from the casket and looked up at the camera. Her face, now visible in all its contours, was anguished, imploring. A chill ran down his spin.

He stared at the face on the screen, and for an instant he felt as though she was staring back at him. Then the camera turned to another section of mourners.

He was reeling. It seemed like a small chamber in his mind had burst open, spilling light in all directions. A strange peace settled over him. It was a self-absorbed notion, certainly. He knew that one person could not reach out to another over a span of seventy-two years. But it was a warm, calming sensation he was feeling, and he didn't want to dismiss it. He wanted to hang on.

O'Banion was married but had no children, and he was faithful to his wife, that much Riley knew from an earlier section of the documentary. So this beautiful and somehow familiar creature couldn't have been the gangster's daughter. And he had no mistress, so that explanation wouldn't account for her presence at his graveside, let alone explain her terrible grief.

Her dark hair, pale eyes, and lightly freckled skin suggested Irish heritage, that unusual combination of physical traits found almost exclusively in those who can trace at least one ancestor to the west of Ireland. Given the ethnic community in which O'Banion lived, there was nothing surprising about that. Riley's own daughter, Lizzie, just sixteen, had that same coloring and that same ripening beauty. They both looked a little like Audrey Hepburn, only with pale eyes, pale blue in Lizzie's case and almost certainly pale blue in the case of the girl on the screen.

WHEN THE PROGRAM cut to a commercial, he inhaled deeply and tried to think through what was happening. Maybe the pain pills for his back were responsible. (The doctor had said that they might make him a little goofy.) More likely it was exactly what it seemed to be: his longing to escape the strains of the Tanzdahl divorce, for flights of fancy in response to stress had been a lifetime habit with him. Or maybe the poignancy of the moment could be explained by the resemblance between the girl on the screen and his daughter Lizzie. It must have been that resemblance that initially drew his attention. But then hers was a not uncommon Irish face, prettier than most but not unlike a good share of the girls Riley had gone to parochial school with.

It had been a long time since he had experienced this kind of emotional upheaval. In his boyhood, and even as a young man, he had been drawn to mysterious females, a penchant that had usually carried with it an emotional charge. Included on his register of mystery women was a youthful preoccupation with Amelia Earhart, the famous flyer lost during a flight over the Pacific. At age ten, he was convinced that she was still alive on some desert island, her wrecked airplane submerged off a coral reef, her navigator dead in the crash. Time that should have been set aside for studying Latin and mathematics was instead taken up at the public library consuming old newspaper and magazine articles about Earhart and her disappearance. When not rummaging through library stacks, he would daydream his way through school with imaginings of the downed aviatrix, stranded and lonesome, awaiting rescue by a dashing admirer. Someone like him, for example. Visions would dance in his head of him appearing on an uncharted Pacific atoll where he would rescue her from an angry sea, carrying her nearly lifeless—and nearly nude—body to a sandy beach, where he would gently breathe life back into her lungs, taking only such liberties as were necessary to save her life. He had even written President Eisenhower of his belief that Amelia was still alive, pleading that the Navy recommence the search it had abandoned fifteen years earlier.

Barely free of Amelia Earhart, at age twelve he wasted months on the case of the actress Jean Spangler, who disappeared in Southern California in 1949. The Spangler mystery contained all the elements of a film noir thriller. Her former lovers, including a famous Hollywood actor, were interviewed by the police, and two thugs working for Los Angeles mob boss Mickey Cohen were sought for questioning. Riley had plunged headlong into the case—spending countless hours in newspaper archives, even making a failed attempt at an interview with the retired detective who had once been in charge of the investigation. Again he harbored an undefined belief that the dark-haired, blue-eyed beauty was still alive and in need of rescue. When he did a book report on her disappearance, his seventh-grade teacher thought it a very odd choice of topics. Most of the other boys wrote about baseball.

But of all his quests for the mythical female, the case of the Grand Duchess Anastasia of Russia had been the most all-consuming. It had taken over his life for the better part of a school year when he and Betsy were college sophomores. It was thought by some that the sixteen-year-old Anastasia had miraculously escaped from a basement in Ekaterinburg where, it was generally accepted by historians, the entire royal family—Czar Nicholas II, Czarina Alexandra, four daughters and one son—had been massacred by a Bolshevik execution squad.

Joining Betsy in her concern over the obsessive quality of that search were Riley's parents, especially his mother, who, as with the earlier cases, was openly hostile to such nonsense. His father dismissed it as a rebellion against his mother's insistence that he become a doctor even though he had little interest in that course of study, to say nothing of the fact that, as a roaring hypochondriac, he'd be sure to come down with every disease he studied.

Now he was nearly fifty, and though he hadn't chased after a mysterious female for over twenty-five years, he was under just the kind of strain that would set him up for such an escape.

When the Capone documentary recommenced, it passed from O'Banion's funeral onto the gang war that followed, ultimately culminating in the St. Valentine's Day Massacre. But Riley saw little of this. Finally, he turned off the program and started replaying the portion of the tape in which the sad and lovely face of the girl appeared. He sat motionless through the replays, his heart pounding as though he was witnessing a vision. It was that old feeling, that rush of excitement that as a boy would come over him powerfully and often. The feeling that had driven him to search for Amelia Earhart and Anastasia and the others. It was back.

But this time he was no longer a dreamy boy or a moonstruck adolescent. He was a full-grown man with a family and a job and a bad back. Yet in a way it was perfect. He couldn't step into Mayberry, but he could lose himself in a quest to understand, or even to find, that enchanting face, a face filled with sadness and vulnerability at the graveside of Dion O'Banion. A face that seemed to reach out to him from another time.

2

_____

TWO DAYS LATER, Riley sat in the den considering how one would go about establishing the identity of a young woman whose image was captured on an obscure piece of film footage in 1924, nearly seventy-two years earlier.

While in law school, he had moonlighted with a private detective agency, specializing in tracking down missing heirs for probate lawyers. He would hunt for long-forgotten nieces and nephews, grandchildren and great-grandchildren, to satisfy court requirements in connection with the settlement of estates. Digging around in newspaper archives, rural courthouses, and poorly tended cemeteries was wonderfully stimulating to him, a sort of historical voyeurism. He was searching through the past for real people, people who seemed somehow to live again in the present moment. He was the only one at the agency who actually enjoyed the work. So with a brief update on the technology associated with public records and other databases, he figured he would be well prepared to handle the task he had set himself, no matter what obstacles might be thrown in his way.

Because she was not identified in the documentary or in the still photos that appeared in contemporary newspaper accounts, Riley trained his sights on finding a living person who had known or was somehow connected to Dion O'Banion and, through that person, the girl at the graveside.

Mortality tables for her generation indicated that, even if she had been very young at the time of the funeral, it would be statistically likely that she was now dead. But those were just statistics. His intuition, enlivened by the power of wishful thinking, told him just the opposite. And, even if the whole project was childish and quixotic, it was also a vacation from Gus Tanzdahl and his squalid little divorce. In fact, he had hardly thought about that miserable subject for the last forty-eight hours.

The last time he felt this way was twenty-eight years before, in 1968, when he was in the grip of the Anastasia search. But this time he was fixated not on a world personage, but rather on a woman of no fame or notoriety, nothing more than a face of great sadness and beauty in the front row of an entourage gathered to see off a fallen gangster. So, even with his prior experience at the detective agency, this search was likely to be a good deal more difficult than those of the past.

He had spent most of the day before at the public library, pouring through old newspaper and magazine articles, anything he could find that made mention of Dion O'Banion. For a man now largely lost in the shadow of his more famous rival, Al Capone, O'Banion had cut a wide swath back in the 1920s. His prominence in the underworld was similar to that of other high-profile Irish gangsters of the era, men like Owney Madden, Legs Diamond, and Vincent "Mad Dog" Coll. More flamboyant and reckless than their Italian counterparts, the Irish were also less business oriented and less inclined to pass the family enterprise onto the next generation. The most notorious of them tended to rapidly rise to the top of gangland and then go down in a hail of bullets at an early age. Owney Madden proved to be the exception, living to a peaceful and thoroughly corrupt old age in Hot Springs, Arkansas.

Born in 1892 in a sleepy Illinois village not known as a spawning ground for big-time gangsters, O'Banion was the second son of Irish immigrant parents. Sharing a first name with a warm and loving father, Charles, from his earliest days he was called by his middle name, Dion, and was known to friends and family as "Deanie."

As a child he was devoted to his mother and, though known in his school days as a mischievous child who loved practical jokes, there was nothing in his background or family life to presage his rise to the top of Chicago gangdom. In a pattern set by many Irish-American males in their young adulthood, the 1920 Census found Deanie unmarried and residing in his father's home. The census-taker spelled his name "Dean," a usage he seemed to favor and one that would be repeated on his tombstone and again in the files of the Cook County Probate Court. His profession was identified in the census as "Bookbinder," a label that must have caught his fancy in the moment. A few historians speculated that the loss of his mother when he was barely eight, combined with a badly broken leg that left him with a noticeable limp, embittered him against conventional life and spawned the hair-trigger temper for which he would later became famous.

That theory was at best simplistic and, in any case, inadequate to explain the complex psychological profile he was ultimately to develop, a persona that Jimmy Cagney would so artfully mimic. It was true that O'Banion's background could be classified as deprived, at least in the financial sense, but many boys of that same background had suffered as much or more early hardship without turning deadly in later life. And few of them had Deanie's advantages. He remained the object of his father's loving attention, sang in the choir at Holy Name Cathedral, and at one time even had aspirations toward the priesthood. It was said that Deanie was a beautiful child, with rosy cheeks, piercing blue eyes, and strawberry-blonde hair. The women of the congregation were known to weep quietly as he stood high in the choir loft, his cassock and surplice blowing gently in the wind, singing out God's praises in a light Irish tenor. It was the voice and face of an angel, they were heard to say.

In his teenage years, though still bearing the outward countenance of an altar boy, he had grown strong and angular. Living amidst the poverty and vice of the section of Chicago known originally as "Kilgubbin," and later as "Little Hell," he was one of many boys who took up with bad companions, soon becoming their natural leader.

While Little Hell was originally an Irish enclave, the young urchins of Deanie's youth were also of Polish, Jewish, and even occasionally Italian heritage, the latter for one reason or another finding themselves settled on the Irish side of town. Of the Italians, Vincent "Schemer" Drucci, a worshipful O'Banion loyalist, was the most formidable. Together with Hymie Weiss, Louis "Two Gun" Altiere and George "Bugs" Moran, this boyhood clique of swaggering roughnecks formed the core leadership of what ultimately came to be known as the "O'Banionites" or, more generically, the "North Side Mob."

Employing a blend of charm and violence, by 1920 the O'Banionites had risen to a position of nearly unequaled criminal prominence in Chicago. They excelled at hijacking, safecracking, strike-breaking and political fixing, with Deanie managing to corrupt most of the city's officeholders and police authorities along the way. It was during those early years as common criminals that Vincent Drucci, who since childhood had cooked up grand designs for the gang, came to be known as "Schemer," and George Moran, at once the dumbest and most violent member of the gang, became known as "Bugs."

As it was for most gangsters of the time, the advent of Prohibition proved a godsend for the O'Banionites, exceeding in its opportunities even their most fervent prayers. They took to the bootlegging trade with a ferocious abandon. In preparation for assuming full control of the lucrative North

Side, Deanie formed alliances with a number of well-established Jewish gangsters, including Nails Morton, the Miller brothers, and two of the toughest mugs in Chicago, Frank and Pete Gusenberg. So literal and comprehensive was Deanie's belief in swift retribution that when his friend and mentor Nails Morton was thrown by a horse in Lincoln Park and fatally injured, a bereaved Deanie sent two of his boys over to execute the horse, a scene vividly recreated by James Cagney in *Public Enemy.*

He also established loose affiliations with other Irish gangs, most prominently the two unrelated O'Donnell families. He loved flowers and, as a front for his operations co-owned Schofield's, a successful Chicago flower shop from which he supplied extravagant and artistic floral arrangements for the city's many funerals—gangster and non-gangster alike. It was said that for a hundred dollars O'Banion would supply the flowers—and for another fifty he would supply the corpse.

That the police had Deanie and his mob down for some twenty-eight killings by the early 1920s surprised no one who knew him. At the same time, those who knew him best, also loved him. By all accounts he was funny, good-natured, genuinely interested in other people, and unfailingly kind to those who had been pushed around most of their lives. He performed matchless acts of kindness toward the North Side's poorer residents, many of whom were recent immigrants. He was known for regularly distributing money out of his own pockets to those in need, no matter their color, ethnicity, or religion. There was in his voice and manner such a warmth of blessing that few failed to succumb to his charm. And for all the deadly frigidity he could bring to his dealings with other gangsters, he could not bear the sight of a suffering child, often dissolving in tears at the sight. He once sent a crippled boy to the Mayo Clinic for a series of costly operations and, when the treatment was unsuccessful, settled upon the boy's family an annuity sufficient to pay for his lifetime care. There was no sad story for which he did not fall, peeling off money in all directions to help relieve the pain of ordinary people.

And it was Deanie who took Prohibition gangsters out of the sartorial wasteland to which they had been consigned and put them into three-piece tuxedos and top hats. But stylish nightwear was not the only trend he set. Along with Hymie Weiss, he pioneered that perennial gangster favorite, the "one-way ride." And indeed a great many gangster rivals were to take that ride on his instructions before the 1920s were half over.

While Deanie established hegemony over the North Side, a twenty-two-year-old comer named Al Capone was distinguishing himself as the trusted understudy of Southside kingpin Johnny Torrio. Though separated in age by nearly twenty years, Torrio and Capone were both alums of the Five Points Gang in New York City. Torrio, in his early forties by 1924, was a brilliant businessman and organizer, and a person who disliked the wanton violence for which the O'Banionites were best known. In spite of a common misperception, neither Torrio nor Capone was a made member of the Mafia, both being non-Sicilians and, therefore, ineligible for formal membership.

Though less flashy and cosmopolitan than O'Banion, Torrio and Capone shared his openness to people outside their national heritage. Jake "Greasy Thumb" Guzik (the Capone mob's chief financial officer) and Fred "Killer" Burke (the chief triggerman at the St. Valentine's Day Massacre), were respectively Jewish and Irish. This early diversity program, gangster style, reaped large rewards for both gangs over the years, but also had the effect of alienating Capone from Chicago's Sicilian mobsters, most prominently represented by the Genna brothers, with whom O'Banion had a bitter and longstanding blood feud.

At the dawn of Prohibition, it was a cautious but hopeful Johnny Torrio who convened a meeting of the major Chicago gangs and proposed a reasonable division of territory, observing in the process the ethnic sensibilities of the various parties. Though the agreements reached at that summit were to be more conspicuous in the breach than in the observance, the boundaries as initially drawn met with the approval of all in attendance. O'Banion's continuing dominance of the lucrative North Side was confirmed by the agreement, with the proviso that, in light of his nearly uncontested sway over police and politicians, he would arrange reasonable accommodations in support of the other players.

Not agreed to, however, then or ever, was the troubling matter of prostitution. For all his hair-trigger violence—what one writer termed his "sunny brutality"—Deanie was a man of considerable personal rectitude. He neither smoked nor drank. He kept a rosary in his vest, not far from the multiple handguns he carried in special pockets sewn into his signature three-piece suits. He was positively rhapsodic in the presence of flowers and other forms of natural beauty. Uncommon to gangsters of that era, he was faithful to his wife. She considered him to be the gentlest man she ever knew. Given all that, it was no wonder that Deanie was appalled by the business of prostitution. "Let the Italians rot in hell over that filthy business," was how he put it.

To no one's surprise, therefore, he refused to allow Torrio and Capone, or anyone else for that matter, to own or operate whorehouses on the North Side. When they attempted to do so, their emissaries were pistol-whipped, and their real estate burned to the ground. Gentlemen, he was heard to say, did not trade in the flesh of womankind, of which his sainted mother was the standing ideal.

Initially, the bootlegging borders established by Johnny Torrio were honored by all concerned. But the gangster mentality was not well suited for long-term compliance, and when it came to stepping over the lines, Deanie was in a category all by himself. As Chicago's "Arch Criminal," the name bestowed upon him by the chief of police, and as a man who had achieved undeniable success through bribery and violence, he was not about to be inconvenienced in any serious way by "those greasy pimps from the South Side," as he indelicately referred to Torrio and Capone.

There had been some instances of friendly collaboration between the two gangs, such as the joint ownership of the immensely profitable Sieben Brewery on the North Side and O'Banion's stake in a Torrio-Capone gambling establishment in Cicero, but when the opportunity presented itself for the O'Banionites to highjack a Capone or Genna liquor shipment, they just couldn't seem to resist. Nor could the Gennas when the tables were turned. Not surprisingly, therefore, by 1924, tension within the sectional and ethnic alliances so carefully worked out by Johnny Torrio had begun to fray badly.

So successful had Deanie been in his undertakings up to that point—and so indifferent was he to his own vulnerability—that when he discovered through his high-level police contacts that the Sieben Brewery, which he owned jointly with Torrio and Capone, was about to be raided by non-bribable federal officers, instead of stepping up and sharing the loss with his partners (as Torrio surely would have done), Deanie staged an elaborate ruse through which he could salvage his own investment and at the same time set Torrio up for a long jail sentence.

Several weeks in advance of the scheduled raid on the brewery, O'Banion approached Torrio with an offer to sell his interest at a bargain price of $500,000, giving as a reason his desire to retire from the rackets. His section of town would then become open territory, he said, and Torrio and Capone would be free to expand their hugely profitable enterprises in booze and prostitution.

O'Banion seemed unworried about the possible consequences of his deception. If he were found out and faced retaliation, he had little doubt that the superior intelligence and firepower of the Northsiders (they were the first to introduce the submachine gun into mob warfare) would carry the day.

And so the scam went forward. Torrio paid over the $500,000 in cash and assumed management of the brewery. In no time at all, the Feds showed up, seized the plant and equipment, and brought charges that would eventually send Torrio to jail for nearly a year.

Deanie, of course, had no intention of retiring or otherwise leaving the field to any of his rivals. Unafraid, he even boasted around town that he had "rubbed that pimp's nose in the dirt." This was too much even for the peace-loving Johnny Torrio. Maybe he could have overlooked the swindle and the $500,000 loss (close to ten million dollars in 1996), but this business of bragging about one's own treachery was too much. Torrio considered murder to be a tactic of last resort but absolutely necessary in this case. O'Banion just couldn't be counted on to play fair.

In ordinary times, Deanie, the ambidextrous gunfighter who carried three pistols within easy reach, would have been a hard man to kill. His enemies knew that they had only one pass at him, for a failed attempt would bring forth a reply of such bloody ferocity that no one, least of all Al Capone and Johnny Torrio, would have been safe. So on November 10, 1924, during a truce marking the formal mourning period for Mike Merlo (head of the Unione Sicilione and, when alive, the one voice obeyed by all Chicago gangs), Deanie let down his guard.

Now in league with the Gennas, Torrio and Capone decided to hit the normally well-protected O'Banion as he was preparing the floral wreaths for the Merlo funeral, just as he had done with such loving artistry for Al's brother Frank, gunned down by Chicago police two years earlier. Three killers were dispatched, and with one of the Gennas keeping watch outside, they entered the flower shop, and in what would henceforth forever be known as the "gangster handshake"—portrayed in countless plays and movies over the years—one of the three gripped Deanie's extended hand with both of his. Not expecting an ambush, and with a floral utensil occupying his left hand, Deanie was powerless to reach for one of his three handguns. His bullet-riddled corpse tumbled to the floor amongst a bed of tulips and carnations.

Johnny Torrio, normally a man of foresight and sound judgment, turned out to be spectacularly wrong in his belief that O'Banion's death would restore peace to Chicago. What he had not taken into account was the fanatical loyalty of Deanie's boyhood friends, who had now succeeded to the senior leadership of the North Side Mob. In the normal case, Torrio's reasoning would have been sound; the surviving gang members would have made a new deal and kept to it. But not here. No gang in Chicago was less likely to forego revenge than the O'Banionites. They and the populace of the North Side loved Dion O'Banion. They would not rest until his killing was avenged. Before Deanie's body was cold, Hymie Weiss, Schemer Drucci, and Bugs Moran had announced that they knew who was behind the murder. Gang member Louis "Two Gun" Altiere even issued a public challenge to the killers to shoot it out on Madison Avenue.

The funeral for Deanie was unprecedented in its pageantry, the first of the great gangster extravaganzas. An estimated forty-thousand mourners viewed the corpse and more than twenty-thousand showed up for the funeral, walking like family behind the hearse that carried his remains to Mt. Carmel Cemetery.

In accordance with mob protocols, Capone and Torrio, officially denying any knowledge of who would want to kill their pal Deanie, attended the wake and funeral, even sending lavish floral wreaths. But there was no doubt who was responsible, and no doubt that the ensuing revenge would be swift and terrible, probably outstripping in its ferocity anything previously seen in the annals of organized crime. And so it was. After a short breathing spell, Johnny Torrio was gunned down in full view of his wife outside their South Side apartment. In spite of multiple gunshot wounds, including one to the neck, he somehow lived. Only a bullet miscount by the mathematically challenged Bugs Moran saved Torrio from the coup de grace, a final round to the head in what was to have been a staged reenactment of the O'Banion killing. When discharged from the hospital, Torrio packed his bags and left Chicago forever, abandoning his multi-million dollar empire to his protégé Al Capone.

Next, Capone's automobile was riddled with bullets, wounding a bodyguard and chauffeur. Capone had luckily exited the car moments before and was uninjured. Other Capone associates were gunned down in rapid succession, including a chauffeur whose tortured, decaying body was found in a city cistern from which a passing horse had refused to drink. Not long afterward, a cavalcade of ten black sedans carrying Weiss and Moran and twenty other Northsiders rolled past Capone's Cicero headquarters, firing over a thousand rounds into the building, again barely missing Al, who was spread eagle on the floor of the adjoining coffee shop, his bodyguard Frankie Rio draped over his body.

Recognizing his mistake, and adhering to the sound managerial principles of his predecessor, Capone offered the O'Banionites a peace treaty and reparations, but Hymie Weiss would have none of it unless those who had dropped the hammer on O'Banion were turned over for execution. Nothing if not loyal, Capone refused the offer. Ironically, all three of O'Banion's killers were to later betray Capone and, in consequence, forfeit their own lives. Two of them, Albert Anselmi and John Scalise, were bludgeoned to death with a baseball bat wielded by Big Al himself at a party staged in their honor.

In 1926, the momentum turned against the O'Banionites when Hymie Weiss, together with his lawyer and bodyguard, were gunned down in the middle of State Street, in front of the flower shop, which still served as gang headquarters. Forty years later the façade of Holy Name Cathedral, O'Banion's place of worship as a boy, was still pocked with bullet holes from the Weiss ambush. The archbishop had left them there as a shameful reminder of the city's lawless past.

Schemer Drucci followed close behind, killed by a police officer while under arrest. The ongoing warfare claimed hundreds of lives over the next four years. The final blow was struck by Capone on St. Valentine's Day 1929, when a crew dressed as police officers invaded a North Clark Street warehouse and massacred the remaining senior leadership of the North Side Mob, save only Bugs Moran, to whom leadership of the gang had passed after the deaths of Weiss and Drucci. The St. Valentine's Day Massacre was a crime so gruesome that even the broadminded citizens of Chicago couldn't stomach it. They rose up against Capone, and within two years he was convicted of tax evasion and sent to Federal prison.

The assassination of Dion O'Banion, pain in the ass though he was, proved to be a fatal misjudgment for Al Capone.

# 3

_____

T O THE TAPE Riley had made of the documentary, he added copies of newspaper photos taken on the day of the funeral by the major Chicago dailies. The face of the young girl appeared clearly in only one picture, but it was a beauty. She occupied a majority of the frame, almost to the exclusion of any background setting. The faces of the people on her right and left were only partially visible and the background setting was badly out of focus. The newspaper cut line read: "Unidentified mourner at O'Banion Rites." The accompanying article said that the photo had been taken at Schofield's Flowers on North State Street, the shop in which O'Banion was a partner.

That the girl's image dominated the photo would not surprise anyone who has ever watched a professional football or basketball game on television. Photographers and cameramen seem always to find beautiful females in any crowd.

Riley took that single still photo to a commercial lab for digital enhancement, thereby greatly improving the quality of the image. The sharper the lab made the image, the more the girl's youth and beauty were revealed. And the more enchanted he became.

His hope was that some person connected to O'Banion, or the child or grandchild of such a person, could identify her by name when shown a copy of the photo. The search was somewhat complicated by the fact that so many of O'Banion's friends and confederates had lived under aliases and monikers assigned by sensation-seeking newspaper reporters.

Betsy happened into the den as Riley worked. With a Tootsie Pop in her mouth, she walked over to the desk and peered over his shoulder at the list of tasks he had written down on a legal pad. She made slurping sounds while surveying the list.

Riley released a crabby exhale and looked up at her. "I don't suppose I could get you to finish that somewhere else, could I?"

Betsy ignored the question. "Why don't you call the Chicago Library and ask how to go about this?"

That seemed a little simple minded, and he said so.

"Okay, Mr. know-it-all," she said as she turned and headed for the kitchen. Once there, she picked up the phone and dialed long distance information. Less than fifteen minutes later she reappeared in the den and placed before him a sheet of paper covered in the distinctive handwriting that had secured her "A's" in penmanship back at Sacred Heart Grade School. And it wasn't just in penmanship that she got "A's." She got them in everything. An aged Monsignor Kane, who ruled the parish for three decades like a medieval pope, would read the report cards out loud as the students paraded across the front of the room to accept their grades. Riley could still recall the Monsignor smiling at Betsy and reading out: "Elizabeth Bainbridge—Reading 'A,' Spelling 'A,' Mathematics 'A,' Deportment 'A,' Conduct 'A'." By contrast, when Riley arrived at the front desk, the Monsignor would shake his head and mumble in a voice weighed down with disappointment: "Riley McReynolds—Reading 'C,' Spelling 'C,' Mathematics 'D,' Deportment 'D,' Conduct 'F'."

Once, when Edgar McGuirk—class brain and the student directly in front of Riley in the alphabetically arranged line—

was sick at home on report card day, Riley rigged the stack so that he'd get Edgar's straight "A's." But he counted in the wrong direction and instead got his buddy Chasbo Peytabohm's grades—the only ones in the class worse than his.

Riley looked down at the sheet Betsy put in front of him. "What's this?"

Betsy smiled but did not reply.

On the sheet was a single name and address. With a hint of irritation, he asked, "What does this mean?"

Betsy switched the Tootsie Pop to her left hand and pointed to the name. "This is Alistair Kavaeny. A very nice research librarian at the Chicago library helped me over the phone, when I told her what I was after. She consulted some index and came up with his name. He was a cub reporter for a Chicago tabloid in the 1920s and later did a series of articles about the St. Valentine's Day Massacre. He wrote openly of his relationship with Dion O'Banion." She then smiled with gentle self-satisfaction. "And he's still listed as a member of the Retired Newspaper Reporters Association of Greater Chicago, even though he's ninety-two-years-old and lives in a nursing home. So how are you coming along with your crack investigative approach?" she asked with a giggle. "Any progress?"

Riley felt the color rise in his cheeks. He pushed aside the elaborate and useless materials he had been working with. "Thank you," he mumbled under his breath.

He could hear Betsy chuckling as she walked away.

He turned to the computer and typed the name of the nursing home into the AOL Yellow Pages. Up came a phone number, which he immediately dialed. Without any questions, the operator connected him to Alistair Kavaeny's room. A raspy but self-confident voice answered.

When Riley explained who he was and why he was calling, from the other end of the phone came a laugh, almost a guffaw. "Well, what do you know about that. I haven't had one of these calls for almost forty years, maybe longer. Last one, I believe, was when they made a movie about Capone back in 1958, and they wanted a little background on Deanie—" He interrupted his remarks to cough up a wad of congestion. Riley felt himself go a little weak. "Even then, O'Banion had been pretty much forgotten. The whole town was full of Capone experts, but there were very few around who had any interest in Deanie, except for his role in Capone's rise to power. History is written by the winners, ya know." He said this as though he had coined the phrase.

"Could I come to see you, Mr. Kavaeny," asked Riley hopefully, his pulse picking up speed. "I have some pictures I want to show you."

After another coughing spell, the old man said, "Hell, yes. Just don't come between two and four in the afternoon. We've got Lawrence Welk reruns this week."


THAT NIGHT RILEY squirmed uncomfortably in his soft leather chair, surrounded by piles of books about Chicago in the 1920s. His back pain was at its worst at night, and in spite of two pain pills after dinner, a vise-like band had spread itself across his upper back, and an ominous tingling was felt in his left arm. Only a TV documentary on the Battle of Britain and the gritty courage of the British home front during World War II provided a distraction.

At ten-thirty, with the image of Nazi dive bombers freshly imprinted on his drug-soaked brain, he clicked off the TV and trudged slowly to the bedroom, moving with a sideways gait that seemed to ease his painful passage. In sympathy with his master, the family dog, Tuffy, climbed the stairs behind him in a similar sidesaddle motion.

He washed down a muscle relaxer prescribed by the doctor to supplement the pain pills. In order to protect against the risk of kidney stones—a complication he read about in his *Merck's Manual*—he drank two full glasses of water to escort the medicine through his system. As he lay in bed, the pharmaceuticals sent him into a mellow, sleepy state. His back still hurt, but the pain was now blunted, landing with less force. Or at least he cared less about it. Within a few minutes, the book he was reading fell from his grip and dropped painfully onto his face. He brushed it away and, with Tuffy curled against the contours of his body, he passed into unconsciousness.

Betsy's noisy arrival an hour later did nothing to rouse him from the narcotized slumber into which he had fallen. His next semi-conscious recollection was of a hazy, shallow dream in which he and Tuffy were peeing against the wall of a nameless wartime London building, with German bombs exploding all around them. In the dream he was strangely unconcerned about the bombs, intent only on voiding his bladder. Despite what seemed an endless stream, he felt no relief. In fact, the longer he peed in the dream, the more urgent the signal seemed to become.

When the sensation grew unbearable, he came awake and realized that his bladder was about to burst. The two glasses of water had been a bad idea, and he was either going to have to wet the bed or face a new round of back spasms by getting up and walking to the bathroom. He opted for the latter, moving slowly in that direction, stepping gingerly around shoes and clothing shed a few hours earlier.

After passing what seemed a record volume of urine, he took another pill to quell the renewed spasms and slid back into bed. While he waited for the medication to take effect, he picked up the headset of his bedside Walkman and dialed his way through those late-night radio programs so beloved by insomniacs, religious fundamentalists, and conspiracy buffs —groups with which he was starting to feel a new kinship. He stopped briefly at a hellfire preacher, and then moved on to a UFO call-in show where the host was taking first-hand reports of alien abductions. This was not healthy listening for a guy on powerful drugs, he concluded, so he moved to an obscure AM station playing songs from the 1940s and 1950s. He was soon blissfully back to sleep.

He couldn't be sure if it was two minutes or two hours later that he came partially awake in a warm, dreamy glow, rolling gently on a wave of womb-like bliss under the warmth of the down comforter spread over him and Betsy and Tuffy. Through the radio headset he heard the silken voice of Vera Lynn, the singer who had done so much to uphold the spirits of the British people during World War II. She was singing "The White Cliffs of Dover," the brave anthem of a besieged nation during the darkest days of World War II, snippets of which had also been played on the documentary earlier in the evening.

Under any other circumstances, the absurdly sentimental lyrics of that ballad would have seemed embarrassingly dated. The song looked forward to the war ending so that bluebirds could again fly over Dover, and shepherds could return to tending their sheep, and little Jimmy could get his room back again. Wide awake and drug free, he probably would have laughed out loud. But, now, those lyrics were almost unbearably poignant. He felt, in that moment, as if he had been taken back to that time and place. The voice was lush and beautiful, heartbroken but filled with hope. And it was all somehow eerily familiar, its notes and cadences vibrating gently against the walls of his mind.

He stared up at the ceiling, blinking several times in rapid succession. It had to be the drugs, he thought. No wonder Timothy Leary kept seeing God. But the true explanation for what he was experiencing didn't matter; it was valid at some level, whether real or metaphorical. The thought of Vera Lynn and the bluebirds and the shepherds and little Jimmy getting his room back, gave him inexpressible happiness. And coming as it did in the midst of the O'Banion fixation, "The White Cliffs of Dover" and the images of wartime Britain seemed to merge seamlessly with those of the girl at O'Banion's grave-side, the one whose picture he had stared at so long that he knew its lines and contours almost better than his own.

In the morning his back was improved and his mind cleared. The moment had passed, but the grace that had settled upon him in the dark of night was still very much present. With boyish enthusiasm, he told Betsy over eggs and coffee of the music and the bombs and of Vera Lynn and the bluebirds and of little Jimmy getting his room back.

Betsy nodded sympathetically, trying to join in the excitement. But there was only so far she could travel on these strange journeys. She was never very interested in Amelia Earhart, for example, and she positively disliked Anastasia. This new fixation—this face at a funeral in the distant past—actually worried her a little, mostly because of its obvious connection to the strain of the Tanzdahl case. Riley's pain at having to tear into a young mother afraid of losing her only child ran so counter to his normal sensibilities that he might actually be going off his rocker. That she didn't want to happen. It wasn't that she was surprised by this latest go-around. It was one of his strange charms that he seemed to have a foot in another world. But this time it seemed to carry a special charge, an energy that could singe them all.

Betsy privately thought that his mother's expectations of her children, especially of Riley, were behind the fantasy life he seemed to turn to during times of stress. Maureen McReynolds, proud of having raised five children, four of them wild boys, was still alive at eighty-seven. And she was still trying to run her favorite son Riley's life from a nearby nursing home.

Betsy said a silent prayer and looked across the table. Riley was busily scratching out a series of notes, uncharacteristically ignoring the morning paper. He took a slug of orange juice, smiled excitedly and said, "Will you drive me to the train station? I'm off to Chicago."


BETSY DROPPED HIM at the Amtrak Station in St. Paul where he had reserved a seat on the Empire Builder, a passenger train that traveled through some of America's most beautiful scenery. It made no practical sense to choose rail over air travel, but it seemed fitting for this trip. He was entering another time, a time long past, when railroads were at their mightiest.

Awash in nostalgia, he inhaled the distinctive and distantly familiar smells of a train terminal and recalled the many business trips his father had taken in the 1950s on this train. His grandmother, Helen Riley McReynolds, would drive his father to the station and bring Riley along, a treat rarely afforded his siblings. The "Riley" name had been bestowed on him because of his resemblance to her, physically and emotionally. A lifelong bond had existed between them, and when she succumbed to Alzheimer's in her mid-seventies, his was the last face she recognized. Her small apartment just a block from their family home had been for him a sanctuary from the larger world, a small museum of another time, of faded photographs of great-grandparents and even a thatched cottage in county Tipperary. It was clean and tidy and smelled faintly of toast and coffee. And it was a place of perfect love—love untouched by any form of discipline.

Apart from his bond with Grandma Riley, as the baby of the family special privileges seemed to regularly come his way. Sometimes, when his parents didn't think he was listening, they would refer to him as their "surprise child," which in the vernacular of the time meant, he eventually concluded, that he was the product of that most unreliable of all forms of birth control, the "Rhythm Method." Sort of a happy accident.

As he and his grandmother would watch the Empire Builder disappear over the horizon, with his father waving from the back platform, she would grow sad and remind him that it was from this station in 1945 that she and his father had seen his uncle Desmond, her youngest son, off to World War II—a war from which Desmond would not return. He had been one of the last casualties in the European conflict, and his death had had an effect on the McReynolds family that was nearly impossible to measure. It is sometimes said that the Irish die better than other people, and Riley thought there might be something to that. But the Irish were also among the least able to let go of their dead—those ordinary, often deeply flawed mortals transformed by death into sainted heroes. Riley's uncle Desmond could not have occupied a larger space in the life of his family if he had lived to old age. That he had died defending his country only added to the legend. He became the family's noble archetype, a role model frozen in time. "Be like your Uncle Desmond," Riley and his brothers would hear from their grandmother every time they turned around, even to the point where the boys would mimic her behind her back, referring to their uncle as Saint Desmond or, worse yet, "Old Dead Desmond." But on orders from their mother they never kidded about Desmond within hearing of their father, who could hardly hear his brother's name spoken without choking up.

As a child, Riley would sit on his grandmother's lap for hours as she talked about his father and what a good brother he had been to Desmond, and about how heartbroken he had been when the black-bordered telegram arrived, the one that began with sad greetings from the president. Grandma would cry a little at such times as she glanced over at the picture of Desmond sitting on the mantel of her fireplace. The young Riley would hide his face and refuse to look, for Desmond, even in the uniform of an Army major, bore a stunning resemblance to his own father—a man who could never die.

As youngsters, John and Desmond McReynolds had been fixtures in the boxing gyms of North Minneapolis, and later they worked their way through college by staging exhibition matches at county fairs, taking on the lumberjacks and farmhands of rural Minnesota. John was the aggressive slugger, Desmond the counter puncher. And though Desmond was to gain greater fame in the ring, even being listed for one glorious month among the nation's top ten light-heavyweight contenders, John retained the role of mentor and protector in a brotherly relationship that could not have been closer if they had been identical twins.

Desmond's death in the war had nearly killed John McReynolds. And two decades later the wound would be reopened with the death in Vietnam of his oldest son. When Jamie was sacrificed, it was Desmond's death all over again. It was too much even for a strong man to bear, and his father's heart burst with grief. He was dead at fifty-eight.

BOARDING THE CHICAGO-bound train, Riley made his way through the dining car and back to the passenger compartments, where he settled in with his briefcase on the seat beside him. Before opening any files, though, he watched the other passengers enter and make their way down the aisle. He knew why he was here, but wondered why anyone else would choose this mode of transportation, other than the phobics who would sooner walk to Chicago than get on an airplane.

As the train left the station, Riley pulled from his briefcase a copy of the latest documents filed in the Tanzdahl case. Less than two pages into it, however, he realized that he could ruin the whole trip if he mixed it with anything to do with Gus Tanzdahl. So he stuffed the file back into the briefcase and replaced it on his lap with a biography of Al Capone. An attractive woman in her early thirties, who was making her way down the aisle, strained with a heavy suitcase. Men of all ages on the train must have felt their muscles twitch as they debated becoming temporary porters, jumping into the aisle to offer assistance. Riley's slightly awed glance at this newly arrived passenger was surely noticed by her. Being the object of male attention could not have been new to her. She had no doubt been stared at her whole adult life and, by the look on her face, had developed a protective shell, an air of practiced indifference.

This brief encounter brought to mind an experience earlier that summer when his daughter, Lizzie, had gotten her first

pair of contact lenses to correct a significant case of nearsight-
edness. Having refused to wear glasses after age twelve, she
was that day getting her first clear look at the world in several years. As she and Riley left the optometrist's office and
walked through the mall on their way to the parking lot,
Lizzie, just sixteen and heartbreakingly beautiful, began
clinging to her father's arm. "Dad, why are all these people, all
these men, staring at me?" she asked, vaguely alarmed.

Riley guided her to a bench and sat her down next to him.
He smiled tenderly and, with moistened eyes, held her hand in
his. "It's because you are a beautiful young woman now, Lizzie
darling. Those men have been staring at you for well over a
year, but you haven't been able to see them until today." He
then creased his brow, looked her hard in the eyes, and in the
tone of a fatherly oracle, said, "I have only one thing to say
about this important passage, and I want you to remember it
for the rest of your life. All men are evil."


THE EMPIRE BUILDER glided through hills and valleys formed
by the breathtaking majesty of the Mississippi River, along
routes that were once a golden highway of luxury travel. At
LaCrosse the train turned further east into Wisconsin and
set a course for Chicago. Soft background music played in the
passenger car, mostly older tunes. Riley gave no thought to
the Tanzdahl divorce. The world seemed right as he slipped
into a short, restful nap.

The countryside flattened as the train made its way east,
through the gently rolling hills of southern Wisconsin. When
they passed Madison and dipped south, the surroundings
lost their idyllic quality, becoming more industrial, and by
the time they reached the outskirts of Chicago, the charm of
the countryside had given way to the grimy reality of a modern industrial center.

Entering Chicago by rail was especially appropriate for
this trip, for this was the city as it had been when O'Banion

fought it out with Al Capone. Like most railroad rights-of-way, it was a time tunnel through another era, vast stretches unaffected by the urban renewal and social engineering of the intervening years. Railroads, especially as they snaked their way through the large cities of the industrial belt, were like guided theme parks for the amateur historian.

Union Station, gray, vault-like and imposing, and at one time the locus of the Midwest's most fashionable traffic, now sat as a relic of another era in the heart of downtown. In front of the station Riley caught a cab and instructed the driver, a man about his age, to drive to 738 North State Street. The driver opened his log to record the address, but then paused in reflection. He turned around and peered into the back seat. "That's a parking lot, mister," he said.

Riley gave a timid smile and nodded. "Yes, I guess that's right, but it didn't used to be. It used to be—"

"Schofield's Flower Shop," interrupted the cabby. Curiosity creased his face. "If you don't mind my asking, why do you want to go to that address? You a historian or something?"

"No," answered Riley. "I'm a lawyer from Minnesota taking a little break from my practice." He didn't want to be more specific. It was a little hard to explain.

"Hmm," muttered the cabby as he flicked on his blinker and nudged his way into afternoon traffic. "If you're going to 738 North State Street, and it's not to park your car, you must be checking out something to do with the old O'Banion Mob. I'd bet anything on that."

Riley was surprised. The Capone-O'Banion wars of the 1920s were clearly part of Chicago's history, but between the ordinary passage of time and the city's desire to erase its lawless and violent past, very few people knew much about Al Capone's lesser-known rival. The average Chicagoan would express familiarity with the St. Valentine's Day Massacre, but by that time O'Banion had been dead for nearly five years. So how in the world did the first person he ran into in Chicago know that the address of a paved-over parking lot had once been the headquarters of Dion O'Banion and the North Side Mob?

"You're in luck, pal," the cabby said as he gazed at Riley through the rear view mirror. "I'm a high school history teacher. George Jensen's my name. I make a few extra bucks in the summer by hacking and driving a limo that takes visitors on tours of famous historical spots. It drives the Chamber of Commerce crazy that we include gangster spots, but the tourists love it." He gave a self-satisfied smile. "I go to that address every Tuesday and Thursday in the summer with a limo full of tourists, mostly Asians and Europeans with cameras strung around their necks. There's nothing left to show them of the flower shop—it was torn down back in the late sixties, but I can point out the spot on the face of Holy Name Cathedral where bullets fired at Hymie Weiss ripped into the face of the church."

Without looking back, but now in a more serious tone, he said, "You don't look like a tourist, and I assume you're not going there on a legal matter." When the cab stopped for the light at Michigan and Randolph, he turned his body fully around in the seat and faced Riley. "Well?"

"No, I'm not a tourist. This may sound a little strange, but I'm researching the story of a young woman who I'm sure had some importance in Dion O'Banion's life. Other than an old reporter I'm scheduled to see later today, I don't have anything to go on beyond a few old pictures that were taken at his funeral. That's why I wanted to start at the address where the newspaper said the first picture was taken. You know, kind of looking for inspiration. Pick up a little karma maybe."

"Well, you won't get any karma there," said the cabby with the certainty for which high school teachers are famous. "O'Banion's service wasn't held at the flower shop, it was held over at Sbarbaro's Funeral Home on North Wells."

The cab swung west and, after a short ride, pulled up to the spot where Sbarbaro's Funeral Home had once stood.

From inside his briefcase Riley pulled out one of the newspaper photos—the one supposedly taken before the footage at the cemetery had been shot. The caption under the picture identified the scene as O'Banion's casket being carried to the waiting hearse, through throngs of mourners. He scanned the surroundings for a common marker, a landmark to verify that he was in the spot shown in the photo. There weren't any. Not a tree, not a building, not even a street lamp. But this had to be the spot. The address was a match, and George Jensen, cab driver and history teacher, said it was so.

Disappointed at the lack of the visceral response he had expected to feel at the site where the newspaper had her once standing, Riley asked George if he had time to run him out to Mt. Carmel Cemetery, where he knew the documentary footage had been shot and at least one of the newspaper photos had been taken.

George winked. "I can take you all over town if you don't mind paying the fare."


WITH THE AFTERNOON sun beginning a slight dip to the west, the cab pulled through the wrought iron gates of Mt. Carmel, one of Chicago's oldest and most renowned cemeteries. Here could be found the mortal remains of statesmen, bishops, artists, industrialists, and more gangsters per square foot than anywhere else in the country. Freshly laid gravel crackled under the tires as the cab moved slowly over the winding roads, with George Jensen and his passenger scanning the landscape for the O'Banion gravesite. As they rolled down one curving slope and up another, Riley felt the restful sensation that usually overtook him when in a cemetery. All his priorities shuffled into place. The small guilt about devoting so much time and energy to this adventure melted away. The residents of this real estate were free of the ambitions and insecurities of life. Those challenges, so important in the moment, didn't count in any lasting sense. That's what these folks would say if they still had within them the spark that separates the living from the dead.

After twenty minutes of aimless circling, George did what no man ever wants to do: he went to the administration building and asked for directions. In accordance with family wishes dating back three-quarters of a century, the attendant wouldn't disclose the grave's location, but by that time Riley had figured out, by reference to the Capone biography he carried in his briefcase, the general area in which the grave had to be found.

Three minutes later they were at the gravesite, marked by an obelisk and simple headstone bearing the name, "Dean O'Banion." Across the cemetery was another, surprisingly modest grave, surrounded with a hedge that obscured the simple word "Capone." Off in the distance, a gravedigger in a dirty tan work outfit was rolling out a line of fresh sod over a recently closed grave.

As they approached O'Banion's final resting place, Riley bowed his head and made a reflexive, abbreviated sign of the cross. George Jensen did likewise, though from the awkward sweep of his hand Riley could tell that George was not a Catholic, or at least not a cradle Catholic. A good sign of the cross was like a good tennis backhand. If you didn't learn it at an early age, you would never master the fluid motion that comes only with neural programming in a young and impressionable brain.

If there was a hell, Riley thought as he knelt before the grave, he hoped Deanie wasn't in it. He had killed a lot of guys, it was true, but they were all in the same business he was and would have done him first if they had had the chance. Deanie never hurt a woman or a child or a member of the square world. In fact, when he wasn't fighting other criminals, his mission was to bring a little beauty and cheer into the drab lives of ordinary people. Sure, he was a psychopath, strictly speaking, but a lovable psychopath who did a lot of good in his short, violent thirty-two years on earth.

Riley hoped that divine providence was taking all that into account, balancing the good with the bad.

There at the graveside Riley entered into the O'Banion mystique in a way that was impossible by merely reading history books or even contemporary newspaper accounts. But, oddly, he felt none of the emotional charge that had come over him when he first watched the funeral films, when he first saw the young girl's face. He should have been fired with excitement at this moment as he stood on the ground where she had stood, but he wasn't. Maybe it had been the drugs he was taking for his pain back then. But he didn't think so, for in life's most important matters he had always relied on emotional cues. And he hadn't been on painkillers when he went chasing after Amelia Earhart or Anastasia.

He held a hand above his eyes to block the sun as he quizzically scanned for landmarks that might verify that the pictures in which she had appeared had, in fact, been taken here at the cemetery rather than downtown, as the newspaper had mistakenly indicated.

Just then, the gravedigger appeared behind them, leaning against his shovel and wiping perspiration from his forehead. Much older up close, his skin was parched and deeply lined, his teeth few and uneven. He seemed to have a hunger for human conversation of the kind so often found in those in solitary occupations. A pint bottle of cheap whiskey protruded carelessly from his back pocket.

"Howdy," he said, nodding in their direction, squinting against the afternoon sun. He pointed down to the headstone. "You interested in Dion O'Banion?"

Riley perked up. "Yes," he said as he moved closer to the man. "Is there anything you can tell us about him?"

"Well, he ain't one of our big draws. Nothing like Capone, for example." He nodded in the direction of Capone's grave across the cemetery. "The Italian gangsters outdraw the micks, that's for sure. Maybe it's the whole Irish guilt thing, you know where they want to forget their part in the gangster years. The Jews are the same way, I guess." He turned his head and spit in the direction of an adjacent grave.

"Yes," said Riley, smiling politely. "But what can you tell me about O'Banion? Does he have any relatives or old associates who visit?"

"You're the first I've seen in twenty-five years," replied the gravedigger as he peered at the headstone. "The story is that his widow came in the early years, but she's long dead. And, anyway, she's supposed to have married a rich real estate guy and tried to forget about being a gangster's wife." Staring at the ground contemplatively, he searched his memory. Finally he looked up. "It probably don't matter, but this wasn't where he was originally buried."

"What?" said Riley.

For the first time, George Jensen turned his attention toward the scruffy man.

Sensing his importance, the gravedigger peered teasingly off in the distance. "Well, that's right. The bishop—you know, the head priest—said that criminals like O'Banion mocked everything the church stood for, so they couldn't be buried in no sacred ground." He then raised a hand encrusted with thick calluses and fresh dirt, and with a boozy motion, pointed to another section of the cemetery. "That's where they used to bury the gangsters, right over there in the unconsecrated section. And that's where O'Banion was first put."

Riley stepped closer to the man. "How'd the body get over here, then?"

"After a few months, Mrs. O'Banion had him dug up and replanted, right in this hole, right down the row from the Archbishops' Mausoleum." He pointed his shovel up the hill at the giant, foreboding mausoleum that formed the centerpiece of the cemetery. "And once he'd been moved, no one dared mess with the grave."

Riley and George Jensen chuckled lightly at the notion of Deanie enjoying his eternal rest right next to the princes of the Church. Mischievous even in death. He would have loved that final laugh at the expense of established powers.

Riley turned back to the gravedigger and slipped him a ten-dollar bill. "Would you take us to the site where he was originally buried?"

The man stuffed the bill in his overalls and happily complied. He hadn't been in such demand for years.

As they approached the original gravesite—the unconsecrated ground of another era and another theology—Riley could feel the old familiar excitement start to rise in his chest and up into his throat. When he caught sight on the horizon of an older building recognizable from the documentary footage, he knew he was in the spot where the film had been shot—the spot where she had stood, frightened and inconsolable. He pulled the enhanced photo from his briefcase and, using the building as a fix on the skyline, stood in the exact spot she had occupied when the picture was taken.

His face flushed. A strange but recognizable stream of energy coursed up his spine. The hair on his arms stood on edge. There could be no doubt about it.

George Jensen looked over at Riley. "Hey, man, you all right?" he said, reaching in Riley's direction as if to break a fall.


BACK IN THE CAB Riley opened his briefcase and pulled out his notes on Alistair Kavaeny. "George," he said, "this crime reporter I mentioned is living over at a place called St. Dunstan's Nursing Home. His name is Alistair Kavaeny, and I want to go over and see him."

George nodded and headed east on the Eisenhower Expressway. Fifteen minutes later they pulled up to a nondescript building with a brick foundation topped off by 1950s style aluminum siding. A set of false Romanesque pillars, grafted onto the structure decades after the original construction, framed the building's front entrance.

George flipped the meter and turned to the back seat. "You want me to wait while you talk to this guy?"

"No thanks," said Riley as he fished through his pockets for $96.00. He then stepped out of the cab and looked through the glass-encased front door to be sure there were signs of life on the other side. When he saw an orderly in a white uniform pass through the lobby, he handed the fare through the driver's window and shook hands with George Jensen.

George winked. "Here's my card and cell phone number if you want me to come back for you." He then burned away from the curb, making a wide U-turn amidst a flurry of horns and flashing fingers.

The narrow foyer of St. Dunstan's opened into a converted lobby that was plain but spacious. Seating arrangements were clustered around the room, and a TV mounted on the wall closest to the receptionist's station was running more or less permanently. Riley checked in at the front desk, asking a homely and bored receptionist if he could see Alistair Kavaeny. Without saying anything, or even looking up, she handed him a visitor's pass, which he fastened to his shirt pocket. He then crossed the room to a small, flesh-colored couch, where he settled back to await the arrival of an escort.

The scent of brewing coffee was heavy in the air, and the sound of dishes being stacked could be heard from an adjoining common room. One corner of the lobby was given over entirely to an elaborate birdcage that ran from floor to ceiling. Within the spacious cage were birds of varying sizes and colors, perhaps two-dozen in all. Some were perched high in the air, singing happily, while others sat in artificial nests tucked into the corners of the metal cage. The birds must have been chosen for their beauty and compatibility, for not a one seemed to be anything short of contented. It was a stroke of genius, he thought, to grace the common areas of a building in which lonely and suffering people were clinging to the last threads of life with these exemplars of joyful surrender.

His aviary meditation was broken by the approach of a young nurse's aid, wearing a candy-stripe outfit that made her nearly as cute as the captive birds. Her smile was open, unguarded. "I understand you are asking to see Mr. Kavaeny," she said, now adopting a mildly scolding tone. "He overdid things yesterday at water aerobics, so he's confined to his wheelchair today. But I'll take you to him."

They made their way down a series of long passageways flanked by carts overflowing with soiled laundry and elderly residents slumped in wheel chairs. The residents, who looked up in confusion at the passing couple, wore sweaters and heavy sox even though the temperature in the hallway had to be at least eighty degrees. Riley's forehead had started to bead with perspiration. The smells of old age—faintly stale, like fruit gone bad—were thick in the air. He felt a little nauseous. Nursing homes were the same everywhere, he concluded, St. Dunstan's being indistinguishable from Loretta Heights in Minneapolis, where his mother was living out a bleak and painful existence.

At the end of the last corridor was a wider passage and beyond that a recreation room in which a tall man with a lively expression sat facing the door in a wheelchair. "Hey, McReynolds, I'm glad you found it," he shouted like a game-show host welcoming a new contestant, simultaneously extending his right hand.

Riley picked up the pace and grabbed enthusiastically for the old crime reporter's hand. "Thanks for agreeing to see me, Mr. Kavaeny," he said as he pulled up a chair directly facing him.

"Call me Stairs, kid. That was my nickname in the news room." He cocked his head jauntily in the style of a 1930s movie. His yellowing eyes were set deeply in a face ravaged by age, sun, and tobacco. Tan spots dotted his face and the backs of his hands, and gray stubble grew, untrimmed, from both ears. A tuft of hair, unattractively encased in a block of nasal discharge, protruded from one nostril.

It was all mildly sickening. This was not a good place for a hypochondriac, Riley thought. The diseases a person could pick up in a place like this were beyond calculation. So he automatically switched over to breathing through his nose. He had read in one of his medical journals that the membranes of the nose are specially equipped to filter out infectious agents.

The nurse's aid reached down and propped up the old man's headrest, smiling down at him as she worked. The look that passed between them was playful, affectionate. Obviously pals, the years between them seemed to represent a barrier only to the accidents of friendship, not its essentials.

She then gave the old timer's arm a squeeze. On her way out of the room, she winked at Riley.

Before another word passed between them, Kavaeny looked in both directions as if to be sure they wouldn't be overheard by the staff. "You got a cigarette, McReynolds?" he asked in the raspy, labored voice. His loose dentures made a clacking sound as he spoke.

Riley smiled and shook his head. "I don't smoke, Stairs."

"Ah, shit," the old man grunted. He then reached into a plaid canvas bag hanging from the wheelchair and fished out a tightly wadded five-dollar bill. He handed it to Riley. "I'll give you all the information on O'Banion you want, but you've got to bring me a pack of Lucky's before dinner." At that he released a thunderous fart, one that almost lifted his emaciated body off the seat of the wheelchair. He either didn't hear the explosion or he didn't care, for there was no acknowledgment. An elderly woman seated behind them glared over at Stairs. She then got a firm grip on the tires of her wheelchair and propelled herself from the room as though competing in the Senior Olympics.

Riley winked at his gaseous host, signaling his assent to the cigarette request. He would have agreed to anything, as the man sitting before him was almost certainly possessed of the information he so desperately wanted.

The Lucky Strike issue settled, Alistair Kavaeny pulled tight his food-stained bathrobe, paused briefly to search his mind, and brought forth the only period in his life that had vested him with any importance. He started the remembrance in 1922, the year he was assigned to the crime beat for a small North Side tabloid. He had been down at the courthouse covering the arraignment calendar one summer morning when O'Banion was downtown paying his judges their weekly stipends. Accompanying Deanie on his rounds were his two main lieutenants at the time, Hymie Weiss and Schemer Drucci. Bugs Moran had just been released from a stretch in the joint and had yet to demonstrate the nerveless violence that would soon gain him entry to the gang's senior ranks.

Young Stairs Kavaeny, freshly graduated from Loyola University with a degree in journalism, had the kind of round Irish face that reminded Deanie of himself at that age. He favored the young reporter with some inside dope about a recent unsolved killing in Cicero, on condition that the source not be identified. Stairs honored the agreement and made it a point to spin the resulting article in a way that was highly damaging to one of O'Banion's known enemies. From that point on Stairs became a mascot to the North Side Mob and a willing conduit of information, and misinformation, on the crime pages of the papers for which he wrote.

Deanie would sometimes take him on his North Side rounds and let him hang out at the flower shop while he trimmed tulips and sang sentimental Irish ballads. Stairs said that Deanie was the nicest man who ever lived when dealing with ordinary people, such as customers and those who worked at the flower shop, but that when he was challenged by another member of the underworld, he would instantly turn vicious and homicidal.

Riley let the old reporter run on for forty minutes, but when Stairs seemed to be getting drowsy and started repeating himself, it was time to get to the point. Reaching into his briefcase, Riley pulled out the enhanced photo of the girl taken at the funeral. He handed it across to Stairs.

In a palsied motion, the old man raised a pair of reading glasses to his eyes. He bent down and silently inspected the picture for what seemed a long time. Then he looked up at Riley. "I haven't seen this picture for over fifty years. It was taken by a photographer employed by another newspaper, a competitor. I was standing right next to him, so sad and frightened I could hardly think straight. Capone and Torrio were standing to the photographer's left. Capone bent over and whispered to the photographer that he'd be sorry if Al's picture appeared in the newspaper. So the guy shot the front row of mourners instead, catching Weiss and Drucci and Moran giving the death stare to the Italians."

Riley was careful to let a moment of quiet pass. He had been taking notes with a pencil, and he now used it to point to a small figure at the center of the front row, the one leaning on the arm of an unidentified older man. "Tell me, Stairs, who was this girl in the front row?"

His heart began to slam against his chest as he awaited the answer. Stairs straightened his eyeglasses and leaned forward to get a better look. There was a slight twitch of his head, and then a tear formed under one eye, where it sat briefly before washing over the lid and running down his cheek, finally disappearing under the collar of his ragged, turned-up robe.

"Oh, my God," he said softly. "That's Bridey Reaves."

An involuntary smile formed on Riley's face. He had a name. The mystery of her identity was at least partially solved. Now for the follow-up. "What was her relationship to O'Banion?"

The old man squinted against the late-day sun pouring in through the west windows, drenching the space where they sat. For an instant, an antiquated fear, the remnant of an earlier time when people didn't talk about such things, creased his face. But it soon vanished, and he sat up straight and inhaled deeply. "She was the daughter Deanie always wanted but never had. The person he loved most."

Riley squirmed in his seat, a raft of questions tumbling through his mind. "Was she his niece?"

"No, no blood relation. Her parents were killed in a car accident when she was fourteen, two years before Deanie was killed. The Reaves' were immigrants from Ireland, and she was their only child. Her mother and father were parishioners at Holy Name, across the street from the flower shop where Deanie was an owner. When her parents died, the Immigrant Aid Society set up the funeral and brought Bridey into Schofield's to choose flowers. Deanie was there that day, and he was instantly smitten by the beautiful young orphan."

The old man then turned down his mouth in a gesture of irony. "I know what history thinks of him, but Deanie was the most soft-hearted person I ever met when it came to widows and orphans. And that little girl just stole his heart. He became her protector and her surrogate father. There wasn't anything in the world he wouldn't do for that child."

A cart carrying a line of small paper cups filled with fruit juice was being pushed through the room. The old reporter, now lost in another time, waived off the volunteer steering in his direction. Rubbing his forehead with tobacco-stained fingers, he struggled to maintain his train of thought. "Deanie knew it would be hard to adopt Bridey because the welfare people would try to stop it, what with his reputation and all the bad publicity he got. But he became her father in every way but the legal papers. He put her up in a convent with the nuns who taught him back in grade school. Paid all her bills. Took her everywhere. Showed her off like she was his natural daughter." His eyes glistened at the memory, and he shook his head almost imperceptibly. "I was a little bit in love with her myself. Everybody was."

Riley didn't bother to take notes. He would remember every word. Still trying to appear casual, he asked, "Was her real first name Bridget?"

Stairs paused momentarily, staring up at the ceiling. "No . . . no," he finally said. "Everyone thought that was her real name. Some even called her Bridget. But her real full name was Anna McBride Reaves. I think her mother's first name was also Anna, so her family took to calling her Bridey because of her middle name."

The old reporter shook his head nostalgically as he gripped the rails of the wheelchair and stared at the floor. "Deanie's funeral was the last time I ever laid eyes on her. She remained under the protection of Hymie Weiss for a while, but the way he was shooting up Capone's people, it was obvious that it was just a matter of time before he was killed. So Bridey fled for her life."

Riley leaned forward in his seat, puzzled. "Protection? Why did she need protection?"

Stairs shot him a look of incredulity, as though Riley had been around in 1924 but had somehow missed what was common knowledge to everybody else. "Well, Deanie gave the $500,000 to Bridey . . . you know, the money he chiseled from Capone on the Sieben Brewery. He told her she should have it in case anything ever happened to him." Stairs Kavaeny's head bobbed back and forth, and he pointed an index finger almost in Riley's face. "Deanie was fearless, but he knew he was on the spot . . . knew that there was a good chance he'd get knocked off at some point, and he couldn't stand the thought of that girl being left penniless."

Riley's eyes were as big as saucers. "How did Capone find out she had the money?"

"Everybody on the North Side knew," he said dismissively. "Some small-time hood who Deanie used as a wheel guy every now and then overheard him telling Moran about it one day on the phone. That little turd sold the information to Capone right after Deanie got whacked." He curled up his mouth in disgust, still angered by the ancient betrayal. But then he chuckled slyly, and said in a whisper: "He was the first one Weiss killed."

He then turned somber again, pulling a handkerchief from the pocket of his robe and wiping away a stream of liquid that had formed under his nose. "Nobody saw Bridey after that, after she fled town. We assumed she had been killed. Capone's guys were pretty efficient."

A tall orderly with a cross on the lapel of his white jacket came over to where they were sitting. He had been standing nearby, within hearing distance, at the adjacent nurses' station, apparently making notes in patient files. When the dinner bell rang, he started rounding up residents. He looked over at Riley. "I hope you didn't agree to buy him any Lucky Strikes," he said.

"No, certainly not," said Riley, winking at Stairs. Rising from his seat, Riley moved closer to the wheelchair. He put a hand on the old man's bony shoulder. "Thanks, my friend. If you think of anything else that might help me find what happened to her, will you please give me a call?" He pulled a business card from his wallet and slipped it into the pocket of the reporter's robe.

The orderly nodded absently at Riley and started pushing the wheelchair in the direction of the dining hall.

Riley left St. Dunstan's by a side door and walked across the street to a gas station, where he bought a pack of Lucky Strikes. Stairs found them under his pillow when he returned from dinner.

# 4

---

A T 7:30 SHARP each Thursday morning, the Partners
Committee of Cosgrove & Levi met in the firm's main
conference room. The committee was comprised of the
twelve most senior partners, only a few of whom actually had
anything to do with firm management. The actual day-to-day
managerial authority resided in the Management Committee, consisting of the managing partner and the heads of the
four major practice groups: Corporate & Banking, Real
Estate, Litigation, and Tax & Estate Planning.

Riley owed his membership on the Partners Committee to
the portfolio of business he controlled rather than to his time
with the firm. That portfolio generated annualized gross
billings in the neighborhood of three million dollars, which
was attributable almost entirely to two clients. The first was
CT Preventive Imaging, Inc., a regional medical diagnostic
concern with a fleet of over-the-road vehicles equipped with
the latest in mammography technology. The vehicles circulated throughout the region much like bloodmobiles used by
the Red Cross, administering breast examinations for
women unable or unwilling to travel to a distant facility. CT
Preventive Imaging was a hugely successful venture found-

ed, owned, and led by the most unlikely of characters from Riley's past, Charles T. ("Chasbo") Peytabohm, a friend from childhood, who prior to his current business success had been a gambler, con man, occasional cat burglar and, for several years of his adult life, the guest of the state government at a local correctional facility. During his last stretch up the river he had enrolled in a vocational training program in order to qualify for an early release. Of all the programs offered to inmates by a nearby community college, Chasbo was most drawn to mammography technology. He thought that handling women's breasts would be a pleasant way to serve out his parole.

Upon release in 1981, he was fully accredited as a mammography technician, but because of an understandable bias against male technicians, especially ones who had done hard time, Chasbo had been unable to land a job in the industry. Ever the entrepreneurial visionary, Chasbo could see that a largely untapped market existed for an enterprise willing to provide that important service to especially remote locations. Lacking the capital to purchase necessary start-up equipment, and having a background that made a bank loan unlikely, he turned to what most people would consider an unconventional source of financing. He cleaned out an upscale jewelry store in a late-night burglary, fenced the goods through a former prison mate, laundered the proceeds through a series of dummy corporations, and purchased the necessary equipment.

The rolling mammography venture caught fire immediately, soon ripening into one of the most profitable enterprises in local memory. With Chasbo's business success came a bid for social acceptance. He went overnight from Chasbo T. Peytabohm to "C. Taylor Peytabohm," a name less likely to lead inquiring minds to his rather extensive, though non-violent, criminal record. He took on all the outward trappings of upper-class respectability, even ceasing his lifetime habit of throwing up on people he didn't like, a skill he had first mastered back at Sacred Heart Grade School, where he and Riley commenced their lifetime friendship. On the golf course and at a wide array of cultural events, Chasbo cultivated bishops, bankers, corporate executives, and his main referral source, board certified gynecologists. The name C. Taylor Peytabohm came to grace the letterheads of some of the area's most prestigious charities, and he was welcomed into membership at several local golf clubs with less than rigorous screening protocols.

But, true to the habits of a lifetime, this reinvention of his persona did not include the elimination of certain deeply imbedded character traits. Thus his taxes were chronically late and self-servingly calculated, his books and records were suspiciously confusing, and his hiring practices were blatantly discriminatory—skewed heavily in favor of young females with prominent breasts. He argued that the latter job requirement was an occupational necessity and, therefore, exempt from the requirements of Title VII. All this misconduct created substantial legal needs, and who better to oversee the delivery of those services than his best buddy Riley McReynolds.

Riley's other major client, accounting for approximately 1.5 million dollars in annual billings, was The Stoddard Trust, a large but low-profile real estate development firm that did business in twenty-eight states, including six states in the Midwest. Originally established as a Massachusetts business trust, Stoddard's executive offices were located in Boston, but its current chief executive officer, Evans Pedersen, was a native of St. Paul and a University of Minnesota graduate. Some years back, prior to Pedersen's association with the Trust, Riley had used him as an expert witness in a large real estate fraud prosecution, and as a result, they had become good friends. When Ev Pedersen was later appointed CEO of The Stoddard Trust and moved his office to Boston, he offered to make Riley the Trust's principal outside counsel for the Midwest region.

When Riley made his deal with Cosgrove & Levi, he was able to leverage these two personal relationships into sizable client accounts. He did little actual legal work for either client, restricting his active practice largely to white-collar business crime. But the accounts were opened by him, and it was clear to everyone concerned that he controlled their roughly three million dollars in annual fees. On any given day, at least five of the firm's seventy-five lawyers were working full time on files associated with those clients. Income from the two accounts, together with that generated by files Riley handled directly, made him the fifth largest revenue producer in the firm and, in the pragmatic calculus of the legal services industry, a partner with considerable clout. For all of that, his book of business was small in comparison to the firm's over-concentrated reliance upon Gus Tanzdahl.

As Riley rose from his desk and made his way into the hallway on this overcast morning, his secretary, Skeeter Swenson, the young woman who had been with him in his last job at The Lindbergh Life & Casualty Company, handed him a file marked "Partners Committee." Like Riley, Skeeter had been implored to remain at The Lindbergh after the incident in which the CEO betrayed his duty of loyalty to a victimized employee. This was no small compliment considering that she had once told a powerful member of the company's board of directors that he acted like a "a real dickhead." She was bright, loyal, and utterly uninhibited—just the kind of person he was most drawn to. Compared to some of the names she had called Riley over the years, he thought the member of the board of directors had gotten off light.

As Riley took a deep breath and turned in the direction of the conference room, Skeeter tossed back her head of thick blonde hair and slapped him smartly on the back. "Give 'em hell, big boy."

\* \* \*

AROUND THE HEAVY mahogany table in the main conference room, the members of the committee were loosely gathered— some feisty, some sleepy, most preferring to be someplace else.

Off at a side table was Blanche Emersen, Ladge Wilkaster's administrative assistant, a small, chinless woman so stiff and officious that she looked always as though she might tip over. Wilkaster himself sat at the head of the table, flanked by Vic Laslow, chair of the Corporate Practice Group, and Barney Bost, the firm's administrator.

Though an attorney by training, Barney Bost did not practice law in the conventional sense, instead overseeing the firm's staff and administrative functions, including human resources and facilities management. Though without status in his own right, he carried the reflected authority of Ladge Wilkaster in all he did. He deferred broadly to the department heads but adopted a bossy and condescending manner with other firm employees—lawyers and non-lawyers alike.

As a major patron of the arts, Ladge Wilkaster had caused the firm over the previous decade to invest heavily in an art collection of a distinctly contemporary nature. Each painting hung in a location assigned by Barney Bost and was flanked by a side panel detailing the history and background of the artist and the work, expressed in the kind of pompous language so beloved by abstract art collectors. Longing for acceptance into the most fashionable cultural circles, Ladge and Barney held to the post-modernist bias against poets who can rhyme, artists who can draw, and composers who can carry a tune. Freed of any objective standard, therefore, Riley thought Barney was as entitled to call himself an expert as any other cultural snob.

In his role as curator of the art collection, Barney had, without notice, hung a grotesque portrait of an amputated limb outside Riley's office, just above Skeeter's head. The accompanying side-panel told of the painter's short and troubled life, which ended in a fatal drug overdose at a young age.

In text composed by Barney, the side-panel described the painting as *"A raw yet sensitive and fully unique rendering of life's brutalities, in which the painter endeavors to disturb our prosperous complacency and establish the principle of interlinear co-optation, which he would have completed had he not first succumbed to the despair of an indifferent world. This work—lyrically evocative and faintly hypnotic—crackles with a languid resignation to the vicissitudes of the everyday struggle and is, at one and the same time, a melancholy yet supinely thematic harbinger of the glorious rapture inherent in the quiescent life spirit."*

What the hell that meant was anyone's guess. No one seemed to know.

Skeeter and Riley were unified in their belief that having to work with people like Barney Bost was disturbing enough to their quiescent life spirit without having an amputated limb hanging on the wall as a reminder. So they took it upon themselves to transfer the offending work to a nearby broom closet, replacing it with a large blowup of Skeeter's high school graduation picture. In the adjoining panel Riley entitled the replacement work, "Hot Cheerleader in Green," and described the photographic subject as *"A raw yet sensitive suburbanite, who in her distaste for artistic pretension foreshadows the disquieting certainty of one day disturbing the prosperous complacency of an inelegant yet somehow languid art curator."*

Barney was not happy about the playful iconoclasm of the firm's two proudest philistines. Even Ladge Wilkaster, a man of occasional mirth, failed to join in the intended spirit. They were amused neither by the insult to their artistic sensibilities nor by the rough time the amputated limb was receiving in the broom closet, where the night crew was using it as a doorstop. To make matters worse, Riley had corrected the grammar and diction in Barney's original side-panel and returned it to him with a grade of "D-."

A compromise was eventually reached in which Skeeter's senior class picture was removed and the amputated limb was relocated to Barney's office. The wall behind Skeeter's desk now boasted a large painting of a picture window, something she was always bitching about not having.

As the remaining members of the Partners Committee trickled in one by one with agendas and legal pads tucked under their arms, Riley flashed a good-natured smile at Barney. Still smarting over his bad grade, Barney put his nose in the air and looked away.

The partners' conference room was lined with an imposing expanse of dark paneling, interrupted by inlaid bookcases on which a collector's edition of *The Minnesota Reports* was neatly stacked. The well-oiled pale leather bindings of the antique volumes stood in sharp relief to the surrounding mahogany walls. At the end of the room were two long, narrow windows, inset with thick grids, giving the room an Oxonian feel.

Riley sat near one of the windows, directly across from two large color portraits of John Levi and Arlie Z. Cosgrove, the local attorneys who nearly seventy years before had formed a lucrative partnership to handle bond offerings for the area's municipalities, school districts, and large corporations. One a North Side Jew and the other a Mt. Curve Wasp, they had initially been fierce competitors. But when their squabbles over the same territory became financially counter-productive, in the best Midwestern tradition they shook hands and joined their operations, commencing what was to be a long and profitable collaboration that ended only when Arlie Cosgrove, at age seventy-five, died of a heart attack in the arms of a high-ticket working girl in downtown Minneapolis.

The heirs of John Levi eschewed the law, instead becoming educators, surgeons, and diplomats, while Arlie Cosgrove's only child, Arlie Z. Cosgrove, Jr., known since boyhood as "Junior," managed to squeak through night law school and, after four tries, pass the Minnesota bar exam. Junior Cosgrove was one of the few truly stupid people Riley had ever met.

When Arlie died, there was a movement to expel Junior from the firm, but the effort lost traction when Junior threatened to use his name and substantial family connections to open a competing enterprise. His mother was an heiress to the Holbein fortune, and the Holbeins were first cousins to the firm's second biggest clients, the Van Studdiford's, so there you were. The Cosgrove & Levi elders ultimately arrived at the conclusion that it would be easier to continue Junior's sinecure than to suffer his mother's enmity and the loss of business that would be sure to result from his departure. Besides, Junior didn't require much pay for the little work he did. As a result of his father's unwillingness to allow his only son to establish a separate identity, Junior's attempts at self-validation were expressed through remarkable sexual promiscuity and an avid pursuit of cultural fashion. Junior wanted to be loved and he wanted to be hip, in that order. He was sort of a well-dressed Billy goat, roaming about the premises in search of female companionship. If there was a social, sartorial, or cultural trend that Junior had missed over the years, Riley couldn't think what it was. No slogan, no air-headed cliché, was too sophomoric to find its way into Junior's lexicon.

He was proactive, he cut to the chase, got to the bottom line, pushed the envelope, thought outside the box, and owned his own feelings. He called people "Babe" (men and women alike), did his own thing, did Vegas, did lunch, and did his best friend's wife. He wore wide investment-banker suspenders even though his pants had never once fallen down and he knew nothing about investment banking. In the 1980s, he kept his eye on the ball, went organic, got it on, got it off, got a life, chilled out, kicked back, and teed it up. He joined the men's movement, where once a week he and his warrior within got slathered with face paint and made strange noises while hugging elm trees. In the early nineties, he followed his bliss, got on with his life, worked 24/7, referred to himself in the third person, and framed every declarative statement as the answer to a question he had just asked himself. He took a meeting, took lunch, took R&R, joined AA, converted to born-again Christianity and started screwing his secretary. His wardrobe tended toward office-casual with a sporting twist and his hairstyle was modeled on Eminem, save only the blonde frosting. It took a direct order from Ladge Wilkaster to forestall the placing of a tattoo on the back of one hand and a metal ring in one earlobe. "Awesome" became his favorite word. When Junior agreed with someone, he looked that person hard in the eye and said, "You rock," or, worse yet, "You rule."

His latest conversion was to a highly westernized version of Buddhism, which had him believing he was the reincarnation of Gregory Rasputin—a prospect that Riley found altogether plausible.

Sloganeering had been greatly discouraged in Riley's family of origin, his father considering it a substitute for thought. So, though he felt sorry for Junior, and even liked him in a pitiable sort of way, he could barely stand to be in the same room when the clichés came pouring forth like molten sewage. But because Junior was scorned and ridiculed by the firm's meanest elements, he was automatically assured of Riley's friendship—a phenomenon that had less to do with saintly decency than it did with his late father's practice of turning to him in moments of unkindness or intolerance and saying "Whatever you do to the least of my brethren." Because that gentle scolding seemed to carry with it the promise of eternal damnation, his lifetime adherence to the biblical injunction was not an example of spiritual loftiness so much as it was a practical tradeoff. In any case, he had come to like Junior and to be fascinated with his peculiar frame of reference.

When Junior caught Riley's eye at the other end of the table, he thrust both thumbs in the air and mouthed the words, "H-e-y, B-a-b-e." Riley nodded and smiled, but he did not reciprocate the gesture. It would take the finding of Bridey Reaves to get his thumbs in the air.

With the exception of Junior, the lawyers in the firm were of uniformly high intelligence and legal sophistication, having been hired from the upper reaches of their law school classes. A solid majority were also good people, likeable and fair-minded, though approximately one out of five was as venal and obnoxious as could be found anywhere in the legal world. One of five probably wasn't bad, Riley thought, but that twenty percent was unfortunately concentrated in the firm's management structure where political and policy decisions were made. It is often said that there are no politics like academic politics, but whoever coined that expression was never a partner in a law firm.

Representatives of the individual departments tended to sit together at these meetings. More often than not, those closest to the door were the litigators. The trial department consisted of eight partners and eleven associates. To outward appearances, the trial lawyers were stoic and self-possessed. In their speech there was an air of precision mixed with a hint of challenge. They were the gladiators of the profession, and no matter how much they might intellectually respect the "desk lawyers" in the firm, they couldn't help but look upon them as mere solicitors, not quite fit to join the barrister ranks.

The senior trial attorneys in the firm numbered only four, all scorched-earth, ball-busting veterans. And when things got ugly, it was to the trial lawyers that the other partners in the firm turned. Having prosecuted and defended over two hundred cases in a career that spanned a quarter century, Riley was numbered among the senior trial counsel. Like his colleagues, he affected an air of perfect self-assurance when about to go to trial, but beneath the calm exterior there coursed a sea of nausea and loose stools. In spite of the obvious correlation between the first day of trial and his intestinal upset, he invariably interpreted the symptoms as the emergence of a long-simmering colon cancer.

The twelve members of the Partners Committee, ten men and two women, were about evenly divided between older partners—gray eminences with pocket hankies and courtly manners—and a newer breed, mostly in their forties and early fifties. Unlike the old timers, the younger partners were less concerned about civility and more concerned about their own advancement. In this respect, their natural leader was Ladge Wilkaster and they followed him like a herd of livestock.

In addition to being the chair of the Charitable Gifts Subcommittee, Riley had been assigned to chair the Partner Mediation Task Force, which was charged with resolving monetary disagreements between individual partners. Not surprisingly, the docket of that committee was riddled with the firm's most truculent elements. Fee disputes most commonly arose between "originators" (those who claimed credit for bringing a client to the firm) and "producers" (those who actually did the work). In all but the most clear-cut cases, assigning financial credit under this system was tricky business. The problem was compounded when a client relationship went back many years and the originating partner had little ongoing contact with the file. The one saving grace was that Riley was joined on the committee by Benton Hubbard, now seated to his left at the conference table. A former Lutheran seminarian and for three years a staff lawyer with the Ethical Practices Board, Ben Hubbard was ideally suited to the business of the committee.

An "originator vs. producer" dispute was currently raging between two lawyers who were inclined to let their disputes spill over into every meeting they attended, including today's. The producer, George Stonequist, who Riley had known since high school, was the firm's most notorious "pencil pusher," often recording ten hours of billable time after being in the office scarcely half that long. Although Riley found that practice to be reprehensible, and could not bring himself to engage in it, on payday he never turned down his proportional share of the loot. He figured that made him at least a half a hypocrite.

Loud, sloppy and ill tempered, with a comb-over hairdo and half his breakfast dripping from his tie, George Stonequist was the living embodiment of those qualities that cause ordinary people to believe all lawyers are assholes. With a finger-jabbing certainty, George was given to dogmatic statements of law and fact that turned out, with an astonishing consistency, to be flat wrong. As Ben Hubbard put it, the best thing that could be said about George Stonequist was that he was unbearable.

For all of that, Stonequist was an unequalled genius for certain types of legal matters. Possessed of a photographic memory, he was more than willing to stage a demonstration for anyone inclined to doubt it. He was, moreover, a stunning success as a marketer of legal services. When prospective clients appeared in his sights, George pursued them with a sort of despotic charm, rarely failing to land at least a portion of their business. He was, in all respects, a partner to contend with at Cosgrove & Levi.

Riley had never been in a meeting with George where his cell phone didn't ring at least once with a breaking development on one of his cases or news of a new account. By reason of George's friendship with Gus Tanzdahl, a good slice of the Tanzdahl Industries account was also credited to him. Gus thought George was a "winner."

But like many driven men, George had his idiosyncrasies, the strangest of which was a collection of vintage Speedo bathing suits, which he accumulated the way other people collect stamps or model airplanes. As proud of this peculiar indulgence as the firm was mortified, a chatty George once gave an interview to a local newspaper that was featured in the following Sunday's variety section, accompanied by color photos of George standing next to his Speedo collection. It was just after the appearance of that article that his second wife left him for good.

In contrast to George Stonequist was Scott Stearns, the "originator" in the current dispute, a courtly but feisty man who had unquestionably brought the client, Bayard Van Studdiford, into the firm some thirty-five years earlier. Once a lion in the Twin Cities legal establishment, Stearns was now pretty much a spent force. Workdays consisted of sitting in his museum-like office surrounded by awards and newspaper reprints documenting the arc of a long and successful career. Stearns had little ongoing involvement in the Van Studdiford client relationship—now handled almost exclusively by George Stonequist.

So, under the rules of the firm, Riley had the disagreeable duty of ruling against a man he deeply admired in favor of a collector of Speedo bathing suits whom he deeply loathed. As irritating as these duties were, though, they were as nothing compared to the strain of the Tanzdahl divorce case, of which he was now repeatedly reminded as each department head reported the number of new Tanzdahl Industries files opened in his area.

At the completion of the Tanzdahl Industries update, Ladge Wilkaster commenced a line-by-line analysis of the firm's recent furniture purchases, which was promptly interrupted by the ring of George Stonequist's cellular phone.

Scott Stearns, loser to Stonequist in the Van Studdiford fee dispute, squinted down the table at his nemesis. "That's a rude interruption, George. Were you born in a barn?"

Junior Cosgrove thought this was a very funny remark, and he roared with laughter.

"Shut up, Junior," said Ladge Wilkaster.

"Leave him alone, Ladge," said Riley.

"Rock on!" said Junior, giving Riley another thumbs up.

"Shut up, Junior," said Vic Laslow from across the table.

"I didn't say anything rude," said Stonequist.

"Did too," said Scott Stearns.

"Did not," shot back George.

"Everybody shut up," shouted Ladge Wilkaster, banging an ashtray on the table.

*What the hell am I doing here*, thought Riley. This was like being in a sandbox. He scanned the room for an escape hatch.

Twenty minutes later, before bidding farewell to the new furniture, Ladge passed around an amortization schedule of the firm's fixed assets in the Sioux Falls office, a document so dull that even the tax lawyers could not bear to look upon it.

This was too much. When Ladge wasn't looking, Riley slipped out a side door.


BACK IN HIS OFFICE, he began work on the monthly billing statements for The Stoddard Trust. The Stoddard relationship was smooth, uncomplicated, and hugely profitable. This was owing in large part to Ev Pedersen's careful and detailed management of the myriad service relationships contracted for by the Trust. It had been a banner month for the account, including the opening of twenty-eight new transaction files, matters that would keep half the real estate department busy for the foreseeable future. Three associates and two young partners were getting their first taste of Stoddard work. The work done by the firm, though extensive, was exclusively of the transactional variety, where the lawyers had little need to interact with senior personnel of the client, let alone understand its carefully guarded internal workings. It was a privately held company and thought to be philanthropic in its leanings, but its actual ownership was deliberately obscured. No one outside the senior management ranks seemed to have any idea who they worked for. On those rare occasions when a board resolution or other document was necessary in connection with a transaction, the Cosgrove & Levi attorney handling the file would simply notify Riley, and he would call Ev Pedersen. The document would materialize within twenty-four hours.

Cosgrove & Levi handled no litigation for the Trust and, as a result, had no need for access to company secrets or other non-public information. On those rare occasions when Stoddard found itself in litigation associated with a transaction that had been handled by Cosgrove & Levi, on instructions of Ev Pedersen, Riley would have the file packaged and sent to Channing & Hollis in New York, the Trust's principal outside law firm.

For Riley, the Stoddard relationship was a stroke of amazing good fortune. "Grace" is what the nuns back at Sacred Heart would call it. "Sheer dumb luck" is what Ladge Wilkaster called it as he sought each quarter to renegotiate Riley's slice of the compensation pie, even hinting furtively that, while the Trust admittedly came in the door because of Riley's prior relationship with Ev Pedersen, it was the high quality of work performed by the firm's real estate department that kept the client happily in the fold. So happily that it would be unlikely to move its business even if Riley were no longer with the firm. This Riley took to be warning that he had a lot at risk should he try to ditch the Tanzdahl case. In this "carrot and stick" approach, it was also pointed out to Riley that his standing in the firm had taken a quantum leap when Gus Tanzdahl insisted that he handle the divorce case. It may have done political wonders for him within the firm, but being Gus Tanzdahl's handpicked champion continued to rest uneasily on his soul.

Thoughts of the Tanzdahl divorce seemed always to send his mood spiraling downward. The case stuck in his mind like motor oil, eerily reminiscent of the feelings that came to torment him in the late stages of his time at the Lindbergh Life & Casualty Company, where a lazy and crooked CEO betrayed his obligation to protect a young employee from harassment by the company's most profitable customer, resulting ultimately in the employee's suicide. Through a combination of naiveté and self-interest, Riley had played an enabling role in that tragedy. He was more than normally uncomfortable, therefore, with career decisions made under the influence of monetary considerations.

To clear his head that morning, sitting at his desk he slapped himself across the face in the style of his hero Joe Frazier in those old shaving cream commercials. He then cleared his throat, sat up straight in his chair, and once again struck himself smartly on the cheek. "I needed that," he mumbled to himself.

When he opened his eyes, Skeeter was standing before him, a stack of files under her arm. "They have some really good medications for people like you."

Riley blushed, smiling awkwardly. "Geez, Skeets, don't sneak up on me like that."

She dumped the files in his in-basket as the phone on his desk rang. They both looked down at the caller I.D. and saw that it was Chasbo Peytabohm returning Riley's call from earlier in the day.

Skeeter headed for her desk and picked up the receiver. In an officious voice, she said, "State Parole Board." After a brief silence, in which she listened to Chasbo's reply, she burst out laughing. "Don't call me names, you tit-handling ex-convict."

Riley sat back in his chair, happy that two of his closest friends, people from two different worlds, liked each other enough to carry on like that. They actually had a lot in common, though Skeeter had never been in prison, and she had never deliberately thrown up on anybody.

"Yeah, well you can put it in the same place, big boy," she said into the phone as she swiveled in her chair and reached into her purse for a piece of gum.

Riley picked up the phone. "Hey Chasbo, what's happening?"

"Is this phone tapped?" asked Chasbo.

"Nope," said Riley. "Even if it is tapped, they can't use the conversation against you. I'm your lawyer, remember?"

"Oh, yeah, that's right. It's just a habit left over from the old days." Chasbo then redirected his attention to someone who had entered his office, covering the phone receiver with his hand. Muffled remarks could be heard on the other end. Finally Chasbo returned. "What do you want, counselor," he said. "I'm a busy CEO with heavy shit going down—balance sheets and cash flow statements and all that stuff."

"I just wanted to make sure you're coming to the Cosgrove & Levi reception at the Millar's Club tonight. Ev Pedersen from The Stoddard Trust doesn't go to public events, and I need a big client there to show how important I am, even if the client is a complete piece of dogshit."

"Yeah, right . . . I'll be there, but you tell Skeeter that she has to treat me with the respect I deserve."

Riley looked out at Skeeter and nodded. "Oh, I think you can count on her to treat you the way you deserve."

THE RECEPTION AREA of the very traditional Millar's Club was enlivened by colorful flowers, bouncing balloons, and waitresses wearing curly judicial wigs. With its dark mahogany paneling, heavy oaken beams and indirect lighting, the space looked like a turn-of-the-century funeral parlor in which a group of clowns had been turned loose. Ladge Wilkaster thought that the setup incorporated elements of the old and the new in an eclectic mix sure to appeal to the aggressive entrepreneurs who had come to dominate the firm's clientele.

In a gesture to the past, the large portraits of Arlie Cosgrove and John Levi had been temporarily relocated to the club, where they stood upright on large easels flanking a massive Tudor fireplace. Skeeter had proposed attaching a written side panel to Arlie Cosgrove's portrait paying tribute to his legendary reputation for sexual conquests within the secretarial ranks. But seeing Junior across the room, Riley vetoed the idea.

Once a bastion of the WASP ascendancy, the Millar's Club had evolved over the years into a gathering place of a different sort. No longer organized along racial or religious lines, the club had become a mixed collection of lawyers, corporate managers, and free-wheeling entrepreneurs. Replacing the aged scions of the Yankee establishment in the high-backed leather chairs lining the club's main parlor were a mass of lawyers and cigar-smoking venture capitalists.

By seven-thirty, the brightly festooned reception area was filling with Cosgrove & Levi's best clients and prospective clients: male and female, large and small, black and white, gay and straight.

Entering the reception area, each guest was pinned with an embossed name tag and given a copy of Gus Tanzdahl's autobiography, *The Making of a Champion, the Gus Tanzdahl Story*. In the suck-up move of the century, Ladge Wilkaster had the firm purchase two-hundred copies for distribution to its best clients at tonight's gathering. *The Making of a Champion* was ghostwritten by a local journalist two years earlier for a cash fee but no authorial credit, and consisted largely of a string of biographical facts meant to showcase Gus's rise from humble origins to the top of the corporate ladder. Along the way, the reader was served a run of mindless clichés passing as business wisdom.

Gus had ordered a 10,000-copy print run, but when, to no one else's surprise, a market failed to develop among local bookstores, he was left to dispose of the books as best he could. This he did with embarrassing resolve, fobbing off copies on everyone in sight, including the seventy-five lawyers at Cosgrove & Levi, all of who were required to prominently display a copy in their offices.

The previous summer Gus had hosted an open house at his northern Minnesota cabin for the sixty other families with homes on Lake Minneowla. Following an evening of food and entertainment, Gus handed the guests personally inscribed copies of *The Making of a Champion* as they got into their boats for the ride home. The guests, who had had quite enough of Gus by that time, politely but unenthusiastically accepted the tendered books.

At first light the next day, Gus made his way to the front dock for a round of calisthenics, only to be greeted by a lake surface littered with so many copies of *The Making of a Champion* that he initially mistook the sight for an enormous school of dead carp. Only the brightly colored American flag adorning the book's cover clearly identified the debris as Gus's memoirs. The hurriedly summoned Tanzdahl grounds crew mounted a valiant rescue effort, netting as many copies as possible before they sank to the lake's bottom. But, alas, they couldn't save a good many, so when the ice that formed the following winter melted away in a spring thaw, Lake Minneowla gave up her dead in prodigious numbers. The sunken volumes rose to the surface like the gas-filled corpses of a massive shipwreck. At final count, over a hundred copies of Gus's autobiography had been chucked overboard.

Riley smiled at the memory and made a mental note to tell Skeeter the story over dinner.

C. Taylor Peytabohm, CEO of CT Preventive Imaging, arrived late in a limousine driven by an ex-convict with whom he had shared a cell during his last trip up the river. Despite Chasbo's stunning financial success, the managing directors of the Millar's Club had blackballed his application for membership several years before. That initiative was mounted before Chasbo became one of Cosgrove & Levi's largest clients, and it had been led by none other than Ladge Wilkaster. In spite of confidential balloting, Chasbo knew exactly who had engineered his rejection.

"Riley, my man," shouted Chasbo as he made a garish entrance into the reception area. "How they hanging, kid."

Riley looked at Chasbo, smiling the way one does at an eccentric but lovable relative. "Hi, Chasbo, how are you?"

"Not too bad," said Chasbo, bouncing on the balls of his feet and surveying the room. Without turning in his direction, Chasbo gestured toward his chauffeur and said, "This is the Weasel."

Riley extended his hand tentatively. "Hello, Weasel," he said politely. He had a vague recollection that he had once prosecuted the Weasel, but he could not be sure. There had been so many.

Chasbo's outfit could best be described as Disco Chic: checkered sport coat over a tan silk shirt with the three top buttons unfastened, revealing a gold medallion resting on a tuft of chest hair. A diamond-studded watch glistened under the bright ceiling lights. Shifting his weight from foot to foot, Chasbo rolled his shoulders, and leaned into Riley. "Say, man, how's Betsy these days? She need her tits examined?" He smiled lustily, wiggling his eyebrows.

"Very funny," said Riley, feigning offense. "That's the mother of my children you're talking about." In spite of the many differences between them, Riley had long ago accepted Chasbo as a close friend and trusted him implicitly, at least in all matters unrelated to women, money, and social etiquette.

There was no earthly reason, given his family background, that Chasbo should have turned to a life of rebellion and larceny. Born of a highly educated and prosperous Kenwood family, from the outset he preferred the company of household servants and workmen to the dancing school crowd that formed the core of the Lowry Hill social set in the 1950s. And when he entered Sacred Heart Grade School—an eclectic collection of the privileged and desperately underprivileged—he promptly associated himself with the school's most troubled elements.

Riley, who seemed to find a home with all components of the Sacred Heart landscape, was Chasbo's only friend from the right side of the tracks. That friendship, forged in the rough-and-tumble precincts of Sacred Heart, was augmented by another four years at St. David's Military School in St. Paul. But even the rigors of a military boarding school had failed to tame Chasbo's counter-cultural tendencies. Riley's father—a man who had grown up on the wrong side of town and was noted for broad-mindedness—thought Riley would be better off divorcing himself from Chasbo's company. Even Chasbo's own parents seemed baffled by their unusual son, openly speculating that he may have been a changeling.

Riley put his hand on Chasbo's shoulder and implored, "Please behave yourself tonight. These are important people for Cosgrove & Levi."

Chasbo chuckled mischievously.

Riley flashed a stern, I'm-not-kidding look, squeezing Chasbo's arm tightly. "I mean it. You can't embarrass me. I've told Skeeter to keep an eye on you."

"Yeah, who's going to keep an eye on her?" said Chasbo as he continued scanning the crowd. His face suddenly tightened as he stared in the direction of the bar.

Riley tried to follow his line of sight. "What are you looking at?"

"There's that little prick Gus Tanzdahl. I hate that son-of-a-bitch."

"Whoa," said Riley. "I'm representing him in his divorce, so let's not have a scene."

Chasbo's expression changed abruptly. He looked over at Riley and smiled wickedly. "Remember that time back in the dorm when we pissed in his humidifier?"

"What do you mean, we?"

Chasbo ignored the question. "Yeah, I heard he's ditching his young wife for that snob Trudi Hansdale. Remember Trudi from the university, that well-bred skag with no chin? I think she had a crush on you, buddy. Did you ever get a little of that stuff?"

"Come on, Chasbo, you're making me sick. Just be nice, will you? This is a classy crowd."

"Yeah, right, classy guys like Gus Tanzdahl. Ellen's a nice kid. I know her mother, Renee Murseth—she's worked in employee benefits at Preventive Imaging for years. She handles all our insurance information and claims. Nicest person in the world." Chasbo's face reddened as he again stared over at Gus. "Tanzdahl's pulled some rotten shit on that girl over the years. I've heard all about it from Renee. I hope Ellen takes him to the cleaners, gets every cent he's got."

Riley noticed that Gus Tanzdahl had caught sight of Chasbo and was moving quickly away from the bar to avoid him. Chasbo loved to embarrass Gus whenever they found themselves together in public.

"Look at that dumpy little chickenshit running away," said Chasbo, his face taut.

He then looked back at Riley and rubbed his hands together. "I'm gonna go socialize."

Riley gave a prearranged nod to Skeeter, who fell in behind Chasbo.

Not fifteen minutes later, as he stood talking to a federal judge and a group of law clerks, Riley felt a tug on his sleeve. He turned to see Skeeter gesturing for him to join her in the hallway. His heart sank. Out in the hall he asked, "What did he do?"

Shaking her head and giggling, Skeeter said, "Oh, my God, you should have heard his conversation with Ladge Wilkaster."

Riley squinted, the lines around his eyes creasing. "Do I really want to hear this?"

"I think you better," she said. "Ladge started to kiss up to him right in front of these other clients . . . you know Bayard Van Studdiford and that stuffy bunch. He was telling Chasbo what a great businessman he was and what a privilege it was for Cosgrove & Levi to represent him. He was laying on all the usual crap."

Riley steeled himself and nodded for her to continue.

"Chasbo knows that Ladge was one of the club officers who blackballed his application for membership here, and he wasn't buying into the flattery."

Riley looked around nervously. "Yeah . . . so what happened?"

"Well, when Ladge finished gushing, he put his hand on Chasbo's shoulder and said, 'Taylor, I'd like you to join these other distinguished gentlemen on a blue-ribbon client-advisory panel I'm establishing. What do you say, my friend?'"

Skeeter choked back a laugh. "Chasbo looked at the other clients and then back at Ladge, and said, 'Oh, blow me, Wilkaster.'"

Riley wiped his forehead with his cocktail napkin. He looked at Skeeter, who was now bent over with laughter. He was afraid she might wet her pants. They were both laughing uncontrollably.

When he recovered his composure, Riley headed for the dining room, using a side entrance to avoid Wilkaster. He entered the room behind a three-piece music ensemble playing background music, keeping an eye out for the managing partner.

Before he got ten steps into the room, Ladge emerged from a group of clients and put a lock on Riley's arm. His face burned red against the high white collar of his custom-made shirt, and his voice trembled with anger. "McReynolds, do you know what that awful friend of yours, Taylor Peytabohm, said to me right in front of a group of our best clients?"

Riley pretended not to hear the question, pointing to the musicians and cupping a hand behind his ear in the style of Ronald Reagan crossing the White House lawn. Smiling dumbly, he continued toward his table.

But Ladge was having none of it. He grabbed Riley's coat and repeated the question, this time in a louder voice. "Well, do you know what he said to me?"

Riley tilted his head helplessly, not sure what to say. Finally he shrugged and smiled weakly. "I hear he wants a BJ."

AS THE EVENING wore on and the demon rum worked its magic on the guests, those in attendance became less formal and more outgoing. Being relatively new to the firm, Riley was acquainted with some of the clients only because he had advised them on the landslide of recent government regulations or represented them in connection with grand jury investigations where they had potential criminal liability. He had helped a number of them out of some pretty serious jams. By and large they were not eager, at least when sober, to be reminded of the peril in which they had so recently found themselves. Encountering their former savior was like running into a doctor who had cured them of an embarrassing disease. But when alcohol loosened their inhibitions, these eminent businessmen gave themselves over, if not exactly to gratitude, then to a sloppy form of camaraderie that made Riley's skin crawl. At the first opportunity he fled their company.

The only thing that could have kept him at this party would have been if Ev Pedersen of The Stoddard Trust had been in attendance. But Ev—and for that matter the entire staff of the Trust—avoided social gatherings the same way they avoided publicity. So Riley was free to make a clean break. He had fulfilled his duty to the firm.

He went looking for Chasbo, and finally found him twirling about the dance floor all by himself to the accompaniment of a string quartet, spilling his drink in all directions as he executed a series of solo maneuvers. After downing five Martinis, Chasbo had decided to express his deepest feelings through the magic of interpretive dance. The musicians looked on with a kind of wonder at this drunken hoofer, not the kind of man they expected to meet at the Millar's Club.

Riley gestured for Skeeter and the Weasel to help get Chasbo off the dance floor and down the stairs. They then guided him out the front entrance and into the waiting limousine.

As the limo departed the circular driveway—now lined with guests attending the wedding reception of a Lutheran bishop's daughter in another part of the club—Chasbo stuck his head out the back window and shouted: "So long, Riley. Don't let the meat loaf!"

# 5

---

I T WAS ODD that the criminal cases Riley regularly handled—tax evasion, securities fraud, industrial espionage—failed to penetrate the wall that stands sentinel to the conscience of a modern lawyer, while his one and only civil case, Tanzdahl v. Tanzdahl, tore at his conscience.

Unpleasantness seems always to accompany contested divorce actions, but there was something special about this one, at least for him. It was not the staggering unreasonableness of Gus Tanzdahl—just about everybody in a high-stakes divorce was unreasonable. And it wasn't the amount of money at stake, for he had dealt with sums that large on many occasions as a lawyer. It wasn't even Riley's assumption, vigorously denied, that Gus was contesting custody of his child solely to leverage a favorable financial settlement.

What it must be, he thought, was the mismatch between the contestants, made worse by the special vulnerability of this young woman who, discarded by her husband, was clinging desperately to custody of her only child, a child who by all accounts she loved dearly. It was the "boy and his mother" angle that seemed to be getting to him. The notion that he was employing his skills and influence to frighten a young mother into renouncing her lawful share of a family fortune, was more odious to him than the acquittal of any criminal he had ever represented. He saw in Ellen Tanzdahl's eyes the same maternal love he saw in Betsy's whenever Lizzie or Teddy were at risk because of illness or danger, the same instinctual love that sent mothers into a burning building or roused them from a deep sleep at the sound of a distant cough. It was no wonder that he had always ducked child custody cases, for to him they were a trespass upon sacred ground. Should one venture into that space in the name of the law, it had better be for the purest of reasons. And preserving Gus Tanzdahl's fortune or, for that matter, the Tanzdahl Industries account for Cosgrove & Levi, didn't seem to him to qualify.

The emotional strain was relieved only during those blessed interludes in which he could jump into the search for the girl at O'Banion's graveside, the girl with the sad pale eyes. It was no wonder, therefore, that it was to that matter that he was most compellingly drawn. He could jump into the Bridey Reaves mystery the way his partners jumped into their golf games or hunting trips. And on this sunny afternoon in early July as his partners headed for the links, Riley pulled from under his credenza the briefcase in which he kept the growing materials relating to Dion O'Banion and Bridey Reaves.

He had already gone to the public library and scoured the catalogue for books on how to track missing persons, with a particular emphasis on people who had deliberately vanished. He searched under key words and expressions and found a listing for what seemed an ideal reference work—a thin paperback entitled *Twenty Successful Disappearances and Why They Worked*. But when he checked the status of the seven listed copies, he found that all but one had been stolen, no doubt by people for whom the book was more than an academic treatise. The notion of library users stealing a "how to" manual on their way to a new life struck him as so funny that he laughed out loud at the lobby terminal, drawing a loud "shush" from the librarian. When he checked out the one surviving copy, the reference clerk looked up at him cryptically, and whispered, "Are you leaving town?"

The book was a primer on the subject of intentional disappearances, though like other writings on that subject, it was geared toward today's world rather than that of seventy-two years before. The all-important initial steps the young Bridey Reaves must have taken in 1925 would have been at least somewhat different. And the trail that she would have laid down in those crucial early years would long ago have grown cold. Nevertheless, while systems and methods had changed, human nature had not, and human nature was the single most important factor driving the choices made by a fleeing person, especially choices made at the unconscious level. People of all backgrounds and descriptions tend to behave in predictable ways, and it is on those ways that skilled trackers concentrate their searches.

Riley had called Alistair Kavaeny that morning, catching him on the way to a shuffleboard tournament. Knowing that Stairs remained the best source of potentially helpful information in the search, Riley called him every few days to cultivate the relationship. Because a man in his nineties was bound to recall information in bits and pieces, Stairs promised that he'd record his memories as they occurred to him. And he had been as good as his word. The small spiral notebook kept next to his bed was already filling with notes about O'Banion and, more importantly, the occasional recollection relating to Bridey.

Such was the case in this morning's call. Stairs relayed that in the late 1930s—roughly a dozen years after O'Banion's death and Bridey's flight from Chicago—he had heard a rumor that a minor hood from the West Side, John Michael O'Caskeny, had been bragging around town that he "popped" some broad who had made off with Capone money in 1925. Stairs said he remembered thinking at the time that, because he knew of no other woman who had run afoul of Capone in a monetary way, the guy could have been talking about Bridey. On the other hand, he also remembered dismissing the rumor as nothing more than the boasting of a drunken hood, "a guy who never amounted to anything."

Riley filed the information away for possible follow-up and, undeterred by rumors of Bridey's death, set about following the procedures recommended by the search materials. He started with the most far-reaching sources, of which the Social Security Death Index ("SSDI") was the most prominent. Except in the most menial of jobs, it was difficult after the mid-1930s to enter the American workplace without at some point being assigned a social security number. Bridey had fled Chicago well before passage of the Social Security Act, but if she had ever had a job after the mid-thirties, she probably would have been issued a card. And because the Social Security Death Index listed the deaths of cardholders who passed away after 1965, if Bridey had died since then she might appear in the index under whatever name she was then using.

That she would have kept her own name, however—let alone used it to apply for a social security number—was highly doubtful. And if she was packing the $500,000 O'Banion was rumored to have given her, there would seem to have been no need for her to work.

As expected, a search of the SSDI yielded no death record for an Anna McBride Reaves, A.M. Reaves, Bridey Reaves, or any of the same variations using the more common spelling "Reeves." None of this was surprising.

He turned next to the statewide death indexes, which when comprehensively surveyed, can plug the holes in the SSDI. Again, nothing under Bridey's real name or its common variations.

Next he checked marriage and drivers license records, city directories, Lexis/Nexus databases, insurance claim indexes, name-change petitions, cemetery and funeral home records, and a full range of other, more obscure databases, ancient and modern, from which he might tease a clue. Again, not a speck of useful information.

Thus he concluded that she had successfully changed her identity during her flight, or that she had been found and killed almost immediately. Despite the passage of nearly seventy-two years, the thought of that beautiful young girl being murdered filled him with a terrible revulsion.

The second phase of the search had commenced with a call to the Convent of St. Agnes, in which Bridey had lived during the two years between the death of her parents and the O'Banion murder. Long past its prime, that community of women—once numbering eighty-three nuns and four hundred girls housed in a five-story, turn-of-the-century building —was now reduced to three nuns living in a convent that was a converted single-family home on Chicago's North Side. There they tended to the legacy of an order that had once been a large and important presence in Chicago.

The previous Wednesday he had set aside all pending matters to race down to Chicago (this time by commercial airliner) to meet with the last of the order. In what seemed a paradox, the youngest of the three nuns, a thirty-four-year-old Ph.D. candidate at the University of Chicago, acted as his primary interface. The second nun, a fifty-something veteran of the civil rights movement, toiled daily in Chicago's most crime-ridden neighborhoods and was generally unavailable. The trio was rounded out by ninety-two-year-old Sister St. Catherine, the sole member of the group to retain the saint's name she had taken at the time of her final vows in 1927. She alone wore the distinctive dark blue habit of the order, with white piping on the headpiece and sleeves, giving her something of the look of a naval admiral.

In dealing with these three women Riley was reminded of how far removed from reality the historical stereotype of nuns was. Polarized portrayals—ranging from the saccharine roles played by Ingrid Bergman to the image of parochial school knuckle rappings in the 1950s—were equally false. Far removed from the popular myth of subservient church ladies standing guard over traditional religious orthodoxy, there had been no more consistently progressive element in American society. When the cardinals and archbishops refused to leave their chancery palaces to face the burning social issues of the 1960s, for example, it was these determined women, in their stubborn fidelity to authentic Christianity, who stood the picket lines, emptied the bed pans of the sick and dying, and taught at-risk children how to read, write, count and pray their way into the promise of American life.

Sister Meghan, the Ph.D. candidate and St. Agnes archivist, was the one to step forward and process Riley's request for any extant documents relating to the twenty-six months in which the child Anna McBride Reaves had lived on the fourth floor of the old convent, just adjacent to the postulants' wing. Short, thin, and slightly graying at the temples, Sister Meghan was the very soul of no-nonsense efficiency.

The St. Agnes records for the period from the beginning of World War II (when the convent had taken in an influx of war refugees) to the late 1950s (when the order lacked the funds to upgrade the convent to conform to modern fire-code standards), were stored in boxes shelved in chronological order in the backroom of the main facility. Records for the periods prior to that time, including those for the years Bridey had been in attendance, were stored in a small frame structure behind the main residence, a neglected out-building that had once served as a detached garage. It had not been opened for decades.

Together, Riley and the young nun walked out through the kitchen of the residence, down the decaying back stairs, and across a short span of patchy grass. The sound of inner city youngsters shooting baskets could be heard across the alley, accompanied by a round of trash talking by a group of spectators who stared menacingly at Riley. They shouted a series of discourtesies about his lack of skin pigment and unfairly characterized his relationship with his mother. Riley thought they might be less hostile and more sympathetic if they actually knew his mother. Just the day before, on a visit to the nursing home, she had scolded him mercilessly for going off on another "missing woman" search.

When Riley's face tensed at the abuse, Sister Meghan looked over at him and smiled reassuringly. "Don't worry, this is sacred space in the neighborhood. Bullets might fly between the gang-bangers, but these kids never give us any trouble. They know we're here to help . . . and, besides, I'm friends with their mothers."

At that she handed Riley what looked like a surgical mask for protection against dust, mold, radon, and whatever else might have insinuated itself into the stale air of the tomb-like garage. They donned their face gear and, with a wink and a sign of the cross, Sister Meghan turned the lock. As she pushed open the double doors the hinges screamed in protest. With Riley clinging ungallantly to the sleeve of Sister Meghan's cotton sweater, the two trespassers cautiously advanced into the semi-darkness, the only illumination being a single flashlight and the beams of afternoon sun, thick with floating dust, stealing in through the open door. A small rustling sound from behind a row of stacked boxes caused them to stop in their tracks and stare in that direction. Instead of the giant rat Riley had instantly visualized, a tiny chipmunk emerged from the corner and ran into the open space at the center of the room. There it made a confused circle and headed for the door.

They giggled nervously and then continued deeper into the garage, following the beam of Meghan's flashlight toward a far wall, against which three rows of boxes were packed floor to ceiling. Though he was crouching behind Meghan, Riley somehow managed to walk into a thick cobweb that spread itself across his face, from his forehead to below his chin. He let go of the nun and swatted hysterically at his face, certain that a poisonous spider had crawled up his nose and was about to take his life. He had read of such things in his *Merck's Manual*.

Sister Meghan howled with laughter. After convincing Riley that there was no spider in his nose, they moved to the far wall and commenced an examination, one by one, of the ancient, decaying boxes.

Riley soon entered into the moment. It was as though he had discovered a secret passageway, a small door into another time, another world. He shook with an involuntary chill.

Two hours and a couple of fresh-air breaks later, Sister Meghan reached into a moldy and unstable stack of boxes and extracted one with faded lettering on the outside. When the flashlight's beam fell upon the writing, they could plainly see: "1920-1925 (Resident Students)." They looked at each other triumphantly. Together they carried the box into the house, being careful to hold it from below to prevent the weight-bearing bottom, weakened by years of neglect, from giving way. To clear the back door, Meaghan took over sole custody and turned sideways as she passed into the kitchen, and then into the dining room. Gently, she placed the box on the table in the center of the room. She then brushed away a thick coat of dust.

His heart pounding in his throat, Riley watched silently as she reached into the box and started to make her way through the tabbed files, all neatly arranged according to the year in which each girl first arrived at the convent.

The file marked "1922" was in moldy but good condition. Meghan pulled it carefully from the box and opened it on the table. With a sweep of her arm she invited Riley to examine its contents.

He looked at her tentatively, wide-eyed. She nodded her permission.

He stepped forward, raised a pair of reading glasses to his face, and peered down at the files for 1922. There had been only eighteen resident students admitted in 1922, so the files took up only half the box.

When he got to the "R's," there was only one file. It was
marked "Anna M. Reaves." He separated the thin, yellowing
folder from its neighbors, and as he did so, a pouch attached
to the back flap gave way from age, releasing a small, com-
pact document that fell on to the table. The word "Passport"
was embossed on its front.

With a shaking hand, he opened the passport to a photograph of a handsome man in his mid to late thirties. Sitting
on the man's lap was a young girl who appeared to be about
ten years old. Riley beamed at the image, for smiling out at
him from the creased, sepia photograph—safe and happy in
her father's embrace—was the unmistakable likeness of the
girl in the front row at O'Banion's graveside.

Riley's eyes glistened as he brushed dust from the surface
of the photo.

Sister Meghan also looked down at the picture, but with a
sort of detached curiosity. She then looked up at Riley. "Is
this the girl you're looking for?"

Riley swallowed hard but didn't take his eyes from the
photo. "Yes . . . it is."

When he told her of the circumstances that caused Bridey
to flee Chicago—of her parents' death when she was fourteen, and O'Banion's death two years later—the poignancy of
the moment broke over the efficient, supposedly unsenti-
mental nun, and she, too, teared over.

When the moment passed, they set about inspecting the
remainder of the thin file. First was a sheet of paper, yellowing and dry like an old leaf pressed into a schoolbook, on which
was chronicled the death of Bridey's parents at the intersection of Fullerton and Clark on a snowy afternoon in December
of 1922. It described the short odyssey of the orphaned child as
she was shuffled between foster homes by the Department of
Child Welfare, before being rescued by The Immigrant
Assistance Society, headed at the time by a man listed as "C.
O'Neill." The chronology recorded that O'Neill had worked
with Bridey's father, John Reaves, at a manufacturing plant

west of the downtown area. It was Mr. O'Neill who had made arrangements for the parents' funeral at Holy Name Cathedral, and it was he who took the young orphan into Schofield's Flower Shop to buy a flower for each parent. It was during that visit to the flower shop that the childless Dion O'Banion was smitten by the grief-stricken girl.

The chronological file notations then became cryptic, containing a lot of ecclesiastical jargon, some of it in Latin. Sister Meghan held the faded paper under a beam of light streaming in from a side window. As she read the strangely constructed narrative, her head nodded knowingly.

"What is it?" Riley asked.

She put the file back on the table, removed her glasses, and looked up at him. "Someday I'm going to write a book about the deviousness of file keepers, especially the inventive nuns of this order, who were compulsive about their records but unwilling to share their secrets with future researchers." She shook her head and smiled cryptically. "These notations indicate, in code, that after the pledge of a substantial sum of money for the construction of a chapel in the north cloister of the old convent, Mr. Dion O'Banion gained special admittance for this young girl. Some things never change, huh?"

Together they read down the "progress log," three sheets describing Bridey's performance in a wide range of academic subjects, including elocution, mathematics, sacred theology, comparative literature, and history.

Why she was not adopted out to some Chicago family could not be divined from the brief notations in the file. Once again, however, Sister Meghan considered the coded entries and concluded that Bridey had been spoken for by a well-connected Chicago family awaiting necessary civil approvals. When she read further and noted the regular visits of Mr. and Mrs. O'Banion, including outings to the zoo and amusement park, she felt confident that it was to them that Bridey had been promised, subject only to "complications relating to Mr. O'Banion's business activities."

Noticing that the last page of the log was darker in color, Riley turned it over and found another, surprisingly well-preserved, sepia photo of Bridey. At the bottom was a handwritten notation: "Anna M. Reaves—date of birth, November 10, 1908."

Riley shook his head sadly. Dion O'Banion—Bridey's benefactor and surrogate father—had been murdered on her sixteenth birthday.

In the posed, rather formal photo, Bridey stood a tall fifteen-year-old, with shoulder-length dark hair restrained by a large white bow. A white, lacy chiffon dress hung on her slender frame, almost certainly a confirmation gown, and a small cross hung from her neck. Though the photo was black-and-white, it was easy to see that her eyes were pale and bright, almost certainly a light blue. Save only for the style of dress, this could have been a picture of his daughter Lizzie or half of her McReynolds cousins or, for that matter, any number of the Irish girls he had gone to parochial school with. Everything about the picture, so superior in quality and detail to the documentary film, verified his initial impressions as to the resemblance. Looking upon that picture of Bridey made him realize how much he adored his own daughter.

Sister Meghan took the file to a small photocopy machine in the adjacent room and made copies of its contents, which, with the exception of a note bearing Bridey's handwriting, he was given the copies. He was allowed to take the original of the note. Riley smiled and slipped the documents into his briefcase.

He then moved to the parlor couch, where Sister St. Catherine, rosary in hand, was mumbling the fourth joyful mystery. Riley dropped down next to her and put his hand gently on her arm. "Sister, can you tell me anything about Bridey Reaves?"

The elderly nun ceased her prayers and turned to him, a smile of great sweetness on her ancient face. She looked like some kind of saint. No one that old, in his experience, had ever been as authentically happy as she seemed to be. Her hand trembled with Parkinson's and her voice was weak, but her eyes, windows to her mind and soul, were bright and clear.

She nodded affirmatively and then explained that she had been a novice during the twenty-six months that Bridey had resided at the convent and had been heartsick when she suddenly disappeared. Though special friendships were discouraged, she said it had been impossible not to form a quick and deep attachment to the winsome and beautiful new girl on the fourth floor. And yes, she said, she remembered Mr. and Mrs. O'Banion picking up the freshly scrubbed, neatly dressed child on Saturday mornings for outings around Chicago. But it had never occurred to Sister St. Catherine then that the bulky men who seemed always to accompany Mr. O'Banion to the rectory—the ones who stood shuffling their feet and avoiding eye contact with the giant crucifix on the lobby wall—were the notorious Hymie Weiss and Bugs Moran, two of Chicago's most feared killers.

# 6

---

IT WAS WARM and soggy outside, eighty-five degrees on
way to a daytime high of ninety-two. But inside the
ornate chambers of the Cosgrove & Levi conference room
it was cool and dry. From the oil portrait hanging on the
north wall, the piercing eyes of John Levi stared down upon
the opposing sides assembled for the deposition of Ellen
Tanzdahl.

At one end of the large mahogany table sat the court
reporter, a heavy-set woman with a jowly face beneath a
frothy confection of reddish-orange hair. A stenographic
machine stood at her side, and, before her on the table in two
carefully arranged rows, were the business cards of the four
lawyers and two paralegals whose attendance she would formally note for the record.

Ellen Tanzdahl sat in a chair to the court reporter's immediate right, and on Ellen's right was her attorney, Clinton
Tarrymore, a seasoned veteran with an excellent win-loss
record and a reputation for thoroughness and civility. Riley
had known Clint for a quarter-century and had a high regard
for him, both as a person and as a lawyer. Tall, angular and
Lincolnesque in bearing, Tarrymore strove to bring reason

and objectivity to domestic cases, knowing that to do otherwise nearly always resulted in unnecessary heartache, emotional bloodletting, and excessive attorney's fees. But his devotion to fair play was not so all-consuming that it overrode a ready willingness to throw elbows with the best of them should that approach become necessary.

The long relationship and professional respect that existed between Riley and Clint Tarrymore, together with their shared belief in the mannerly resolution of disputes, would ordinarily insure that this litigation would proceed smoothly, at least as to procedural matters.

Riley sat directly across the conference table from the witness and just to the right of Gus, who insisted on being present during his wife's testimony. Gus chose a seat directly within Ellen's sight line. He stared across at her, chewing gum and sneering at the ingrate who had dared reject his settlement offer—a woman he viewed as little more than a street urchin he had raised to a life of luxury.

Though twenty-nine years old, Ellen Tanzdahl looked to be barely out of her teens. Thick waves of lustrous brown hair framed her attractive, unblemished face, and natural dark eyebrows and lashes set off a pair of soft eyes falling somewhere between green and gray. Her complexion, still cushioned by a thin layer of baby fat, was lightly dusted with freckles. A small ski-jump nose curled gently upward above full lips, now covered by lipstick that was only slightly too dark. An abundance of now-healed piercings—tracks left by face metal worn during her life on the streets—were still visible on both earlobes and above one eyebrow. To someone unfamiliar with her past, these small desecrations would go unnoticed. But to Riley they were the scars of a ruined childhood.

He had seen pictures of Ellen Tanzdahl in the file work-up prepared by Sara Hall, but those pictures—taken at a charity event the previous spring—failed to fully capture the youthfulness of her appearance. The features, coloring, and manner of this young woman, especially when viewed through the narrow lens of his Bridey Reaves preoccupation, put him more in a mood to protect than to attack. But then most of the pretty young women he encountered these days reminded him of Bridey, whose face had come to occupy almost all his waking hours. Now included in the ambit of resemblance were not just his daughter Lizzie, where the similarity was pronounced and obvious, but also the family's cleaning lady, the receptionist in the courthouse lobby, and the canine beautician who gave Tuffy his monthly bath and haircut. It was a testament to his obsessive nature that even his own image, viewed each morning in the bathroom mirror, reminded him somehow of the forlorn face at Dion O'Banion's graveside. Betsy was right when she described him as overly fixated.

Seated between Clint Tarrymore and the court reporter, Ellen Tanzdahl fidgeted nervously in her seat, carefully avoiding eye contact with Gus, who stared at her across the table like an angry parent. It was a warm day, and she was dressed in a plain cotton dress held up in the front by a thin strap tied around her neck. Her bare shoulders, thin and freckled, added to the impression of youth and vulnerability.

Sara Hall, by contrast, was dressed in a gray pinstripe skirt and jacket worn over a plain white blouse fastened at the neck with a gold medallion. Sara referred to this ensemble as her "get down to business" suit. And she was wearing her game face, staring stiffly at the other woman. The men in the room might get a little starry eyed over the busty ingénue in the witness chair, but not Sara Hall. She was from the hardball school of litigation.

Gus was turned out in the kind of casual golfing outfit favored by thirty handicaps belonging to second-tier country clubs. He had thus far been excluded by the old-money crowd at Somerset and Woodhill, people who placed a premium on good manners. But that would soon be fixed, he thought, just as soon as he was rid of this ungrateful tart and united in holy matrimony with Trudi Hansdale, a woman with robust social credentials.

Riley had failed to persuade Gus to stay away from the deposition, to go play golf and let him handle things. Prior to entering the conference room, he had explained to Gus that the purpose of the deposition was to develop facts from the other side and to telegraph just enough damaging information to arouse a desire for settlement. It was not a time, he had made clear, for personal interaction between the contending parties. Arguments were not won at depositions. Gus was thus instructed to be seen and not heard during the testimony. And, consistent with Riley's strong belief in the civility of such proceedings, Gus was specifically cautioned to keep his gestures and body English to a minimum. He had nodded his assent but with a noticeable lack of enthusiasm.

Several years back, Clint Tarrymore had shed the portions of his practice dealing with personal injury and criminal matters in order to concentrate entirely on matrimonial law, developing in the process a substantial practice and reputation. He represented only women. Thoroughly familiar with the controlling law and capable of putting on a persuasive case on occasions when a case had to be tried to verdict, he was not a man to be underestimated.

Though considerably younger, Sara Hall was his equal in legal knowledge and nearly as good a courtroom performer. But owing to her combative style, she was less well regarded by the family court establishment. This fact no doubt influenced Ladge Wilkaster in the scheme he had devised to enlist Riley as lead counsel in the case. Riley had not made an appearance in the family court for over a decade, but he was respected by courthouse personnel, from the judges on down. During weak moments, he attributed that standing to character and talent, but he knew that those qualities, held in equal measure by less popular lawyers, were not the explanation. Rather, his credibility was traceable to a long history of fair dealing with friends and adversaries alike. When in the prosecutor's office, he had routinely cautioned eager young crime fighters bent on bullying their way through cases, that all the ability and hard work in the world would count for nothing in the absence of the respect of the people who ran the courthouse. That included not just the judges, who were sucked up to by everyone, but more tellingly, the court clerks, bail evaluators, probation officers, deputy sheriffs, court reporters, and even the janitors.

Of course, there might come a time in any lawsuit when shouting and table pounding would be called for, but absent a palpable outrage by opposing counsel, it was rarely appropriate during the first deposition of an opposing party—especially a sympathetic party like Ellen Tanzdahl.

When the court reporter finished arranging her narrow stenographic paper, she administered the oath to the witness and nodded to Riley.

Riley looked across the table at Ellen and commenced the examination. "Good morning, Ms. Tanzdahl, my name is Riley McReynolds, and I represent your husband in this matter. As your counsel has no doubt explained, the purpose of this examination is to allow us to gather information relevant to the issues in the case. If at any time a question I ask is not understandable to you, please feel free to request a clarification, and I will be happy to provide one."

Ellen nodded and said, "I understand."

Riley then reached into a stack of documents and pulled out the first in a series of brown Manila folders. He opened it, made a check mark in the upper right-hand corner, and commenced the questioning. "Would you please state your name, age, and current address for the record?"

The witness took a deep breath and sat forward in her chair, her thin, girlish arms resting on the table, her fingers nervously intertwined. The keys of the stenographic machine tapped lightly as she answered, "Ellen Murseth Tanzdahl, twenty-nine years old, and I live with our child at 783 Charlottesville Trail, Orono, Minnesota." She then looked over at Riley, doe-eyed, as though she had just completed a recitation in grammar school and was hoping for a gold star.

Riley was struck by her nervousness and lack of sophistication. It was even greater than he had first imagined. It was a stretch to believe that a person of this timidity could have survived months on the street ten years earlier as Gus contended. Riley was glad she was represented by an attorney of Clint Tarrymore's grit and competence. If she had hired an incompetent lawyer, of which there were a good many practicing in the local courts, the case would be like shooting fish in a barrel.

"Are you presently employed?" Riley asked.

Before she could answer, Gus, who had been glowering at her across the table, leaned forward and shouted, "Working? Are you kidding, Riley? This little whore hasn't made a penny since she stopped dealing drugs ten years ago, just about the time she started leeching off me."

Ellen collapsed back into her chair and buried her face in her hands. Clint Tarrymore didn't even look at Gus; instead he nodded to the court reporter to confirm that Gus's outburst had been entered into the record. He then turned to Riley, who was glaring at Gus.

"How do you want to proceed, Riley?" asked Clint. "Will Mr. Tanzdahl be going on his way, or do we recess the proceedings long enough for me to ring up Judge Hammergren for an order ejecting him."

Riley signaled for the reporter to go off the record and, without speaking, seized Gus by the arm and pulled him out of his seat and toward the door.

"You greedy little cunt!" Gus screamed at her over his shoulder as Riley gave him a hard shove into the hallway. Sara Hall closed the door behind them and took up a position behind Gus.

"I guess you weren't paying attention during our visit this morning, Gus," said Riley through clenched teeth, his face inches from Gus's, the veins in his neck red and pulsating. "I hope you enjoyed yourself in there because that little performance will go down as your first serious self-inflicted wound."

Gus's self-satisfied smile melted away. He hung his head slightly.

"We're just lucky this was not a video deposition," said Riley. "If Judge Hammergren were to see a tape of that puerile demonstration, not to mention the charming, off-the-record epithet you hurled on the way out, you could measure the damage to your case in the millions."

Harvey Aingren, who had been sitting in the reception area, rushed down the hall when he saw his boss emerge from the conference room.

Gus shuffled his feet and looked off into the distance, but the small smirk tugging at the corners of his mouth gave him away. "That little tramp!" he said. "She has the nerve to come in here looking like Shirley Temple. It makes me want to puke."

"You're right about that, Gus," said a freshly arrived Harvey, breathless from his exertion.

Riley glared over at Harvey, and then back at Gus. "Tell your trained squirrel to get his ass out of this hallway, before I personally remove him."

Gus nodded at Harvey, who turned and walked back down the hall.

Sara stood off to one side, expressionless, her eyes glued to the floor.

Riley looked Gus hard in the eyes. "You're about to hit the links, my friend. You're not going to be in the same room with Ellen again until the day of the final hearing, if I can help it. I'm going to run this case, not you—and if you don't like it, you can go down to the Merchants Exchange Building and hire one of those professional bullies who enjoy making things as ugly as their half-witted clients will allow. It will cost you big time in the end, of course, but you'll have the petty satisfaction of tearing her to pieces."

Gus took a deep breath and let it out slowly. He then gave a shallow nod, but still didn't look at Riley. "All right, I'll leave," he said, his eyes on the floor. "I can't stand being anywhere near that bitch, anyway." He pulled his pastel golf pants up over his soft, rounded belly and looked down the hall. "I'll go over to the corporate department and visit Vic Laslow or George Stonequist. They're more respectful of the firm's biggest client. Over there they know how to make a client feel appreciated."

Riley said nothing but kept his eyes glued to Gus, still waiting for a grown-up answer. But Gus kept at it: "The corporate guys know where their bread is buttered. They'd never embarrass me the way you just did. If it wasn't for our long friendship, I'd think about taking my business elsewhere."

*Friendship, he calls it,* thought Riley as he moved a little closer into Gus's space. "You do what you have to do, Gus, but as long as I'm leading this case, it will be conducted according to my standards. If you want to replace me, just say the word." He glanced over at Sara. "We've got lots of good lawyers in this firm and some of them have styles that are more to your liking."

Gus stretched to his full five-foot-six height and, in a quick makeover, produced the smile that had carried him through so many business negotiations. It amazed Riley how fast people like Gus could switch affects, going from tough and intimidating to soft and charming. It was the skill of the sociopath. He was reminded of Churchill's observation that the Nazi's were either at your throat or at your feet. These types cared little for pride or the opinion of others so long as in the end they got their own way.

Gus winked and slapped Riley on the shoulder. "Just a little theater to let her know she's in for some hurt. Nothing against you, old buddy, you're fully in charge." He flashed a broad, toothy grin and feigned an air of contrition as he reached out for a handshake. "I promise I'll be good."

Riley recoiled at the touch. His facial expression remained unchanged. Mechanically, he accepted the extended hand. Then, in a flat voice, he said, "Have a good day, Gus. Go down and see the corporate people, play a round of golf. Do anything you want, but don't show up anywhere near this conference room. You understand?"

"Hey, you bet, Riley. I've got it, man."

# 7

_____

THE EAST WALL of the family den was dominated by tall leaded-glass windows, through which the morning sun spread itself in a spectacular medley on the beige carpeting. The house itself sat upon some of the highest ground in the western suburbs, commanding a view of Highway 169 and, beyond that on the distant horizon, the skyline of Minneapolis. It was Saturday morning, and Betsy was attending a two-day, overnight seminar, leaving Riley to preside over the household. Teddy was still asleep, Lizzie was in the shower, and Tuffy was serving a time-out in the basement for humping the mailman and pooping in the living room.

Up since six, Riley had already shaved, showered and tossed down a light breakfast that sat uneasily in a stomach still knotted over Gus Tanzdahl's tacky performance. The whole thing was ugly and disturbing. How in the hell did he get stuck in this mess? he wondered. He tried not to think about it.

Twin briefcases sat quietly in the corner, one menacing, the other inviting. The first was stuffed with discovery materials and research on the Tanzdahl divorce. It was smooth and shiny, and had embossed across its front: "Cosgrove & Levi, Ltd." The other briefcase—the one given to his father upon graduation from law school in 1936 and passed on to Riley at his graduation thirty-five years later—was shabby and creased with age. It bulged with materials compiled in his ever-widening search for Bridey Reaves. The two brief-cases were like rival puppies begging for attention, one representing the heartaches of the real world, the other symbolizing the capacity of the human spirit to soar to heights of imagination.

He sat back in his chair, took a last swallow of the room-temperature coffee, and watched the cars on the highway below speeding in both directions. Even on a Saturday morning the drivers seemed to be in a pointless rush. He could remember, as if it were yesterday, when that highway was a sleepy two-lane conveyance and the only speeders were teenagers sporting ducktails, nylon jackets, and loads of attitude. They drove hot cars with shiny full-moon hubcaps and back ends that pointed in the air at what seemed an impossible angle. Their mufflers could be heard for miles as they roared up and down the highway at all hours of the day and night. As a youngster Riley never understood those guys with their strange automotive customs and fast girlfriends with breasts that pointed straight out from their chests.

They were tough guys, those greasers in the hot cars, and they were often looking for trouble. But they were always nice to him because they wanted no trouble from his three older brothers, who as a group constituted a sort of in-house goon squad in that part of town. Although Riley despised fighting outside the controlled setting a boxing ring, he kind of liked having three brothers who enjoyed it. It allowed him to mouth off to just about anyone in town with near impunity, for though he didn't share their love of fisticuffs, he did share their name and a strong family resemblance. How he could have been so temperamentally different from those mugs, however, was beyond him.

His meditation was broken by the sounds of hungry birds frolicking about an empty backyard feeder. He had promised Betsy that he would refill the feeder in the early morning so that "God's outdoor friends," as she called them, would be properly nourished while she was gone. He rose slowly from his chair, careful not to twist his still-healing back and passed through the French doors with a sack of birdfeed in his arms. Hop-scotching his way over a flagstone walkway, he was confronted by a flock of birds circling in a criss-cross pattern above his head, one or two even dipping frighteningly in his direction. He felt like Tippy Hedron. And talking nice to them didn't do any good. They must have known that he, unlike Betsy, didn't really like them—or any of God's other outdoor friends either. He dumped the birdseed into the feeder and ran for the house.

Inside, he removed a note from the refrigerator reminding him that Teddy and Petie Portland had a baseball practice at eight-thirty, and that Teddy needed to be clothed and fed before being picked up by Petie's mother. Even when Betsy was home, Riley had taken over all sports equipment responsibilities after she sent Teddy, at age five, to his first hockey practice with his jock strap on the outside of his hockey breezers. The coaches felt so sorry for him, they let him play on the first line that day.

At the appointed time, Petie Portland's mother, a crabby woman with the faint outlines of a mustache on her upper lip, leaned out the driver's window of her SUV and looked Teddy up and down. "Oh, I see Teddy is wearing the same clothes he had on yesterday."

"He looks pretty good to me," said Riley, embarrassed. He felt inadequate in the childcare department and inwardly cringed at the rebuke.

Mrs. Portland put the car in gear. "Well, I suppose he'll get by," she said smugly, as though resisting the temptation to report Riley to the child welfare authorities.

Before jumping into the van, Teddy threw his arms around Riley's neck and squeezed with all his might, letting out an affectionate squeal that was a nearly perfect imitation of the sound Betsy made each morning as she hugged her loved-ones goodbye. Riley held Teddy's small, bony body tightly, clinging a few extra seconds. He knew these hugs had to be cherished while they lasted, for as sure as anything in this life, one day soon Teddy would come to believe that public displays of family affection were for dorks, especially a father's hug. That's just the way it would be. But until that day Riley was going to capture every one that came his way.

He waved to Teddy as the van door closed and smiled at Mrs. Portland. She did not smile back.

In the house, he picked up the Cosgrove & Levi briefcase and withdrew a stack of materials assembled for him that morning by Skeeter. The first item in the file was a stack of pink slips representing phone messages of various descriptions. He sorted through the pile, prearranged by Skeeter into three categories: "Client calls," "Charitable Gifts Committee," and "Personal."

From the first stack, he quickly tossed aside three calls from Gus Tanzdahl, on the self-serving assumption that Sara Hall, the designated call returner, had already responded or soon would. He returned the next call, one from Ev Pedersen concerning the progress of a Stoddard Trust transaction in St. Paul.

He then turned to the Charitable Gifts Committee stack. The calls all appeared to be from representatives of charitable organizations seeking contributions from Cosgrove & Levi. He was about to mark the whole pile for referral to the staff administrator assigned to the committee, when he noticed the name "Paul Giel" on one of them. A small twinge registered at the base of his spine. Good lord—there was a name from the past. Paul Giel had been a local icon, everybody's favorite All-American in 1953 when Riley was just a seven-year-old boy and the area's most worshipful football fan. Though they had lived in the same community in the intervening years, the name of his one-time idol had hardly entered his mind after Giel, also an All-American in baseball, had signed a pitching contract with the New York Giants and abandoned football forever.

Amidst the fierce but poorly understood feelings surrounding his part in the fate of Ellen Tanzdahl's young son, Josh, Riley's own boyhood was much on his mind these days. The bond between four-year-old Josh Tanzdahl and his mother— a bond threatened by a reckless and selfish man who had selected Riley as his instrumentality—was clearly behind this unusual emotional fragility. It was a measure of that fragility that any story or TV program involving vulnerable children brought a lump to his throat these days. Even advertisements and commercials with small children in them produced that effect. And not just Hallmark commercials. He had become a sort of weeping embarrassment around the house.

Betsy said his mind and body and subconscious were trying to tell him something, that they were pointing in a revealing direction. But he had never put much store in those theories of deeper meaning. As far as he was concerned, the only thing he was being told was that Gus was an asshole. And he had known that for thirty-five years.

But there was no question that the unexpected sight of Paul Giel's name on that pink slip transported him back to his boyhood, to a defining time in his and his family's lives— a time nearly forty-three years before. Polio was loose in the land in 1953. And it was just this time of year, late July, the beginning of dog days, when the epidemic swept through the community like a mythological beast, devouring children at will. It had already called on several homes in the neighborhood, and on a sunny Tuesday afternoon it made a stop at the large brick house on the corner, the one belonging to the seemingly invulnerable McReynolds family. And there it carved out the youngest child.

Maybe it was because he had gone swimming at the public beach in violation of his mother's instructions, or maybe it was exposure to one of the other stricken boys in the neighborhood. But his sister and brothers had also been exposed, and they were left untouched. Something in his makeup had made him, amongst all the family, uniquely vulnerable. What it was, no one knew.

The cloudy memory of that time so long ago still haunted him—the sudden raging fever, the aching legs and shallow, labored breath, the stark hospital setting viewed hazily through a plastic bubble filled with life-sustaining oxygen. In the distance, lined against the walls of the hospital ward, he could see other children, some emitting a deathly rattle, others fated for iron lungs and wheel chairs. And at his bedside he could see his father's face, twisted in agony. All this remained at the surface of his memory, renewed and reconsidered so many times over the years that it could have happened yesterday.

In those first days in the ward the oxygen tent would be lifted only to administer penicillin injections. On those occasions he could hear the panicked voice of his mother begging the nurse to be gentle and demanding yet another session with the beleaguered pediatrician. Even his older brothers stopped razzing him when it was said that he would probably not live. The searing pain forming in a tightening band around his chest is what first alarmed the doctors. Even before the pain reached his legs, when his fever was barely 102 degrees, an ambulance rushed him from his bed at home to the isolation ward at St. Mary's Hospital. The wail of the siren, he remembered, took his mind off the blinding headache climbing up the back of the neck and clawing at his temples.

That siren was to be his last unclouded memory for ten days, though the sounds of many sirens were to intrude on his sleepy delirium. But for all of that, there was a strange peace inside that tent. Family quarrels and boyish rivalries disappeared from his consciousness as his mind gave itself over to the singular task of staying alive. Though he couldn't have named it then, it must have been the mysticism of the dying. From inside that bubble, he glimpsed a sculpted wooden crucifix above the bed of each child. And next to the common doorway stood the blessed lady in all her porcelain perfection, a pale-blue veil framing a face of unspeakable sweetness. As his lungs struggled for breath, his spirit was free. There were no tunnels or lights, no ancestors lining the passage, but the prospect of passing from this earthly existence held no fear for him.

When liberated from the tent days later, the fever, once 104, had dropped to an unalarming 100. The pain in his chest and legs had gradually receded, and the crisis his parents would not name—the "P" word they dared not speak—had been defeated. The long days and nights of return to normalcy were nearly as blurred, for his conscious mind was only gradually regaining ascendancy. On the eighth day his mother knew he had turned the corner when he developed a desperate crush on a tiny blond nurse on the day shift who ministered to him with a special devotion. But, alas, he was seven, and she was twenty-one and a favorite of all the interns.

The night shift had its angels, too, though for some reason they were as dark-haired as the day nurses were fair. And they were less clearly recalled because of the faint lighting and intermittent consciousness. One dark-haired beauty would be glimpsed only as she wiped perspiration from his forehead at intervals throughout the night, her starched white cuffs and lavender scent announcing her ministrations. She would then sit next to his father, speaking words of reassurance to this lovely man who never left his boy's bedside, sleeping only in catnaps on a chair beside the bed.

Even for a second-grader, a brush with the great mystery seems to rewire the mind. Through that experience he had come to realize the power of kindness as a healing force. It was the doctors, then all men, who applied the technology; but it was the nurses, then all women, who presided over the healing. And though he would never admit it to anyone else, it did not escape his awareness that the many imaginary illnesses he was to suffer later in life were probably just an expression of his longing for the life-giving female, whether she came in the uniform of a polio ward nurse or in the person of a famous aviatrix or Russian grand duchess . . . or in the confirmation gown of an orphaned girl in Chicago.

If he had not been the family pet before the illness, he certainly was afterward. Among the many favors bestowed on him was the prize most coveted by his brothers, the seat next to his father at the Saturday afternoon football games at the University of Minnesota's Memorial Stadium. And one game in particular stood out above all others. Under a brilliant sun pouring down upon the greenest grass Riley had ever seen, on that day so long ago, the All-American Paul Giel passed, kicked, and ran like the wind in a performance of skill and beauty rarely equaled in college football, almost single-handedly defeating a nationally ranked Michigan team by three touchdowns. And as the freshly recovered seven-year-old boy and his father thrilled to the sight of that performance, he somehow knew that he had been spared for a reason, that the ferocious love of his family and the healing touch of women in starched white outfits, glimpsed through a fever-drenched sepia landscape, had delivered him to that moment of perfect happiness at Memorial Stadium—a moment in which the sun shone brightly, God was in his heaven, and he was snuggled into the folds of his beloved father's camel's hair overcoat.

Now, forty-three years later, the middle-aged lawyer enthusiastically reached for the phone and dialed the number scrawled on the pink message slip. When he heard the voice on the other end say "This is Paul Giel," it was suddenly 1953 again and the past forty-three years had not happened. The cares of the present day—of firm politics and evil men who use children as pawns—seemed to melt away in the warm glow of the voice on the other end of the phone, the voice from an earlier, better time. Whatever had happened in their respective lives in the interim, no matter what accomplishments Riley may have racked up in life and in the law, they counted for nothing. For in that instant he was a seven-year-old boy again, and in his mind, the man on the other end of the phone was a young college student wearing a maroon and gold uniform. And the sun shone on the grass at Memorial Stadium, and his father lived again, and he believed that all the current stress in his life would have a happy ending.

And like a seven-year-old afraid of making a fool of himself in front of his hero, he stammered and stuttered and wished that he could reach for his father's hand. He probably said some dumb things in that conversation; he couldn't remember. Something about the Heisman Trophy and the Little Brown Jug passed his lips, but he wasn't sure if the words had made any sense. Even the All American's warm and modest manner was not sufficient to unscramble his thoughts.

Paul Giel must have wondered how it could be that a man so confused and inarticulate could be the high-profile former prosecutor and senior litigator at Cosgrove & Levi, from which his foundation was seeking a charitable contribution. But if he did think that, he was too kind to say so. He was every bit the modest and decent guy those old press clippings had said he was.

On the authority of its chairman, The Charitable Gifts Committee of Cosgrove & Levi made a generous contribution that day.

SUNDAY DAWNED BRIGHT and cheerful, the surrounding landscape bursting with rich summer colors as Riley and Teddy made their way through the countryside. Teddy sat in the front passenger seat, punching away at a hand-held computer. Father and son were on their way to visit eighty-seven-year-old Maureen McReynolds, Riley's mother and Teddy's grandmother. As they pulled off the county highway and passed under the brick-pillared entryway to the Loretta Heights Senior Residence, the serene beauty of the rolling landscape and the sight of nuns in white habits moving quietly about the grounds, confirmed the difficult but necessary choice Riley and his siblings had made when they insisted that their strong-willed mother leave her apartment and take up an assisted living arrangement.

Maureen had been thirty-eight when Riley was born and, as the youngest child of an older mother, he had been showered with inordinate attention and affection. His four siblings teased that he was a mama's boy, spoiled beyond hope. And there was truth in their taunts, though he thought it a relative judgment; after all, his older brothers were less family oriented than he was. But whatever the case, there was no doubt that upon the death of his father nearly thirty years before, Riley had become his mother's principal moral support. And in recent years, as Maureen became increasingly enfeebled, their roles as parent and child had almost been reversed. This had been a mixed blessing, affording the emotional rewards of helping those we love, but also a little unnerving, for his mother had always been a woman of unmovable will, the backbone of the family. It was she, not his softhearted father, who commanded obedience; and it was she who held the family together during its greatest challenges. Now, in her old age, the sweetness that had always existed under her hard-shell exterior had been released in great torrents.

Though still beautiful at the time of her husband's death, his mother never looked at another man and, to this day, spoke of him in the present tense, as though he were present to her at all times. When, in her mid-eighties, she was beset by a series of small strokes that closed off selected chambers of her mind, the iron will that had characterized her life gave way to a childlike willingness to be led. Only in the arena of family relations did her once-fierce independence still burn hot. With four surviving children, three daughters-in-law, one son-in-law, and eighteen grandchildren, she had lost formal control of the clan, but on those rare occasions when misunderstandings or bad feelings erupted between family members, she would convene a summit meeting at which attendance was mandatory. Her remaining powers were then concentrated upon working a reconciliation, and she rarely failed to accomplish her mission. She could no longer give spankings or call time-outs, and she no longer had the power of the purse, but she could still assign guilt like a mother superior.

Some weeks earlier, during another weekly visit, Riley had aroused her anger when, to make conversation, he had described his latest search for a missing female, this one disappeared in 1925. He had forgotten that his mother severely disapproved of his boyhood searches for Amelia Earhart, Anastasia, Jean Spangler, and the others, scolding him for wasting time on what she called "childish nonsense." But he was not quite prepared for the ferocity with which she greeted his newest fixation. Coming out of her sweet docility, she had lit into him as though he were a small child playing too close to traffic. Even the nurses were surprised by the force of her upset, speculating in a later medical conference that the strokes she continued to suffer might have slightly deranged her.

As a result, Riley had vowed then and there to stay away from the topic of missing women. This took some doing, as it was still the thing he thought most about, at least when it came to Bridey Reaves.

As Riley and Teddy pulled slowly into the Loretta Heights parking lot and made their way to Maureen's corner room in the medium support unit, he rehearsed this week's agenda of items: The Loretta Heights food menu, Teddy's recent athletic accomplishments, his brother Ian's purchase of a lake home.

"Hi, Mom" he said warmly as he tapped gently on the door. Teddy hid behind his father, a little spooked by the Coke-bottle glasses Grandma had been wearing since her cataract surgery.

His mother looked up at them, blankly at first, but then with a wide grin as she recognized her son and grandson. She moved forward in her rocking chair and extended her arms to Teddy "Come here to Grandma, Billy," she said. One of the side effects of the strokes had been a reshuffling of names, Teddy having been transmuted into his cousin Billy. It wasn't that Maureen didn't know which child she was talking to; it was purely a matter of semantics. The brain circuits that assign and track names had simply been taken out in one of the strokes.

Teddy clutched Riley's hand and peered up at him, seeking a reprieve from this disagreeable duty. Riley looked down and gently shook his head, so Teddy dutifully moved to the rocking chair and accepted a hug and a wet kiss from this giant-eyed, ancient woman whom he had not known during her years of arresting beauty and glowing self-confidence.

When Teddy squirmed from her embrace, Riley bent down and kissed his mother on the forehead. "How are you feeling today, Mom?"

She took hold of his hand and looked up. "Oh, just so-so, honey. Everything hurts . . . and there's not much to do here . . . Loretta Heights is filled with old people." This was her customary opening, and it was intended to induce shame on his part for her lonely circumstances. If allowed to progress, it would end in another heartbreaking plea that she be allowed to move in with him and Betsy. Riley knew that there was a time when a standard household was composed of three and sometimes four generations, and that in some quarters that was still regarded as a neglected ideal, but he had serious reservations about it in this case. Apart from the fact that he and Betsy could never provide the care his mother needed, Betsy was wise enough to know that, in spite of her love for Maureen, a mother-in-law living above the garage was a bad idea. Especially this mother-in-law.

So before her plea could gain traction, Riley changed the subject. "I saw that Madge Henderson's funeral was on Thursday at Sacred Heart," he said.

Being altogether Irish, the deathwatch was one of his mother's favorite activities. Madge Henderson had once been Maureen's neighbor and bridge partner. Maureen and Mrs. Kilmartin, whose room was down the hall, could occupy a full day making lists of all their dead friends and enemies. They would watch old movies in the recreation room, excitedly pointing out who and under what scandalous circumstances the various actors had died.

Maureen nodded. "Yes, I know Madge died. She was a good bridge player but a terrible gossip . . . may she rest in peace." She made the sign of the cross.

What it was about Madge Henderson's death that caused Maureen to take up the very topic Riley was trying so hard to avoid, was anyone's guess. But something did, and his mother was off and running. Her eyes narrowed and her facial muscles tightened. "I talked to Betsy yesterday, and she said you went out of town again on that crazy mystery search, and that you even missed one of Billy's games." Her voice grew louder and her blue-gray eyes, swollen to unnatural proportions by the magnifying glasses, bored in on him.

"It's *Teddy*, Mom. Billy is Ian's son, remember? And I don't want to talk about how I spend my time. That's my business." He diverted his attention to the patio, where Teddy had gone at the first opportunity to avoid the sights and smells of the elderly.

Before he could change the subject, his mother lifted her hand, and in a palsied motion, pointed a finger in his face. "You're too old for that kind of nonsense, Riley. You wasted enough of your life as a boy chasing after that Grand Countess."

"*Duchess*, Mom, *Grand Duchess*," he said, looking at her accusing finger, so close to his face that his eyes were crossed slightly.

She was not about to be sidetracked. Her finger stayed in his face. "Your obligation is to your family, mister." She started poking at his shoulder, and her voice became shrill. "If your father were alive, he'd be furious that you're neglecting your family."

Good Lord, thought Riley, she was really flying today. What the hell had gotten into her, invoking his dead father? Talk about playing your trump early.

He finally managed to distract her by talking about the one subject to which she assigned even more importance than his boyish fantasies. Money. It galled her that she didn't have free access to cash—real cash, the kind that she could stash under her mattress like Mrs. Kilmartin did. But Riley knew that as lovely and bucolic as Lorretta Heights was, no senior care facility anywhere in the world was a good place to keep much in the way of cash.

"I need cash for all kinds of things here at this old people's home." She pinched her nose when she said "old people's home" in spite of being the oldest resident in her wing.

Riley looked puzzled. "Like what kind of things do you need cash for?"

"Oh, you know . . . I can't think of all of them now, right off the top of my head, but there are a lot of things. They come up all the time."

In truth, there was nothing to spend money on at Lorretta Heights. Not even vending machines. But it would have been unkind to remind her of that. Instead he said, "How much cash do you need, Mom?"

She perked up and considered the question for a moment, stroking her chin with an index finger. "How about two-hundred thousand dollars?"

Riley flinched. "*Two-hundred thousand dollars!*"

She reconsidered briefly, and then said, "Oh . . . excuse me, what was I thinking? . . . One-hundred thousand will be enough."

Riley suppressed a laugh as he reached into his wallet and pulled out a five-dollar bill. "We'll compromise, Mom, here's five bucks."

Maureen snapped the bill out of his hand, slipped it under her mattress, and climbed onto the bed to sit sentry. Within minutes she had fallen into a light nap.

Riley sat back in his chair, watching her sleep. As a result of wasting muscles and deep facial lines, her once-elegant face had collapsed in on itself, making her appear even older than her eighty-seven years. She had cared less for her appearance than most women of her generation, but her natural beauty, shared by her three sisters, had paid rich rewards over the years. In keeping with an old Irish custom, all four girls in her family had been christened Mary: Mary Eileen, Mary Alice, Mary Kathleen, and Riley's mother, Mary Maureen. Not a single one was ever called Mary. The oldest of the sisters, Eileen, now long gone, was widely regarded as the most beautiful girl in St. Paul. At seventeen she had resisted determined sieges by both Richard Arlen, later a famous actor, and her young Summit Avenue neighbor, F. Scott Fitzgerald, viewing both as having no future. Like Zelda, Eileen was beautiful and insane. In fact, the Carr family used to say that Zelda had been a Southern replacement for Eileen.

Maureen was the third of the Carr sisters, and though less breathtaking than her oldest sister, she was beautiful by any conventional standard and was possessed of an indefinable charm that made her the first choice of half the eligible bachelors in St. Paul. So, when she rejected them all—industrial barons, high-born Summit Avenue Anglicans, surgeons, lawyers, and professors—in favor of a shanty Irishman from north Minneapolis who was putting himself through law school by boxing at county fairs, her family was appalled. Boxing was regarded as coarse and vulgar by the lace-curtain Carrs. But with his winning smile and movie star good looks, John McReynolds soon became a family favorite. John and Maureen were married at St. Luke's Church in 1938, and in a flash Maureen transformed herself from a flirtatious St. Paul debutante into a Minneapolis housewife and mother.

Following the reception, the Carrs saw Maureen off at the Lake Street Bridge, waving goodbye as though she were disappearing into Eastern Europe. Such were the cultural divisions between the two cities in those days.

Maureen's one non-negotiable demand of John was that any sons she bore would attend St. David's Military School and any daughters the Sacred Heart Convent, each a pillar of the St. Paul Catholic ascendancy. Thus did Riley follow in the footsteps of his three older brothers, straddled between two narrowly elite cultures—Lowry Hill in Minneapolis and Crocus Hill in St. Paul.

Now, more than a half-century later, he sat looking at Mary Maureen Carr McReynolds curled up in her bed, so much smaller than she had once been, deep in an aged sleep. Her practical usefulness long spent, she was now a vessel of pain and confusion but also of undiminished love for her children and grandchildren. She could no longer tend to a large, expensive household; domestic helpers and workmen no longer jumped to her command. And the man who had taken her west into Minneapolis—the man for whom she still held a ferocious love—was long ago buried at Resurrection Cemetery, under a marble headstone on which both their names were chiseled.

Riley listened to his mother's soft, wispy breath and watched the once-graceful hands, now a mass of bony knuckles under thinly stretched skin, gripping the rosary given to her during the Great Influenza Epidemic of 1918. From across the room, he could feel the power of her all-consuming love—a love that would last for as long as she drew breath, and perhaps beyond.

He gazed across the bed to the large oaken dresser that had followed her for nearly a half century, atop which were arrayed photographs representing a pictorial record of her life. Three pictures of her family of origin—father, mother, three sisters and a brother—sat next to an oversized photo of John McReynolds with one arm around the shoulder of his mother, Helen Riley McReynolds, holding up for the camera a freshly minted law degree. Next in line was their formal wedding picture taken at St. Luke's, bridesmaids petite and elegant standing in sharp relief to the groomsmen, three tall, dark-haired McReynolds brothers and two heavy-set Northside bootleggers for whom John and his handsome but doomed brother Desmond had been beer truck drivers toward the end of Prohibition.

The remaining pictures were of Riley's siblings and a single group shot of Maureen's grandchildren taken on her eightieth birthday. Riley's two surviving brothers and his lone sister were assigned one photo each (usually high school graduation). But he got three, one as large as his parents' wedding photo. He winced at this reminder of his privileged status as the baby of the family. But then he had been the one who stayed by his mother's side as she grew old and unreasonable. And as the only lawyer in the family, he tended to what was left of a once-considerable fortune earned by his father over the years, most of which had been consumed by a lavish household and the private educations of five ambitious children.

Legal and financial questions gave Maureen an excuse to summon Riley to her bedside on a thousand pretexts. But he always came when she called. Whether driven by devotion or guilt, or a combination of the two, he couldn't be sure.

He stared at the images of his brothers, all cocky and handsome. Though dark-haired and freckled like him, they were more like each other than he was like any of them. Maybe it was his being the youngest, with his sister serving as a buffer between them. He had idolized his brothers and good-naturedly endured their teasing. Then, as now, he was closest to Ian, the brother nearest in age and the one who had been both his protector and tormentor growing up.

Just three years older, Ian was the most mischievous of the boys, missing no opportunity to play tricks on his younger brother. Riley was an inveterate sleepwalker, the only one in the family. He often awoke in distant corners of the house, curled up on a couch next to a radio he had somehow managed to turn on. Of these nocturnal wanderings he could remember little, save only on those occasions when his father, who growing up had served the same rescue function for his sleepwalking brother Desmond, interrupted his wanderings.

Riley was just thirteen when a freshman in high school, and he would turn in for a good night's sleep by around 9:30 each night. Ian, at sixteen, was less in need of sleep and, in any event, tended to do his homework late in the evening. Therefore, it was usually about 11:30 before he retired to the room they shared. By that time Riley would be deep into the kind of sleep from which quick awakening is nearly impossible.

As Ian would button his pajamas with one hand, with the other he would poke at Riley's shoulder, and say, "Get up, or you'll miss the bus!" He would then continue his preparation for bed as Riley, in a fog of formless dreams, arose slowly from his bed and started mechanically putting on his school uniform. "God," he'd say as he dazedly buckled his pants and tightened his school tie, "I feel like I just went to bed."

Ian would smile sympathetically as if to confirm that there are some nights when a guy just can't get a good rest no matter what. That Ian continued to undress as he spoke, did not register in the few sections of Riley's brain that were awake. Then, as Ian was hopping into bed, Riley would stumble to the kitchen, where he'd pour himself a bowl of Wheaties and a glass of orange juice, the whole time failing to notice that the house was dark and he was the only one not fast asleep.

On one occasion he actually went out the back door and into the pitch darkness of a moonless night, and then down the block to the bus stop, where he stood for several confusing minutes awaiting a bus not scheduled to arrive for another eight hours.

Eventually he would come awake and trudge, downcast, back to his bed. He never snitched on his brothers, but Ian's smirks and giggles at breakfast the next morning would inevitably give him away.

His siblings never got polio, nor were they sleepwalkers or nearsighted, like him. They didn't bounce their knees when nervous, and they never once chased after a missing female. But then they weren't the baby of the family or their parents' favorite, either. So it all seemed to balance out in the end.

*Enough of family reminiscences*, he thought. Looking out at Teddy running about the patio with another boy who was also visiting his grandmother, Riley felt a rush of gratitude for all that he had. For his mother and surviving siblings, of course, but most of all for Teddy and Lizzie and Betsy. The whole world could fall apart, so long as he had them.

Maureen seemed to be passing into a deeper sleep. Riley quietly rose from the chair and tiptoed toward the hall. As he passed through the doorway, his mother's voice came from the bed, strong and commanding: "Remember, you've got a family. No more silly searches."

# 8

H EY, SKEETS," YELLED Riley as he entered his office, tossing his briefcase onto the couch. "When's Mick Goerdan supposed to be here?"

Skeeter stood by the door with notepad in hand. "I'm ten feet away, and I've got perfect hearing. Why are you shouting?"

Riley looked up. "Sorry, I thought you were in the file room."

Skeeter looked down at the day's calendar. "He'll be here at ten-thirty."

Mick Goerdan had been a robbery-homicide detective with the Minneapolis Police Department during Riley's time as a prosecutor. Following retirement from the department in 1990, he did a year as an investigator with the county attorney's office and then went into business for himself, working primarily for criminal defense lawyers he personally knew and liked, all of them former prosecutors. With a pension in place, Mick was financially secure and under no obligation to get involved in things that didn't interest him.

Riley had always liked Mick Goerdan, though he had often had to decline prosecution in cases where it was clear that

Mick had exceeded his legal authority. Those occasional differences between them were not so serious as to cancel out a three-generation relationship between his family and Riley's. Both clans had lived on Minneapolis's North Side during the Great Depression, where Riley's father ran around with Michael Goerdan, Sr., when they were boys. Mick was nine years older than Riley, but because of a special fondness for Riley's older brother Jamie, later killed in Vietnam, Riley came within the small circle of people to whom Mick was unreservedly loyal. Their only point of ongoing contention was Riley's long and inscrutable friendship with Curt McBraneman, a drug-dealing vigilante whom Mick had once personally placed on the Minneapolis PD's list of most dangerous criminals. There was a time, many years back, when Riley worried that his two hot-tempered friends might one day kill each other.

More a man of instinct than science, Goerdan's years on the force enabled him to assess guilt and innocence with an uncanny accuracy. But because street intuition is not an articulable form of probable cause recognized anywhere in the U.S. Constitution, Mick was constantly at odds with the system in which he worked. At fifty-eight he was just old enough to have been trained in the "old" methods of crime detection, so when the law of criminal procedure took a turn to the left, Mick became a resourceful expert at finding alternate grounds on which to stop and search those who had fallen under his suspicious eye. Minor traffic violations would do nicely for rolling stock, and where he felt a need to enter a dwelling without benefit of a warrant, he was renowned for using what came to be known in the department as "Mick Goerdan Probable Cause." He'd send his partner to the back door of a dwelling while he went to the front. When he knocked on the front door and yelled, "Can I come in?" his partner at the back door would shout, "Sure, come on in." At the subsequent hearing he'd testify, accurately if not honestly, that he'd been invited into the premises—where with an amazing frequency he'd find drugs, contraband, or other evidence of serious criminal activity.

Like many old-line police officers of his generation, Goerdan had started his public service in the pre-Miranda era, back when uncooperative murder and rape suspects were routinely interrogated in the wee hours of the morning while being held by their ankles over the Tenth Avenue Bridge, which spanned the Mississippi River at one of its most turbulent points. The suspects were given to understand that a failure to be forthcoming might result in their washing up as far south as Baton Rouge. Those days were long gone, and the judges of the county were decidedly mixed in their opinions of Mick, the more liberal amongst them publicly railing against his "rubber-hose tactics." But, without exception, when those same judges came under serious threat from this or that dangerous psychopath, they quietly requested that Sergeant Goerdan be assigned to the case. And they left the crime-fighting techniques entirely to him.

In his later years with the department, and during his time as a private investigator, Mick had switched from being a head-cracker to an expert researcher. Although well trained and competent with the computer and the high-tech databases now widely available on-line, he continued to produce his most creative results through witness interviews and an eerie ability to place himself in the mind of another person. In a bank fraud case just concluded by Riley, Mick had uncovered a witness (a former clerk in the accounting department of a rural bank) who provided dispositive defense testimony in the acquittal of a bank officer accused of wire fraud. No computer ever designed could have turned up that witness, nor for that matter could the prosecutor's best investigators.

Now, having lifted the rock on the short, unhappy life of Ellen Tanzdahl, Mick would report on whether Gus's claims of unfitness had any merit—whether she had, in fact, been a hooker, drug user, and corrupter of the public morals.

Promptly at ten-thirty Riley heard Skeeter yell, "Yo, Micky," in her best Rocky Balboa voice. Mick was Italian on his mother's side and looked a little like Luca Brazzi.

Mick wiggled his eyebrows lustily as he passed her desk.

"Yeah, in your dreams, you old goat," she snorted.

Without being announced, he sailed into Riley's office and headed for the couch.

"Don't bother knocking, numb-nuts," said Riley without looking up from the memo he was drafting.

Mick dropped onto the couch and propped a heavy-booted foot on one of Cosgrove & Levi's finest coffee tables. While Riley delivered the memo to Skeeter, Mick dialed a number on his cell phone and began jotting notes on the back on an envelope. When Riley returned, Mick was conning some low-level clerk at the County Recorder's Office into providing confidential information that he had no business getting.

"Thanks, honey," he said as he clicked off his cell phone. He then sat up on the couch and pulled a thick wad of papers from the inside pocket of his sport coat. He rustled through the papers until he came to the "M's."

"Let's see now," he muttered, "Mason . . . Marduke . . . McMahon . . . ahh, here we are, McReynolds."

Riley leaned forward with his hands folded patiently on the desk. "Okay, Mick, enough theater. What did you find out?"

Mick looked up with a smug smile. "Well, let me put it this way: You could probably say that Tanzdahl is technically correct, but the reality is not nearly as bad as the spin he's put on the facts."

Riley thought it highly unlikely that Ellen Tanzdahl was the tramp described by Gus. He didn't know what she might have done in the past, but unless it was something really awful, she could hardly be a less suitable parent than Gus. He was disappointed, though, at the news that there was any truth to Gus's claims. So disappointed, in fact, that he was having trouble formulating even a single coherent sentence. He could feel his jaw tighten and his teeth start to grind. He didn't want to have to go after her in court. It didn't feel right.

The poise for which Riley was famous seemed to desert him when his mind turned to this tawdry business of using a small child as a pawn in a high-stakes financial battle. And the strain was showing on his face.

Mick rose from the couch and walked over to the chair facing Riley. He sat down and leaned forward. "Listen, man, the facts are not that bad. Just sit back and I'll tell you what I found out."

Riley sighed and shook his head. "It almost doesn't matter, Mick. If you've come up with anything, Gus Tanzdahl is going to insist that we use it. That's his right as the client. But it's slimy."

"But wait, Ellen Tanzdahl wasn't that bad—"

Riley cut him off. "Don't you see, Mick, that's almost worse. If she were truly unfit . . . if she were an unreformed junkie or a hooker or something like that, it would make what I have to do easier because I would be watching out for the interests of a four-year-old kid. Or at least I could tell myself that, as bad as Gus might be, he was no worse than she was, so maybe the boy should be in his custody."

Goerdan took a deep breath and exhaled audibly. His expression was one of sympathy mixed with surprise.

Riley leaned back in his chair and steeled himself for the information he was about to hear. "Okay, let's have it."

Goerdan flipped through several pages in a small red notebook. "Let's see, when she was eighteen, Ellen Murseth, now Ellen Tanzdahl, ran away from a home in which her alcoholic father regularly beat up her mother and had recently started knocking her around, too. She headed to the Southwest part of the country, where she and two other girls a few years older were picked up for 'soliciting with intent to commit prostitution.'"

Riley put his hands up to his face as though he were about to weep.

"Now, wait a minute, goddammit, it gets a little worse, but then it gets better," said Mick. "When the cops booked her they found a dime bag of grass. Because the cops knew the people she was with when they arrested her, it was assumed she had gotten the drugs down in Mexico—but they couldn't prove that. So she pleaded straight up on the marijuana charge, and the government dropped the solicitation, for which they didn't have any real evidence anyway. They had basically used it as probable cause for the stop and search. She was sentenced to time served, two days for possession of the marijuana. The plea bargain provided that the offense would be dropped from her record after a year if she had no new drug-related charges during that time. But, as so often happens, there was an administrative screw-up and the record was not expunged when the year was up. That's probably why Gus found it."

"That's it? There was nothing else?"

Goerdan raised his hand, palm up, to signal that he wasn't through. "The records are a little unclear but there was a later charge called 'indecent exposure in the presence of a child,' which was suspended administratively on condition she attended a series of classes at some women's center. That must be what Tanzdahl was referring to when he said she had a sex offense involving children."

"Indecent exposure in the presence of a child?" Riley muttered, incredulous. "So Gus was right? What the hell were the facts?"

Mick shook his head ambiguously. "Well, it was exposure only in the derivative sense. This one was really bogus. When you study the police report, which I got a copy of from a guy I used to know down there, you see that she was in a car with four other kids, and they mooned a motorist at a stop sign. You remember mooning and streaking were popular with kids during those years. The problem was that the guy they mooned was a Baptist minister and a member of the local school board."

135

"Mooning? She got charged with indecent exposure just for mooning?"

"Yup, it's a community standards kind of thing . . . this was the wrong town to drop your trousers in. If they had been local kids, nothing would have happened. Shit, if that standard had been in effect around here in those days, half the suburban kids in Minnesota would have a record."

"So, how did they get 'in the presence of a child' into the charge?"

"You'll love this. There was a school bus behind them at the stop sign, which they didn't even know was there, and it had some grade-school kids in it. The report said the kids loved it—they laughed hysterically—but the minister went nuts and swore out a complaint against everyone in the car for indecent exposure, and he used the school bus to invoke the 'involving a child' section of the statute."

Mick twisted his mouth and let out a sardonic laugh. "This is pure chickenshit, but because they offended a community elder, they got charged with an offense that was nothing more than horseplay. And Ellen probably didn't even hang her ass out like the other kids in the car did, because she was driving. But whatever the case was, she got charged along with everyone else, and she was too naive to know that the case against her was weak. So she pleaded guilty along with the others."

Riley rose from his chair and walked to the window. He stood looking out at some of the least interesting scenery in Minneapolis. To his left was a parking lot and, directly in front of him, were the backs of several turn-of-the-century, three-story buildings, one of which had a commercial mural from the 1940s painted across its east face. Though faded, he could just make out that the painting had been of a smiling Betty Crocker-type figure holding a small child on her lap. It had been an ad for a baby formula that had long since passed out of use.

Without turning from the window, he asked, "If we were to cite that conviction in the custody part of the case, would it stand up?"

"Yeah, I suppose. First impressions are important, even when they're based on misleading information. Once planted early in a case, those impressions die hard. Just the label used in those old charges make her look like some kind of deviant." Flipping through the last of his notes, Mick looked over at Riley, who was still at the window. "I can see where using this stuff would throw a scare into her, which is what your client seems to want to do. It's very effective ammunition for that purpose."

A cramp rolled through Riley's midsection. He returned to his desk and stared hard at Goerdan. "That is exactly what I didn't want to hear. A nineteen-year-old on the run from an abusive father gets some minor charges that would be meaningless in any other setting, but with language like 'indecent exposure in the presence of a child,' 'controlled substances,' and 'soliciting to commit prostitution,' Gus has just what he wants."

Mick looked puzzled. "But this can be explained away by her attorney in his pitch to the court and the custody evaluator. It doesn't actually prove she's an unfit mother."

"That's not the issue. Just alleging this stuff in court documents will humiliate her, especially if the allegations are picked up by the newspapers . . . and believe me, the newspapers love a jet-set domestic squabble like this one. You know the way people read these stories; they see the words 'indecent exposure in the presence of a child' and automatically conclude she's a child molester . . . and that first impression never goes away. They don't sort though the detailed facts." Shaking his head in frustration, he made his way back to his desk. "I'd rather you had told me that she had been dealing heroin for the Cali Cartel . . . or that it was a case of mistaken identity, another 'Ellen Murseth'—so I could either go after her in good faith or get this slime out of the case. Instead, I'm exactly where I didn't want to be, where Gus is going to make us use this stuff as a club. It makes me sick." He put his elbows on the desk, and dropped his face into his hands.

Mick Goerdan had never seen Riley so rattled over a case they had worked on together. There were plenty of matters in the old days where the facts were upsetting, but in those instances they had both been on the side of the good guys. Riley's role had been as an enforcer of justice. Here he was being called upon to twist the system, to extort a financial settlement from a young mother.

Riley finally looked up and said with dutiful reluctance, "All right, give the report to Sara Hall. She's working on a first draft of the motion to change custody. I don't even want to see the damn thing until I absolutely have to. And by the way, tell Sara not to file or serve any of this stuff until I've approved it. I've got to think more about this."

Mick nodded and started toward the door, then stopped and looked back. "Listen Riley, you've got to let go of this thing. You're just doing your job. It's not up to you to decide fitness. He may be a better parent than she is. Let the court decide." Again he turned toward the door, but again he paused. "And here's some other free advice: try to figure out what's got you so worked up about this particular case. Your reaction is exaggerated, way out of proportion. It's none of my business, but are you having trouble at home or anything like that? You're way too involved here—you're reacting like a damn participant rather than a lawyer. You're not Joshie Tanzdahl, for Christ's sake. None of this is happening to you personally."

Riley nodded and sighed, more with embarrassment than understanding. "You're right, Mick. I'm sorry. I don't honestly know what's going on. There's nothing wrong at home, other than that Betsy is understandably a little angry about me being gone all the time on the search I told you about. Don't worry, I'll snap out it."


AFTER MICK LEFT, Riley changed gears and went to work on a grand jury investigation of one of his healthcare clients. But before he got two pages into the file, the phone rang.

He picked up the receiver and heard the stiff, officious voice of Blanche Emersen, secretary to Ladge Wilkaster and Barney Bost. "Please hold for Mr. Bost," she instructed.

Riley rolled his eyes and slammed down the phone.

Less than a minute later, Barney Bost barged into his office. "Dammit, McReynolds, I have to talk to you."

Riley looked up, wondering why it was that nobody waited to be invited into his office. "If you want to talk to me, Barney, trying calling yourself rather than playing the big shot by having Blanche do it. You're not the president of General Motors, ya know."

Barney tossed off the rebuke. He took a seat and began stroking the arms of the chair. He cleared his throat; his expression turned official. He then got up and walked back to the door. He peeked out at Skeeter's desk, and then softly closed the door. "I'll get right to the point here, McReynolds. Ladge and I had a talk, and we want you to tell your secretary that she should be more . . . well, more deferential to the lawyers in the firm, especially the partners. She should not address them by their first names."

Riley groaned. *Good God, not this crap, not today.* Skeeter was one of the best-liked people in the office—by lawyers and support staff alike. When she wasn't joking playfully with other employees, she was listening to their troubles. She had one of those faces and smiles that people are drawn to. Every law firm should have at least one like her. The only people she ran afoul of were tight-asses like Barney and Ladge.

Barney continued. "She should model herself on Blanche Emersen, who is a shining example to the younger secretaries. She's the very soul of professionalism . . . not the kind to go around taking liberties like Ms. Swenson does."

Riley smiled ruefully. "*You* tell her that she should be more like Blanche Emersen, Barney. And let me know when you do it—I want to watch."

"And speaking of professionalism," said Barney as he reached into his coat pocket, "Blanche was quite offended to find this left behind in the photocopy machine when she came in on Monday morning." He passed a sheet of paper across the desk. Riley peered down at it, moving his head in a circular motion in an effort to identify the image. For a moment he thought it might be a print of a new addition to the art collection.

"What is it?" he finally asked, looking up at Barney.

Barney affected an expression of mild disgust. "I believe it's a photocopy of your son's rear end. It seems that he sat on the photocopy machine without his pants on. You did have him at the office with you over the weekend, didn't you?"

A look of recognition now crossed Riley's face. He remembered that Teddy and his friend Petie Portland *had* come to the office on Saturday, and, sure enough, he had heard them giggling and horsing around near the copy machine outside Ladge's office. He turned the sheet on its side. "Yeah, by God, this is Teddy's butt," he said as though he had just solved a difficult crossword puzzle. "It's definitely a Bainbridge keister—very much like Betsy's. We McReynolds don't have shapely butts."

Barney leaned forward in his chair, smiling weakly. "That's very interesting, McReynolds." His smile then turned to a snarl. "But I don't give a damn about your family anatomy. Just be sure this kind of stunt doesn't happen again. Blanch is a consummate professional, and she shouldn't have to put up with this kind of crudity."

"Crudity? For God's sake, Barney, they're seven-year olds." A smile stole across his face. "It could have been a lot worse. The boys could have photocopied their wienies. But they probably didn't know how to work the magnification button." He chuckled in tribute to his own wit.

"Very funny, McReynolds," said Barney as he rose from the chair and headed for the door. On the way out of the office he broke stride to straighten a picture hanging over the couch. He then looked back at Riley. "Please try to remember that dignity is essential in this operation, and Ms. Swenson has to be made to understand that she has to behave like a professional. I don't care what she does outside the office, but when she's at Cosgrove & Levi, we expect decorum."

He then opened the door, walked through the seating area, and turned into the hallway.

As he rounded the corner, he collided gently with Skeeter, just returning from lunch. "Yo, Barney, what's happening, dude?" she said with a smile.

Barney expelled a short huff. As he stepped around her, Skeeter punched him high on his arm. "Have a good day, big boy."

# 9

---

RILEY HAD HOPED he'd get lucky, hoped he'd find someone right off who knew what had become of Bridey
Reaves. To that end he had placed a notice in the per-
sonals section of fourteen carefully chosen newspapers, requesting information about a woman born in 1908, with an
Irish accent, who may have gone by the name Anna Reaves
or Bridey Reaves or some variation of those names, and who
left Chicago in 1925. A partial physical description was
included, along with a P.O. Box and e-mail address to which
responses could be sent.

Over 160 replies were received, of which the vast majority
could be eliminated as cranks. Others were from people who
said they had known Bridey, but on closer examination, they
could be eliminated by reference to details Riley had deliberately withheld for purposes of verification.

Sixteen replies were from professional psychics who gave
wildly conflicting accounts of her life on the run, save only
that all sixteen concluded that Bridey was dead. All sixteen
also said that Bridey could be contacted in the afterlife for
a nominal fee, payable by credit card, check, or money
order.

Three responders said that they were Bridey, but their claims were easily disproved by reference to physical characteristics or personal history. One said she was Bridey's reincarnation.

Having exhausted the shortcuts—the easy, obvious, and rarely successful avenues of inquiry—it was now time for the heavy lifting, the unglamorous grunt work of picking up a trail that had gone cold more than seventy years before.

Assuming that Bridey hadn't been caught and killed by pursuing Capone operatives—a sizable assumption in its own right—the most likely scenario, based on the course followed by a majority of people making a getaway, was that she changed her identity as soon as she was physically out of Chicago.

In 1925 it was a good deal easier to disappear than it would be in 1996, or, for that matter, at any time after the passage of the Social Security Act. Bridey could easily have selected any name that popped into her head and started a new life in another part of the country. Unless she applied for a passport, she wouldn't even have needed a birth certificate, and it would have been an easy matter to obtain a secondary identifier such as a driver's license or library card. And as long as she stayed away from friends, relatives, and locales with which she was previously associated, those searching for her would have had considerable difficulty picking up her trail. No doubt her pursuers kept a watch on the St. Agnes Convent, hoping to intercept mail, phone calls, or other forms of communication. And though it would have been initially impossible to get to O'Banion's widow because of the bodyguards posted by Hymie Weiss and Bugs Moran, there would almost surely have been a Capone operative watching her from a distance in the hopes that Bridey would make contact there.

Riley knew from his days as an investigator that the centerpiece of any search going back this far would be the psychological factors involved. For no matter how smart such people on the run might be, they nearly always slip up by leaving behind at least one important marker. And that marker most often involves the selection of a new name. Though they typically shed their given names in favor of something with an entirely different sound, the new name is nearly always drawn from some aspect of their past, some association that is consciously or unconsciously of importance to them. Identity changers tend to fall into the same patterns as ordinary people choosing a pin code for an ATM or long-distance calling card. An astonishing number of otherwise clever people can be counted on to use a backwards configuration of their own birth date or phone number. And those who make it their business to break such codes rarely have to try more than four or five combinations before they're able to hack in.

In the case of changed identities, the least shrewd and most commonly used practice is to take a mother's or grandmother's maiden name. Riley knew from Bridey's passport, found in the records of the St. Agnes Convent, that her mother's maiden name had been Cavanaugh, and her maternal grandmother's maiden name had been McBride. Those names, therefore, went to the top of the search list. He also phoned Sister Meghan and talked her into providing the legal names (as opposed to the church names) of the novices with whom Bridey had been close during her stay in the convent. It was possible that she had selected one of those names; after all, they were legitimate names of real people who had retreated from the world and had little use for their legal identities. Thus, there would be little chance of tripping over the real owner of that identity.

Armed with that information, he recommended the search, using the same index and source materials previously consulted when searching the names "Reaves" and its anglicized iteration, "Reeves." There were thirty-eight names of novices in 1925. All were searched. All came up negative, as did the Cavanaugh and McBride angles.

For sentimental reasons, and thinking that Bridey might in a moment of carelessness, have taken the name of her surrogate father, he searched the name "Anna McBride O'Banion" and several of its variations. Again nothing.

Having exhausted the frontline choices without result, he would now have to widen the circle—flail about, take guesses. Informed guesses, but guesses nevertheless.

Prior to her parents' deaths, the family had lived in an apartment near Halstead and Armitage. Her parents were killed in a car accident at Fullerton and Clark. The original St. Agnes Convent stood on Wells, near Superior. Combinations of all those words—with and without Anna, Ann, Reeves, Reaves, Bridey and McBride—were likewise run through all available indexes, to no avail. He had several hits out of that pool of names—some dead and some alive—but they were easily eliminated in reference to gender, race, age or other immutable characteristic. Death records were found for all the novices, save only Sister St. Catherine, whose real name turned out to be Mary Shaw.

The thrill of the chase was still upon him, but the unlikelihood of success sometimes made the effort seem hopeless and, therefore, a little foolish. Once outside the circle of high-potential markers, searches of this kind had little chance of success. He had already run upwards of fifteen hundred separate inqiries, if one included all the data bases searched under the various name combinations. All for naught.

Still, the dreamy fun of it all, the spine-tingling prospect that he might break a seven-decades old mystery, supplied just the kind of distraction he longed for. He had fallen into a strange but happy form of bondage to the girl with the pale eyes.

The Anastasia mystery—dead though Anastasia turned out to be—had distracted him from physics, organic chemistry, and a medical school education that undoubtedly would have ended in a hypochondriacal meltdown. Now, as he prostituted his talent, influence, and good name to an odious man in an uneven tug of war for a small boy, he was again in the chase for the mythical female, the woman whose ghostly presence had been someplace at the center of his heart since he was a small child. So, in the end, it didn't really matter how unlikely he was to find the owner of that haunting face, just so long as there was even a distant chance.

Betsy suggested that it might be time to grow up and face this latest stress like a grown-up, a mature and realistic man. But Riley had always considered being a grown-up to be a vastly overrated commodity. Seeing much of life through the eyes of a boy had its drawbacks, but in other ways it was quite wonderful. Many things that seemed dull and unremarkable to grown-ups, like the swirling pattern made by the cement in front of his house, could be fascinating to him, filled somehow with quiet fun.

And he didn't much warm to the word "man" either. It was a hairy, thick-knuckled word, with a strong body odor. Better to keep in touch with the intuitions of youth, no matter how imperfectly remembered. That's what made for a rich life. It was no accident that Wordsworth had always been his favorite poet.

Still, there were drawbacks to his behavior in this instance. His mother, for example, seemed to be viewing this newest search as an insult to her personally, even more than she had with Anastasia and Amelia Earhart. And even the long-suffering Betsy was running out of patience. Skeeter was the most straightforward of the bunch. "You're fucking nuts," was how she put it.

But on this sunny afternoon, as he sat alone in his office, he did what he was compelled to do, and the search pressed ahead in an ever-widening sweep, radiating outward from the known tidbits of Bridey's early life. He stared at the file, trying to divine from its scanty contents the next wisp of information from which a clue might be tortured.

He examined a small sheet of yellowed paper that had been given to him by Sister Meghan. It was a handwritten note Bridey had sent to the Mother Superior at age fifteen, in

1923. Too faded to photocopy, Meghan had given him the original. The handwriting was girlish but somehow elegant. In the note Bridey apologized for giggling in church the previous Sunday and asked for permission to help Sister Monica, her favorite novice, tend to the garden behind the convent. Given its clarity, sincerity, and humility, real or feigned, it must have accomplished its purpose, for it could be seen that Bridey had the gift of persuasion. In another time, she might have become a lawyer herself.

He turned next to the passport. It showed that she had been born in the Village of Turlough, in County Clare, Ireland, a small community that his atlas placed just north of Shannon. He pulled a pencil from a yellow holder Lizzie had made for him in fifth grade and scribbled in a column on the left-hand margin of a legal pad: "Clare Ireland," "Shannon Ireland," "Shannon Turlough," "Clare Turlough," "Clare Shannon," and "Shannon Clare." He then ran each name through the consolidated indexes. To his surprise, he got a death-record hit on a "Clare Turlough." His heart jumped slightly as he read across the column: "Clare B. Turlough, born Feb. 12, 1908; deceased Jan. 18, 1937."

He slumped back in his chair and looked out the window at the grimy building with the faded mural. "It's probably not her," he muttered to himself. But the chances of those two names (the county and town in which she was born) being found together and in combination with her actual year of birth and the spelling C-L-A-R-E rather than C-L-A-I-R, would at the very least be a sizeable coincidence.

The place of death for Clare Turlough was listed as Omaha, Nebraska. Turning from the computer, he reached for the phone and dialed up a law school classmate, Clay Huston, a senior attorney in the Omaha prosecutor's office. Clay was not in, but Riley managed to find Greta Gustafson, a paralegal he had once worked with on the extradition of a Minnesota felon from Nebraska. She agreed to run a quick check on the death records and call him back.

Riley paced the office, talking loudly to himself. He wanted the mystery solved, but at the same time he dreaded the news that Bridey might be dead.

When she heard his solitary ramblings, Skeeter got up from her desk and leaned through the doorway. "I understand you're harmless, but other people might get the wrong impression." She closed the door.

Ten minutes later he lunged for the ringing phone. "I've got your information, Riley," said Greta. "I don't know what you're up to, but here goes: The deceased was five-foot-seven, 130 pounds, small boned, thin legs. She had dark hair and pale-blue eyes. Hmmm . . . I've never seen the descriptor 'pale-blue' used in a homicide file. Those eyes must have been really pale. Anyway, she had no known middle name, but the middle initial was 'B.' She was believed to have been foreign born, somewhere in the British Isles, and died of suffocation in what was classified as an unsolved homicide." She rustled papers on the other end, and sighed with afternoon fatigue. "It says there were no signs of sexual assault, which is unusual when the victim is a prostitute, as this summary states she was. There's a marginal note that directs the reader to the full homicide investigation files."

After more shuffling of papers, Greta said, "That's all I can get you on such short notice, but I talked to Clay during a recess in the case he's trying, and he said that if you want to come down he'll retrieve the original investigative files from the police archives. A murder file, as you know, is never really closed, even one nearly sixty years old."

ON SATURDAY MORNING, Riley caught the first plane for Omaha, rented a car at the airport, and drove downtown. Though he assigned no meaning to it, a large, dark sedan left the airport at the same time he did and arrived at the courthouse just as he was going through the front entrance. There were many explanations for this small coincidence, most of them benign, so he did nothing more that make a mental note.

Together with his old classmate Clay Huston, he dove into the archives of the Omaha Police Department and the Douglas County Attorney's Office in search of anything relating to the unsolved murder of Clare Turlough. A thick file jacket—dusty, brittle, and curling from age—had been resurrected from the bowels of the police archives. Segregated into sub-files, the jacket contained all official materials generated by the police investigation fifty-nine years earlier, including the notes of the investigating officers. Those notes indicated that the murdered woman had been discovered in a cheap boarding house near the stock yards on January 18, 1937. The location was listed as a known domicile of itinerant prostitutes. The coroner's official report attributed the cause of death to "*Suffocation complicated by alcohol intoxication. Probable homicide.*"

The official inventory showed that the following items were booked into the property room as evidence:

1. One pair of dark leather shoes with low heels, size 6.
2. One pair of imitation gold earrings in the shape of four-leaf clovers.
3. One white silk dress with a blue and green flower pattern.
4. One pair of women's underpants.
5. One garter belt.
6. Two tan nylon stockings.
7. One bra (white), size 34B.

Attached to the coroner's report was a photo static copy of the death certificate signed by F. Benson, M.D. A footnote indicated that Dr. Benson was a second-year surgical resident at St. Joseph's Hospital, which Riley calculated would have made him roughly twenty-eight years of age at the time, roughly the same age as Bridey.

The coroner's report described "*A poorly nourished female in her later 20s or early 30s, with signs of incipient alcohol-*

*induced liver disease, without scars or birthmarks that could be used in identification. There were no deformities, fractures, or signs of violence to the female genitalia. Although alcohol was detected in the stomach contents expelled at the time of death, suffocation was not attributable to aspirated vomitus. Oxygen deprivation was imposed by an outside agent."*

The county attorney's summary noted that no drivers license, social security number, birth certificate, or other evidence of identity could be located for the victim, the crime scene having been cleared of identifying data by person or persons unknown. The first officer on the scene, Detective Lieutenant Patrick Clebourne, attached to the Robbery/Homicide Division, together with his partner, Sergeant William Kunz, identified the deceased as one Clare Turlough, a twenty-nine-year-old woman personally known to Sergeant Clebourne as a prostitute with whom he had had a prior contact in connection with a robbery investigation. The summary went on to state that, *"Inability to confirm identity or next of kin from fingerprints or birth records suggests that the name used by the victim was an alias, though by reason of an accent testified to by Detective Clebourne and the victim's landlady, it is likely that she was foreign born, most probably somewhere in the British Isles."*

Brief notations entered by the file clerk six weeks after the coroner's inquest showed that the investigative file had been reviewed by one Gavin Emmetts, Esq., an Omaha attorney with known connections to the "Capone Organization" in Chicago. If Emmetts also talked to the investigating officer, no notes of that conversation survived. From a distance of fifty-nine years, a mob lawyer reviewing the police file strongly suggested that, if Clare Turlough was Bridey, her mob pursuers, who may also have been her killers, had not recovered the rumored half-million dollars, at least not at the time of the murder. They might well have been keeping tabs on the file in an effort to determine whether the money turned up. Or it might just have been their desire to confirm that they had gotten the right person. Or none of the above. But all that, combined with the boasting of John Michael O'Caskeny in 1937, as recalled by Stairs Kavaeny, only served to harden Riley's suspicion that Bridey Reaves had, in fact, been slain while on the run from the mob. This was by no means certain, but the likelihood of a woman of Bridey's age and exact physical description—with no record of birth and bearing the name of a small village in Ireland in which she just happened to have been born—being someone else, was extremely remote. Add to that the fact that a lawyer associated with the Capone Mob had tracked the police investigation of a low-end prostitute in Omaha, and the odds became astronomical.

Riley turned over the last page of the file, not expecting to find anything, when his eyes fell upon a brown envelope stapled to the back of the file jacket.

He looked up at Clay Huston, who nodded permission to open it. The aged seal securing the flap broke into pieces at the first touch. He reached inside and carefully removed six crime-scene photos. His mouth went dry and his heart pounded as he neatly arranged the photos on the table surface.

The first two were black and white close-ups of Clare Turlough's body on a filthy, disheveled bed, her lifeless eyes open but unfocused, dark, viscous fluids draining from her mouth. He went weak with nausea and grief as he viewed the pictures, one by one. He felt like a ghoul trespassing upon a grave that hadn't been disturbed for nearly sixty years. With trembling hands, he placed the photos side by side under a magnifying lens attached to the table. The face, frozen in death, was rigid, and it had begun to darken by the time the photo was snapped by the assistant medical examiner. Dark hair, clotted with sweat from her last desperate exertion, framed the death mask. The eyes, strikingly pale, stared lifelessly out at him.

He reached into his briefcase and pulled out the enhanced newspaper photo of Bridey and laid it alongside the crime-scene pictures. Joined by Clay Huston and Greta Gustafson, he compared the images. Riley knew from having viewed hundreds of crime scene photos during his time as a prosecutor that the years between age sixteen and twenty-nine can bring about substantial physical changes to just about anyone. But even discounting for the toll that hard living must have taken on this woman's appearance, there was a striking resemblance between her and the sixteen-year-old Bridey Reaves.

A seasoned prosecutor of homicide cases himself—often where the deceased was in a state of advanced rigor mortis or even partial decomposition—Clay Huston offered a firm opinion that the pictures were of the same woman. Greta Gustafson agreed. They looked over at Riley sympathetically. He seemed to be coming a little unglued.

Through a title wave of emotions—including grief, disappointment, revulsion at the photos, and a roiling anger— Riley concluded that Clay and Greta were probably right. Years as a lawyer had taught him that ninety-nine times out of a hundred things are what they seem to be. And the sad, abused woman lying dead in the forgotten police photographs sure seemed to be the once-beautiful girl who had stood, innocent and inconsolable, at the graveside of Dion O'Banion.

He excused himself, walked down the hall to the men's bathroom, and threw up violently.


REPRODUCTIONS OF THE CRIME-SCENE photos were prepared by the archives custodian and given to Riley along with copies of the relevant reports. He declined copies of the autopsy photos, which showed the bloated corpse from several angles, dissected like a medical school cadaver, grisly beyond description.

Driving home from the airport in Minneapolis, he had an hour to grieve the abrupt ending of his latest dream. Disappointment mixed with horror as the image of the dead woman flashed through his mind like a malevolent strobe light. He wished he had not seen those photos, had not unearthed a mystery with such a sad and gruesome end. The fascination he had felt for the pretty girl in the crowd, a girl he had wanted to reach out to across time, had been replaced by an unnerving sense of revulsion.

He had known girls from his youth—grade school and high school, and even college—who were pretty and innocent when young but later succumbed to addiction and prostitution. It hurt to think of the innocent Bridey Reaves reborn through fear and adversity into the squalid and twisted corpse of Clare Turlough. That it had happened six decades before did nothing to lessen its horror.

After switching lanes and exiting Highway 169, he drove past a baseball field and a small corner church from which the bells were calling the faithful to evening prayers. The feeling that he had foolishly wasted a great deal of valuable time broke over him. What had seemed such a good idea just weeks before now seemed only strange and dark. He felt embarrassed and stupid. The sandcastle he had constructed in his mind had collapsed and washed out to sea. His critics and detractors, especially his mother, had all been right.

But it was true that he had solved a long forgotten mystery, even if it was one that no one else on earth gave a damn about. Maybe Stairs Kavaeny would want to hear about it, and possibly Sister St. Catherine, but it would be pointless and cruel to sadden them with these melancholy developments.

At least Betsy would be relieved to have him back. She had been graciously tolerant, just as she had been with Anastasia and the other lost beauties. At such times she treated him as though he was a boy with an imaginary friend at the dinner table, which probably wasn't far from the truth.

But his mother—that would be something else altogether. She would crow, "I told you so. Remember I told you to grow up and stay away from that kind of silliness." Her voice played in his head.

After a minute or two of sitting numbly behind the wheel in the driveway, he trudged into the house and collapsed in self-pity onto the couch. His daughter, Lizzie, walked by and looked down at him with her own pale Irish eyes and said, "Another wasted trip, huh Dad?"

He wanted her to sit down next to him and listen to the whole disappointing tale, of how the girl he had first noticed in a documentary because she looked like Lizzie had come to haunt and obsess him, and of how he had spent hours and days and weeks chasing after a beautiful ghost who it turned out had been dead for nearly sixty years, the victim of a cruel murder. But when he started to unburden himself, Lizzie nodded absently and said, "I'd love to hear all about it another time, Dad, but what I'd like now are the keys to your car. Me and Jenny are going to the mall."

"Jenny and I," he corrected as he obediently reached in his pocket and handed over the keys, even foregoing his standard cross-examination about who she was going with and when she'd be home. He was too tired, too downcast.

Seven-year-old Teddy, who had been in the kitchen listening to Betsy talking on the phone with Riley's sister Molly, came over and sat beside him on the couch, resting his head on Riley's shoulder. After a few silent moments, he peered up at his father with large, round eyes and said, "I don't care what Mom and Aunt Molly say, Dad. I don't think you're crazy."

"Thanks, pal. I'm glad at least one person understands." He reached down and put a bear hug on his pride and joy.


RILEY WENT TO BED that night in the confirmed belief that the dead prostitute buried under the headstone bearing the name Clare Turlough was in fact Bridey Reaves. But he emerged from the shallow, ragged sleep that followed with a nagging sense that he was not one hundred percent certain. He couldn't let go just yet.

So he sat down and reviewed the bidding. There was no doubt in his mind that Bridey had taken the name of her birthplace, Turlough in County Clare, when she fled Chicago. The age, the spelling of the first name, and the fact that there was no birth record in the 1900 to 1912 timeframe for a woman of that name, made the coincidence too remarkable to bear any other interpretation. And the striking physical similarity between Bridey and the dead prostitute—together with Clay Huston's professional opinion that they were one and the same person—made it all but certain.

Still, he couldn't fully detach, couldn't bring himself to consider the mystery fully solved. The spell cast by the grieving face of the sixteen-year-old girl, first glimpsed in the blistered footage of the television documentary, had not been broken. And though he didn't think the O'Banion money meant anything to him, what little evidence there was relating to that aspect of the case suggested that it had not been recovered by the Mob. Otherwise, why would the lawyer Gavin Emmetts have been tracking the murder investigation?

The money was no substitute for Bridey, but it might serve as a justification to continue a search that had provided such an effective distraction to the Tanzdahl divorce case. And so he called in an old favor from a forensic artist in Colorado, Norman Pennington, a man he had used in several murder cases where the victim's remains were in such a state of advanced decomposition that they couldn't be identified. Armed only with a human skull and such other bits of information as could be discerned scientifically, and aided by lasers and a chart of facial landscape points, a team consisting of Pennington, a forensic anthropologist and a former medical examiner, was able to create a portrait of the nameless victim, right down to the finest detail. When the resulting portraits were reproduced and distributed to national missing-persons databases, almost without exception they generated positive identifications from friends or next of kin. Validation through DNA and dental records then quickly followed.

There was no accessible skull to work with here, and there were no next of kin. So for Pennington to form an opinion, the photos of Bridey—newspaper, documentary, passport, and confirmation day—would have to contain sufficient definition to allow for computer, laser-based, and manual comparisons with the crime scene photos of the Omaha murder victim officially listed as Clare Turlough.

On arriving at the office a few days after sending the materials to Pennington, Riley pushed aside a thick memo from Sara Hall marked "Tanzdahl Divorce—Drafts of Custody Motion," replacing it on the desk with a certified copy of Clare Turlough's Nebraska death certificate. While awaiting Pennington's formal findings, he could think of almost nothing else, least of all the Tanzdahl case.

He straightened the death certificate in front of him on the cleared desk top, pressing its corners as though tidiness might coax it into giving up its secrets. He examined the seemingly routine entries, line by line. The physical description (*"5'7," 130 lbs."*) could have fit thousands of women in that area at that time. The description on Bridey's childhood passport from nearly twenty years before the Omaha murder was of little value as to height comparisons. And her height at the time of O'Banion's funeral, as judged by the known height of Hymie Weiss, who stood to her immediate right in the newspaper photo, made her closer to five-five in 1924. But she was only sixteen at the time and could easily have grown two inches while completing adolescence.

*"Eyes: blue. Hair: black/dark brown."* Those markers, too, were shared by thousands of women, though the police report had described the eyes as *"pale blue."* So, on the whole, that feature tended to confirm the identity.

He reached into his briefcase and removed the crime scene photo provided to him on his last Omaha visit, and stared into the lifeless eyes of the murdered woman. The sight produced in him nothing of the visceral reaction that the earlier photos and images of Bridey had. Even Bridey's passport

photo, taken when she was just a ten-year-old girl, and first
viewed by him at the St. Agnes Convent, had moved him to
tears. The death photo he was now looking at was stunning
and sad and even horrible, but from the evidence of his gut,
it was like any other photo of a stranger.

He scanned back and forth between the digitally enhanced
newspaper picture and the dead face at the crime scene, com-
paring on each the nose and mouth, the distance between the
cheekbones in relation to the length of the face, the shape and
configuration of the ears, the size and architecture of the eye
sockets, the length and slope of the forehead, the curve of the
hairline. There was unquestionably a remarkable resemblance. But then the most eminent forensic scientists and
handwriting experts in Europe, fifty years before, had testified that Anna Anderson, the claimant Riley had most closely
followed in his quest for Anastasia, had displayed similarities
so great to the grand duchess that she could only be the missing Romanov daughter. But DNA later showed them to be
plainly in error. Anna Anderson was, in fact, the Polish peas-
ant woman the royal family had claimed all along. So such
evaluations, made by the naked eye, were highly unreliable.

He could only hope that Norm Pennington could isolate
enough detail in the Bridey photos to make a comparison
that would satisfy modern science. That was his only hope,
for none of Bridey's DNA could be obtained—not so much as
a lock of her hair. And in any event, the likelihood of obtain-
ing a court order to exhume the body of a 1937 murder victim would have been one in 10,000. Courts do not consider a
lawyer's mid-life crises to be sufficient grounds to disturb the
grave of a woman who had been buried for fifty-nine years.
An exhumation request to the Nebraska courts, moreover,
would almost certainly be picked up by the newspapers, and
his peculiar obsession would be exposed to the world. He
couldn't bear to think of the effect that would have on his
marriage, to say nothing of the reaction it would bring from
his mother. And, anyway, Bridey's parents had been killed in

the car accident in 1922 and were cremated, so no comparator DNA would be available.

A handwriting expert would also do him no good. He had the specimen of Bridey's handwriting from the convent file, but no sample existed for the dead woman. Nothing had been found at the death scene—not a letter, not a laundry list, not even a signature on a driver's license.

So, as Skeeter opened the morning mail at her desk, it was back to the death certificate he went, living a few more precious moments in another world. He picked up a magnifying glass, and as he started to scan the remaining entries on the certificate, Skeeter entered the room with an armful of files.

She saw him bent over the magnifying glass. "Holy shit," she said, rolling her eyes and trying to suppress a laugh that might hurt his feelings. "Maybe I ought to get you one of those deerstalking hats that Sherlock Holmes used to wear, so you can be the undisputed dweeb of the century."

Riley lowered the magnifying glass. "If you had to put up with Gus Tanzdahl, you'd be a little nuts, too."

Skeeter set the files in Riley's in-basket and sat down in the chair facing his desk. "Yes, I understand that, Riley," she said in a tone normally reserved for children who had scraped their knees and were pretending not to cry. "But we have to be sure that we don't go completely around the bend."

The muscles around Riley's mouth tightened. Whenever either Betsy or Skeeter used the pronoun "we," especially when referring to a matter in which he was the only participant, he knew he was being patronized. And it embarrassed him. His mother told him he was now the laughing stock of the family, and his daughter, Lizzie, begged him not to talk about this subject in front of any of her friends for fear they would laugh at him behind his back.

He sat looking at Skeeter, not knowing what to say, let alone how to explain his Junior G-Man magnifying glass.

Skeeter returned his glance with a mixture of humor and pathos. She then held up a brown paper envelope with a circular logo and the words FORENSIC ANTHROPOLOGY CONSULTANTS, INC. in the upper left corner. The envelope had been opened by her but not read.

Riley's heart leaped into his throat. "Why didn't you tell me right away? What does it say?"

Skeeter put a pair of glasses up to her face. Her eyes grew wide and one eyebrow arched as she straightened the pages of the report and turned to the final section, where she knew the conclusion would be found. She took a deep breath and read: *"The female figure pictured in the several photos supplied from passport, newspaper, documentary film, and convent files, all taken before 1925 (herein 'Comparator Photos'), are confirmed to be of the same person, an adolescent female of somewhat unusual features and coloring.*

*"The woman pictured in the crime-scene photos found in Homicide File No. 3712063 of the Omaha Police Department, identified therein as Clare B. Turlough, is not the same person pictured in the Comparator Photos referenced above. The level of certainty assigned to this conclusion is of the highest scientific order."*

The woman buried as Clare Turlough in Holy Cross Cemetery in Omaha was not Bridey Reaves. Good lord, she had faked her own death.

# 10

RILEY WAS BEAMING as he packed his suitcase. He felt like a man reborn. The search was back on, and any extant leads concerning Bridey's next move after faking her own death in 1937, would have to be found in Omaha.

Using the earlier photos—with an emphasis upon the passport photo in which Bridey and her father appeared—Norm Pennington had prepared a set of age-progression drawings: artist's renderings of what she would have looked like at ages twenty-nine, thirty-nine, fifty, seventy-five—and eighty-eight, the age she would be if still alive in 1996. The passport photo of her father had been invaluable to Pennington in calculating the manner and rate at which she would have aged over the years.

A call to Clay Huston secured the necessary approvals to gain unrestricted access to the old police records relating not just to the Turlough homicide but also to the police personnel involved in the case. And so Riley had hopped a plane to Omaha and proceeded directly to the courthouse. Now, as the sun rolled over the vast Iowa plains, across the wide expanse of the Missouri River and up the misty stone walls of the Douglas County Courthouse in Omaha, Riley sat hunched over records first compiled in 1937.

The stunning news that the woman buried in Clare Turlough's grave in Holy Cross Cemetery was not Anna McBride Reaves, late of the Village of Turlough, County Clare, Ireland, meant that somebody had gone to a great deal of trouble to switch the two identities. Attempts by Mick Goerdan to find any trace of the dead prostitute's actual identity had come up completely dry, lending additional weight to the conclusion that it was only in death that she became Clare Turlough. How all this had come to pass could only be guessed at.

Whether the scam had thrown the mob off Bridey's trail was also anyone's guess. But successful or not, the ploy had been elaborate and ingenious and, in Riley and Mick Goerdan's judgment, could not have been pulled off by Bridey alone. She had to have had at least one accomplice in the design and execution of the scheme, and that accomplice must have had sufficient authority or contacts to manipulate an official police investigation.

What then had become of Bridey after she successfully faked her own death? What new identity had she assumed as she fled Omaha? In the years between her flight from Chicago and the faked death in Omaha, the Social Security Act had passed. Therefore, taking yet another false identity would be more complicated than simply assuming a new name. The great likelihood was that, having effectively killed off the Clare Turlough persona, she would have employed the method still in use in modern times—a method well known to Riley from his days at the detective agency. It involved finding the name of a deceased child with a birth date close to one's own. This was normally done by searching cemeteries or obituaries. The deceased child would have left no paper trail beyond certificates of birth and death. Since those documents were not cross-referenced, the death certificate would be invisible to anyone dealing with Bridey under her new false identity, unless that person suspected the ruse and took the trouble to manually cross-reference the two documents in a laborious state-by-state check. For that reason, sophisticated identity-changers invariably select a child who was born in one state and died in another, thereby greatly compounding the burden for any tracker.

The Social Security Administration did not establish a database of deceased cardholders until 1965, so there would have been no chance in 1937 that an application for a social security card in the name of a dead child would have met any resistance with that agency.

But trying to discover the identity Bridey assumed would be nearly impossible without first determining who it was that had assisted her in the scam. With that objective in mind, Riley sat at a long table in the bowels of the Douglas County Courthouse, carefully examining a stack of decaying files transported from police headquarters on instructions of Clay Huston.

On a yellow legal pad he noted in sequential order the names of all persons mentioned in the file, including the landlady, the investigating officers Patrick Clebourne and William Kunz, the emergency-room physician who signed the death certificate, the coroner, and the three funeral home employees involved in the burial of the woman who in death had become Clare Turlough.

Riley copied substantial portions of text from the investigative files, paying special attention to the description of the crime scene and the attempts by police to marshal information relative to the deceased woman. Of special interest was the fact that the room in which the victim was found contained nothing in the way of papers or other materials in any way connected to her. There was no identification on or around the body or in the room itself, one of many small chambers housing prostitutes employed by a local madam. Either the victim had carried no identification or the space had been swept clean before the police arrived. This didn't surprise the investigating officers, given the use to which the room was being put. Fingerprints of the victim were taken but could not be matched with any existing records in Nebraska or any other jurisdiction.

The chief investigator, Patrick Clebourne, a former vice officer, was able to identify the victim by reason of a prior investigative encounter. The police report and death certificate noted the date and place of birth for the deceased as "unknown," and surviving family members as "none found." The proprietress of the rooming house, a well-known madam in the Omaha area, confirmed Clebourne's identification.

Beyond the clothing she was wearing at the time of her death, only an inexpensive crucifix was found on the dead prostitute's body. With this as the sole indication of her religious affiliation, the police department chaplain applied for and received a burial allowance from the local diocese, thereby securing her a plot at Holy Cross Cemetery.

Investigative notes detailed the leads followed in the homicide investigation. Interviews with pimps, johns, psychos, and assorted miscreants from the area were summarized, including two with inmates of a mental hospital in Council Bluffs who had confessed to this and several other crimes, all of which would have been geographically impossible for them to commit. None of those contacts yielded information upon which a credible prosecution could be based.

Detective Clebourne and his partner, Sergeant Kunz, concurred in the theory that Clare Turlough had died at the hands of an unknown john in a moment of rage. It was a sadly familiar end for many street prostitutes.

The detectives also noted that they had staked out the funeral home and gravesite for seventy-two hours in the hope that remorse would draw the killer to the body. No luck there, either. Only the mortician and a couple of gravediggers were in attendance.

Riley next turned to the individual participants in the investigation, starting with Patrick Clebourne, whose personnel file now sat open before him. The file contained performance appraisals spanning a seventeen-year career with the Omaha Police Department. A veteran of World War I, Clebourne had enlisted in the army on his eighteenth birthday, just in time to fight and be wounded in the Battle of the Marne. He stayed in the army as a military policeman until 1925, when he joined the Omaha department as a patrolman. After eight years as a uniformed officer he was made a detective, serving first in the vice unit and later in Robbery-Homicide.

It was in the latter capacity that Patrick Clebourne found himself the first officer on the Turlough murder scene. File notes of a Captain Fitzsimmons indicated that he had been Clebourne's immediate supervisor during his service with the unit—service that, according to the file, came to a bloody end on November 10, 1939, roughly two years after the murder of Clare Turlough. A tersely worded memo noted that Officer Clebourne had been fatally wounded on that date while posted to a robbery stakeout on the city's near north side.

It did not escape Riley's notice that Patrick Clebourne had died in the same manner, summary execution, and on the same date, November 10, that Dion O'Banion had been assassinated eighteen years before. November 10 was also Bridey's birthday. Like O'Banion, Clebourne had received multiple gun shots to the body and a single finishing shot to the head. Though it probably had no meaning to the officer making the entry, the memo noted that a single sprig of lilies was found in the dead man's hand. The officers who investigated Clebourne's murder attached no significance to that odd fact, probably assuming that Clebourne was holding the flower at the time he was shot. But it immediately suggested to Riley that, if Clebourne was tied into Bridey's escape, if he had been in any way helpful to her, the lilies had been left by his killers in memory of the world's most violent florist. Lilies were Deanie's favorite flower; in most surviving pictures, a sprig can be seen attached to the lapel of his suit jacket. In a similar gesture, when Machine Gun Jack McGurn, Al

Capone's chief triggerman and the mastermind of the St. Valentine's Day Massacre, was assassinated in a Chicago bowling alley in 1936, a valentine was found in his right hand. Such were the macabre rituals of the underworld.

The last entry in the Clebourne personnel file was a summary of the final accounting done relative to the deceased officer's accrued pay and benefits, including a life insurance payment that, because of the absence of a designated beneficiary or locatable next of kin, reverted to the Policeman's Benevolent Association.

To let some of the new information sink in, Riley took a break and walked the halls for twenty minutes. He then went up to the main lobby for a cup of coffee, which he sat drinking while reading a copy of Friday's Omaha newspaper. As he turned the pages of the sports section, he noticed a large, black automobile idling across the street from the courthouse entrance. The windows were tinted, but he could make out at least two people in the front seat. It could not be considered strange that a vehicle was sitting outside a major urban courthouse, but this looked very much like the car he had noticed behind him on the way downtown from the airport the previous week. His days as an investigator had sensitized him to surveillance techniques and had also endowed him with a bit of a sixth sense that seemed now to be sending a faint signal.

His rising anxiety was probably the result of too much coffee combined with the disturbing nature of the material in which he was immersed. But then again, who could say? Even though the grisly events he was researching were almost sixty years in the past, it was possible that the people behind those events had a long institutional memory, especially where a large sum of money had yet to be accounted for.

These dark speculations were a little far fetched, he knew, but the sight of that car was making him uncomfortable. He stood at the window for a few minutes, staring out at the passing traffic and every so often checking to see if the car had moved along. Finally it did, turning north on an adjoining one-way street, perhaps in response to a dispatch call. A small aerial protruding from the trunk, now noticed for the first time, allowed him to tentatively pass it off as a police vehicle. Relieved, he went back to the archives for another trip into the past.

Again at his seat, he turned to the personnel file of Sergeant Bill Kunz, Clebourne's partner, which contained considerably more background information than Clebourne's file had. By all appearances, Kunz had been a serious and conscientious young man who had joined the Omaha Police Department after an inner struggle with a family tradition, a tradition that in the ordinary course would have had him following his father and grandfather into the Lutheran ministry. As a youngster, Kunz had played trombone in the school band and was the starting quarterback on a conference-winning football team in a small town in central Iowa. At age twenty he married his childhood sweetheart, Louise, whose father was also a Lutheran minister. His youthful rebellions were confined to marrying outside his immediate religious tradition—though not far outside, for both families were Lutherans, his Missouri-Synod and hers Wisconsin Synod. In those times, in that part of the country, the union qualified as a mixed marriage.

Informed by religious sensibilities and a natural sense of compassion, Bill Kunz and his wife felt deeply challenged by the widespread suffering of the Great Depression and decided that their commitment to humanity could best be expressed in practical rather than churchly endeavors. Thus Bill became a police officer, and Louise, after finishing her training as a practical nurse, became an independent midwife.

The file indicated that the couple had raised one child, Nancy Fiona Kunz. Both Bill and Louise lived to a comfortable old age—long enough to see the birth and maturing of three grandchildren. Louise died at age eighty-one in 1992, followed by Bill six months later, both of natural causes. Their daughter, Nancy, had attended Creighton University, earning a bachelor's degree in 1951 and an M.D. in 1955.

After several years as a patrolman with the Omaha Police Department, Bill Kunz was assigned in July of 1935 to the Robbery-Homicide Division, where he was paired with Detective-Lieutenant Patrick Clebourne.

In combing through the Turlough murder file and the personnel records of both Clebourne and Kunz, Riley could find little to suggest that Kunz had been anything but a quiet understudy to his partner. His signature appeared routinely on reports complied by the investigative team, but Clebourne had clearly taken the lead in all matters associated with the Turlough file.

After the close of the Turlough murder investigation, what had once been Bill Kunz's fast-track climb to promotion within the department seemed to have come to an abrupt halt. He remained on the force through November of 1939, the month in which Pat Clebourne was killed by unknown persons while on a stakeout in which Kunz was covering the back of an apartment building thought to be the headquarters of a local burglary ring. Kunz stayed on the force only long enough to participate in the unsuccessful follow-up investigation of Clebourne's murder and to be the chief witness at the coroner's inquest. He then resigned from the department, entered a Lutheran seminary, and ultimately became the pastor of a small congregation just west of Omaha.

In a gesture that must have been mildly shocking for its time, the file indicated that his daughter, Dr. Nancy Kunz, had taken a hyphenated name after her marriage to a medical school classmate, thereby making it an easy matter for Riley to go to the local phone directory and find a listing for "N. Kunz-Smithson." Having no leads of greater promise, he went to the pay phone in the hall and dialed up Bill Kunz's daughter. When she agreed to see him, he packed up his briefcase, hailed a taxi, and set out on the twenty-minute drive to her West Omaha home.

During the short cab ride he again saw the black car following at a distance of one or two blocks, at all times keeping at least one car between itself and the taxi. Riley had learned surveillance techniques when with the detective agency, and he could see that the black car was observing those same time-honored procedures. In addition to keeping a discrete distance, at no time did the car draw close enough for him to make out the license plates, though from the plate's color and design he could tell that the vehicle was not registered in Nebraska.

By the time he arrived at Dr. Kunz-Smithson's home, there was no sign of the car.


NOW A WIDOW herself and recently retired from a forty-year career as a family practitioner, Nancy Kunz greeted Riley at the door of her modest suburban home. She was plainly curious about who he was and why he had requested a meeting with her.

While she was in the kitchen getting refreshments, Riley scanned the walls of the small but nicely decorated living room, adorned with pictures of Nancy Kunz's three children at various ages, along with several of her late husband, Dr. Rupert Smithson.

Riley periodically glanced out a front window to see if the black car was anywhere to be seen. It was not.

Though sixteen years older than Riley, Nancy Kunz was youthful in appearance and manner. Her hair was light in color, having gone largely gray, but in a way that is less noticeable in natural blondes. The pictures of her on the living room wall confirmed this impression; she looked much as she had when younger. As he stood scanning the picture ensemble, he paused at a photo of Nancy standing next to her father at her medical school graduation in 1955. Bill Kunz

had aged dramatically between the time of his last department photo in 1939 and the 1955 picture Riley was now viewing. The idealistic visage and jaunty smile of a former time
had been replaced by the grim and wounded look of a man
who seemed to be bearing a great burden. His hair had gone
completely gray, almost white, and deep furrows creased his
ruddy face.

Nancy served Riley a Pepsi and seated him comfortably in
a chair next to a window air conditioner. She then leaned forward and squinted in the style of the trained physician.
"Now, then, Mr. McReynolds, what in the world do you want
with me?"

Riley appreciated the directness. He put on his business
face. "Thanks for agreeing to see me, Dr. Kunz. I promise not
to take up much of your time." A small stream of perspiration
that had formed in his right armpit began dripping down his
ribcage. He was not sure if the nervousness was owing to the
embarrassment he felt at the strange mission he was about
to reveal or from excitement at having found a real live
human being who might have information about Bridey
Reaves.

He cleared his throat. "I'm on what some people would consider a fool's errand, I guess. Or at the least a little fanciful."

Nancy Kunz, her gray hair pulled severely back off her
forehead, fastened her eyes on him, the smallest hint of a
smile trying to break through. It was easy to tell that after
forty years of general practice, this woman, who still exuded
uncommonly high levels of self-confidence, was not likely to
be surprised by much. Nor did she seem in the least bit put
off by the man sitting across from her nervously palming a
can of Pepsi.

Nancy stood about five-foot-six and peered at him through
a set of bright green eyes as though he were the only person
in the world. She had fine features, which seemed to have
been spared the normal thickening of advancing age. Her lips
were full and well defined, and when she smiled he could see

rows of small, straight teeth. Only her hair marked her as a woman over sixty. Everything about Nancy Kunz was reassuring, even cozy. Riley could feel his discomfort melting away under the sway of her presence. But then he had always preferred the company of women. They were so much nicer than men.

The fatigue of five hours of pouring over old files in a musty basement, combined with the strain of the worrisome black car and the guilt he felt at being away from home, made him so grateful for Nancy Kunz's warmth that he had all he could do not to go over and sit on her lap, or invite her to the senior prom, or confide in her about how no one understood why he was doing all this—including himself. He felt like Richard Dreyfuss in *Close Encounters of the Third Kind*. He knew he had to do something but didn't know exactly what it was or why he had to do it. And telling a stranger might be just what he needed.

As Nancy smiled at him across the table, his body let go of the tension and unhappiness of recent weeks. Here was a woman just enough his senior to engage his sense of dependence and need for reassurance but not old enough to be his mother. Though he knew it was an exaggerated reaction, she seemed a living validation of the process in which he was immersed, a process in which he had felt all alone until now. And the only thing Nancy Kunz had done, for God's sake, was to smile and give him a Pepsi.

So he started talking. It all came tumbling out, beginning with the Tanzdahl divorce case and the emotional toll it was taking, and then moving into the TV documentary, at which even the seasoned physician looked a little puzzled. He resisted mentioning the black car for fear she would think him an outright mental case.

For twenty minutes information poured forth in no particular order. Several times during the data-dump he feared that he might have lost her, that she might have joined the ranks of his mother and Betsy in their belief that he should see a counselor and maybe get on some psycho-active medication. But Nancy Kunz's bedside manner never faltered. It was only when he spoke the name Clare Turlough that her controlled exterior seemed to crack slightly, her expression turning from one of serene professionalism to personal engagement, as though a long-buried memory had been tapped.

An emotional charge had passed between them. He could feel it. His pulse started to race. The fatigue and pessimism of earlier in the day, the embarrassment of a moment ago, seemed to vanish.

Encouraged, his tone now changed to one used by equals. "Clare Turlough was a woman who was murdered in 1937 in a flop house near downtown," he said, scanning her face for signs of recognition. "Your father was one of the investigating officers, and I was hoping that you might be able to tell me something about the case."

Though her poise did not falter, the tiny lines in the facial terrain, so easily recognized by trial lawyers accustomed to cross-examining witnesses, were now plainly in evidence. And while the memory, whatever it might prove to be, did not appear to be pleasant, he knew in his gut that it was important to this intense and intelligent woman with whom he had so quickly bonded. It also signaled the end of the one-sided nature of their relationship; transference had abruptly turned into counter-transference.

Riley allowed a brief silence to pass. Nancy Kunz broke eye contact for the first time, gazing wistfully out the window, shaking her head in a barely detectable motion. An aged golden retriever with a gray face and cloudy eyes lumbered into the room and leaned heavily against her, barely looking over at Riley. Nancy reached down and began stroking the dog's ears. She then looked back at Riley, who was now as much her counselor as she had been his moments before. The interpersonal transaction between the seasoned professional and the fatigued, disorganized seeker had passed into history.

She looked him hard in the eyes. "I don't know who you are. But you have a nice face, and"—she hesitated and let out a small sigh—"I feel a little bit like I've been waiting for you to show up for a long time."

She pushed aside her glass of iced tea and placed her hands, palms down, on the table, almost prayerfully. "First, I need something from you," she said, narrowing her eyes in an intense but trusting expression. "I need more of a description of what you're up to and a promise that whatever comes of what you're doing, you won't do anything to harm my father's reputation."

Riley quickly nodded. "I agree." He cleared his throat and took a sip of Pepsi. "I'm searching for a woman who disappeared in 1925 because of a dispute between two Chicago crime bosses, Al Capone and Dion O'Banion. That search has led me to Omaha and the Clare Turlough case. I didn't know anything about your father before this afternoon, and I still don't have any interest in him except to the extent he may have said or written something about that case. There appears to be a substantial possibility that the woman who fled Chicago in 1925 took the name Clare Turlough but then transferred it in 1937 to a dead prostitute buried over at Holy Cross Cemetery—the woman whose case your father helped investigate. Everything I've been able to piece together, including the dead woman's lack of a past, suggests that she was used—or rather her death was used—to divert the Capone Mob from its pursuit of the real Clare Turlough, who I think was actually Bridey Reaves, the girl I first saw in a documentary about Chicago crime."

Nancy Kunz nodded politely, but only half-knowingly. She switched her weight in the chair, and the wrinkles around her eyes deepened as she scanned the ceiling. It was as though she was tapping into a deep reservoir of memory.

The window air conditioner purred contentedly in the background, insulating their small space from the blistering July afternoon and filling the room with a cool, gentle breeze.

To Riley, it was stunningly reminiscent of the cozy feel of his grandmother's small apartment just blocks from his boyhood home. That dear old woman, her young grandson's biggest fan, would sit before her air conditioner on hot days, fanning the cool air into her face and down the neck of her print dress. Nancy Kunz wasn't a grandmotherly figure, and he was no longer a boy, but her house felt just about as cozy.

Nancy's gaze finally left the ceiling and returned to Riley as the gates of the past opened wide. She started in: "My father was the finest man who ever lived. He went into police work the way most people today would go into the Peace Corps or a religious vocation. And it isn't just his adoring daughter saying this; I've talked to scores of people, before and after Dad's death—people of all types who knew him in different settings—who said the same thing. That he was kind and honest and brave and the best friend they ever had."

Her lower lip began to quiver. The controlled visage of the veteran physician slowly gave way to a sixty-five-year old woman who missed her father. She shook her head and wiped moisture from her eyes.

Riley let a moment pass and then said, "That sounds like the man whose personnel file I just read. It was filled with testimonials from people he had helped."

She was grateful for that. Arching her back and sitting up straight, she inhaled deeply. "Well, now that we have that out of the way, we can get on to the Turlough case, the reason you're here." She leaned forward, her face resting in her open palms. "I certainly don't know all there is to know about that case, but from what I overheard as a youngster, I know that something dishonest happened and that Dad blamed himself for breaching his duty as a policeman out of friendship for Pat Clebourne. He kept saying to my mother that it was a harmless betrayal, but I know it ate away at him. And when he was much older, and passing into mild senility, Dad said things that made me believe that the woman whose body was identified as Clare Turlough was in fact someone else, a prostitute who had been killed by an angry customer. The reason I know that is because Pat Clebourne—who was 'Uncle Pat' to me when I was a girl—was often at our house with a beautiful woman named Clare Turlough. I was only seven or eight at the time, but I adored her. And it was obvious to me that she and Uncle Pat were in love."

These words fell on Riley's ears in a way that caused all sensory data—the hum of the air conditioner, the sight of the beverages on the table and the pictures on the wall, even the throbbing ache that had been building in his head when he first arrived—to pass out of existence. He heard only Nancy's voice.

She paused momentarily, but Riley remained still. He didn't want to break her train of thought. She started back in. "I saw the picture of the dead woman in the newspaper, the woman who was identified as Clare Turlough. Mind you, I was only about seven at the time. But I knew she was not the pretty lady who came to our house with Uncle Pat. She looked like her—I remember that—but she was not as pretty. I can't give you a very good description of either of them now, but I knew at the time that the woman in the newspaper was not the sweet lady Uncle Pat told me to call 'Aunt Clare.'"

Riley now felt at liberty to probe gently. "Did you say anything to your father about that? And did you ever see her after the time of the murder?" His heart was slamming against his chest. He prayed that the phone wouldn't ring, that the dog wouldn't bark, that nothing would interrupt her reminiscence.

"I never saw her after that time, and I rarely saw Uncle Pat either. That hurt my feelings because I knew he was still my dad's partner, even though I knew there was trouble between them." She squinted and nodded in his direction. "And, yes, I did say something to my Mom and Dad about the picture in the paper. My dad said I was mistaken, and that I should not think about it or mention it to anyone ever again. It may sound funny to you, but I adored my father so much that when he gave me those instructions, I actually did put it out of my mind until many years later. You probably know that Pat Clebourne was killed during a stake-out that he and my dad were handling a few years later."

Riley nodded.

She put her hand up to her chest and again seemed on the verge of tears. "My father was so shattered by Pat's death that he left the police department forever. He felt he should have done something to protect Pat, because he had been receiving threats from people who were trying to get information from him. At the time of the shooting, Dad was still mad at Pat about dragging him into falsifying reports on the Turlough murder, and he feared that that had made him less vigilant about Pat's safety. "

She leaned back in her chair and ran the fingers of both hands through her hair. She reached for another memory. "I know there was more to it. And even though it's hard sometimes to separate childhood memories from imaginings, I know it involved that Turlough business. I sensed it at the time, and I came to know it beyond any doubt when Dad got older and started to slip. He'd stroke his head while sitting in a wheel chair at the nursing home, repeating the name Turlough over and over again in a voice filled with regret. I know in my heart that it was that case that caused Dad to betray his duty. And right or wrong, he thought it was that case that got his partner killed."

Her expression was a blend of nostalgia and sorrow. The carefully constructed borders of her persona seemed, like his, to have collapsed. They no longer looked or sounded like two professionals exchanging information. It was more like they had grown up together and provided mutual support during an uneven childhood. Nancy Kunz was his new best friend, ranking only slightly below Betsy, Lizzie, Teddy, and Skeeter. And he thought they would always be friends. They were kindred souls wandering in a common wilderness, joined at an unforeseen intersection.

He didn't want to let her go, this decent woman with the bewildered girl buried deep at her center. He sensed he might have set free a long imprisoned memory for this good woman. Perhaps that was why this was all happening.

Nancy tapped her fingers on the table. "Through what I picked up on over the years and a strong intuition, I came to believe that the Turlough matter was the source of all Dad's grief. After he died, before putting the house up for sale, I went up to the attic and found among the boxes containing his papers an old suitcase filled with files and notebooks kept by Pat Clebourne. Pat had no relatives, so his few personal effects were turned over to Dad—a scrapbook he had kept and several files filled with notes that didn't mean anything to me."

Riley sat transfixed, his nerves tingling. "Do you still have the suitcase?" he asked, bracing for a turndown.

Nancy smiled. "I do. Sit still and I'll go get it."

He could hear her rumbling about in the attic. He sat still, not daring to move a muscle. The noise finally stopped and footfalls were heard coming back down the stairs. She rounded the corner to the living room with a wide grin and made her way to the seat next to him. She placed the old suitcase filled with dusty files between them on the table.

"Here goes," she said, lifting out a scrapbook and opening its cover. Photos of Pat Clebourne in the early stages of his military service and others from his days as a patrolman with the Omaha Police Department, were mounted on heavy brown paper in the first section. Next were pages filled with snapshots, some of which fell off the page when exposed to the air. Many pictures were of Pat Clebourne and Bill Kunz during the years they were partners. Near the end of the scrapbook was a series of black-and-white snapshots of Nancy's parents, Bill and Louise, standing at an amusement park next to Clebourne and a woman who seemed to have been caught unawares by the photographer. She was a young woman with dark hair and pale blue eyes.

A huge smile danced across Riley's face as his eyes feasted on the image, the unmistakable image of Bridey Reaves.

Nancy, too, smiled as she pointed to the figure in the picture, "Aunt Clare."

# 11

——————

I T WAS AFTER FIVE when Riley arrived back in Minneapolis. To add to the frustration of a two-hour delay in the Omaha airport, there followed a thirty-minute walking tour of the airport parking ramp. Having failed to note the level or section where he parked, he was forced to search four different floors.

As he exited the ramp, a pickup truck next to him exhaled a cloud of dense, noxious smoke into the closed space. Driven by a man who appeared to be in his early thirties with long greasy hair, the pickup sported a bumper sticker reading: "How's My Driving? Call 1-800-EAT SHIT."

Sensing a disapproving stare, the driver looked over at Riley with a menacing sneer. For the first time since high school, Riley was tempted to flip the guy the bird. He knew that fatigue and impatience spawned confrontations of the kind that he was now getting dangerously close to.

Only the prospect of the next day's headline: "Former Prosecutor Held In Ramp-Rage Incident," settled him down. That and the fact that the guy looked like he might be carrying a gun.

It was not a good reentry. He hadn't wanted to leave Omaha, and he didn't like being back in Minneapolis. He wanted to go back and sit by Nancy Kunz's air conditioner.

At home, Betsy had had their contractor knock out another closet to give the downstairs a more open feel. Riley liked lots of separate rooms; she liked open spaces. With the closet gone, he looked around for a place to hang his coat, finally tossing it over the railing leading to the upstairs.

He wanted to get mad about this latest desecration of the building's original design, not to mention the expense, but he couldn't. Betsy was too pleased and excited. And the sight of her immediately lifted his mood. As he watched her move about the space where the closet had been just that morning, he thought of how a quarter-century of marriage had done nothing to dull the sensation of her love. Marrying a girl he had known since infancy seemed a little strange, sort of uncosmopolitan, but there it was. And what a blessing it had been: She brought cheer to his melancholy, courage to his anxieties, health to his hypochondria.

Betsy sat down beside him on the couch and planted a big kiss on his cheek. "Thanks for not throwing a tantrum over the missing closet. I promise it will be the last one."

"It will have to be. The only ones left are supporting walls. If you take one of them down, the house will collapse."

She smiled mischievously. "That's what the contractor said."

Her expression then turned serious. "I'm sorry to lay this on you right away, but Sara Hall called and said that she needed to talk to you about something important that came up when she was reviewing documents for the Tanzdahl subpoena, but that you should first check your e-mail for copies of the child custody documents that were served on Friday. And she said she wanted you to call her tonight, no matter what time it was."

She tilted her head sympathetically, acknowledging the pain of his reentry into the real world and the loathsome case in which he was enmeshed.

With the mention of child custody, his headache returned and his spirits plummeted. The reentry process was awful. He lifted himself off the couch and went downstairs. There he booted up the computer and dialed into his office e-mail account. After scrolling through several administrative memos, he came to copies of documents that Sara Hall, without his authorization, had served on Ellen Tanzdahl's attorney shortly after he had left for Omaha. Interestingly, none of the documents had been filed with the court, which meant that Sara was giving Ellen Tanzdahl a taste of the humiliation she would be in for publicly if she didn't accede to Gus's demands. The papers had been served on Ellen's lawyer, but they would almost certainly have been faxed to her by Clint Tarrymore.

What Sara had done here was not a tactic Riley favored in most cases—and certainly not in this one. But she was just the kind of hardball player to make use of it. Being the family law expert, she knew how to get people's attention, and he couldn't second-guess her strategy so long as she was being faithful to the facts as they knew them.

He scrolled down the language of the change-of-custody petition. The early paragraphs were drawn as he expected, with a bare assertion of Gus's belief that he was the more suitable parent to hold primary custody of the child and requesting an evaluation by the department of court services. But when he reached the second page of Gus's supporting affidavit, to his horror, he found a list of factual assertions based upon information "recently discovered by Mr. Tanzdahl," including "a documented history of drug abuse, prostitution, and lewd conduct in the presence of children."

Riley let out a gasp that could be heard all the way upstairs. Mick Goerdan's report had obviously been used to throw this specious slime into the petition. He was sure he had left instructions to hold off on any allegations of this type until he had considered which, if any, of them could appropriately be used. This was just plain cruel and irresponsible—and a gross and unfair exaggeration of Ellen Tanzdahl's mildly wicked past.

He was sickened to see his name appear as lead counsel on a document with such a foul stench to it. Sara was tough, but she wouldn't have done this on her own, he felt sure of it. Or, at the very least, she would have used her name on the petition, not his. This had Ladge Wilkaster's fingerprints all over it.

Closing the file, he reached for the phone and dialed Sara's number. When he got her voice machine, he left a message for her to call him immediately.

He then trudged upstairs to dress for a dinner engagement with Judge Henry Peters and his family. His mood having plunged another two levels, he looked over at Betsy with a face filled with anger and defeat. His soul-sickness over the Tanzdahl case had just doubled as a result of this attack made in his name.

As he selected a necktie from the closet, he tried to transport his mind back to Omaha, and away from the document he just read. Without thinking, he said, "I have a new best friend, a sixty-five-year-old retired doctor in Omaha. She's the daughter of one of the police officers who investigated the Clare Turlough case back in 1937."

Wrong comment. Wrong subject. He knew it instantly. The small fibers around Betsy's eyes and mouth tightened at the mention of Clare Turlough. She threw him a blistering look.

They had made a deal that, when home, he would focus entirely on the affairs of the family, and that as hard as it might be, he would not bring his obsessions into the family space. It was plain to both of them that he had just violated that deal.

Could this return home be any worse, any more discordant, he wondered. In the early days of the search, he had tried to draw Betsy into his enthusiasm. He sat her down to watch the documentary, and he had shown her the enhanced photographs he obtained from the Chicago newspaper. He hoped that she'd fall under the same spell that had been cast on him. But it hadn't worked. To Betsy, Bridey Reaves was just another face in the crowd—a pretty face, of course, but nothing more. None of it made her heart leap.

Betsy considered this period in their lives to be an especially inappropriate time for him to get wrapped up in something so childish and impractical. Unlike him, she was firmly grounded in the present. For all her finely tuned sensitiv-
ities—to plants and animals and people of all descriptions—
she didn't understand what he was talking about when he
dreamily speculated that time might be an illusion, that
what we call memory might actually be glimpses of a present
reality unfolding elsewhere. To her, life was linear, sequential. The Battle of Britain had been fought and won more
than fifty years before, so she didn't get all misty over Vera
Lynn and the White Cliffs of Dover. In fact, if Riley didn't
stop playing that damn song about the bluebirds and the
shepherds and little Jimmy getting his room back—playing
it in the car, in the house, even on his headset in the middle
of the night—she was going to destroy the CD. And though
she was reluctant to admit it, she didn't care much about the
pretty girl in the front row of Dion O'Banion's funeral, the
girl who seemed even less interesting than Anastasia or
Amelia Earhart. At least they had been famous.

This was one of the few times that Betsy and her mother-
in-law were of one mind on a matter affecting the family.
Normally they were players in a subterranean, barely conscious competition for Riley's affection. But this time, Betsy
thought Maureen McReynolds was right: he was too old for
this kind of nonsense.

Oddly enough, it was Skeeter, normally a hard-edged skep-
tic, who seemed to be on his side. But then what did she have
to lose; it wasn't her family that was being neglected. For
whatever this search might symbolize, to Skeeter it was a
welcome relief from the tedium of typing briefs, interrogatories and endless correspondence. So even though she had lots
of fun at Riley's expense over his strange preoccupations, she
was enjoying the chase, wasn't much worried about his mental health, and actually shared some of his wacky optimism
that in the end it would all have some meaning.

When Riley noticed Betsy set her jaw at the mention of Clare Turlough, he took a seat on the bed and went to work tying his tie.

"Did I have any calls when I was gone?" he asked without looking up from the half-Windsor he was nervously trying to execute.

Betsy cleared her throat loudly. "Yes, when Teddy and I were leaving for his soccer game, alone . . . you know, the game where I was there with twelve dads—"

"I know, I know. I'm sorry I missed his game," said Riley contritely. "I promise I'll make every game from now on."

She looked like she'd believe it when she saw it. But she did understand what he was going through in the Tanzdahl case. Not the confidential parts, of course; she knew nothing beyond what appeared in the newspapers. But that was enough to know that it was exactly the type of case for which he was spectacularly unsuited. The solution, though, was not to revert to childhood fixations on missing women. It unnerved her that the man who functioned with such a principled maturity day in and day out, a man who hadn't missed more than two of his kids' events in sixteen years, seemed to be on the verge of losing his soul over this thing.

She sat down next to him with a look of impatience. "Nobody's been more tolerant than I have about these things. When we were kids, I was the one who defended you when your brothers teased and your mother scolded, just as she's doing now. And I'm not saying, like your brother is, that you're into some kind of sick 'Harold and Maude' thing. I don't have it in me to be mean about it, but"—her voice cracked slightly—"this one kind of hurts."

The thought of wounding the person who had loved him unconditionally his whole life was nearly unbearable. The full force of his selfishness washed over him. He took his eyes from her and looked down at his knee, now bouncing rapidly.

Betsy reached over and grabbed his face, forcibly turning it back toward her. "I can understand a dreamy temperament. Dreamers make life interesting, and they sometimes even accomplish things for the world. But this is something more, something different. You're somehow in love with a girl from another time, someone who if she were alive at all would be a withered old woman." She shook her head in exhaustion. She was so close he could feel her breath on his face. "I can't do time travel, Riley. I've got both feet on the ground, and thank God I do. In some strange way you feel responsible for this woman, and you're chasing after her as if she were one of our family. But she's not! She's a dream or a symbol that somehow takes you away from the stress of living in a grown-up world. It's a mental trick, that's all it is."

She still had a vise-like grip on his face, so when he finally spoke it was through puckered lips. "I understand, darling, I really do," he squeezed out.

She paused briefly, trying to maintain the serious mood, but then started giggling involuntarily. Finally she released his face and stood up, staring at the ground between them.

Riley stretched his cheeks to restore circulation and, knowing he was far from off the hook, started back in. "But you know the good part is I haven't fallen in love with some chorus girl or one of your bridge partners or a student at the law school, or anything like that. Maybe Bridey qualifies as some version of love, but she's hardly anything that's a threat to you and me. And it'll all be over soon, I promise. These things always die down eventually."

He lowered his head to peek under her downcast eyes. "You know it'll work out. I feel like I'm already alienated from my mother over this, and I can handle that. But if you were to pull away from me, I think I would lose my mind—at least the part of it I still have."

She smiled weakly and gave a nod of assent. "I wish my competition were a chorus girl. I'd know how to handle that. Instead I get some wrinkled up old woman who's probably deader than a doornail."

"Hmm . . . a chorus girl," said Riley, wiggling his eyebrows lustily.

"Yeah, just try it, you dried-up old fart."

While Betsy finished getting dressed, Riley ducked downstairs and went on-line to see if anyone had posted a reply to his most recent query about a pretty woman with dark hair, pale-blue eyes and a soft Irish accent, last seen in Omaha, Nebraska, in 1937.

A MOMENT OF EMBARRASSED silence passed as the elegantly attired steward stood waiting for Riley to approve the small splash of wine poured into a tasting glass. Betsy jabbed an elbow into his ribs and cleared her throat audibly. He looked down dumbly at the solitary mouthful of clear, white wine, a particular favorite of Judge Peters' wife, Margaret. Henry Peters was one of the senior judges in the county and, like Riley, he knew nothing about fine wines and their associated rituals. Also like Riley, he had ordered a Pepsi.

With Betsy's prompting Riley reached for the proffered glass, pretended to sniff its aroma through nostrils inflamed by summer hay fever and took a small sip. He looked up at the steward and pronounced the wine—which he thought tasted like battery acid—just perfect. In addition to Judge and Mrs. Peters, their son Billy, who had a ferocious crush on Lizzie, had come along. Lizzie sat between Billy Peters and Teddy.

Riley and Henry Peters had been friends as far back as law school, and it was that long friendship that had occasioned tonight's dinner, not professional brown-nosing. More fanatical than Riley on matters of propriety, Henry Peters used any social occasion with a practicing lawyer to pull out a pocket calculator and segregate the evening's charges—including tax and gratuity—into two distinct columns. He once famously turned down a twenty-five cent loan from a junior prosecutor to use a pay telephone, fearing that it would be perceived as a bribe.

The waiter served the wine to the adults around the table, ignoring Teddy's extended glass. Riley casually scanned the long, dimly lit restaurant, checking out the other diners. He didn't see anyone he knew, which was unusual given the small town nature of the Twin Cities. As his glance passed over a corner table near the entrance to the kitchen, a faint sensation of recognition caused him to look back. The people at the table included a woman of late middle age, a young woman with thick brown hair facing away from him, and a boy in a sailor suit seated between the two women. The boy was busily coloring cartoon figures on a children's menu.

Though visible only in profile, when Riley looked closer he thought he recognized the younger woman as Ellen Tanzdahl. He correctly pegged the older woman as Ellen's mother and the boy's grandmother. A chance encounter with an opposing party in a public place was not new to him, though since his departure from the prosecutor's office such encounters were less frequent. And in the typical case, it rarely mattered. But this was different. In light of the change-of-custody petition having been served by Sara Hall—replete with the poisonous and unfair allegations concerning Ellen's past—the sight of her made him very uncomfortable. He rearranged his chair on the pretext of getting closer to Margaret Peters. His face and profile were now out of Ellen's line of sight.

The dinner passed in friendly conversation and good food. Margaret Peters was recounting her afternoon round of golf as they awaited the arrival of dessert, when mid-sentence she went mute, staring over Riley's shoulder with a puzzled look.

The rest of the table also fell silent. With a look of uneasy curiosity, Lizzie's eyes were fixed on a spot behind her father.

Riley turned and looked up. Ellen Tanzdahl and her young son stood next to his chair, the small boy's hand gripping his mother's tightly, his large brown eyes gazing at Riley. The boy's grandmother stood several paces behind her daughter, looking as though she wanted to be someplace else. Ellen was flushed and trembling.

This was a nice restaurant, quiet and elegant. A raised voice, such as the one he feared he was about to hear, would be likely to seize the attention of everyone in the room.

Ellen Tanzdahl, a shy and unsure young woman who found herself trapped in a nightmare proceeding in which the only decent thing in her life could be taken away, had marshaled all her anger and courage to confront one of her husband's hired tormentors. It was not lost on her that the gray-haired eminence seated across the table from Riley, whose picture regularly appeared in the local newspaper, was the chief judge of the county specialty courts. He seemed a living symbol of Riley's connections in the halls of justice.

"Hello, Mrs. Tanzdahl," said Riley tentatively, rising from his chair.

Ellen's lips quivered as she stared silently at him, maintaining a firm grasp on her son. She took a deep breath and said in a voice cracking with emotion, "I thought you might like to meet the little boy who has a whore and a drug dealer for a mother. I mean . . . like . . . shouldn't a man who wants to steal a little kid away from his mother, at least have to see the kid somewhere along the way? Or don't you get paid for that kind of time?"

The boy looked up at his mother—adoringly, Riley thought—and then back to him. Mercifully, he didn't know what any of those words meant, but still his expression started to turn from curiosity to confusion.

There was no point in Riley trying to explain the mix-up in the documents served on Friday, which she had obviously received copies of. He shook his head almost imperceptibly and, in hopes of deflating her mounting resolve, nervously started to make introductions around the table. He turned toward the people at his table but, before he could speak, she stepped back into his line of vision as though there was no one else in the room besides the two of them and the small child.

Now in a louder voice, she said, "My lawyer gave me a copy of the papers you sent to him." Color rose in her neck and up into her face. "I didn't know until I read those papers what a horrible person I was—that I was a street prostitute and a drug addict, and dangerous to Joshie." At that, she tightened her grip on her son's shoulders and a small sob choked off her words.

Riley stood motionless, feeling the eyes of everyone in the restaurant upon him. He felt like a boy who had carelessly killed a bird with a new slingshot and had been found out.

Partially regaining her composure, Ellen continued: "I've never been any of those things you said about me. I was messed up for a few months when I was nineteen . . . but you twisted it all into a bunch of lies. I trusted some dumb people back then, but I've never deliberately hurt another person in my whole life. That's something you can't say, can you Mr. McReynolds?"

The boy had now become frightened. He grabbed at his mother's arm with both hands, trying to pull himself up toward her.

Without taking her eyes from Riley, Ellen leaned down and lifted the boy into her arms, resting his small rear-end on her hip. They both looked small and vulnerable and injured. The boy threw his arms around his mother's neck and pressed his cheek against her face.

In spite of the tears, Ellen's voice was growing stronger. "I don't know how anyone could be so mean. When my lawyer found out that you'd be on the other side of the case, he told me that we should be happy. He said that you were a decent man, and that we wouldn't have to face any of the slimy tricks some lawyers use."

Henry Peters started to rise from his chair to leave the room, but his wife grabbed his arm and slammed him back into his seat. Young Billy Peters looked over at his mother as if awaiting instructions on what to do next. Lizzie sat frozen, her eyes glued to the pretty young woman with tears pouring down her cheeks. Nearly the whole restaurant had gone quiet and was staring at their table.

Ellen Tanzdahl's mother stepped forward and gently tried to pull her daughter toward the doorway. But Ellen stood firm, determined—perhaps for the first time in her life. She pulled away from her mother's grip and began shouting, "I don't know how many people you had to fool to get that reputation, Mr. McReynolds, but no lawyer in the whole world ever pulled a meaner trick."

The child had now planted his lips on his mother's cheek, and was not letting go. He had never seen her this way, and it scared him. When the grandmother tried to lift him from his mother's arms, he only squeezed her neck more tightly.

Ellen would not yield to her mother's urgings. She went right on talking. "My husband hasn't seen Joshie for over a year, and the last two times he was with him he spanked him both times because he made noise when Gus was on a business call. My God, Joshie was three-years old! That's the man you want to have my baby—" Her words were interrupted by a sob. She turned and handed the child, now nearly hysterical with fear and confusion, to his grandmother.

She then turned back to Riley and looked him hard in the eyes. "I don't know why you did this to us, but as far as I'm concerned you're every bit as evil as my husband." She then pointed down at Teddy and Lizzie. "But, you know what? I still hope that you never know what it's like to face the possibility of losing one of these beautiful children of yours. And I hope God will forgive you for what you're doing to me . . . because I never will."

Riley reached for her arm to tell her that he was sorry for the way things had been handled, that it was a mistake that it had happened when he was out of town. But she recoiled at his touch, her hands in the air as though backing away from a snake.

He stared at the ground and shook his head. Betsy tugged on his sleeve to get him to sit down. A waitress holding a dessert tray stood frozen off to the side of the table.

Ellen then turned toward the door and ran from the restaurant.

Riley dropped back into his chair, downcast. When he finally looked up, the others avoided his eyes—except Lizzie, who glared at him from across the table.

As they drove home, Lizzie silently stared out the window of the car. She was a McReynolds, so unlike her mother, her deepest feelings were expressed as anger rather than hurt. At a stop sign Betsy turned to the back seat and tried to explain how lawyers are required to fight for the interests of their clients even when they don't personally like or agree with them.

Lizzie cut her off mid-sentence. "Mom, did you see how scared that little boy was? And how much he loved his mother? My God, that girl didn't look much older than me." She then looked at Riley and screamed, "What kind of a monster are you?"

Riley looked up through the rear-view mirror at his first-born child, his precious daughter. He tried to speak, but the words caught in his throat. He drove into the night, hardly able to make out the lines of the highway.

# 12

---

A FTER A SERIES of delays resulting from Gus Tanzdahl's claims of illness, business emergencies, and scheduling conflicts, Clint Tarrymore had had enough. In late July he served Gus with an order to show cause why he should not be held in contempt of court for failure to appear for a pre-trial deposition.

Having been spectacularly unsuccessful in getting Gus to understand that he had a legal obligation to submit to sworn examination, Riley was secretly pleased that Gus would now have all this explained to him by a family court judge. And not just any family court judge, but Judge Gertrude Hammergren.

Like most bullies, Gus was good at dishing out punishment but not very good at taking it. He knew that his arsenal of obfuscation, misdirection, and intimidation—all of which had served him well during his long career in business—would be of limited usefulness in the formal and controlled surroundings of a sworn deposition. Smoke screens of the type Gus was famous for laying down would do nothing but arouse Clint Tarrymore's competitive instincts and lawyerly curiosity. A perfect gentleman under most circumstances, Tarrymore could turn nasty when provoked. Though Clint had initially believed that there would be at least partial cooperation, Gus's behavior had now convinced him otherwise.

So it was a new man they were up against in Clint Tarrymore. And in some perverse way Riley felt relieved to be free of the delusion that he could bend this client's will to his own standards, especially when one considered that Ladge Wilkaster, filled with fear that Gus would transfer the Tanzdahl Industries account to another firm, was enabling his mischief all along the way.

The case had been newly assigned to Judge Hammergren, a recent appointee to the family court and a sixteen-year veteran of the county attorney's office, where she had specialized in domestic abuse and sexual assault cases. Whatever could be said about Gertrude Hammergren's devotion to due process and the rule of law, there was nothing in this judicial pick from which Gus Tanzdahl could take any comfort. During her early years as a prosecutor, Gert had found herself under Riley's tutelage as she rotated through the major crimes unit, but that old friendship paled before her deeply held conviction that wealthy and powerful men often take advantage of their less sophisticated wives when it comes to the ownership and management of family assets. She had a nose for such strategies and, when the scent was picked up, she was like a heat-seeking missile. In the lottery of judicial assignments, Gus could scarcely have done worse.

In spite of having all that explained to him, Gus could not be persuaded to play by the rules, to surrender to the radical egalitarianism of the modern court process. So it was a real eye-opener for him when Gertrude Hammergren signed an order commanding his appearance before her on the 26th day of July 1996, to then and there show cause why he should not be held in contempt of court and transported to the adult detention facility until such time as the scales of ignorance dropped from his eyes. Not even Ladge Wilkaster had trouble understanding the judge's directive and its broader meaning for Cosgrove & Levi, whose attorneys had a good many other cases pending before Gertrude Hammergren. Thus Ladge belatedly joined Riley in demanding Gus's cooperation.

Stripped of Ladge's contrivance and with a jail sentence looking him in the eye, Gus appeared in Judge Hammergren's courtroom on the appointed date. Dressed in a yellow sport shirt and blue polyester golfing slacks, the expandable waist of which hugged his protruding belly, Gus reclined backward in his chair at the counsel table. An impatient smirk creased his face. Harvey Aingren, fat, oily and sycophantic, sat behind him in the gallery.

Ellen Tanzdahl and her mother sat off in a back corner of the courtroom, well removed from the counsel table, Ellen looking young enough for a guest spot on American Bandstand. Riley nodded politely in her direction, but she looked away.

At the appointed hour, the bailiff gaveled in Judge Hammergren, who made her way from the door of her chambers to the bench with the stride of an NFL nose-tackle. Stout in build, with a strong face and wiry dark hair shot through with gray, Gertrude was the walking embodiment of judicial authority. Above her left eye she carried a scar earned during her early days with the county attorney's office. When serving a rotation on the felony arraignment calendar, an obstreperous and slightly unhinged defendant had been routinely asked by her in open court if he was represented by counsel. He replied, "Yes, I am represented by God." Gert rolled her eyes and asked if he had "local counsel." The guy caught her with a right cross, knocking her half-way across the courtroom. It took four deputy sheriffs to restrain him and eight stitches to close the gash. Though the county's insurance policy would have paid for cosmetic surgery to repair the resulting damage, Gert refused it, wearing the wound like a German dueling scar.

From the bench Judge Hammergren surveyed the assembled parties without expression. She then opened the court file and nodded to the counsel table. As counsel for the moving party, Clint Tarrymore rose from his seat, buttoned his jacket and reached for the legal pad on which he had sketched out an outline of his remarks. But before he could open his mouth, Gert Hammergren turned to Riley and said in a tone that was at once sarcastic and threatening—and very unlike the one she had used three days before when they exchanged war stories over beers at a bar association meeting—"Mr. McReynolds, we don't see much of you in family court, so perhaps you need a little instruction on the importance we place upon cooperation between the parties to the cases that come before us."

Riley knew that the opening act of this judicial performance was not in reality directed at him personally, but was rather a bit of guerilla theater for which Gertrude was famous. Like the assassin who disables the bodyguard before taking out the intended target, she made it a studied practice to let recalcitrant clients know at the outset that the lawyers they viewed as the protectors of their dignity would in fact be quite helpless before the power of the court.

Riley rose from his seat and in his most humble voice said, "Good morning, your Honor. I appreciate the court's concern along those lines. I can only say that Mr. Tanzdahl"—he looked down at Gus, sitting uncomfortably in the adjoining chair—"is the chief executive officer of one of the state's largest companies, with many demands upon his time." This short recitation was the one Ladge Wilkaster had urged Riley to put forward with Judge Hammergren. What Ladge didn't know, and what Riley did not tell him, was that it would be hard to imagine an explanation more likely to inflame the passions of this particular judge—a prospect that Riley privately relished.

Gus nodded agreement, as if to say that these petty proceedings were a hindrance to industrial progress and a waste of his valuable time. "I've got more important things to do," he mumbled under his breath to Sara Hall, sitting to his left.

Judge Hammergren turned in her seat and glared down at Gus. "Get on your feet when you speak in this courtroom, Mr. Tanzdahl," she said.

When a stunned Gus failed to instantly comply, she shouted, "I said remove yourself from that seat, Mr. Tanzdahl, or I will have the deputy sheriff assist you."

All eyes turned to the entrance to the jury room, before which stood a beefy, six-foot-six, overfed deputy sheriff who was having a pretty slow day and would love nothing more than to manhandle an arrogant business tycoon who made more money in one day than he did in an entire year. This overgrown crime-fighter, well known to Riley from his days with the prosecutor's office, stood bouncing on his toes, staring hungrily at Gus, rotating a large deaths-head ring on his finger.

Gus looked up at Riley pleadingly as if he expected him to explain to this deranged civil servant what an important man he was and why people just didn't talk to him that way.

Riley gave a helpless shrug. Gus was on his own, facing a judge unequaled in her ability to administer a painful asswhupping without leaving any marks or contusions on the court record. Her contempt was conveyed entirely by tone of voice, facial expression, and shortened time intervals. Any appeals court that might have occasion to review the fairness of these proceedings would be hard pressed to find any abusive or improper behavior in the stenographic record. Riley had witnessed mortifications of this kind rain down upon a deserving litigant during any number of trials and hearings over the years. He had felt the bitter taste of judicial disapproval himself on occasion. But in this case, despite the wounded look, he was feeling an inward jubilation. And it was positively therapeutic that Ladge Wilkaster, whose last trip to a courtroom was when he was sworn into the bar thirty-five years earlier, got to see life in the real world.

Deep reserves of gall and arrogance seemed to drain from Gus's face as he stood at the counsel table, his head bowed like a whipped puppy.

Sitting quietly in a modest tan outfit, Ellen Tanzdahl perked up and watched in wonder as the all-powerful husband who was trying to steal the thing in life that she most valued, was reduced to a whimpering supplicant by this symbol of American justice. Riley watched as a healthy color seemed to return to Ellen's cheeks. The muscles surrounding her eyes and mouth gradually transformed her face from one of timidity into one of resolve. Despite all Clint Tarrymore's pep talks, it was only now that Ellen's belief in herself and her chances for a fair shake started to take shape.

Riley had witnessed many such epiphanies in his years as a prosecutor—witnesses who summoned the courage to do the right thing, children who reported their abusers, rape victims who, in a defining moment, found the strength to turn the tables. Such was the look now taking shape on Ellen Tanzdahl's face. And if Gus had missed it, he was the only one in the room who did.

Gertrude Hammergren leaned forward in her seat, and as she brushed a strand of unruly hair from her eyes, she stared acidly at Gus. "Mr. Tanzdahl, consider yourself fortunate that I do not make a finding here and now that you have deliberately evaded and obstructed the discovery process in this case, for if I were to do that you would find yourself across the street in the company of the kind of people you don't run into very often in your paneled boardrooms and executive jets."

She then leaned back in her high-backed leather chair and crossed her arms over her ample breasts. A smile tugged at the corners of her mouth as she moved from the role of bad cop to that of benevolent and impartial fact finder. "What I'm going to do is send you back out into the world with a charge to leave no stone unturned in your search for assets germane to this action, followed by full and truthful testimony in a sworn deposition." She now pointed a short, beefy finger directly at him. "Should you disappoint me in this regard, I will expect a renewed motion by Mr. Tarrymore, one seeking the most punitive sanctions available to this court, including an all-expense-paid trip to the adult detention facility. I think it goes without saying that I would be kindly disposed toward any such motion."

Riley tapped Gus on the shoulder to signify that he should acknowledge the court's instructions. Gus's golf shirt was warm and moist to the touch; he had sweated right through it. Riley could feel Gus's body trembling as he leaned down to his ear and said, "Say 'Yes, your Honor.'"

Gus looked up at him with a mixture of confusion and gratitude. He then turned back to the bench. "Yes, your Honor."

"Good!" said the judge in the sunny inflections of a morning talk show host. She then looked alternately at Riley and Clint Tarrymore. "Do counsel have anything else for the record?"

"No, your Honor," they replied in unison.


AND SO IT WAS a seemingly compliant Gus Tanzdahl who sat in the conference room of Tarrymore & Gleason on the day and hour specified in the order issued by Judge Hammergren three days earlier. Of all the roles played by Gus over the years, that of contrite and cooperative witness was the one for which he was most obviously miscast. A Nixon operative from the Watergate era was said to have had a large sign above his desk that read: "If you have them by the balls, their hearts and minds will follow." That bit of practical wisdom was doubtless true in most cases, but not so with present company. Clint Tarrymore had Gus by the balls, surely, but his heart was elsewhere and his mind was busy cooking up dodges and evasions, not dissimilar to the ones he brought to the many business transactions to which he had been a party over the years. He was constitutionally incapable of playing it straight.

Sitting to Gus's right at the large circular conference table was Sara Hall, dressed in a dark pantsuit. Riley sat on Gus's left, though at this stage of the proceedings he was merely playing a supporting role, the lead having been passed to Sara as the family law expert. Riley brought little to the table, and inasmuch as physical proximity to Gus made him feel as though he had been dunked in an oil slick, he had tried unsuccessfully to absent himself from what promised to be a long and tedious day of financial testimony. He and Sara had spent most of the previous day at Gus's office going over the questions he was likely to be asked and coaching him on the proper way for a witness to handle himself when testifying.

Like most business tycoons, Gus believed that every encounter with another human being was a chance to persuade or intimidate that person into adopting his point of view. Such people were always at risk of incurring self-inflicted wounds. They had a hard time understanding that their charm and forceful personalities would be of no value under such controlled circumstances, that none of their body English or voice inflection would make its way into the written transcript.

Sara had spent hours firing questions at Gus and then explaining to him why his proposed answers were wrong-headed and unresponsive. Gus seemed to have come to understand that every word of testimony he spoke would later appear in black and white on the deposition transcript, and that the rambling speeches that came so naturally to him in ordinary circumstances would be counterproductive here. Lastly, they hammered home that he should answer only the precise questions asked and not volunteer information not specifically requested.

By the end of that training session, known in the industry as "sandpapering the witness," they thought they had put to Gus all the questions—or at least all the areas from which questions would arise—that would be thrown at him the next day by the very able cross-examiner Clint Tarrymore. Because the case thus far from Tarrymore's side had concerned itself with the allocation of marital property and not with the fitness of either party to be the custodial parent of the minor child, it was reasonably anticipated that matters of character would be touched upon during the follow-up deposition set for two weeks hence. This belief was reinforced in its reasonableness by Ellen Tanzdahl's short history of wildness during her late teens and her understandable reluctance to commit any of those facts to the record prior to a full effort being made to settle the case. In addition, Gus had assured Sara and Riley that his life was an "open book," and that any of the nuisance claims against him as CEO of Tanzdahl were of no consequence and were, in any event, well known to Cosgrove & Levi as Tanzdahl's primary outside counsel. A check of the firm's Tanzdahl and Tanzdahl Industries files confirmed that no significant litigation had been brought relating to Gus.

It came as somewhat of a shock, therefore, when Clint Tarrymore, ignoring the mountain of information relating to Gus's financial interests, moved directly to the custody issue. After identifying for the record the persons in attendance at the deposition and walking through a short litany of ground rules, Clint opened up with the heavy artillery.

"Mr. Tanzdahl, in reference to the allegation made in paragraph three of your petition that you are the person best suited to assume exclusive custody and control of your son, Josh Thomas Tanzdahl, I ask you if in the last five years you have been the subject of any complaints in either administrative or judicial proceedings charging you with gross sexual improprieties in the Tanzdahl Industries workplace?"

Riley, who had been doodling on a legal pad during the introductory formalities, looked over at Sara. She tilted her head and shrugged.

Gus's face turned red. He stared across the table.

Clint Tarrymore smiled. "Did you understand the question, Mr. Tanzdahl, or would you like me to repeat it?"

Gus's anger mixed with a touch of panic. He turned to Riley, then to Sara. They both stared back at him in curious expectation. He had assured them just yesterday that there were no such complaints.

Gus bit his lower lip and turned to Sara as though she, being a woman and all, could somehow save him from this line of inquiry. Sara did a good job of suppressing the disgust she felt, not so much at the prospect of his having committed sexual improprieties, but rather that he had been stupid enough to withhold that information from his lawyers.

"Would you like me to have the court reporter read the question back to you, Mr. Tanzdahl?" repeated Clint.

Gus fidgeted in his seat. "Well . . . I never had any kind of a verdict or anything like that against me . . . along those lines . . . but of course every now and then the CEO of any large company becomes the target of gold diggers who pretend to be offended by a little workplace high jinks."

Clint reached over to a neat stack of files sitting on the table and extracted one from the pile. He opened the tan jacket and ran his finger down the first page. Without looking up, he asked, "Was a nineteen-year-old woman by the name of Lorina Ferrell one of those gold diggers, Mr. Tanzdahl?"

After a long defiant silence Gus nodded his head.

Clint Tarrymore leaned into the table, shortening the distance between them. "You're going to have to make an audible response for the record, Mr. Tanzdahl. Is your answer yes or no?" Clint seemed to be smirking, as he peered over his half-moon reading glasses.

"Yes . . . I would put that woman in that category."

Clint nodded as his eyes returned to the open file. He turned a page in what appeared to be a summons and complaint in a lawsuit that had been commenced by service of the complaint but settled before filing with the court. He deliberately placed the open file on the table so that Riley could see the letterhead of Hadley & Baxendale, a firm that specialized in defending workplace harassment claims. Clint rightly surmised that the Cosgrove & Levi lawyers had no knowledge that Gus was two-timing them with another firm. "Well, let me ask you this, do you believe that the CEO of a large publicly held company should personally set up a surprise birthday party for a nineteen-year-old secretary on the executive floor, and then unveil a birthday cake in the shape of an oversized male sex organ standing straight in the air? Would that qualify as office 'high jinks,' Mr. Tanzdahl?"

This was one of those moments when a witness's lawyer wants to slide under the table. Riley pretended to be taking notes on his legal pad. But instead of taking notes, he was sketching out what he thought a penile-decorated birthday cake might look like.

Sara stared at Gus, who said nothing.

"Let me see if I can stir your memory a little," said Clint. "It says here that the 'aforesaid birthday cake had a dab of whipped cream on the end and that the word Lorina was written in green frosting along the shaft'. Does that help jar your memory, Mr. Tanzdahl?"

Riley could tell from the lilt of his voice that Clint was having the time of his life. It wasn't often that a trial lawyer came into possession of information this juicy with which to humiliate a lying sack of shit like Gus Tanzdahl. And the shame of it was that Gus could have spared himself this and what was sure to follow by simply taking Riley's advice at the outset and not seeking a change of custody. Had he left that issue alone, none of the evidence now stinking up the record would have had any relevance to the distribution of marital assets. Riley was just angry enough at Gus's refusal to take his advice—to say nothing of his anger over Gus's denials that there was any damaging evidence against him—to take some small satisfaction in his present agony.

Gus sat silently in his chair, his face red, his carotid arteries distended and throbbing.

"Weeeell . . . Mr. Tanzdahl, what say you?" asked Clint.

"Yes," said Gus, clearing his throat. "But the way it's written there by her shyster lawyer, it sounds much worse than it was. That girl had only been on the floor for two weeks, and let me tell you she was plenty game, and she was making eyes at me from the first day she arrived. There was no reason to believe she'd take offense at a little fun. It was like an office initiation, and she was just a bad sport about it."

There it was, thought Riley, the bloated ego and deluded self-absorption displayed by so many successful businessmen. Somewhere along the way, the line between fantasy and reality had been sufficiently obscured to allow this short, paunchy, homely man to believe that he was the possessor of a magnetic sex appeal, even to a young woman roughly the age of his own children. It would be amusing if it were not so pitiful.

Clint turned the next page in the file, and again without looking up, said, "I see that there were affidavits filed in that case from six other women who were part of the Tanzdahl Industries support staff. Apparently they were very bad sports also, for all of them, under oath, said roughly the same thing: that they considered your actions to be cruel and degrading, and injurious to the complainant, Lorina Ferrell, who they say ran from the room in tears." His voice now dripping with sarcasm, Clint asked, "Were those women all gold diggers, too?"

Riley knew from his time in industry that the conduct described in the complaint was probably the God's truth, and that Gus's only miscalculation on that occasion had been the resolve of the young woman victimized by his puerile misbehavior. He thought back to his time at The Lindbergh Life & Casualty Company, where he steered clear of office events at which liquor was served, knowing that as sure as night follows day some half-wit in senior management, usually the CEO himself, would drunkenly act out his most juvenile fantasies—usually with some woman half his age, someone like Lorina Ferrell. Those parties were a train wreck waiting to happen, and he didn't want to be anywhere near the scene of the crime. What amazed him back then was how seldom such behavior resulted in complaints, formal or informal. It was as simple as people needing jobs, apparently.

Gus now leaned into the table and stared acidly at his inquisitor. "Yeah, they were all gold diggers, and I fired every goddamn one of them!"

Sara reached for Gus's arm to slow him down, but he pulled away.

"Yes, I see that," continued Tarrymore calmly as he reached for three more files in the stack. "Among them would be the women who filed the wrongful termination complaints contained in these three files, I believe, all of whom settled for substantial sums of money—the precise amounts being subject to confidentiality stipulations demanded by you as a condition of payment. But even more interesting, I think you will agree, Mr. Tanzdahl, is the parade of horribles—as we say in the law—contained in the exhibit attached to the Ferrell complaint. It recites in some detail the fourteen prior instances of improper conduct charged against you."

Clint licked the index finger of his right hand and turned several pages in his file. He then adjusted his glasses, squinted at the page, and shook his head in mock sadness. "You've been a very bad boy, Mr. Tanzdahl. Either that or you have been unfairly set upon by a remarkably large throng of gold-digging women. And I haven't even gotten to the rooftop swimming pool yet."

Gus's face turned scarlet. His hands shook as he rose from his seat and leaned into the table, glaring at Clint Tarrymore.

Clint looked up but didn't move or even blink. Instead, he glanced over at the court reporter and said, "I should like the record to reflect that Mr. Tanzdahl has left his seat and is leaning across the table in a state of great upset, apparently one of those attempts at intimidation for which he's so famous." He then looked up at Gus with a small, contemptuous smile. "But I don't scare quite as easily as your young wife or a nineteen-year-old secretary, Mr. Tanzdahl."

Riley lifted himself partially out of his seat and put a hand on Gus's forearm, urging him back into his seat. But Gus jerked his arm free. He stared down at Clint. "At least I was never a junky and a hooker like that little slut you represent, you bottom-feeding scumbag."

Clint again looked over at the court reporter to be sure that every word was going into the record. Sara was rolling her eyes in disbelief. Riley flashed a time-out signal to the court reporter and then looked over at Tarrymore. "I think that's it for today, Clint. I'll talk to you tomorrow about further examination on this subject. Perhaps we can complete the discovery having to do with parental fitness through written interrogatories. This is getting a whole lot uglier than is good for anybody."

Clint smiled. "Sure, Riley, we can talk tomorrow. But as of now, this deposition should be considered in recess, subject to recall at any time Ellen Tanzdahl chooses." He slipped his reading glasses into his vest pocket, and casually straightened the files sitting before him. He then looked directly at Gus and said, "You will also be receiving, later this week, a notice of the deposition of Rider McLaine, the former controller of Tanzdahl Industries, who we anticipate will testify that he was fired when he refused to approve your fraudulent expense reports for over $300,000 in purely personal expenses for the year 1995, including the transport in the corporate jet of your family dogs to a canine obedience school in Malibu, thereby defrauding the Internal Revenue Service and, of course, Tanzdahl Industries shareholders out of a lot of money."

Clint turned to Riley. "If the testimony in that deposition turns out to be as we expect, we will then note the deposition of the present officer at Tanzdahl who succeeded to Mr. McLaine's responsibilities as guardian of the corporate treasury. It appears that the present incumbent is less fastidious in the discharge of his duties than his fired predecessor."

Clint then gazed meditatively out the window at the far horizon and said in the tone of a law professor: "Of course, that testimony will almost certainly be considered by Judge Hammergren to be relevant both to Mr. Tanzdahl's actual compensation and to his fitness as a role model for his young son."

At this, Gus broke free and attempted to hurl himself across the table. The gesture was more theatrical than real, for the table was a full four feet in width and Gus had never been much of an athlete. What's more, if Gus had made it across the table, Clint Tarrymore, a former starting tackle for the University of Wisconsin, would have cleaned his clock in a matter of seconds, probably by tossing him through the glass panels of Tarrymore & Gleason's conference room.

Riley knew exactly what Clint was up to. It was a tactic he used himself on special occasions. Get your opponent so riled that he loses all self-control and not only makes a fool of himself but often blurts out self-destructive statements of the type Gus did just moments before.

Clint's motivations were not chiefly personal, though he was obviously taking enormous pleasure in these events. By forcibly letting Gus know that he was willing to return fire, and then some, he could reasonably expect Gus to withdraw the custody petition, which would lessen the emotional pressure on Ellen enough so that she could press her case for an equitable division of property. And even if Gus were not cowed by this display of damaging evidence, so long as Clint could keep Ellen's courage up, he was prepared to air this growing body of incriminating evidence in court.

Riley and Sara reached for Gus, now sprawled across the conference table with his ass in the air like a man awaiting a prostate exam. After getting him to his feet, Sara packed up their open briefcases as Riley firmly moved Gus out through the glass doors.

In the parking lot, Riley tried to explain why persisting with the change in custody action would be a disastrous course, not just to the divorce case but also to potential criminal exposure arising out of the falsified expense reports.

Gus conceded nothing. As to the expense reports, he considered the company, even after it went public, to be his private piggy bank. The worst that could happen, he said inaccurately, was that "some of the expenses would be disallowed and, as for those gold-digging bitches with their complaints and affidavits, he'd make every one of them wish she had never been born."

It was almost impossible to measure the revulsion Riley felt for his client at that moment. He had all he could do not to toss him up against the car and beat him to a pulp. He stared at the ground as he shook with anger and self-loathing that he was in any way associated with this man. He barely heard the words as Gus continued to spew invective and threaten to turn up the heat on his slanderous assault on his wife's character. "I will now play my trump card," he hissed.

When he could stand to hear no more, Riley turned away and, grabbing his briefcase from Sara, got into his car and drove away.


WHEN HE RETURNED to his office later that afternoon, following a two-hour swim to burn off the anger generated during the disposition, Riley found a manila envelope with his name typed on the front cover but no return address or other evidence of the sender's identity. As he unsealed the back flap, he shouted in the direction of Skeeter's desk, "Where did this envelope come from?"

"Beats me," she said, making her way into his office. "It was sitting on my desk when I got back from lunch."

Riley opened the envelope and pulled out several sheets. After examining them, he looked up at Skeeter. "These are photocopies of Ellen Tanzdahl's medical records."

"So?"

Riley scanned the entries on the second page. "It looks like she was treated for gonorrhea at this clinic. Good God, what next in this damnable case?"

Skeeter took a seat. "But we already knew she had a few wild years. A little dose of the clap shouldn't make things any worse . . . you know, the poor kid slept around before she got married. It can happen."

Riley turned back to the report. "Yeah, but this timeframe wasn't when she was a kid on the run. This was two years ago when she was already married . . . and was already a mother."

"Oh," said Skeeter, "congratulations, I think you just won the case."

Riley looked puzzled. "This is strange. Copies of medically privileged documents show up anonymously, apparently showing that Ellen Tanzdahl committed perjury in the answers to the interrogatories we sent last month. She was asked if she'd ever been treated for a medical or psychological condition that would bear upon her fitness as a parent, and she swore she hadn't." He tapped a pencil on the desktop and looked over at the phone.

"Most people don't even know what's in their medical records. Maybe she thought she was being truthful," said Skeeter.

"Give me a break. How likely is that?"

"I don't know. I just know from my old public health class that that disease is almost symptom-free for women until a lot of damage has been done." Her eyes squinted in curiosity. "Say, how could anyone have gotten those records anyway? Did you subpoena them?"

"No, I didn't. Not yet . . . but Gus was demanding that we get her medical records—almost as if he knew what was in these documents. And he sent his own medical records in to show that he was clear of any physical or psychological problem." Riley sat back in his chair and massaged his neck in the spot where a tension headache was gaining strength.

"These records for Ellen had to have come from Gus. He or someone working for him probably pirated them." He looked across the desk, shaking his head. "See if you can track down that little prick Harvey Aingren. I have a feeling he's involved in this. I think he's on the golf course with Gus and Ladge "

Several minutes later, without putting her hand over the receiver, Skeeter yelled, "I've got that little prick Harvey Aingren on the phone."

Riley picked up the phone. "Harvey, I don't suppose you or Gus would know anything about some private medical records that showed up mysteriously on my desk this afternoon?"

"Gee, I don't know what you're referring to, McReynolds," Harvey replied in a mock boy scout voice. "Whose records are they?"

"I think you probably know whose records they are, but I'll tell you. They're Ellen Tanzdahl's records, and they seem to show that she was treated for venereal disease a couple of years ago."

A small theatrical gasp could be heard on the other end. "Imagine that! And she wants to have custody of Gus's child. It's an outrage. And as you can see from Gus's medical records, which you should feel free to turn over to Ellen's lawyer, that he has no such sordid history."

Riley felt sick. Could this thing get any uglier? A recent case of gonorrhea seemed utterly incompatible with the character of the woman he had recently questioned under oath. "So you're saying that you and Gus know nothing about where these medical records came from?"

"That's exactly what I'm saying, McReynolds. But whatever the source of the records, you've got an obligation to act on this information. It seems to me that the custody evaluators would be interested in information like that. So, go do your duty, mouthpiece."

Riley said nothing. The silence was filled first by Harvey. "And, there's another thing we require of you, McReynolds.

You're a big buddy of Chasbo Peytabohm, or as he calls himself these days, 'Taylor Peytabohm.'"

"Yeah, so what?"

"Well, use your influence to get him to stop harassing Gus. Over the last month whenever he gets a chance—at receptions and CEO forums—he takes after Gus in the most insulting way. He's a real problem, and he's your friend. We demand that you to get him to back off." Harvey was sporting a whole new attitude. Gone was the servile flunky of an earlier time.

Riley chuckled sarcastically. "Apparently you don't know Chasbo very well, Harvey. He doesn't take orders from anybody. Gus will have to solve that problem on his own."

"No, I don't think so," said Harvey snidely. "Gus is sure you can influence Peytabohm in a positive way. So, we're holding you accountable."

Riley's face darkened. "Accountable?" he shouted into the phone. "Accountable! you say? You can bite my ass, Harvey, you little pimp . . . you hear me?"

But Harvey didn't hear him. He had hung up.

# 13

B ETSY PICKED LINT off his sleeve as Riley adjusted the
Baggies lining the pockets of his sport coat. He
straightened himself, cleared his throat, and lifted the
brass knocker on the massive front door of Studdiford House,
the three-generation-old estate of Bayard Van Studdiford
and his wife Weezie.

Bayard carried no title, but as the eldest son of a long line
of coupon-clipping Surrie Road aristocrats, he was expected
to reside in the ancestral home. The Van Studdifords were
charter members of the local nobility, heirs to one of the
areas great fortunes in lumber and railroads. Together with
other members of the clan and a few old-line area families,
they lived in a residential section high above Lake
Minnetonka.

The towering and stately wonder of Studdiford House,
three stories of golden stone which seemed to subtly change
color with the slant of the evening sun, was lovely to behold,
a symbol of another era. Tall, narrow windows flanked the
large front portico and reached upward to a row of second-
floor balconies. The third floor blended seamlessly into a roof
of gray slate arranged in a steep configuration. The whole

scene was bathed in a blend of setting sun and carefully placed floodlights casting an eerie glow from the closely cropped hedges lining the building's facade. The overall effect, borne of a mixture of the expensive and the practical, certified to its old-money status. Homes of similar grandeur, constructed by those of recent wealth, could be found in abundance in the surrounding area, but the desperate perfection with which they were designed and built marked them as creations of the nouveau riche.

Betsy was quickly inspecting Riley's outfit for spots, stains, wrinkles and the occasional laundry tag he neglected to remove from a sleeve or collar. "How did you ever leave home looking this way?" she said. "A gray herringbone jacket does not go with brown pants and black loafers."

Riley looked down at his coat, pulling on the sleeve to get a better view. A Band-Aid covered a recently discovered blemish on his wrist, which he had tentatively identified as an early-stage melanoma. Betsy said it was a freckle, but then what did she know; she had never been sick a day in her life.

"The salesman said this sport coat was brown," Riley said defensively as he pulled at the fabric.

"Yeah, well, you've been had again, slick," she said, shaking her head. It was true that though he saw vivid colors and shadings all around him, they didn't happen to correspond to spectrum norms. When given his first color perception test back at the university, a crabby public health nurse held up a mosaic of colorful stones and asked what number he saw. When he could find no number, they moved him over to a line of oddballs who were given special attention in a side room. His buddy Chasbo Peytabohm was also assigned to that room, but not because he was colorblind. Too impatient to wait in the urine specimen line, he had grabbed someone else's cup off a passing cart and turned it in on his own. The specimen, it turned out, had originated in the Homeless Clinic next door. When it was analyzed, it showed that Chasbo had a sexually transmitted disease and, worse yet, was three months pregnant. Chasbo was recalled to give a new specimen, this time under the watchful eye of a male nurse. His student file was marked with the first in what would ultimately become a record-setting series of entries. The section analyzing his MMPI alone ran nearly thirty pages.

Betsy gently pushed Riley's arm down when she saw the hostess approaching inside the foyer. The massive door swung open to reveal Weezie Van Studdiford, tall and stately, and resplendent in a coral floor-length evening gown held together with jeweled clips at several strategic points. Though only three years older than Riley, by reason of her dress and demeanor Weezie could have passed for his aunt. It was said that Weezie had been born old, and there was some truth to it. But for all her stuffy grandeur, she was full of irreverent fun.

Riley smiled and extended his hand, which was warmly accepted. Weezie leaned toward each of them and delivered a glancing kiss.

It was a tribute to Betsy's popularity that they had been invited back in light of the social boner he had committed at an earlier Van Studdiford dinner party. Tonight he had come prepared to handle the culinary challenge that had so embarrassed everyone on that occasion.

Betsy and Riley had known Weezie on and off since dancing school nearly thirty-five years before at Lakeridge Country Club, where flat-chested, pre-pubescent debutantes received their introductions to society. Weezie had been a toothy, homely girl in those days, but in the fullness of time had grown into a passably attractive woman. And in spite of her husband Bayard's serial infidelities, she had provided him with a gracious home and two well-adjusted children.

Then, as now, Bayard was a pleasant but colorless man who had fallen into the tedious pattern of the idle rich set by his father and grandfather before him. The family boasted patrician lineage, but like most wealthy Midwestern families, the truth was more complicated. Purged from the family history was Bayard's great-grandfather, an illiterate fish merchant who had wandered up the Mississippi River from New Orleans shortly after the Civil War. He had later gotten lucky on a mining claim in Northern Minnesota.

Though Riley liked Bayard, he avoided spending much time with him. Bayard was a man so tiresome that after a few minutes of conversation most of his listeners resolved to either flee or take their own lives. But as the Van Studdiford family interests constituted one of the largest Cosgrove & Levi client accounts, ranking just behind Gus Tanzdahl and his associated companies, there was nothing to do about it. As a Cosgrove & Levi partner, it would have been unthinkable for Riley to decline a dinner invitation from any member of the Van Studdiford family, but most particularly from Bayard and Weezie.

After making inquiries about the health and welfare of the McReynolds children (even remembering the names and ages of Lizzie and Teddy), and summoning a white-coated waiter to take their drink orders, Weezie Van Studdiford moved to the next guest in line.

As Riley watched a small group of guests make its way down the stately hallway, he felt a poke in the lower back. He turned to find an already well-oiled Trudi Hansdale, Gus's high-society girlfriend, smiling up at him as she sipped on her third Martini. She was adorned in an expensive lightweight outfit, through which the outlines of her generous breasts could be seen in nearly perfect detail. They were expensive breasts, that pair, being the result of surgical augmentation performed several years before as a Christmas present to her husband, Bronley "Biff" Hansdale. That was back when they were still speaking to each other.

Looking Riley up and down, Trudi snickered, "I hear gray and brown are coming back this season, Riley." She tried to smile but her many facial surgeries had left her virtually expressionless. A gruesome trifecta of collagen-injected lips, twice-tucked chin line, and Botox-paralyzed forehead made her look like some kind of wax effigy.

Riley had known Trudi for a long time and had never liked her. Unpleasant in the best of circumstances, she was unbearable after a few drinks. As far back as college, she had felt the need to comment on his visually challenged outfits. He was irritated enough on this occasion to consider reminding her of the time she had attended a party at his fraternity house thirty years earlier, where she got so loaded that she mistook an ashtray off the dance floor for the ladies' commode, and took a pee in it. But that would have been cruel, and he almost never made cruel remarks, even to Trudi Hansdale. The ashtray caper had been during her brief foray into bohemian life with the fine arts crowd at the university, where she had taken up avant-garde poetry following a rebellious year at Miss Carstairs finishing school in the rolling hills of southern Virginia. By the beginnings of the Ford Administration Trudi had grown tired of tormented existentialists, starving artists, and her own bad poetry, and reassumed her role as the privileged daughter of a Wayzata billionaire. Thus did she come full circle, joining the Junior Assembly and the small equestrian circles of the local gentry. The only creative writing she did now were those ubiquitous thank-you notes that circulate mercilessly amongst the well-to-do.

At twenty-eight Trudi landed her first husband, Biff Hansdale, who in the best old-money tradition had left in seventh grade for six years of boarding school, followed by four years at Amherst, two years at Harvard Business School, and five years on Wall Street. He then returned home to attend to the family fortune. He, too, had been at dancing school as a youth, well before he adopted the distinctive stammer that privileged Midwesterners seem to acquire somewhere between the western suburbs of Minneapolis and Cambridge, Massachusetts.

In spite of living the comfortable life that marriage to Biff guaranteed, Trudi was by no means happy. So when Gus

Tanzdahl hit on her one night at the Symphony Ball, she gave herself over, body and soul, to his rakish charm and vulgar suggestions. Their mutual attraction—she to him a symbol of the station to which he had always aspired, he to her the noble savage who had assembled one of the area's great fortunes—resulted in a bodice-ripping love fest under a raised platform on which a musical ensemble was performing the first movement of Rachmaninoff's *C-Minor Concerto*. Poor old Biff was dispatched with a cruel efficiency by Trudi's lawyers, and her betrothal to the still-married Gus was put out on the Lake Minnetonka grapevine as an accomplished fact.

As Trudi continued to sneer at Riley's outfit, Betsy said, "He's a little color blind." To forestall the comeback she knew Riley was formulating, Betsy felt an urgent need to head him off.

Trudi looked over at Betsy for the first time, tossing a tight, feline smile in her direction. "Oh, hi, Bainbridge," she said a little snidely, using Betsy's maiden name in a custom popular amongst the cool girls back in the early sixties when they had first known each other. She had resented Betsy for her beauty and popularity then, and Trudi's resentments tended to be of the lifetime variety.

Betsy paid no attention. Trudi was obviously stuck in the mean stage that had first emerged in adolescence. Betsy simply refused to engage with such people. Trudi had suffered from the delusion that they had been girlhood competitors, a notion that had never occurred to Betsy nor to anyone else with functioning eyesight.

Trudi threaded her hand through Riley's free arm and the three of them walked down an ornate central hallway, flanked on both sides by a series of formal rooms. As they rounded the corner and headed toward the patio, Riley thought about how much more he had liked Trudi when she was peeing in fraternity house ashtrays. That short phase had been her one brush with real life.

At the end of the hallway stood large leaded-glass doors, topped by a single arch that reached nearly fifteen feet to a plaster relief ceiling. Beyond the doors was a broad patio commanding a panoramic view of Lake Minnetonka. The evening was perfect for a gathering of this type, with the temperature a comfortable seventy degrees and the breeze strong enough to cool against the fading sunlight but not so strong as to displace even a strand of hair from the carefully groomed guests.

Beyond the expanse of manicured lawn, running about the length of a football field, sunlight glistened off the waves of the lake. Directly across the bay, sitting regally atop a fortress-like embankment, was the baronial home of Ward Crosshaven, an embittered man whose wealth and influence had failed to keep his favorite son Brad from a prison cell for dealing drugs. That was just after he had played a central role in a tragedy at Riley's former employer, The Lindbergh Life & Casualty Company. Not all was well in the land of the rich.

As he stood peering across the lake, Riley was approached by Ladge Wilkaster and Thompson Van Studdiford, Bayard's youngest son, who had just graduated from law school and was about to sit for the bar exam. "Riley, Thompson is thinking about going into criminal law—against the wishes of his parents, I should note—and he wanted to meet you."

Riley and Betsy shook hands with the earnest young man with green eyes twinkling below an unruly mass of reddish-brown hair. Young Van Studdiford resembled not just his parents but a good many other guests at the party, for the Van Studdifords were one of four wealthy families (the others being the Holbeins, the Hartswirths, and the Parrys) that had been intermarrying for four generations. In spite of producing a good many talented offspring over the years, this practice had also spawned more than their share of slow-witted look-alikes with extra digits.

Trudi Hartswirth Hansdale—herself the issue of a union between double cousins Muffy Holbein and Parry "Puck" Hartswirth—had the dubious genealogical distinction of being her own third cousin. Into this rarefied genetic scramble was now coming Gus Tanzdahl, a short, fat, common-as-dirt plebeian, who was about as welcome in this extended family as the heartbreak of psoriasis.

By all appearances, Thompson Van Studdiford had escaped the worst ravages of the family's furious inbreeding, and to Riley's delight, he turned out to be a charming conversationalist. They talked pleasantly about his professional ambitions and where he was applying for jobs and, for a moment, Riley thought that the evening might not be a total loss. That prospect was cruelly dashed when Trudi again walked up and butted in, her face close enough to Riley's to launch the smell of stale cigarettes and gin.

Paying no attention to Thompson (her second-cousin-once-removed) she looked at Riley furtively, the way people do when addressing an accomplice. "I'm hoping you can wrap up this nuisance of Gus's divorce in short order, Riley."

The young man raised his eyebrows and excused himself.

Trudi looked around, and her voice dropped to an intimate whisper. "Gus and I are hoping to be married in Naples over Thanksgiving weekend, and it would be positively dreadful if that little tart he's now married to were to get in the way of our plans."

Riley stiffened at this unattractive intrusion into the sad matter of the Tanzdahl divorce, in part because of the tackiness of the sentiment and in part because of the inappropriate venue. He looked over at Betsy and then back to Trudi. "This isn't a very good place to talk about somebody else's divorce, Trudi. Why don't we change the subject?"

Trudi grunted, dispatching a small swirl of tobacco fumes. She then patted him on the shoulder and said in a stage whisper, "You were always sooo proper, Riley. But let me just tell you one thing before we change the subject. No matter what Gus's strategy might be, there's no way in hell their kid will ever reside under my roof once we're married." With that she flicked her head in the style of Betty Davis, causing the wave of hair sloping off her forehead to sail backwards, in the process exposing the incision from her most recent face lift. Riley couldn't help but admire the artistry of the surgeon, who through a succession of procedures over a three-year period, had turned an essentially homely, slightly horse-faced woman into one who was, if not quite pretty, at least mildly attractive. It was the chin he had built for her in the late 1980s that probably accounted for the greatest improvement, he thought. It had taken some of the meanness out of her look, if not her soul.

As for her crack about little Josh Tanzdahl never living with them, it only confirmed Riley's robust suspicion that Gus's petition to have Ellen declared an unfit mother was little more than a ploy to scare her into renouncing her rightful share of the marital estate.

The familiar unpleasant sensations in his midsection began to return with a sickening force.

"Let's go for a walk," he said to Betsy after Trudi got bored and went chasing after a doctor who had been on the front page of the morning paper and was, therefore, deserving of her temporary notice. Riley put his arm through Betsy's and they headed for the garden.

On the way across the patio, Riley caught sight of George Stonequist talking into his cell phone. He and Betsy cut tightly to the right to avoid George, in the process running into a tall man of stately bearing with whom Betsy had been visiting earlier in the evening. The man extended his hand to Riley. "J.R. Wadsworth," he said. He wore a monogrammed blazer and a red ascot. In an aristocratic stammer that brought to mind Thurston Howell in Gilligan's Island, he said, "Had a nice visit with your wife, old sport, and I wanted to meet you."

Riley took the man's hand and smiled politely, first at him and then at his wife, Lillian Hartswirth Holbein Wadsworth, a jumbo-breasted dowager decked out in absurdly heavy jewelry. She bowed stiffly toward him but didn't smile. Riley bowed back, awkwardly.

J.R. Wadsworth beamed at Betsy. It was obvious he had formed an instant crush on her. He then turned back to Riley. "Knew a McReynolds back at Yale, class of '33. Any relation?"

"1933? Not unless he was delivering bootleg booze for Lefty Kapowitz over on the Northside."

The old Brahmin threw his head back and roared with laughter. Most bona fide blue bloods in Minnesota, in contrast to their Eastern counterparts, cared little for distinctions of class or background. There was a common misperception that they spent all day riding to the hounds and munching on watercress sandwiches. In truth, the real snobs among the Lake Minnetonka set were those who had made their money in the last thirty years and then elbowed their way onto the social register. J.R. Wadsworth, standing there in all his patrician splendor, didn't seem to have a snobby bone in his body. In fact, Riley knew from other sources that he had a history of philanthropy and community involvement to rival the most dedicated social activist. It was one of the many nice things about the Midwest, this egalitarianism among the founding families. Normally, two generations of coupon-clipping in a family is enough to destroy it, but not so with most of these folks. They had remained largely untouched by the vanities that so often befall old wealth.

Out in the garden Riley stood admiring the gothic grandeur of Studdiford House, while Betsy meditated ecstatically upon the array of flowers spanning the two acres of gardens. Flowers excited her so much that they considered stealing a little splendor in the grass behind the garden gazebo, but decided that for reasons of good taste—to say nothing of the seven security cameras continually scanning the grounds—not to give wing to their passion. There would hardly have been time, anyway, as a waiter was passing through the garden ringing one of those little silver bells that tell rich people it's time to eat.

Five tables of eight settings each were arranged in a matrix pattern about the high-ceilinged room known as the "conservatory." Riley half expected Colonel Mustard to walk through the room.

Name cards at each setting specified the arrangement laid down by Weezie Van Studdiford, herself an heiress of considerable magnitude on the Holbein side. Weezie was a tough old girl, and she was ferociously attached to Bayard in spite of his wandering eye.

On one famous occasion, it was said, Weezie hosted an afternoon tea for eight women representing a wide range of backgrounds who, with only one or two exceptions, were unknown to each other. Their only common feature was that they were—or once had been—highly attractive. The guests had passed a lovely afternoon, getting to know each other but secretly wondering what the unifying element might be that brought them. Their curiosity was finally satisfied when Weezie rose from her chair after dessert and tapped a small demitasse spoon against her water glass. "You ladies are probably wondering why I brought you here today," she said in a cultivated and welcoming tone, a broad smile gracing her face.

The ladies nodded their acknowledgment to Weezie and to each other, a soft hum passing through the room. Indeed they did wonder.

Weezie then leaned forward, her smile morphing into a determined frown. "I had you here today to serve notice that each of you has had her last piece of Bayard Van Studdiford." She looked about the gathering of pretty faces, now gone slack with horror. They had all been mistresses of Weezie's husband Bayard at one time or another over the previous twenty years, even overlapping each other in several cases.

Weezie set her jaw and continued, "Don't worry, you'll be allowed to keep the jewelry and other gifts he used to compromise your virtue—not that it took much. And you, Sally"—she now turned a hawkish eye upon Sally Quinlaevin, a knock-out thirty-year-old with a law degree but no need for earned income—"you'll even get to keep the condo in Boca Raton and the marketable securities placed in your trust by my dear husband."

The three or four mature women now in their mid-forties, long since discarded by the youth-worshipping Bayard, could hardly suppress their joy at this spectacle. Several others, however, sat in huffy outrage at what they considered a tasteless exhibition.

Sally Quinlaevin, the current holder of the mistress crown—"Queen for a Day," as Weezie called her—had the crust to indignantly deny the allegation. "Oh, really," said Weezie as she nodded to a waiter standing near the fireplace. He reached over and flipped a switch, causing two ceiling panels to part like the Red Sea. There was a brief rumbling, followed by a movie screen dropping across most of one wall. Another nod from Weezie and the screen came alive with the image of Bayard and Sally engaged in torrid copulation on the balcony of their Boca Raton love nest. They looked like the stars in a Russ Meyer film.

This was too much even for the emeritus members of the group, who rose as one and headed for the exits. Weezie shouted after them, "You're not missing much, girls. The old goat's pretty much out of gas anyway."

How could you not love Weezie after that performance, thought Riley, as he searched for his place card. Passing the table closest to the French doors, he waived at Scott Stearns, who pretended not to see him. Scott had not spoken to him since Riley ruled against him and in favor of the odious George Stonequist in the matter of the fees on the Van Studdiford account. Riley understood his feelings, but the snub still hurt.

Arriving at his assigned table, he was horrified to see that Trudi Hansdale's name appeared on the place card next to his, and next to hers was one for Gus Tanzdahl. Riley quickly palmed his card and switched it with Ladge Wilkaster's on the other side of the table. This had the advantage not only of ducking Trudi but also of seating him next to a dermatologist to whom he could display his suspicious pre-melanoma blemish.

221

As it turned out, his efforts came to naught as Trudi, ignoring the place cards, plopped her ass down right next to him.

"Oh, won't we have fun," she slurred over her fourth Martini, grinning at Riley as broadly as her tightly bound skin would permit. Even the smallest smile caused her hairline to slide back and forth in a Dracula-like motion.

Riley tried to strike up a conversation with the woman on his other side, but she was hard of hearing and didn't seem much interested in getting to know him. Besides that she was from the Hartswirth side of the family, the branch that had taken the worst collective hit from the interfamily nuptials.

As the salad was served, Trudi pulled on Riley's arm and whispered. "Gussie is going to join us later, after a late business meeting."

*Gussie?* Now, he thought he might actually blow lunch right on the table. Besides which, he happened to know that Gussie was not at any late business meeting. He and a bunch of his cronies, including Buck Montrowe, were having a stag party back at headquarters, replete with naked pool nymphs.

Trudi peered around the room in search of someone to gossip about, straining her neck in a way that caused her hair to fall clear of her left sideburn. Riley stared at the small bundle of scar tissue next to her ear, the exact spot where the facial reconstruction had been anchored. It occurred to him that if that small wad of tucks and levers were to come loose and unwind, the whole facial edifice might suddenly collapse. Old Gus might wake up some morning next to Eleanor Roosevelt.

Riley stopped staring at Trudi's ear when she leaned into him. Still looking off at a table on the far side of the room, she said, "I hope Binky McFairlane doesn't drink too much wine with dinner. She might start humping Garrett Minstad right on the table." She turned her face to Riley and gave a knowing wink. "Remember when they got caught in the closet at Korwin's New Year's Eve party last year?"

"No, I don't, Trudi. I missed that party." Riley and Betsy hadn't accepted a New Year's Eve invitation for over twenty years.

Trudi didn't hear his answer. Her questions were nearly always rhetorical, and in any case her attention had been seized by another, equally banal, thought. "Daddy loves Gussie, you know. Self-made men are his favorites. He's so excited about our engagement."

Riley looked at her blankly. He had never met Trudi's daddy, and knew only the common folklore about him, which was that he was filthy rich and led a largely useless life. Riley thought about how empty and purposeless one's existence would have to be to look forward to having Gus Tanzdahl for a son-in-law.

Trudi picked at her salad, occasionally winking and waving at other guests, simultaneously emitting a high-pitched but unintelligible sound from her throat. She would then turn to him and conduct a one-way gossip session about the person to whom she had just waved. She boasted shamelessly about her children's SAT scores and her new condo in Palm Springs.

Riley wondered what sin he had committed to deserve the tortuous company of this garrulous bag of hot air. His eyes reached across the table, pleading with Betsy to somehow save him. She only got the giggles.

Suddenly Trudi grabbed Riley's forearm and released a small, affected gasp as though she had just remembered something. "I told Gus I wouldn't sign a pre-nuptial agreement, you know? Not for him or any man. So you don't even need to draft one." As she said this, her eyes stared off into the distance as her right hand fondled the pearls of her expensive necklace. Her demeanor became thoughtful, reflective. "It's a matter of principle with me, a core component of my authentic self, my womanhood"—she tossed her head back dramatically—"my goddess within."

*Oh, God*, prayed Riley, *would someone please save me from this air-headed ninny*. Trudi's concept of womanhood, by the way, was pretty much limited to middle-aged white women whose authenticity had vanished in a volley of cosmetic surgery. And imbedded within her assumption that he would be involved in the preparation of a pre-nuptial agreement was the wrong-headed notion that he would ever again represent Gus Tanzdahl in anything. Once was enough, no matter what the cost.

She continued, "I've opened a whole new world for Gus. He's at long last getting in touch with his inner child."

Riley pictured Gus back at Tanzdahl headquarters getting in touch with his inner child, assisted by a bevy of nubile young beauties frolicking naked in his rooftop swimming pool.

Trudi narrowed her eyes earnestly. "I believe I impact Gus in truly positive ways."

"Impact is not a verb," said Riley calmly.

"What?"

"Never mind."

One waiter removed the salad plates and appetizers—marinated liver pate arranged in small pyramids topped by a dab of cream sauce—while another set the main course before each guest: veal forestier surrounded by scrawny sprouts of bleached asparagus. Small bread squares that fell apart when touched rounded out the culinary presentation. As Riley expected, the whole thing, other than the bread, was inedible. He longed for a Milky Way and a Pepsi.

George Stonequist's cell phone could be heard ringing in the distance.

Junior Cosgrove passed by on the way to his table. He slapped Riley on the back and bent down to kiss Betsy lightly on the cheek.

"Hi, Junior, you look so handsome tonight," said Betsy, smiling up at him.

"Oh, Betsy, you rock!" he said, grinning broadly. He then looked down at the food on Riley's plate and made a face. "Yuck! Gag me with a spoon!"

"Shut up, Junior," said Ladge Wilkaster from across the table.

"Leave him alone, Ladge," said Riley.

Junior was right. Tonight's fare was even worse than the steak tartar and caviar Weezie had served last year. Not wanting to hurt Weezie's feelings on that occasion, Riley had quietly shoveled the contents of his plate into napkins, which he then slipped into the pockets of his suit coat. Unfortunately, he hadn't considered the moisture content, and the food leaked through the napkins and into the fabric of his jacket, creating large circular stains that spread like a bad rash. It was those stains that had given him away when he said goodnight to Weezie.

After driving through Wendy's for some real food on the way to tonight's dinner, he lined the pockets of his jacket with Baggies, which he now proceeded to surreptitiously fill with marinated liver pate and veal forestier. Even the dessert of fresh raspberries, studded with those awful little hairy seeds, ended up in his pockets. Just as he was shoveling the last handful of dinner into a Baggie, Trudi perked up and shouted with delight, "Oh, here comes Gussie!"

All looked out through the floor-length windows and saw a large black limousine pulling slowly around the circular drive. When the limo came to a stop, the uniformed driver hustled around to open the back door, from which emerged a wobbly, heavily intoxicated Gus. Unaware of the observing crowd, he stumbled over to the rich foliage lining the driveway, whipped out his business, and commenced relieving himself into the sculpted gardens of Studdiford House.

Riley leaned over to Trudi, his hand resting gently on her arm. "I'm not sure, Trud, but I think Gus's inner child just pissed on Weezie's forsythia."

In the ensuing confusion, Riley grabbed Betsy and headed for a side door, not even bidding farewell to Weezie. He could not bear the prospect of being in the same room with Gus.

Once out the door, they made a mad dash for their car. The Van Studdiford family dogs, having caught the scent of the liver-filled Baggies, followed in hot pursuit.

# 14

---

A  s Riley sat staring at the Tanzdahl file and sorting
   through his jumbled emotions, an ashen-faced Skeeter
   staggered into his office, the back of her hand pressed
theatrically across her forehead. She reached blindly for a
chair.

Riley looked up. "What in the world happened to you?"

She exhaled loudly. "I just walked into Barney Bost's office
to drop off a memo—" Pausing briefly, she seemed to be choking off a gag reflex. She gripped the sides of the chair with
white knuckles and took a long calming breath. "I should
have knocked . . . I really should have knocked. But without
thinking I barged right in, and there was Barney putting it
to Blanche Emersen . . . right on the desk for God's sake!"

She shuddered a little as though experiencing a chill,
shaking her head back and forth while giving off a whistle.

Riley studied her face, thinking that she looked like one of
the witnesses to a heinous crime he used to interview as a
prosecutor.

"It was repulsive," she said, looking over at him. "Like
some kind of porno nightmare. Pants down, files sailing off
the desk, pencils and paper clips flying all over."

Riley put his palms in the air like a traffic warden stopping a speeding vehicle. "Whoa, whoa, not so fast there. I don't need details." His face went slack as he stared down at the Milky Way he had been eating when she came in. He slowly re-wrapped the half-eaten candy bar, tossing the remnant into his treat drawer, where it mixed with randomly scattered Star Burst Clusters, Bubbilicious bubble gum, a Tootsie Roll, and a bottle of Maalox. "I wish you hadn't shared that image with me, Skeets. It is too horrible for me to contemplate."

"Too horrible for you to contemplate!" she groaned, her hand now covering her mouth. "What about me? It's been scorched into my brain. I may have to go on disability for years of psychotherapy to get rid of it."

"Maybe you could try shock therapy. You know, where they hook you up to jumper cables and purge bad memories. The only problem is that it could also fry off a couple of years of good memories."

"It would be worth it," said Skeeter. "The picture of Barney's flabby white ass in the air will haunt my waking hours for the rest of my life."

Riley looked at her sallow coloring and feared she might hurl right on his carpet. He reached for an empty wastepaper basket, but Skeeter waved it off.

Putting on his reading glasses, he opened the official Cosgrove & Levi Policy Manual. After running his finger down the table of contents, he paged through to the section dealing with sexual relationships in the workplace. He scanned the text, puckering his face as he read.

Finally, he gave a confirming poke at the page. "Yes, here it is. This is a paraphrase, mind you, but it clearly says that managers and subordinates are not allowed to hide the wienie at work."

"Stop!" pleaded Skeeter, leaping from her chair. "I can't talk about this anymore. My God, I feel like I just watched a snuff movie. Do you have any idea how unattractive that scene was?" She looked sick again, the corners of her mouth curling downward. "And then, when they heard me walk in, Blanche screamed and Barney fell off the desk. I think he may have broken his wrist."

Riley roared with delight.

"It's not funny," said Skeeter as she started to leave the room.

"Here, take the wastepaper basket."

"Shut up!" she yelled, cupping her hands over her ears.


AFTER CALMING DOWN, Riley could not bring himself to return to the Tanzdahl case. So he turned from the desk and looked under his credenza at the flimsy and worn suitcase once owned by Detective Lieutenant Patrick Clebourne. Until retrieved by Nancy Kunz and given to Riley, it had resided for over a half-century in an attic in Omaha. Riley longed to return to the search chiefly because it provided a respite from the Tanzdahl case, but also because of a mounting sense of urgency for which he had no rational explanation.

So he went to work on the contents of the suitcase. In the first file jacket were onionskin carbon copies of the investigative report on the Turlough homicide, bearing the names of Detectives Clebourne and Kunz. He had seen the original of that same report in the investigative archives of the Omaha Police Department. Pencil notations were scribbled along the margins in Pat Clebourne's distinctive handwriting, but none of the notes shed any light on the true purpose of what he now knew to be falsifications contained in the text. The report had been painstakingly constructed to make it appear both authentic and routine, but the evidence already uncovered by Riley established beyond any doubt that Clebourne had used the occasion of the violent death of a common prostitute with a remarkable resemblance to Bridey Reaves to throw Bridy's Chicago pursuers off the trail long enough for her to flee Omaha.

Several more hours of painstaking review revealed nothing in the way of useful information. This was a great disappointment, inasmuch as these files were his only remaining source of clues.

He dropped his head into his hands and rocked back and forth in glum frustration. Pat Clebourne was a professional and it was he who had engineered Bridey's escape from Omaha. If he could fool the Mob in 1937, he could probably fool Riley in 1996, even with the improved search techniques available to him.

Tired, hungry, and gripped by a headache resulting from examining small, faded print, Riley rose from the desk and, in a gesture of frustration, drop-kicked the emptied suitcase clear across the room. It collided with the wall, bounced off an end table, and tumbled to the ground, a shattered lamp following in its wake.

Hearing the ruckus and naughty language, Skeeter hurried into the office, closing the door behind her. She lifted the lamp back onto the table and reached for the damaged suitcase, one side of which had collapsed under the force of the kick. "Easy now," she said in the soothing tones of a psychiatric nurse.

As she picked up the suitcase it fell into several pieces, revealing a false bottom from which a thin stack of papers was dislodged. They fluttered to the ground, landing randomly in a wide circle.

Skeeter looked up at Riley. They both dove for the papers, which appeared to be pale-green accounting sheets of a kind widely in use in the period before World War II. Riley sat down on the couch, arranging the sheets before him on the coffee table. Skeeter pulled up a chair next to him.

The sheets contained long columns of names written in Pat Clebourne's handwriting. Next to each name was a date falling somewhere between January 1, 1906, and December 31, 1910. Together, he and Skeeter examined the entries, looking for recognizable information or some common feature. But beyond the fact that the entries were all female names common to that era, they seemed to bear no discernible relationship to each other. After twenty minutes, having in mind the methods used at his old detective agency for finding missing heirs, it dawned on Riley that these might well be the birth dates of young girls born close to Bridey's birth date. She had been born in 1908, right in the middle of the range represented by the dates on these schedules.

To test his suspicion, he booted up the computer and went on line to tap into private databases accessible through Mick Goerdan's private user code. Death records for the State of Nebraska were his first stop. He typed in the first name on the list, "A-l-i-c-e A-n-d-r-e-a M-a-c-K-a-n-n" and clicked the "find" prompt. The computer whirred and whistled, and eventually came up with the following entry: "Alice Andrea MacKann, deceased, February 16, 1909, Omaha, Nebraska."

Riley went back to the Andrea MacKann entry on Clebourne's schedule and with his finger traced across the horizontal line to the numbers column, where sure enough, the date "2/16/09" was entered. To double check, he randomly picked four or five other names on the schedule and ran each through the same drill. In each case he got the same result—a name verification and a corresponding date of death.

But in the Nebraska records no birth dates were given for any of the deceased children listed on the schedule, only dates of death. So he switched to the birth records field and ran each of the names, finding, unsurprisingly, that none of the dead infants had been born in Nebraska. That would make perfect sense. If Clebourne had compiled the list for the purpose Riley suspected, selecting children who had been born in one state and died in another would make tracing them immeasurably harder, especially in 1937 when public records of this kind were the exclusive province of government units operating independently of each other.

Pat Clebourne had almost certainly compiled his list from gravestones and cemetery records, which in most instances would include the birth date and birthplace of the deceased. And, indeed, in running the same selections through the Nebraska death records he determined that all five had been buried in Omaha-area cemeteries—two of them in the same cemetery as the nameless prostitute who went to her grave as Clare Turlough.

Given the migration patterns of the 1930s, it was logical to assume that many, if not most, of the children had been born in adjoining states. Thus he went next to the database for Iowa, where he found the birth records for two of the random selections. Pat Clebourne had done his homework. In a time before public databases were privately compiled and made available for a fee to investigators like Mick Goerdan, Patrick Clebourne's methodology was undoubtedly sufficient to confound even the most sophisticated pursuers.

Riley set the three pages of Clebourne's handwritten notes before him, scanning down their columns in the almost certain knowledge that one of those names had been assumed by Bridey as she fled Omaha in 1937. His spine tingled and the hair on the back of his neck stood on end as he moved from name to name, making informed guesses as to which one of the dead infants had been reborn in 1937 as a twenty-nine-year-old woman with dark hair, pale-blue eyes, and a soft Irish accent.

Skeeter looked on in rapt attention.

"One of these is Bridey," said Riley without looking up.

Together they searched the Social Security Death Index, and none of the entries on the Clebourne list appeared. That meant that if Bridey had assumed the identity of one of these dead girls, as Riley now felt sure she had, and then applied for a social security card, the absence of the name in the death index would mean that she was still alive. The other names on the schedule wouldn't appear, of course, because they were dead long before the Social Security Act was passed and no one had since taken up their identity.

The next step—determining a social security number and last known address for any name on the list to which a social

security card had been issued—would require the not strictly legal methods of Mick Goerdan. So Skeeter faxed the three
sheets to Mick with a note reciting Riley's belief that one of
the names on the list would likely correspond to a social security filing. Inasmuch as dead people don't apply for social
security cards, that filing would have been made by an
imposter, by somebody who needed a new identity.

Fifteen minutes later, the humming fax machine kicked
out a note from Mick Goerdan. It contained a single name.
That name corresponded to number seventeen on Pat
Clebourne's list: "Suzanne Sheridan, last known address
1766 Girard Lane, Leavenworth, Kansas. Last payment into
system—October 30, 1945."

By some method—the legality of which was doubtful—
Mick had also obtained a photo static copy of the 1938 social
security application filed by the woman posing as Suzanne
Sheridan. The race, date, and place of birth, and the names
of the applicant's parents all corresponded to the information
contained on the birth certificate of the dead infant, the real
Suzanne Sheridan, who had been born on December 18,
1907, and had actually died on March 1, 1908. The entries on
the falsified social security application were in the handwriting of the woman who had assumed the dead child's identity
and, though he would have Mick Goerdan verify it through a
handwriting expert, the letters were formed in the distinctive Palmer method taught at the St. Agnes Convent in
Chicago. And it appeared to be nearly identical to the school-
girl script appearing in the handwritten note found in the St.
Agnes Convent file of Anna McBride Reaves.

The social security documents disclosed that Suzanne
Sheridan's employer was The Plains Rialto Movie Palace,
Leavenworth, Kansas, and that the last payment was made
into the account in 1945.

Riley's heart jumped into his throat. Not even Gus Tanzdahl could ruin this moment. He was back on the Bridey
case.

\* \* \*

THAT AFTERNOON Riley attended the weekly meeting of the litigation department, but he didn't hear a word that was said.
His mind was in Leavenworth, Kansas, circa. 1945, where a
woman by the name of Suzanne Sheridan lived.

Following the meeting, he barricaded himself in his office,
ignoring the phone slips and an overflowing in-basket. More
than simple excitement was at work here. He felt a sense of
urgency that freed him of the kind of guilt that would normally be aroused by spending office time on a project that
generated no income for the firm. He couldn't have cared
less.

From the shelf behind his desk he pulled a reference volume containing the names, locations, and phone numbers of
the state and municipal subdivisions of all fifty states plus
the federal government. He turned to "K" and found the
number for the Kansas Secretary of State, where corporation
documents are filed. He reached a woman with a genuine
interest in being helpful, especially toward people whose
voices were desperately needy. Within minutes, he had the
information he needed.

The Plains Rialto Movie Palace had operated in the
Leavenworth area for nearly forty years. It was demolished
in 1965 after sitting derelict for three years. It had been
owned by a privately held corporation, itself dissolved in
1965, whose principal shareholders and officers were Vernon
and Elisa Olinger of Lawrence, Kansas. The last corporate
papers on file with the Kansas Secretary of State listed the
attorney for the corporation as Morgan J. Farrington IV, of
the firm Jones & Farrington, also of Lawrence.

Skeeter, who knew not to interrupt during a time of
fevered intensity—his "spells" as she called them—slipped
into the office, closed the door, and dropped quietly onto the
couch, where she could watch and listen.

Riley thanked the clerk, hung up the phone, and turned to
the on-line white pages in search of a Vernon or Eliza

Olinger. Though Skeeter was right in front of him, he failed to notice her or, for that matter, any of his other surroundings. When the Olinger search came up negative, he switched back to the Social Security Death Index. There he found Vernon and Eliza, both dead for more than two decades. Their city of residence at the time of their respective deaths was listed as Leavenworth, Kansas.

Trying to convince a county probate clerk to retrieve a long-closed probate file and read from its contents was a daunting challenge, no matter how desperate the caller sounded or how much charm he turned on. The easier route to the needed information was through the law firm that had handled the Olingers' business affairs, if that firm was still in business. He pushed his chair toward the bookcase so vigorously that he rolled off the plastic floorboard and nearly toppled to the ground. Undaunted, he recovered his equilibrium and grabbed for a directory of American lawyers.

Skeeter sat quietly on the couch, fascinated and amused.

He whipped through the directory until he came to Lawrence, Kansas, where he found an entry for Morgan J. Farrington IV, now eighty-three years old. He was listed at the same address he had occupied at the time he formed and later dissolved—The Plains Rialto Movie Palace.

Riley grabbed for the phone and dialed the number listed in the directory. On the third ring an elderly man picked up. "Farrington," he said brusquely.

"Morgan Farrington, the attorney?" asked Riley as he pulled a pen from his shirt pocket and reached across the desk for a yellow legal pad.

"That's correct," said the voice on the other end, old but strong. "But I go by Morg."

"Morg, my name is Riley McReynolds. I'm an attorney up in the Twin Cities and I'm doing a little research on a probate file . . . looking for a missing heir." This bit of misdirection was designed to facilitate communication with an old-school general practitioner accustomed to such calls. "The woman

I'm looking for used to be an employee of one of your clients, The Plains Rialto Movie Palace, in Leavenworth.

Morgan Farrington cupped his hand over the receiver and coughed hoarsely. He then said, "Yes, I remember The Plains Rialto. It was owned by Vern Olinger and his wife. One of six theaters they ran from the early forties until sometime in the mid sixties, I think." He coughed again, this time a little more vigorously. He then started to recite a lot of information that Riley didn't want to know about.

Riley did not interrupt him for fear of giving offense. Small town practitioners of his age, with most of their clientele long since dead, were often starved for conversation. Receiving an inquiry that took Morgan Farrington back to his glory days was obviously welcome. So Riley listened patiently to a recitation on the economy of "motion picture houses" during the mid-twentieth century, including an endless account of how the drive-in theater craze of the early sixties had virtually wiped indoor theaters off the map.

When the old lawyer finally paused to take a breath, Riley broke in. "That's very interesting, Morg. You know a lot about that subject, and I'd love to hear more about it over lunch sometime when I'm in Lawrence."

Over on the couch Skeeter rolled her eyes.

Before Morgan Farrington could launch off on another tangent, Riley said, "What I need just now is information you might be able to give me on anyone who knew the Plains Rialto employees back in the mid-forties."

Farrington sighed thoughtfully. "Well, let me see, I think Vern had only a couple of employees at the Leavenworth theater. You know, a ticket taker and an usher who doubled as the popcorn dispenser. That location wasn't much hassle for him and his wife because Fort Leavenworth was a training facility for senior officers rather than enlisted men. Vern was at the theater a lot of the time, himself. Yeah, I had a friend back in those days who—"

Riley interrupted. "I'm wondering if there are any surviving relatives or business associates, or any records that might give me a lead on one of the employees who worked at the theater in 1945. Her name was Suzanne Sheridan."

The old lawyer wheezed and coughed. "I don't know that name," he said, "and I wouldn't have any idea where the records are. But Tracy Olinger, Vern's daughter, still lives in Leavenworth. Her name is . . . ah, let me think . . . Ridgeway . . . Tracy Ridgeway. She's a partially retired teacher and librarian, and I think she'd be in the phone book."

Riley scribbled Tracy Ridgeway's name on a legal pad and slid it across the desk to Skeeter. She went to her computer to retrieve the phone number while Riley satisfied himself that Morg Farrington didn't have any additional information that would be useful to him. He signed off by telling the old lawyer how much he looked forward to a long visit about his life in the law.

He then dialed up the number handed to him by Skeeter. After two rings, a young boy who sounded to be about Teddy's age answered the phone. When Riley asked for Tracy Ridgeway, he heard the phone drop on a table surface, followed by a boyish shout of "Grandma!"

The sound of young children could be heard in the background, together with a woman's voice saying, "Why don't you take that outside, Tyler, so it doesn't spill on the carpeting."

She then picked up the phone. "Hello."

Riley swallowed hard and looked over at Skeeter. "Hi, Mrs. Ridgeway, my name is Riley McReynolds and I'm calling from Minneapolis."

"Yes," she said stiffly, as though she suspected a telemarketer.

"I'm a lawyer working on a matter that concerns a woman who used to be employed by your parents back in the mid-forties in Leavenworth. Morg Farrington said it would be all right if I called you."

There was a short pause on the other end. She then said hesitatingly, "Well, I was only a young teenager in the mid-forties, and I knew only a few of the employees. I think we tossed out all the old records when Mom and Dad died. I checked with Mr. Farrington to be sure that was okay." Her tone was a little defensive, the way most people sound at the mention of lawyers and legal proceedings.

To counter that perception, Riley softened his approach further. "Oh, that's no problem at all, Mrs. Ridgeway. This is all informal; I don't need any records or any testimony or anything like that. I was just hoping you might remember a woman named Suzanne Sheridan."

Now there was a long silence, perhaps ten seconds in length. "I think I'll talk to Mr. Farrington and my husband before I say anything more. If you'll give me your number, Mr. Reynolds, one of us will get back to you."

"McReynolds," said Riley, as he flashed a look of disappointment at Skeeter. But he knew this was no time to press her, knew that if he came on too strong she would be likely to clam up permanently. And what's more, that long silence and the edge in her voice made him sure that she had something to say. "I understand, Mrs. Ridgeway, I want you to be completely comfortable. I'll just wait to hear from you and thanks in advance for taking the trouble to talk to me."

MORNING DAWNED CLEAR and sunny in Leavenworth, Kansas. A cab in search of a fare was parked at the curb as Riley emerged from the airport. On the drive to Tracy Ridgeway's house they made all the lights, arriving in fifteen minutes.

Tracy greeted him warmly at the door and installed him in the family den while she went for refreshments. Everything about this visit felt right. Tracy was a retired school teacher and a part-time librarian; that much he had been able to find out from publicly available sources. She looked much as he had pictured her—mid to late sixties, neatly arranged steel-

gray hair, engaging eyes that sparkled with a calm authority. She was taller than most women of her generation—about
five-foot-nine he estimated—and her skin, which seemed to
still show the small scars of early acne, was relatively
unwrinkled for a person her age.

The house itself was large but unpretentious. The back
den, which appeared to have been added after the home's
original construction, was nearly as large as the rest of the
downstairs combined. A bright floral arrangement sat at the
center of a large table with a rotating serving shelf used for
family meals. The smell of coffee and toast mingled with less
identifiable cooking odors. This was a good house—a good
home. He felt sure of it.

Through the broad plate-glass window of the den he
watched a group of young children dash about the yard, playing an impromptu game of tag. It was not hard to pick out
Tracy's grandchildren, for they bore the kind of unmistakable
family resemblance most easily recognized by a stranger.

Photographs of Tracy and her husband and children, and
some recent ones of her grandchildren—including the two
girls and one boy now playing in the back yard—adorned the
walls of the room. The largest and most formal picture had
been taken on her wedding day and showed Tracy and her
husband flanked by her parents. Riley leaned forward,
studying the images of Vern and Eliza Olinger, the Ma and
Pa theater owners who had employed Suzanne Sheridan during the mid-forties. They looked honest and ordinary, just as
he expected.

A refrigerator behind the wet bar off in one corner
hummed quietly, and the clock in the front hallway chimed
11:00 A.M. He was glad to have gotten Tracy's return call so
soon, and glad to be here in this house with a person whom
he was sure had once meant something to Bridey.

He looked up when Tracy entered the room with a tray of
iced tea and vanilla wafers, the clinking of the ice cubes signaling her arrival. She set the tray down on the coffee table

between them and gazed over at him. Her smile was filled with welcome, melting away any residual tension.

She elevated her glass slightly as she settled back into a deep couch adjacent to the table where he was seated. She then took a sip of iced tea and grinned at him. "I've checked you out, Riley McReynolds," she said winking, "and I know you're a good guy. I wouldn't have agreed to see you otherwise. Yours was an unusual call, I think you'll have to agree."

Riley nodded. "I know it must seem that way, so I was thrilled to hear back from you so soon," he said. "May I ask how you got comfortable with my coming to see you?"

"I'm a librarian," she replied, "and you'd be amazed at the kind of information we can dig up with just a name and general location. Beyond that, Morg Farrington checked you out with a lawyer friend of his in St. Paul. I won't say who, but he had very nice things to say."

Riley tilted his head to show that he was impressed with the speed and efficiency of her due diligence. A sensation washed over him that this was all meant to be happening in accordance with some plan. But he thought this probably wasn't a good time to get metaphysical. He moved over to the couch where Tracy was sitting and turned toward her. "Well, you know all about me and I can't wait to hear about you. I'm ecstatic to be sitting next to somebody who knew Suzanne Sheridan."

Her smile remained firmly in place, but her overall expression turned contemplative. She glanced out the window at the children playing in the yard before nodding her assent to the topic that had brought them together. "I was about the age of my granddaughter out there . . . about ten, when I first met Suzanne. She was the most charming person I'd ever known, and the most beautiful, too, with her dark hair and dazzling ice-blue eyes. She seemed to captivate everyone who crossed her path. It was remarkable to me then, and it's still remarkable to me now because she was not in the least bit aggressive. In fact, she was almost shy, or a least careful in

239

the way she interacted with people. But everyone was drawn to her, almost magnetically." Tracy beamed at the memory. "She was so dear to me during those few years. It was an awful time. I was awkward and homely and dismissed by most of the world. She was a savior, almost like a saint. She made me feel I was her special friend and that everything I said and did just swept her off her feet. I reasoned that if Suzanne loved me, then I must be lovable no matter how things seemed, no matter how other people treated me."

At that she blushed, color rising in her cheeks. She leaned down in embarrassment and swept her open hands across her face. "I'm sorry," she said, looking over at Riley, who was staring at her in rapt attention. He nodded his understanding.

She cleared her throat. "For all of that, I can't tell you what became of her. We all lived in Leavenworth then, and I only know that I was heartbroken when she suddenly left in late 1945. Outside my own parents, Suzanne was the only person in the world I truly loved. And even though I was crushed when she left, I somehow knew that it had to be that way, and that it didn't have anything to do with me. She was so afraid of something." Her smile was replaced by a look of resigned sadness. A tear formed in one eye and escaped its confines, running down her cheek. No attempt was made to brush it away.

"What was she afraid of?" asked Riley. "Did she say?"

Tracy shook her head. "I never knew, but there was always something in the background. She was very cautious, and I remember she hated having her picture taken. I thought she was just shy, but I now know it had to have been something more than that."

Riley asked, "Did she have any women friends in the area that you know of?"

"Almost nobody," she replied. "Every now and then she would eat lunch at the corner drugstore with one of the other girls who worked next door to the theater, but she deliberately didn't get close to anybody. That's one of the reasons I felt so special. She loved me when nobody else seemed to. We had funny, affectionate nicknames for each other, sometimes they were taken from movies we saw together. That was a defining period in my life. I think that if I hadn't had that kind of relationship with a grown-up woman, I would have sunk into the kind of adolescent despair that ruins so many kids."

Riley nodded sympathetically. "What caused her to leave town, do you—"

Tracy, who had been staring off into the distance, suddenly came alive with a recollection. "—I do remember, and this is in response to your last question, that she had a gentleman caller, as my mother referred to him. Which was kind of funny because I don't think he ever actually called on her when my mom was around." A smile tugged at the corners of her mouth. "To my mother, all unmarried men were divided between gentleman callers and brutes. Brutes only wanted to 'have their way' with girls."

They both giggled knowingly. Riley's mother had the same attitude and the same vocabulary. The poor guys who had dated his sister had to go through a cross-examination from Mama to convince her that they wouldn't soil her daughter's innocence. His sister was his pal, but Riley had never thought of her as being anything close to innocent. The boys' mothers should have been the ones cross-examining his sister.

Tracy continued. "Anyway, I knew Suzanne was in love because of the way she looked and acted. She had always been sweet, but in the summer of 1945, I think it was, she started doing her hair up all special, and bought new clothes. And even though she tried to keep it a secret, I knew that it was an officer from Fort Leavenworth because I would see her whispering with him when he'd come by the movie theater. I remember the look on his face—he was just on cloud nine when he looked at her. That guy had fallen hard. And so had she. She didn't seem afraid when she was with him, so

241

tall and handsome in his uniform. But I could never get her to tell me his name."

Riley could well imagine Bridey's continuing fear of the mob after what had happened to Pat Clebourne, and why she would be cautious and protective about any man she loved. "So what did this guy look like . . . this mystery Army officer?"

Tracy winked. "He was the most handsome man I ever laid eyes on . . . with the exception of Freddie, of course." She pointed to her husband's picture on the adjoining bookshelf.

Riley glanced over at the picture. Freddie seemed to have a face of great kindness, but handsome he was not.

Tracy looked back, all smiles. "I was only a geeky kid in 1945, too tall for my age, with a mouthful of metal braces and a face full of pimples. But I used to read all the movie magazines, and I knew what a good looking man was supposed to look like—"

Riley broke in with an information-gathering device he first learned as an apprentice investigator. "Tell me this, Tracy, which movie star did he look like?" Just about everyone looks at least a little like some famous person—an actor, a politician, an athlete—and that resemblance can serve as a shorthand identifier."

Tracy looked at the ceiling and bit her lower lip. "Oh, my God, that's right. He looked like Tyrone Power . . . but he was tall like Gregory Peck." She giggled shyly. "In retrospect, he was probably about six-foot-one, but that was pretty tall for those days, and he looked even taller when he was all decked out in his dress uniform."

Riley nodded. "Tyrone Power? So he had dark hair?"

"Yup, I even remember showing Suzanne a picture of Tyrone Power from one of my movie magazines and saying he looked like her mystery officer. She and I saw a movie together one night that starred Tyrone Power and Betty Grable. And I remember kidding her about the resemblance and how she was like the girl in the movie who Tyrone Power's character fell in love with. I even teased her by calling her Mrs. Tyrone Power."

Tracy beamed at the ancient memory, now so vividly recalled. "This is a lot of fun—I like it. It makes me feel good." She then leaned in his direction, a look of happy curiosity on her face. "Where did you come from, Riley McReynolds? Are you like one of those angels on TV, the ones who go around making people happy."

Riley smiled shyly and rearranged himself on the couch. He had never been called that before, but maybe he *was* an angel for Tracy. Maybe that's the way that sort of thing really unfolded in the grand plan. Maybe he was an unknowing instrument of some grace intended all along for a Kansas grandmother and an Omaha physician.

"I don't think my wife would classify me as an angel these days, and I *know* my mother wouldn't. They both think I've lost my mind, running around the country after a woman whose image appeared for a few seconds in an old documentary—the image of a girl who, if she were still alive, would be eighty-eight years old."

Tracy gave an understanding nod and reached across to pat his arm. "Well, you're an angel to me, and even if you are a little crazy, I'm half tempted to join you in your delusion. I would give anything to look into Suzanne's sparkling eyes again, the ones that reached out to a lost child in a way that no one else did." Tears gathered again in her eyes.

Riley shuffled his feet and finally looked over at her. "You'd be most welcome to join the search, but your friends and family would say you had entered into the delusional system of some crank from Minnesota undergoing a mid-life crisis. Don't psychologists have a name for that—when two people have a shared delusion?"

With the encyclopedic knowledge of librarians the world over, Tracy said, "*Folie á deux.*"

"Right," said Riley. "That's what they'd accuse you of. And when my loved ones heard that I ran off with a Kansas grandmother I'd just met, in search of an eighty-eight year old woman who is probably dead, I think my wife would petition for the appointment of a guardian. Our families would have us both in straightjackets."

As her grandchildren ran through the room, on way to the kitchen, Tracy and Riley laughed like a couple of school children who had just become best friends, talking about family and career and the empty spot they both seemed to have at the center of their hearts.

When it was time to head back to the airport, he walked slowly to the front door, not wanting to part company with this living reminder of Bridey, perhaps as close as he would ever get to the real thing.

At the doorway, they spontaneously embraced. Then, as he headed for the waiting cab, Tracy grabbed his arm and let out a small gasp. When he turned back, she looked at him wide-eyed. "I nearly forgot. When she vanished in 1945, I felt sure that she was pregnant, even though she never said so. I just had a sense that she was. And the handsome officer, the Tyrone Power look-alike, was long gone."

# 15

---

SARA HALL had left an urgent message when Riley was in Kansas, but when he called back upon his return in the late evening, a recording said that she was unavailable. In no mood to take up the matter of *Tanzdahl v. Tanzdahl* even a moment before it was absolutely necessary, he was relieved that she had not answered the phone.

Leaving the world of Bridey Reaves to reenter the world of Gus Tanzdahl was never fun, but the unpleasantness was especially acute on this occasion. He could actually feel the energy drain from his body.

The disembodied voice on Sara's machine slogged through a series of options from which the caller was invited to choose. Riley sat tapping his fingers as he awaited completion of the list. It was late evening, and the house had settled into a peaceful quiet, broken only by the soft hum of the kitchen refrigerator and the sound of an occasional passing car. A single light burned above the breakfast nook where he sat. Teddy had come downstairs when Riley first arrived home, complaining that he couldn't get to sleep no matter how hard he tried. Within minutes of curling up on the couch in the den, he was out cold. Teddy's sleep pattern differed from Lizzie's, who from the time of earliest childhood would get up from whatever she had been doing when fatigue overtook her and, without a word to anyone, disappear into her bedroom. It didn't matter if it was in the middle of dinner or while visiting with guests or during the stunning climax of a TV program. She would just soundlessly repair to her large, cozy bed, from which she would not arise for eight and one-half hours. Her dietary habits were equally unconventional. She'd go for two or three days eating almost nothing, and then, as though some life-saving mechanism deep in the reptilian brain was sounding an alarm, she would open the refrigerator and graze indiscriminately for what seemed like hours. In a moment of parental panic, Riley had taken her to the pediatrician for a nutritional evaluation but, like most of the doctors he consulted in connection with his own imaginary illnesses, this one only laughed.

He took a deep breath and exhaled slowly as Sara's phone options ran down. At the sound of the beep he started in: "Hi Sara, this is Riley. It's 11:40 P.M., and I just returned from—" He started to say that he had been in Kansas, but as the firm had no business in Kansas, he felt a small twinge of guilt for missing the Tanzdahl document review that day in favor of an activity that had nothing to do with the firm. "—ah, anyway, I just now freed up and wanted to return your call. I'll be available first thing in the morning for—"

At this, Sara, whose speaker phone broadcast messages in progress, picked up the phone. "Hi, Riley. I'm glad you called," she said hurriedly. Sara was always wired and, to his disappointment, she seemed hell-bent on doing business in spite of the lateness of the hour. He pulled a legal pad from his briefcase.

Without stopping to take a breath, she launched into the matter at hand. "I spent the last couple of days looking through the Tanzdahl Industries files that the paralegals pulled from our file room in response to Clint Tarrymore's subpoena." She paused. "We've got a hell of a lot of paper on that company."

A conversation at any time of night or day with Sara was a manic affair. Most of the partners who worked with her would eventually tell her to slow down, or even to keep quiet. But she meant well, and Riley could never bring himself to snap at her or any of the other associates. So, he just sat and waited for that inevitable moment when she had to take a breath. At the first sound of air being inhaled, he leaped into the opening. "I don't think there's much we can accomplish between now and 7:30 A.M. when we'll both be in the office anyway. So, why don't you just give me the highlights, Sara, and then we'll go over it more thoroughly tomorrow."

Sara paused, then chuckled. "Yes, of course. I didn't realize how late it was, and I've been so immersed in this crap all weekend that I've had trouble letting go."

Sara had been number six in her class at Columbia Law School and had the gray matter and guts to become an exceptionally good attorney. She also had the physical and psychological resources required of great trial lawyers, and perhaps more importantly, she seemed unencumbered by any sense of gender-based limitation. She was supremely indifferent to such issues—not to the discrimination encountered by almost all women in the legal profession at some point along the way, but to the idea that such attitudes could take her down personally.

"So let me just give you a thumb-nail sketch of the problem," she said. "As you instructed, I did a complete sweep of all our firm's files, cross-indexing to any numbers that would indicate a connection to Gus Tanzdahl or Tanzdahl Industries. I even threw the net wide enough to pick up closed and inactive projects, where the files were stored off-site because of their age. Given the long time span of the Tanzdahl relationship and the fact that we have represented Gus and his affiliates in virtually everything he's done, you can imagine the number of hits we got. Under the present coding system—the one we've had in place for the last eight years—this is a fairly easy task because the search engine can cross-reference against any of about twenty key words and number identifiers. Under the old system it was a little different, in that the initials of the client and the originating attorney would precede a series of digits that signified the year the file was opened and the department with primary responsibility for it."

A loud buzz was heard on Sara's end, signaling a high-priority call under her elaborate phone system. "Hang on just a minute, will ya, Riley?" she said. Without waiting for an answer, she put him on hold.

He sat rubbing the back of his neck, speculating on what kind of information might have turned up. He thought of hanging up and leaving the phone off the hook. Tomorrow morning would be time enough to get this stuff, but as he resolved to do just that, Sara got back on the phone. She offered neither an explanation nor an apology for the interruption.

She took a deep breath, signaling that the next string of words would probably be a long one. "So anyway, Riley, this approach ferreted out just about every file, dead or alive, that had a Tanzdahl fingerprint on it. Most of the files we looked at were inconsequential and I was quickly able to eliminate them. Then there's another category of file that is marginal, but I don't think they'd be of much interest to Clint Tarrymore. But we might want to throw them at him anyway, just to tire him out."

Riley sat listening, massaging his aching temples, wondering if she was ever going to say something that justified this late-night confab. "Where are we going with this, Sara?" he finally asked.

"Just hang on, let me get to the big problem." She cleared her throat and paused briefly.

Riley's mind was sluggish and overstuffed with facts relating to Bridey Reaves, but not so much so that he didn't suspect, even before Sara finished, that she had found documents that were embarrassing or even incriminating to Gus—documents that might have to be turned over to Clint Tarrymore under his subpoena.

Sara started back in. "Well, I'll tell you where we're going, Riley. One item that turned up really caught my eye. The filing system, in all its hyper-efficient sensitivity, spit out Stenham Investment Company, a file that went back nearly nine years and doesn't seem, on its face, to have anything to do with Gus Tanzdahl or Tanzdahl Industries. But Ladge Wilkaster had coded it under the old system with his own initials, followed by the initials of the client, Brad Stenham, and a 'GT' in parenthesis preceding the numerical file digits."

Riley recognized that coding system as the one briefly in use in the late eighties. He had seen other files with that mechanism come across his desk. The "GT" designation indicated that Gus Tanzdahl had made the referral. Brad Stenham, who now had a number of other files open with the firm, was the actual client of record, but Ladge placed the 'GT' designation in the coding to insure that he would get personal billing credit for fees generated by the account as a Tanzdahl referral. That was innocuous enough; Gus had doubtless made many such referrals over the years.

"That designation simply indicates that Tanzdahl was the referral source," said Riley. "Under the old system, Ladge was always careful to tack on the initials of his client in order to get credit at the time the bill went out."

"Right," said Sara, "And there were other files like that . . . maybe fifteen or twenty, but I was easily able to determine that those were arm's length referrals that Gus had no personal stake in. This Stenham file was the only one that had to be looked at carefully, because it was a corporation set up to buy and sell stock in a fairly small portfolio of companies, most of them headquartered in this area. Because the corporate department handled Stenham's SEC regulatory compliance, including its insider trading filings, the file is packed with statements showing its various stock holdings over the years."

Over the phone Riley could hear the shuffling of papers. He visualized Sara's efficient and inelegant fingers, with chewed-down fingernails, whipping through the inventories attached to the reporting documents. As he listened, he could also feel the beginnings of a churning deep in his gut. He feared this conversation was about to take an ugly turn.

Having found the page she was looking for, Sara said, "I've got the inventory and trading schedules for the first five years of the company's existence sitting right in front of me, lined up side by side for comparison." There was a brief moment of silence on both ends. "If you're not currently sitting down, Riley, now would be a good time to do so, because there is a perfect—and I mean perfect—overlap between the securities owned and traded by this little company and the list of companies in which Gus Tanzdahl is a reporting insider under Section 16 of the Securities and Exchange Act. And—surprise, surprise—the common stock of Tanzdahl Industries accounts for the largest single block of stock held by Stenham Investment."

She paused to let this information sink in. "And let me tell you something else, these guys have made a bloody fortune—in up markets and down markets, and no matter what kinds of securities they were trading: stocks, bonds, options, warrants, puts, calls, you name it. Brad Stenham seems to have a real knack for reading the market in the securities of these particular companies."

Riley was already a half-step ahead of Sara. The markers of an insider-trading conspiracy were plainly in evidence here and, at the very least, as lead counsel in the case he would have no choice but to conduct an internal inquiry to determine whether any of these trading profits had gone to Gus. If it turned out that they did, a good part of the file would have to be turned over to Clint Tarrymore.

"And I'll tell you another small fact that adds to the smell," she said, "two years into the life of the file it got re-coded, and the former reference to Gus Tanzdahl—the "GT" initials—were removed. Someone even removed the file initiation sheet that was in use at that time, which was a violation of the firm policy manual. So, in effect, what would have been the fourth volume of this file has a whole new numbering system, and though the file is still open, that last volume is nowhere to be found. I think whoever worked the switch-over simply neglected to remove the first three file jackets from the shelves. That fact, combined with the hair-trigger sensitivity of our new software, accounts for this damn thing popping up in the document search as we reply to Tarrymore's subpoena."

She probably had it right, Riley thought. Except for a moment of carelessness during the file conversion process, there would be no way that the Stenham Investment Company file would have ever come to their attention. Information on investment companies of this type was normally protected by an internal firewall that prevented firm employees not directly involved with the client's files from any access. Were it not for Tanzdahl fingerprints left in the initial coding system, there was no way, formal or informal, that he and Sara would have come into possession of this information in a routine document search.

The headache that had been building in the back of his neck now moved over the top of his head and concentrated itself in a throbbing mass just above his right ear. Added to his concern over what looked to be an insider-trading scheme, was the likelihood that Ladge Wilkaster, the lawyer who opened the original file and benefited so richly from the fees generated by it over the years, had attempted to alter the original coding at a later date.

Through his fatigue Riley summoned a small hope that it was innocent incompetence rather than venality that accounted for Ladge's actions.

He stuffed his notes into his briefcase, and said, "In the morning, pull all the insider trading reports for Tanzdahl

Industries from the time it went public. Also check to see if our corporate department prepares Gus's insider filings for the other companies where he is or was a director. That may take you back to the period before Tanzdahl Industries went public." Riley scanned the ceiling as he considered other sources that should be consulted. "And have an associate compile a list of executive officers and directors for each of the other companies in which Stenham Investment Company has taken a substantial position. We may find some additional overlaps."

"What about the tax implications of all this, if it's what it seems to be?" asked Sara.

"We've already assembled Gus's tax returns for the last five years—as called for in the subpoena—so we can see if the gains and losses reported to the IRS track his insider trading filings or might possibly report gains from Stenham Investment Company. That's not likely to be the case, but you never know. The problem with this kind of scheme is that, completely apart from the securities violations, you automatically end up committing tax fraud unless you're dumb enough to incriminate yourself in your tax return."

"Yup," said Sara as she furiously took notes.

"This is a damn mess. I'd like to think that it's just a series of coincidences, but I've been a lawyer long enough to know that this much smoke means there's some fire."

Sara said, "Got it." She then started to move on to the child custody issues.

Riley stopped writing and set down his pen. "I've heard enough for now, Sara. If you lay any more bad news on me, I won't sleep a wink tonight."

"Right," said Sara. "You go to bed and get some sleep. I'm going to go on-line for a bit and check on some cases on privilege to see how we might creatively interpret the language of the subpoena."

Riley trudged upstairs, shedding his clothes along the way. He then collapsed in bed, where for the remainder of the night he didn't sleep a wink.

\* \* \*

MOST OF THE WAKING HOURS between one and six A.M. had been given over to pointless rumination about the problems turned up by Sara Hall and the political fallout likely to result from the decisions he would have to make. And, of course, he was concerned about how the matter of Ellen Tanzdahl's recent venereal disease would further complicate the custody issue.

After hours of tossing and turning, at 4:35 A.M. he picked up the headphones of his bedside Walkman and casually surfed the radio waves. He stopped briefly at a bible-thumping evangelist and then at a call-in talk show where a nocturnal caller thought he was turning into a werewolf. Ultimately, he settled into an oldies music station, where he was treated once again to the brave and silken voice of Vera Lynn, pouring out the sweet and hopeful lyrics of "The White Cliffs of Dover." In this twilight state, with Tuffy curled up at his feet and Betsy's warm body touching his, the somehow familiar voice flowed like honey into the deepest recesses of his mind. It amazed him that a small cluster of notes, arranged in a certain sequence, had the power to transport a troubled mind into an almost womb-like serenity The anxieties of the preceding hours vanished and the world was once again sweet. Lights cast by the occasional car passing on the street below, eerie and portentous just moments before, now danced happily on the walls of the bedroom.

He thought of waking Betsy to share the moment, but wisely decided against it. She had lost patience with his fantasy life and wouldn't wish to be stirred from a peaceful slumber to hear from Vera Lynn.

So he was alone in this other world—the world he had created as a refuge from the harsh realities of the present. It was a world filled with haunting sweetness, and it seemed to come over him at precisely those moments when his deeply felt values about honesty and motherhood were most under assault from the Tanzdahl mess. It was a world peopled by its own cast of characters. As Anastasia had in another time, Bridey was now playing the lead.

THE PLUSH CARPETING and broad corridors of Cosgrove & Levi gave no hint of the storm that was brewing for its largest client as Riley made his way to the office the next morning.

He fell into his chair and reached for the Tanzdahl file. Moments later Sara Hall appeared at the door, simultaneously knocking and entering. She was wearing a plain black suit with light gray pinstripes, and had pulled her dark auburn hair back into a tight bun. A pair of over-sized horn-rimmed glasses sat engagingly on the bridge of her ski-jump nose. Sara was ready for business.

Dropping an armful of files on to his desk, she said, "Okay. Here are some cases I pulled on attorney-client privilege as it relates to protecting the incriminating evidence turned up in the Stenham Investment file." No doubt she had been chugging coffee and reading cases even as he was floating over the White Cliffs of Dover.

Riley looked up at her and, skipping social formalities, got right down to cases. "So let's assume that Tanzdahl and Stenham and Ladge Wilkaster stretch the truth and tell us that this stuff you found isn't the inside trading it seems to be, and that it is subject to the attorney-client privilege? What problem do we then have?"

Sara wrinkled her face as though contemplating a law school hypothetical. "Well, if opposing counsel is sharp enough, after we identify the documents on which we are claiming privilege, he will demand a review of them by the judge. And that . . . uhh, and that could possibly open us— the firm—to the charge of a bad faith assertion of privilege, which would in turn make us look like a co-conspirator or an aider and abettor in an ongoing crime." She tapped her pencil a few times on the desk. "So the only practical way to protect the client would be to destroy the documents and make no mention of them in our response to Tarrymore—which Gus would probably be happy to do, but you and I wouldn't."

Riley nodded. "That's right. And then, apart from what Clint Tarrymore might do, you and I are officers of the court and may have an independent obligation under the rules to make full disclosure to Judge Hammergren."

She nodded. "So what do we do now?"

"We set up a meeting with Ladge Wilkaster to find out if there's a theory we can legitimately invoke to avoid calling anyone's attention to this information. If there is not, the case will be lost, Gus Tanzdahl will be held in contempt, and that will be the least of his problems. He may be looking at tax and securities violations, some of them criminal. And, I don't need to tell you, this firm will lose close to half of its revenues when and if Gus pulls his business." He leaned forward, elbows on the desk; and looked at her. "Other than that, we've got no problems."

Sara laid out the file materials on the Stenham Investment Company, which appeared to be a rather artless front for Gus Tanzdahl's insider trading. Regrettably, but not surprisingly, those documents yielded no plausible explanation for the strange coincidences Sara had described over the phone. The government filings appeared on their surface to be in order but had about them the kind of pristine consistency rarely found in good-faith filings—the kind of perfection that prosecutors look for. It was those documents that would be used to prove securities and tax fraud if Gus Tanzdahl was the real party in interest to the trades conducted by Stenham Investment.

Riley instructed Sara to prepare a flow chart showing the timing of trades in the stock of Tanzdahl and the other companies for which Gus served as a director, and to identify the person in the Cosgrove & Levi corporate department who handled the preparation and filing of Stenham's regulatory reports. It was the kind of information that every attorney dreaded finding out about a client, but there was no choice but to track it down.

Before she left his office, Sara handed Riley a draft of the memorandum she had prepared for submission to the child custody evaluator assigned to the Tanzdahl case. When she was gone, he settled into his chair and read, with disgust, the spin being placed on Ellen's misadventures as a rebellious teenager. One would think she had been a Manson Family member.

The medical report referring to her recent treatment for gonorrhea had been attached as an exhibit.

Sara was good at this kind of dirty work. But he couldn't fault her too much; she was, after all, doing her job. Still, it was sickening. He took out his pen and scratched across the cover: "Hold this—do not submit until approved by RMcR."

AFTER DETERMINING that Harry Wilford was at his desk, Sara and Riley walked unannounced into his small, windowless office in the bowels of the corporate department. Despite being with the firm for six years—and, therefore, technically eligible for a junior partnership—Harry Wilford's awkwardness and geeky manner had inoculated him against any advancement with the firm. He had been consigned to the status of "permanent associate." Harry possessed a first-rate mind for the kinds of matters found in a law school curriculum and was of great usefulness when an obscure citation was needed to bolster an argument in a difficult case, but when it came to firm politics, people like Harry Wilford, who once populated the upper reaches of the law school grade curves, were virtually helpless in any practical sense. Thus, Harry had been permanently assigned to "securities compliance," an activity so relentlessly tedious, so mind-numbingly repetitive, that only the firm's most boring members could stand to be associated with it.

Down in his basement lair, Harry was starved for human contact and, therefore, thrilled to receive a visit from a senior partner and the iron lady of the family law department. Trying to hide his surprise, he jumped from his seat and cleared away stacks of files from the couch and two chairs crowded into his small cell. Riley and Sara smiled as they stood waiting to take their seats, embarrassed by the enthusiasm with which they were being received.

"What's up, guys?" said Harry as he straightened his tie and took a seat on a small couch against the wall. Before Riley could open his mouth, Sara started in. "We assume, Wilford, that you handle the corporate housekeeping and regulatory filings for Stenham Investment Company. Is that right?"

Harry seemed disappointed by Sara's directness. And he tensed a little at being quizzed this way.

Riley shot her a look. Sara fell silent.

He then smiled at Harry and said, "We're working on assembling some discovery materials in kind of a sensitive divorce case—I can't tell you which one—and we may have to produce regulatory reporting materials that relate to our client. I want to be sure that we don't miss anything. I had that happen about a month ago and caught holy hell from the U.S. Attorney about not being fully responsive to his subpoena. You know how that can be?"

Harry felt a small rush of pride at being a player in such an important matter. "Oh, sure. I know exactly what you mean," he said as if he had been in that same position many times himself.

Sara sat quietly.

Riley continued. "Maybe you could educate us a little on your setup down here so we can figure out what, if anything, we need."

Harry cleared his throat. "Oh, you bet, Riley, I'd be happy to give you a rundown on what we do." He now shifted into the voice of a law review editor trying to impress his faculty advisor. As he described the functions and procedures of the compliance department, his sentences became larded with the nomenclature of legal academia, including uncountable "notwithstandings," "whereupons," and "heretofores." But allowing him to prattle on for a while was a small price to pay for his cooperation.

According to Harry the compliance department lawyers never performed independent inquiries concerning the accuracy of factual information given to them by the insiders. Nevertheless, the transfer of that information into the form prescribed by the SEC and NASD could require considerable skill and judgment. And it had to be done right because the insiders whose reporting they handled were big-shot executives, the firm's best clients.

Riley was developing an admiration for the intelligence of this eager, if somewhat pedantic, young man. With a quizzical expression, he asked Harry if he could illustrate the filing procedures by reference to the Stenham Investment Company account.

Ladge Wilkaster had issued a standing order that information relating to Tanzdahl Industries or Gus Tanzdahl was to be made available only on a strictly "need to know" basis, with his personal approval, but this was a senior partner asking so Harry assumed all political clearances had been obtained.

Harry left his seat and beckoned for Riley and Sara to follow him to the monitor on his credenza. Using a code known only to Ladge Wilkaster and the three lawyers in the compliance department, he opened the Stenham file and brought up the schedules listing stock transactions for the previous year. The details appearing on the screen were more extensive and more carefully footnoted than the summaries seen by Sara.

As they stood looking over Harry's shoulder, Riley shook his head as his eyes passed down the long columns. Sara was furiously taking notes. Trades for the reporting period still underway were top-heavy with the common stock of companies in which Gus Tanzdahl was an insider, including Tanzdahl Industries itself. A hefty profit was shown for virtually every trade. The only losses appearing on the inventories were small trades, deceptively plentiful in number but inconsequential in their financial impact. This pattern, almost always found in sophisticated insider trading schemes, was designed to normalize the appearance of the schedules and avoid the detection mechanisms of the government computers.

Riley asked Harry for a printout of the reporting schedules for the last year. Harry nodded and struck a series of keys, causing the adjacent printer to come awake. Harry looked up proudly and said, "Stenham Investment's sole shareholder is best buddies with Gus Tanzdahl, ya know?"

Riley nodded. "Does Tanzdahl have anything to do with this file?"

This was a big day for Harry; he not only got to hang out with these two high-profile litigators, he also got to drop the name of the firm's most important client, Gus Tanzdahl. "Oh, not in any formal sense," he said with barely concealed pride, "but he and Brad Stenham often come in together before a golf game or when Gus is down seeing George Stonequist on another matter. Tanzdahl sometimes sits with Stenham in the waiting room across the hall when Stenham is signing off on the list of trades."

Riley started to ask a follow-up question when Harry reached into a drawer and pulled out a file containing the Stenham inventories filed for the last three years. The file jacket also contained the original drafts, sometimes typed and sometimes handwritten, submitted to Harry by Brad Stenham for a given reporting period. Harry paged hurriedly through the drafts, pulling one for the current month and handing it to Riley.

Riley ran his fingers down the left-hand margin, noting a series of scribblings made in the small, distinctive handwriting of Gus Tanzdahl. He instantly realized that he was looking at the kind of small act of carelessness upon which large criminal cases so often turn—the scrap of paper destined for the shredder but somehow mindlessly left in the work papers of a criminal enterprise. His mind was spinning with the legal and ethical implications to Cosgrove & Levi of this discovery, to say nothing of his obligation to produce this document in the divorce case. He slipped the original in his file and said goodbye to Harry Wilford.


AT THE TOP of the pile in Riley's in-basket when he returned to his office was a Manila envelope delivered while he was down at the compliance department with Harry Wilford. It contained no return address or other indication of the sender's identity. He unsealed the flap and extracted a two-inch pile of documents which he immediately recognized as photocopies of medical records. Here we go again, he thought.

The cover sheet displayed a letterhead: "Oshlund Internal Medicine Clinic," and several lines down the patient's identity: "Gustav Tanzdahl, DOB 1/16/47." Below that was a chart entry reading: "Penicillin administered for non-specific urethritis."

Next to that entry was a handwritten notation: "11-B7." On an attached Post-it Note were scribbled the words: "See last page."

Riley flipped to the last page, which contained no letterhead and no typed entries, but had in its right-hand corner the designation "11-B7 (Confidential - File Separately)," and below that, circled in red, were handwritten notes reading: "Gonorrheal infection confirmed through gram-stained smear of urethral discharge. Patient reports sexual contact with wife, who he has undoubtedly infected. Spouse's physician, a social friend of patient, has been notified of likely transmission and instructed to summon wife to office for penicillin injection on pretext of pap smear or flu shot."

Next to that entry was another Post-it Note from the anonymous sender, this one reading: "The son-of-a-bitch gave her the clap—and she didn't even know she had it!!"

Riley verified that the date of the treatment notes for Gus preceded the entry in Ellen's medical records by several days. He set the documents down and stared out the window. Now that's hubris, he thought. Gus goes to a cooperative physician, not his regular one, who treats him for an STD and then makes a clandestine contact with Ellen's physician, who on a pretext injects her with penicillin to kill off the microbes that would otherwise ravage her reproductive organs long before any noticeable symptoms appeared.

Riley shook his head in disgust at the venality of Gus challenging his wife's fitness on the basis of a venereal disease that he, himself, had given her.

When Sara had recently let Clint Tarrymore know of her intention to subpoena Ellen's medical records because of possible evidence of a recent venereal disease, Clint reacted by subpoenaing Gus's records. Those records, however, were from his regular medical clinic and did not include the Oshlund Clinic. But they soon would. Riley would have to send them along with the medical records kept by Gus's regular physician.

This whole thing was too ugly for words. Whoever got Gus's secretly coded medical files and sent them to Riley had done so by illegal means, perhaps even burglary. The universe of Gus's enemies—people who hated him enough to go to all this trouble—would make for a very long list of suspects. But Riley's suspicions immediately fell upon Chasbo Peytabohm, who was more than capable of getting even the most carefully maintained medical records. Ellen Tanzdahl's mother, Rennee Murseth, worked in the medical benefits department of Chasbo's company and doubtless had a few tricks of her own to get bootleg medical records. They might well have put all this together when Ellen told her mother of the STD charge Gus was making against her.

It didn't much matter, though, how all this came about. Riley now knew the real facts behind Ellen's venereal disease and, consequently, he could not and would not be a party to suppressing them. In fact, it would secretly be a pleasure to pass Gus's "full" medical records along to Clint Tarrymore.

At six-fifteen p.m. an agitated Ladge Wilkaster took a left into the hallway leading to the litigation department and, without acknowledging Skeeter, barged through Riley's half-open door. He threw his briefcase on the couch and stood over Riley's desk.

Riley looked up from the Stenham schedule he was examining. "Well . . . hello, Ladge, what's got you all worked up?"

"As if you don't know!" shouted Wilkaster, his voice shaking with rage, his face a mask of anger and panic. "Who gave you the authority to go scrounging around in the compliance department?"

It seemed that Harry Wilford had developed seller's remorse about his cooperation with Riley and Sara. He had, no doubt, reported their meeting to his supervising partner, who in turn reported it to Ladge.

Through the open door of his office, Riley nodded to Skeeter. She had been packing up to leave for the day, but when she heard Ladge's opening salvo, she sat back in her chair. In the wordless vocabulary developed between them over the years, his nod signaled that she would be an offstage witness to the conversation that was about to take place. She leaned back and commenced filing her nails, pen and notepad at the ready.

Riley looked across the desk at Ladge, all pink and puffy with agitation. "I'm not sure what you're so exercised about, Ladge. Discovery requests in the Tanzdahl divorce case are being handled in a normal fashion, though I admit that what we're coming up with here is a little dicier." He raised his eyebrows and cocked his head. "I believe we have you to thank for the hypersensitive tracking system that coughed up a rather peculiar trail of evidence, including the Stenham Investment Company trading schedules."

Ladge took a seat in front of the desk, pulled a silk hanky from the breast pocket of his suit jacket and wiped perspiration from his forehead. He gripped the arm of his chair and shook his head back and forth. Over the years Riley had seen hundreds of self-possessed men suddenly stricken with panic when all their careful planning fell apart. If he needed any confirmation of Gus Tanzdahl's tawdry and illegal stock manipulations, this seemed to be it. Ladge's starchy white collar was withering under the flow of perspiration now cascading down his face and neck. He looked like Richard Nixon during his farewell speech to the White House staff.

Loosening his collar, Ladge cleared his throat and looked over at Riley. "We have a firewall established between the compliance unit and every other department of the firm; it's laid out clearly in the policy manual. You have no business with that information, and I'm instructing you to return the originals and any copies to Harry Wilford and make no mention of your silly suspicions of insider trading to anyone—especially not anyone connected with Ellen Tanzdahl."

Riley widened his eyes. "I didn't say anything about insider trading, Ladge."

Ladge broke eye contact and rose from his seat. He walked to the window, where he glared through the glass, his back turned to Riley. "I don't have to be a rocket scientist to know what you're up to here. And I'm telling you you're way off base. Gus Tanzdahl and Brad Stenham are close personal friends, so it's perfectly natural that Gus would have referred him to us to set up his investment company. And Stenham purchasing stock in some of the companies that Gus Tanzdahl is involved with only means that Brad had confidence that Gus was associated with winners. All kinds of people do that, and it's completely legal."

Riley stole a glance at Skeeter, whose head was tilted backward, her eyes rolling to the ceiling. He then looked back at Ladge. "I hope you're right, but if Stenham has so much confidence in Gus's winning ways, why are forty percent of the profits generated from short sales, where Stenham is betting that the stocks will go down in price?"

Unlocking the top drawer of his credenza, Riley pulled out a copy of the schedule bearing Gus Tanzdahl's handwritten notes in the margins. He walked over to where Ladge was standing and handed him the copy. "And how would we explain this?"

Ladge's hand shook as though he was reading the obituary of a close friend. He scanned the entries, including the margin notes, and then took a step back and dropped onto the couch. The schedule hung limply from his hand.

Riley actually felt sorry for him, even felt a little sorry for Gus Tanzdahl who, not satisfied with the fifty million dollars he had already accumulated, felt the need to make a few million more through a little stock manipulation. Riley hoped that Ladge Wilkaster was not so deep into this thing that his career—perhaps even his freedom—would be at risk. Ladge was more pathetic than evil, and in many ways he had been an able managing partner for Cosgrove & Levi, a firm with a spotless reputation.

Ladge put his hands on his knees and forced himself up from the couch with a groan. He seemed a much older man than the one who had burst through the door minutes earlier. He looked over at Riley. "Isn't all this stuff privileged? Aren't we bound to withhold it in discovery? Isn't it really non-existent for purposes of this case?"

Riley shook his head. "Sara's doing some research, but if this is what it seems to be, it's part and parcel of an ongoing criminal enterprise and, as such, under the crime-fraud exception, it loses any privileged status. And even if the schedules were somehow privileged, there's no way we could exclude the company's stock gains from Gus's net worth statement, which we're required to give to Ellen Tanzdahl's lawyer. To withhold it would be a fraud upon the court."

Riley returned to his chair and stared down at his folded hands. "I just hope like hell that you didn't know what was going on here, Ladge. Don't say anything about that now, but know that when the firm's ethics committee sorts through all the evidence, you're going to have some explaining to do."

"Me!" said Wilkaster, suddenly reenergized. "Are you crazy!" He glowered at Riley. In that instant, whatever bond had existed between these two men was dissolved. Ladge's eyes told Riley that he was now the enemy, pure and simple. There would be formal politeness, of course, but never again would they be comrades.

Riley stood up and moved toward his distressed colleague. But Ladge took a step backward. He raised the palm of one hand in Riley's direction, while with the other he stuffed the moist hanky back in his suit pocket. After a brief interval, in which he stared at Riley with an angry, pinched expression, he straightened to his full height and walked from the room.

# 16

IN THE TEN DAYS following Riley's trip to Leavenworth, Tracy Ridgeway had made several attempts, through the resources available to her as a librarian, to pick up the trail of Suzanne Sheridan—a trail that had been cold for roughly a half-century. In a way that Riley wouldn't have expected, this grandmother from Kansas had fallen back under Bridey's spell, joining in the search with a passion to equal his own.

Because Tracy wanted desperately to believe that Suzanne Sheridan, the fairy godmother of her adolescence, had gone on to a life of happiness and security, she suppressed her own doubts about anybody ever being able to solve the mystery. But her skepticism did little to lessen the subjective joy she felt at being back in touch with the memory of the adored friend of her youth. And she had the advantage of not having to care about Dion O'Banion or even Clare Turlough, for Suzanne Sheridan, whatever her past might have been, was as real to her as her own children. She and Riley were now united in a common mission.

So, Tracy had set about tapping into arcane databases with the surgical skill of a career researcher. Riley was doing the same thing—and with the same disappointing results. There had been no payments into the social security system since Suzanne Sheridan's last check from The Plains Rialto Movie Palace, and the social security and state death indexes recorded no deaths in the intervening years for a woman named Suzanne Sheridan with a birthday falling within the indicated range. Moreover, no birth certificate was on file anywhere in the country for a child born to a Suzanne Sheridan of that age and physical description during the period Tracy believed Suzanne-Bridey to have been pregnant.

At a personal expense running into thousands of dollars, Riley had commissioned the assemblage of a private index of death records for white females born, not just in Nebraska or Kansas, but anywhere in the United States between 1906 and 1910, who had died before their sixth birthday. In the process he enriched a number of private genealogists, cemetery associations, private investigators, and even a few county clerks. Absent any tangible clues, that kind of massive canvassing was about the only avenue left to him.

If Bridey had once again chosen the method that she and Pat Clebourne used when she fled Omaha, the new name she assumed from another dead child would appear somewhere in the vast population of that self-styled database, either by way of a second death certificate, if she had later died, or some evidence that the identity was being used by a live person—evidence like an active driver's license, social security account, real estate title, or even something as routine as a library card.

He cross-checked the new list against death records for white females since 1945 (the year of her flight from Leavenworth), for any named person who had, in effect, died twice—once before age six and again as an adult of at least thirty-seven, Bridey's age when she left Leavenworth. Interestingly, within that database there were several such "twice deads," but, by reference to immutable physical characteristics, none could have been Bridey. But like Bridey, those women—whoever they really were, whatever they had been running from so long ago—had also been identity changers. Only his obsession with Bridey prevented him from heading off in search of their stories. Each was a "vanished female mystery" of her own.

If Bridey did, in fact, appropriate to herself the identity of another dead child, Riley's research meant that she was still alive in 1996 and that her assumed name, whatever it might be, resided somewhere in the broader database he had painstakingly compiled.

But there was no evidence that she had again taken that approach. After all, if the Mob had penetrated the Suzanne Sheridan identity, why—she must have reasoned—couldn't they do it again with another identity created by that same method.

It was more than possible, therefore, that she had used some other scheme, such as simply taking the identity of another living woman. But that was risky business even then, and somehow not in character for the cautious Bridey. It was also possible that she had obtained forged identity papers and managed to avoid detection over the years by steering clear of the regular economy and its social security card requirements. Both of those approaches, however, were strictly short-term; unlike the deceased-child method, they did not provide a safe harbor for very long.

Another method—one that carried only temporary risk— was to pull a made-up name right out of the air and then quickly get married. That would have had her taking her husband's surname shortly after assuption of the fake name. And though it would require a forged birth certificate to get the marriage license, the period of exposure would have been miniscule. Without the benefit of modern computerized databases, unheard of in the 1940s, it would have been virtually impossible for her pursuers to track her to the lawful identity made possible by her marriage. Likewise, even with the technology Riley had available to him, there would be no way, short of lucky guesswork, to find the married name she might have taken.

It would have helped if Tracy had been able to provide more information about the handsome young officer who had won Suzanne Sheridan's heart in 1945, the one who looked like Tyrone Power. Though the adolescent Tracy Ridgeway had been of the impression that the officer had somehow deserted Suzanne, leaving her pregnant and uncared for, there was no actual evidence of that. In fact, if the Mob had again picked up her trail, to avoid another Pat Clebourne tragedy she might well have left him out of concern for his safety. It was also possible that he had rejoined her in later years, perhaps after the completion of military service. For all those reasons, if the handsome officer's name could be found there would at least be a concrete lead to follow.

But, alas, not even Tracy Ridgeway—research librarian, wife of a retired army officer, and the only known living person to have laid eyes on the handsome stranger—could find anything about him. That he had looked like Tyrone Power wasn't much help; every hotshot with dark hair in 1945 thought he looked like Tyrone Power, including his father and uncles and the many officers who passed through Fort Leavenworth.

Tracy had taken out ads in various veterans and American Legion on-line publications asking for feedback from former soldiers who had attended officer training at Fort Leavenworth from 1940 to 1945, but had not received a single response. That trail was dead.

Having struck out on the dead-infant database, Riley concluded that the most likely course was that Bridey had gotten married and taken her husband's surname, thus blending seamlessly into the world of real people with legitimate identities. If she followed that course, she could have temporarily taken any name that struck her fancy and lived off the O'Banion money while shopping for a suitable marriage partner. It seemed odd, though, that she would have worked as a ticket-taker at The Plains Rialto if she possessed the small fortune O'Banion was said to have settled upon her just before he was killed.

There was also the distant possibility that she had taken the veil, joined a convent like the one she lived in as a teenager. Maybe she even hopped a boat for China or, more likely, for Ireland or some other spot in the British Isles where friends or relatives might have stashed her away. But if those options had been available to her, she almost surely would have utilized one of them much earlier than 1937, in Omaha, let alone 1945 in Leavenworth.

The most disagreeable possibility—and a very real one at that—was that the Mob had caught up with her, and that she was long-since buried as a Jane Doe in some paupers' cemetery. Even if she had avoided her pursuers again in 1945, however, the odds were that she would have passed away of natural causes by now. Not many people of her generation lived beyond age eighty-five, and she would now be eighty-eight.

The possibilities were endless. And exhausting. He sat slumped in his den, deflated by the long odds. Though this seemed the end of the road, he felt a small measure of pride at having gotten this far. Betsy and his mother notwithstanding, it had not been a waste of time. It had been an interesting and therapeutic diversion during a period of stress. In that sense, it was a journey into the deepest reaches of his own spirit, a trip that everyone should be lucky enough to take.

Lizzie poked her head in the door, breaking his meditation. "The phone's for you, Dad, but don't stay on too long. I'm expecting a call from Justin. "

*Justin? Who the hell is Justin?* he wondered. Lizzie ran through boys with such speed that Riley could hardly keep pace. Just as he would grow fond of one of them, she would decide that his voice was too high or his complexion too spotty or that he lacked ambition. Being beautiful widened a girl's options.

Riley picked up the phone, mindful that he might be displacing a call from Justin, whoever the hell he was. "Hello, this is Riley McReynolds."

"Riley, this is Tracy," came the voice of his favorite librarian. "I was sitting in the kitchen yesterday watching my grandchildren and straining to recall more about my time with Suzanne, when I was struck by a memory."

Riley sat up in his chair and reached for a pen and paper. One of the nice things about Tracy was that she skipped small talk. "What is it, Tracy? Tell me about this lightning bolt."

Her tone was enthusiastic but at the same time reserved, as though she was worried about creating a false hope. "Well, remember the gentleman caller, the young officer I told you about, the one who looked like Tyrone Power?"

"Of course, I remember. Tell me you figured out who he was?"

"No, it's not quite that simple. But I think I have a lead that's at least worth running down."

"Okay, let's hear it."

Tracy shuffled papers on the other end. Sounds of her grandchildren could be heard in the distance. "Okay, remember I told you the gentleman caller looked like Tyrone Power. Well, I now remember that when I couldn't get his real name from Suzanne, I teased her that her name would one day be Mrs. Tyrone Power?"

"Okay. So?"

Static erupted from her portable phone as Tracy moved to the back door to let her dog in the house. She quickly made her way back inside. "Can you hear me now?" she asked.

"Yes, I can hear you, but barely. Could you switch to a hard-wired phone?"

A click registered, and her voice became clear. "Okay, here goes. So, I got thinking that when Suzanne chose a new name after fleeing Leavenworth, that maybe she would have chosen "Power" or "Tyrone" or something that had a connec-

271

tion in her mind to her absent lover. There was nothing promising in the Social Security Index, so I went to the marriage databases we compiled and checked out any brides named Power or Powers in the ten years following 1945. In the Midwest there were lots of brides with the name 'Powers,' but only a few with the maiden name Power, singular. I checked them out and found that none could have been Suzanne because of age—you know, too young or too old."

It all sounded a little far-fetched to Riley but, if Bridey's mind was on the Tyrone Power angle when she left Leavenworth in 1945, there was a certain internal logic to it. It would be consistent with the manner in which she had chosen the name Clare Turlough, for example. It was possible. "So, what did you come up with?"

"Okay," she said, "just be patient a minute. I need a reality test on this theory, and in order to do that you need to hear how my reasoning unfolded. It's a remote possibility, but it's better than nothing."

Riley apologized for his hurried tone. He sat back and tried not to interrupt, biting into his pencil. His leg was bouncing at high speed. Betsy passed through the room and stopped just long enough to place a hand on his knee to slow it down. He looked up and smiled.

Tracy flipped through more pages in her notebook. "All right, just as I was about to throw in the towel, it came to me that it wasn't "Mrs. Tyrone Power" that I called her, but rather the name of the character who was the love interest of the Tyrone Power character in one of the movies we saw together."

"Uh-uh," mumbled Riley encouragingly, in spite of being a little lost.

"I remembered the character was played by Betty Grable . . . you know the pin-up girl with the great legs that were insured for a million dollars . . . which, by the way, was another similarity. Suzanne had great legs, too. I guess I'm getting a little far afield here."

Riley said nothing.

"Anyway, I could remember that the movie was about the war, and that it was not a brand-new release when we saw it. But I couldn't remember the name of the character Betty Grable played . . . you know, the name I started calling Suzanne by. I knew it was a common name, which I think would also make it more attractive to Suzanne for purposes of anonymity. So, anyway, I went on-line and researched the films of Tyrone Power and found the movie right away: *A Yank in the R.A.F.* Betty Grable played a character named Carol Brown."

Riley thought he was following her reasoning, though it seemed remote, even a little desperate. He gave another affirming grunt.

"So I ran the name 'Carol Brown' through the indexes, and you can imagine the number of hits I got. Good Lord, it took me two days to winnow them down to a manageable number of candidates, based on age and race." She now giggled a little and said, "Are you ready for this?"

"Yes, Tracy, I'm more than ready," said Riley flatly.

Sounding like a camp counselor approaching the end of a ghost story, she said, "On August 2, 1946, in a little town in northeastern Iowa, Dr. Axel S. Gifford married a Carol Brown at the Waterford Catholic Church. The groom was forty-two years old and the bride was thirty-eight. And, get this, her middle name was Tyrone." With exuberant satisfaction, she shouted into the phone, "What do you think?"

Riley had been taking notes; the yellow legal pad before him was now a mass of scribbles, arrows, scratch-outs, and exclamation points. He had hoped for something a little more solid than this. Finally he said, "I don't know, Tracy. I guess you're the expert on the events of 1945, so I'm in no position to provide a reality check on your theory. If you think it's worthwhile, then I do too."

"I know, but I'm so punch drunk from all that time in front of the computer that I may be grasping for straws. But I also know that even though I was fourteen and she was thirty-seven back at The Plains Rialto, we were just a couple of girl-friends all a twitter over her gentleman caller who looked like Tyrone Power. And I know, as only a girlfriend can know, that she was madly in love with this guy."

She then turned from the phone, and her tone changed from bobby-soxer back to grandmother as she told one of the children to go back and wipe her feet on the mat outside the door before walking on the carpeting.

Returning to Riley, she said, "So, dear boy, no matter how remote it sounds, my gut tells me it's a lead worth checking. I mean, geez, how many women can there be out there with Tyrone for a middle name? It's just a heck of a coincidence. And maybe Axel Gifford was the gentleman caller who married her when he returned from the war. Anything is possible. "

Riley's knee started bouncing again. Tuffy sat on the chair across from him, staring at his agitated master, his tail thumping against the fabric in sync with the bouncing knee. Riley looked out the window, biting his lower lip. "What's next, Tracy?" he said like a lowly corporal asking guidance from his commanding officer.

Betsy again entered the room and, after one look at the knee bouncing, took a seat at the table, her face a blend of hopefulness and cheer. She just wanted this crazy project over, one way or the other. It was like a fever that had to be broken.

Riley looked over at her. "Just a little while longer," he whispered as he simultaneously listened to Tracy's recommended strategy.

He then said into the phone. "Yes, Tracy, I can go down there later in the week. What town is that in Iowa?"

# 17

---

T HE NEXT MORNING the sound of marching wingtips
echoed off the marble corridors leading to the litigation department, causing Riley to look up from a stack
of billing records and peer out into the hallway.

A phalanx of partners, all in dark suits, rounded the corner
and passed by Skeeter's desk, their eyes straight ahead.

Skeeter leaped from her chair and stood at attention, giving
a snappy salute. At the head of the formation was Ladge
Wilkaster, flanked by Rod Willoughby, George Stonequist,
Junior Cosgrove, and, wearing an Ace bandage that stretched
from his elbow to the wrist of his left arm, was Barney Bost.
Bringing up the rear in the diamond-shaped formation was
Benton Hubbard, the former seminarian and expert on ethical
issues governing law firms.

As he watched the delegation crowd into his office, it
occurred to Riley that, having had twenty-four hours to think
things over, Ladge Wilkaster had decided to fight this one
out. As the others took seats around the office, Ladge posi-
tioned himself at the round conference table near the window.

Riley leaned back in his chair and, with raised eyebrows, surveyed his guests. "You guys are all dressed up. This must be important."

He then looked over at Barney Bost and smiled broadly. "Yo, Barney, how's the wrist doing? I hear that was a pretty bad fall you took."

Barney turned a light shade of crimson as he pulled the sleeve of his suit jacket over his bandage.

The other lawyers, supporting players in the drama about to unfold, looked over at Ladge, who cleared his throat and stared hard at Riley. "This is no time for your smart-ass talk, McReynolds."

Ladge swept his hand in the direction of his confederates. "As the special committee on ethical practices, we've been considering the information you and Sara Hall saw fit to dig up about Stenham Investment Company."

Riley interrupted with a raised hand. "Whoa, wait a minute," he said. "You're off to a real bad start here, Ladge. All this ceremony isn't impressing me too much considering that this is a firm problem—not 'my' problem." He then looked around the room at each member of the delegation, a puzzled look on his face. "And what's this 'special ethics committee' talk, anyway? Where's the regular ethics committee? It looks to me, Ladge, like you got a few of your admirers together to stack the deck."

He then stared directly over at Benton Hubbard sitting on the far end of the couch, his eyes glued to the carpeting, his fingers tapping nervously on the arm rest. "I have to admit, though, that I'm curious how you got a decent man like Ben Hubbard to join your little rump caucus."

Ben Hubbard took a pained breath but didn't look up.

The faces of the other participants looked almost as grim, save only Junior Cosgrove, who looked mindlessly cheery. "That's a kick-ass tie you've got on, Riley," he said.

"Shut up, Junior," said George Stonequist.

Riley looked at Ladge. "All this formality makes me think you might actually have some arguable theory that will permit me to avoid turning in that thieving piece of crap you forced me to represent."

Ladge started to talk, but Riley stood up and cut him off. "You remember, Ladge, you were sitting right there on the couch where Barney has his sorry ass planted right now."

Barney Bost darkened.

"And you told me how, for the good of the firm and the many employees who depend on us, I had to personally represent Gus Tanzdahl. And how you realized it was a breach of the agreement you made with me when I came to the firm, but that it was absolutely necessary to retain the client."

Riley walked around the desk and pulled up a chair directly across from Ladge. "And you probably also remember how I said that I was the wrong guy for the assignment, that I despised divorce work, especially where children were involved, and that I wasn't real crazy about Gus Tanzdahl, either . . . and how I had a low tolerance for vainglorious CEOs who abuse employees and live high off the shareholders."

Ladge looked up and met Riley's eyes, his face flushed a deep red. But before he could say anything, Riley continued. "And remember how I cautioned you that my background gave me an eye for fraudulent practices, and that on several occasions I begged you to relieve me of the case."

Ladge Wilkaster gave a dismissive sneer. "That's all history," he said, "nothing more than Monday-morning quarterbacking. We're here to advise you that a review has been conducted of the transactions that you mistakenly suspect of being illegal insider trading. When those transactions are viewed in a broader context, the trades that appear suspicious to you are nothing more than a series of coincidences. And we"—he now moved his hand in a broad circle that included Riley—"all of us, are bound to maintain attorney-client privilege and not, under any circumstances, pass on groundless suspicions to Ellen Tanzdahl's attorney, let alone to the court. And you will not be relieved of anything, now or at any time until this case is successfully concluded. You will go on representing Gus to the bitter end. My God, taking you out of this case would be like taking Hamlet out of the play."

"Take Hamlet out of what play?" asked Junior Cosgrove.

"Shut up, Junior," said Rod Willoughby.

Riley never took his eyes off of Ben Hubbard, who looked back with an expression that seemed to say, "I had no choice."

The others sat smugly on the couch, nodding agreement with everything that Ladge said.

Reaching into his briefcase, Wilkaster extracted a thick memorandum. He handed it to Riley as though he were serving a summons. "This memo contains a description of our committee's investigation and the resulting findings of fact. There is also a twelve-page analysis of the applicable law, along with controlling authorities on privilege, confidentiality, and the professional responsibilities we owe to these two clients, Gus Tanzdahl and Brad Stenham."

"Gus Tanzdahl has never done anything unethical," exclaimed George Stonequist, self-appointed expert on legal ethics and collector of Speedo bathing suits.

Riley flared. "People with your track record in the ethics department should just keep their mouths shut at a time like this." It was one thing to receive moral instruction from Ben Hubbard, or even from Ladge Wilkaster, but he'd be damned if he'd take it from a full-grown man with a Speedo collection.

George's face reddened, and he jumped up off the couch. Riley stood up and started moving toward him. Ladge quickly stepped between them. "Now, now, none of that. We're all on the same team here." He then smiled broadly, his demeanor suddenly transformed. Reaching over, he placed a brotherly hand on Riley's shoulder. "I want to personally express our admiration for the conscientious manner in which you have handled this difficult case so far, Riley. And I want to apologize for the computer glitch that sent you and

Sara Hall on a wild goose chase. You will both, of course, get full hourly credit for the time you spent in that unfortunate detour."

On cue, the other members of the delegation, other than George Stonequist, arose and, in a burst of collegiality, shook Riley's hand one at a time as though he were a rush candidate just given a fraternity bid.

Riley took a small step backward, fearing that they might be planning a group hug. To rescue him from this embarrassing spectacle, Skeeter popped her head into the office and announced an emergency phone call. Riley nodded acknowledgement, scooted back behind his desk, and started to talk into the dead phone.

Junior Cosgrove gave Riley a thumbs up as the group left the office. "You're the man, Riley!" he said.

AS UNLIKELY AS IT ALL SEEMED, as incriminating as the Stenham documents appeared to be, it was actually Riley's fondest hope that these guys were right, that his suspicions were unfounded. That this whole mess was just a series of coincidences accidentally unearthed by an oversensitive computer. Or, in the alternative, if he couldn't shake his suspicion that an insider trading scheme had been executed with the firm's connivance or, at least, its acquiescence, that the available evidence would not rise to the level where he would be ethically compelled to turn it over to Clint Tarrymore, let alone to Judge Hammergren. He now knew why the lights in the corporate department library had been burning brightly when he drove past the firm's headquarters on Saturday night at eleven. Ladge and his special committee—and God only knew how many trusted underlings—had been researching the case against disclosure.

He returned to his chair and bounced the thick memorandum on his knee. He then stood up and went into the hallway, standing in front of Skeeter's desk, looking a little lost.

She declined to look up at him. Her silence told him that she thought he was being naive. It was obvious that he was going to get no sympathy from her, so he shuffled back into his office and slumped onto the couch. The relative certainty of yesterday, when he thought he had no choice but to blow the whistle and withdraw from the case, uncomfortable though it was, had oddly alleviated some of the anxiety that came with the original discovery. Now he was back into the anxiety of indecision, thinking that there might be a way to avoid exposing his scumbag client. Maybe his personal dislike of Gus had closed his mind to a thorough and objective analysis—an analysis like the one elaborated between the covers of this chunky memorandum.

Even Betsy would caution him to carefully consider all valid alternatives before imploding the law firm and, possibly, his own career. But, strangely, it was not to Betsy that he felt drawn for emotional comfort at this moment. It was to a woman on whom he had never laid eyes except in a jerky, blistered bit of film footage, a couple of newspaper photos and some old pictures found in a file at a Chicago Convent. A woman who might be nothing more than a ghost in 1996—a woman who had become, in life or in death, somehow his moral anchor.

A small smile broke through as he thought about how truly bizarre all this was. He looked over at the pile of Bridey-related documents, now grown to forty-eight file jackets stored in sixteen boxes, stacked on the floor of the office closet. He could see Bridey's face, carrying the wounds of loss and abandonment. Though he had never heard her voice, both Nancy Kunz and Tracy Ridgeway had described it as of medium register, lilting and soft in the style of children born in the south of Ireland. She had never acknowledged being from Ireland to either Nancy or Tracy, but she had also done little to suppress the cadences of her native speech. So he had created a voice to go along with the face and, fictitious though it might have been, it fell gently upon his mind.

It would have been embarrassing to share much of this interior world with anyone else, even Betsy. But as a psychological prop, the search for Bridey didn't seem any sillier than much of modern psychotherapy, with its mind games and role playing and letters to dead parents. Somehow they got that stuff to pass for science, and it must have helped some people along the way. So even though the search for the Holy Grail in the person of Bridey Reeves might be a fantasy woven out of a few flickering images of primitive film, it seemed a perfect godsend at this stage of his life.

Skeeter walked into the office and, slowing her step, sniffed the air. "God, it smells like a men's locker room in here. I hope it's not me," she said, bending her head to catch a whiff of her armpit. "Whew, it's not me," she declared triumphantly. "What is it with men and high tension meetings. I ought to hose you guys down with deodorant every time I know you'll be discussing a nasty topic."

Riley grabbed the fabric of his shirt and took a whiff. "Pure Right Guard," he said defensively. "I think it was Ladge Wilkaster sweating out his exposure on this case. I think he perspired right through all that blue gabardine."

"They're all a bunch of weasels, Stonequist and Wilkaster and Willoughby. You know that, don't you?" said Skeeter, now standing over him. "Why don't you just tell them to take their phony arguments about what a misunderstood guy that sleaze-bag Gus Tanzdahl is and put them where the sun doesn't shine. If you lose your partnership, we can go somewhere else. And I bet Sara Hall would come along."

This surprised Riley. At first, Skeeter hadn't liked Sara, whose single-minded energy rubbed a lot of people the wrong way, especially women in the firm. But Sara didn't mess with Skeeter, not after a little attempted intimidation had backfired early in their relationship. Skeeter had given her such a snootful of her own medicine that she had been nothing but respectful ever since.

Riley looked up and smiled weakly. "It could come to that, I suppose. But I came here for a long-term commitment, and I have a huge financial investment at stake. Besides, ninety-eight percent of the people around here I like and admire. Even Ladge Wilkaster has some good points."

"Oh, God, here we go again," said Skeeter. "No such thing as a bad boy, right, Father Flanagan?"

"No, no," said Riley as he rose from the couch and walked back to his desk. "I learned that lesson back at the Lindbergh. I'm just saying that all the facts aren't in yet, and it may not be as bad as it looked at first. We'll see."

Skeeter walked over to the desk and put her palms on the desktop, leaning down to eye level. "Yeah, but what about Ellen Tanzdahl and her little boy. Are you really going to be a part of what they're doing to her?"

He put his hands up to his face and rubbed his eyes and forehead, leaving a swatch of hair standing nearly straight in the air. "I don't know what to do. If I call their bluff and withdraw from the case, Wilkaster will just reassign it to somebody with fewer scruples, and Gus will have his own way. Or Gus will just go to another firm. And we'll still have to face the decision of our disclosure obligations. Remember, one of those subpoenas was served on the firm in its own capacity." He drummed his fingers on the desk blotter a few times and then looked up at her the way he used to look at Sister St. Lillian, the principal back at Sacred Heart School after a scolding. "There's just no easy way out."


THE BASEMENT TREADMILL whirred beneath his feet as Riley, like a gerbil in its running wheel, hustled to keep up with the speed of the belt. The back injury, still not fully healed, would not permit him to sprint, but he was moving at a respectable jogging pace. Perched on the reading stand attached to the treadmill was the legal brief served on him by Ladge Wilkaster.

As he read, he was reminded of the old law school maxim that if you're weak on the facts, pound on the law; if you're weak on the law, pound on the facts; if you're weak on both, pound on the table. This seventy-eight-page tome, including exhibits, was a table pounder if ever he had seen one. But it was also a skillful handling of the complexities and ambiguities associated with the suspected insider trading scheme uncovered by Sara Hall. Most such issues, no matter how incriminating they appear on the surface, can be deconstructed and massaged and ultimately obscured inside the Byzantine technicalities of insider trading law. And it is those technicalities that will sometimes afford a safe harbor for firms like Cosgrove & Levi when they find themselves in an ethical dilemma.

Knowing that, Ladge Wilkaster and his talented crew had pulled out all the stops in the preparation of these materials. And they had displayed the good sense to frame the discussion in non-adversarial terms to avoid arousing reader resistance, for they didn't have to persuade Riley that Gus was innocent, only that there was enough doubt to relieve the firm and its lawyers of any professional obligation to pass on their suspicions to the opposing party or the "tribunal," which in this case was Gertrude Hammergren.

A good many criticisms could be leveled at Ladge Wilkaster, but lack of cunning was not one of them. He owed his exalted position in the firm not to his skills as a lawyer, for they were modest, but rather to his ability to manage the bloated egos of seventy-five ambitious lawyers. Riley himself was not altogether immune to the artful manipulations of the sort at which Wilkaster excelled. Part of him hoped that there was an ethical escape hatch, a legal way out. For buried deep in his bone marrow, formed during more than two decades in the criminal justice system, was an instinctive loathing for informing on even the most reprehensible client. This ethic had rarely come into play during his years as a prosecutor; if he came upon falsified evidence by a witness for the prosecution, it was in the best interest of his client—that marvelous abstraction known as the "State"—to dismiss the case. But on the defense side of the table the duty was owed to a real person and, no matter what the various ethical codes might say on the subject, being a cause of injury to a client was a highly distasteful act. The only exceptions that came easily to mind were pedophiles and psychopaths of obvious continuing danger to the community. But those exceptions were not present in this case; the larcenous conduct of which Gus Tanzdahl was suspected, odious though it might be, was of the non-violent variety.

So it was with a blend of curiosity and dread that he turned to the opening page of the brief. He noted that the authors conceded at the outset the applicability of the legal and administrative rules governing the obligations of lawyers who find themselves in this kind of predicament. This tactical concession, formulated to appeal to Riley's sense of balance, told him that Ladge and his accomplices intended to make their case primarily on factual rather than legal grounds.

He wiped perspiration from his forehead and smiled with grudging admiration for the artistry with which that first section was constructed. The drafters knew their man. Ladge Wilkaster was intellectually incapable of the complex argumentation found in the brief, so Riley visualized one or two of the more gifted associates fashioning the position that a law firm had to be objectively certain of its suspicions before it was required to produce documents against the wishes of its client, let alone report suspicions of wrongdoing to a presiding court. Not by accident did these young prodigies lead with a case in which a lawyer was sanctioned for going too far in respect to disclosure in a divorce case. Not a bad opening, thought Riley. Unfortunately for them, however, he was well aware of that case and knew that, when fairly read, it actually supported disclosure under the Tanzdahl facts.

He also noted that the cases cited were largely from jurisdictions outside of Minnesota. That approach sometimes meant that the Minnesota courts had yet to face the question at issue, but more often it signaled that the authors found the direct precedents unhelpful. For all of that, the first section of the brief was a work of art, and though it underestimated his familiarity with the area of the law under discussion, it was not without merit.

By far the more important section was the factual analysis. He again wiped his face and neck with the towel slung over the side railing of the treadmill and, as his respiration climbed in tandem with the whir of the treadmill, he dove into that section, the heart of the brief. It quoted extensively from three attached affidavits: one from Gus Tanzdahl, one from Brad Stenham, and the last from Harry Wilford. The central argument in the brief was that the suspicious paperwork Riley and Sara had stumbled upon could be simply explained. It was true, the affidavits conceded, that Stenham Investment Company had traded extensively in the securities of corporations in which Gus Tanzdahl was an insider and that such trades, long and short, had been consistently profitable. And, yes, it would be easy to see how a person unfamiliar with the "Gus-Brad" relationship, might look at the trading schedules and get the wrong impression of their meaning.

But as with so many mysteries, this one had a simple and innocent explanation, according to the brief. It seemed that Brad Stenham and Gus Tanzdahl, lifelong buddies and inveterate betters, had been wagering since college on everything from sporting events to how long it would take an old lady to cross the street. Here, it was contended, they had simply made a $10,000 annual bet that Brad, through Stenham Investment Company's trading in a portfolio of companies in which Gus was an insider, could not outperform a shadow portfolio of stocks chosen by throwing darts at the stock listed on the New York Stock Exchange. The theory was that Gus, in possession of important but unshareable inside information relative to those companies, would have special fun monitoring Brad's performance. The affidavits in support of this explanation submitted by Stenham and Tanzdahl were models of clarity and persuasiveness, containing the kind of elegant syntax that made it all but certain that neither Gus nor Brad had taken any part in their creation. The text of Gus's affidavit was replete with the kind of detail as to times, dates and locations that lends credibility to even the most farfetched scenarios, including an exhibit listing the many wagers between the principals going back more than thirty years. Most of that historical account was probably true, and, in any event, it was impossible to disprove.

The more challenging factual issue, though, was the re-markable success of Stenham's trades in those securities. The affidavits attributed that success to Brad's abilities as a stock analyst, aided over the last several years by a strong market and a run of simple good luck.

The brief even got around to the troublesome absence of the claimed $10,000 in annual wagering income on Brad's tax returns, by saying that his gambling losses for those years had zeroed out the winnings attributable to the Tanzdahl bet, thereby leaving no tax liability. A highly con-venient but not totally implausible juxtaposition of events.

Regarding the most incriminating piece of evidence—the schedule bearing Gus's handwritten notations in the margins of the reporting schedule—the brief soared to its most cre-ative heights. But inventive though it was, it barely passed the snicker test when it claimed that the undated annota-tions had been made well after the dates of the trades, in a timeframe when the inside information had long since been made public. It was, according to them, an improvised score-card, a postmortem on Brad's performance.

Incredulity mixed with admiration as Riley toweled down his face, turned up the speed of the treadmill, and continued read-ing. Harry Wilford, the junior associate who was in hot water for giving Riley and Sara access to the Stenham trading sched-ules, gave his memory a good tweaking when the shit hit the fan and now recalled that he saw Gus and Brad sitting in the reception area doodling on that very schedule well after the public release of the information. He was sure that was the case because he now remembered associating the timing with his son's birthday. For authenticity, in what Riley had to admit was a nice touch, Harris even described Gus and Brad's discussion reminding him of a couple of college boys going over a racing form days after a race had been run.

The remainder of the brief he only skimmed, knowing that the heart of the matter was contained in the middle section. The third and last section, though nicely written, was anticlimactic, consisting of a synthesis of the arguments developed in sections one and two.

Riley had read hundreds of such documents—indeed he had authored nearly that many over the years—and he knew even before he started reading what this one was likely to say. But he hadn't realized how well its authors were going to say it. He shook his head and smiled as he flicked the switch on the treadmill and collapsed onto the adjoining couch, dripping sweat on the pleated fabric. Ladge and his crew had planted doubt, there was no question about that. Maybe even doubt that would justify withholding the information. Not the quality of doubt that would shake his opinion that Gus and Brad Stenham were a couple of sleaze-bag inside traders, but then that was not the test they had to meet. A finding of insider trading turned on subjective intent, just as motivation for seeking a change of custody was a matter of subjective intent. He felt sure that Gus was dirty on both counts but, absent compelling objective proof, his duty was to interpret the rules in such a way as to protect the best interests of his client. It held together, but it also made him feel a little sick. And this stretch, if he could make himself take it, would be followed by a similar pitch to suppress the evidence of what appeared to be Gus's venereal disease. He could only imagine how that one would be spun. There were no circumstances under which he would allow Ellen's infection to be placed into evidence unless Gus's medical condition was also disclosed, no matter what kind of brief Ladge Wilkaster produced.

As he cooled down from the run, he thought about the practical alternatives, about how the just course would be for Gus, recognizing his vulnerability in all this, to authorize Riley to withdraw the custody action and make a generous settlement offer to Ellen—an offer that at least approached one-half of the massive wealth he had accumulated during the marriage. But that was not likely to happen. He knew Gus and knew that, even under a cloud of criminal suspicion, the arrogance that seems always to afflict people of his character would not permit him to willingly part with that kind of money. No matter how bad things might look, Gus would have a hard time envisioning himself as a criminal defendant. Riley felt a small surge of amazement over the immunity to emotional suffering possessed by sociopathic personalities like Gus Tanzdahl. Pangs of conscience seemed to be reserved for people of finer temperaments. It seemed ironic and unfair.

Ellen Tanzdahl's attorney, Clint Tarrymore, now fully realizing that this was not going to be a fair fight, had moved to a wartime footing. An honest and congenial man, he was nevertheless capable of slugging it out with the best of them, and the revulsion he felt for Gus seemed to have aroused a truculence that promised to forever change the tenor of the case, no matter how forgiving Ellen Tanzdahl might be. Riley didn't think he had sent an unconscious signal telling the other side that he was powerless to influence the conduct of his client so they might as well fight fire with fire. But in light of his profound dislike of Gus Tanzdahl, who could really say what might have leaked out around the edges. In any event, Clint Tarrymore was now fully mobilized.

Riley wouldn't think about that just now; he would think about it later. Now he would take a shower, have a Milky Way, and go in search of the beautiful girl with the pale-blue eyes who still beckoned to him out of an ancient photograph.

# 18

---

THE SUN WAS HIGH in a cloudless sky, and a soft, promising breeze brought with it the rich scents of a Minnesota summer. Driving south past Rochester at a comfortable five miles over the speed limit, Riley veered gently to the east, where the flat landscape gradually gave way to the steep, rolling hills flanking the Mississippi River Valley. Starting as a mere trickle from a nondescript lake in the north of the state, by the time the great river passed between the skylines of Minneapolis and St. Paul it had become a mighty waterway bisecting the continental United States. Here, just forty miles north of the Iowa border, the river broadened into a massive blue expanse broken only by land formations spread out on a wide canvas like an artist's bold strokes. Distant hillsides were dotted with Victorian homes built by shipping barons in the late nineteenth century, back when the river was the golden highway of national commerce. Towering stone hills rose to meet him as he descended to pick up the roadway that would take him into Northern Iowa.

With the sight of the great waterway came a complete release of tension. All thoughts of the Tanzdahl case seemed to drain from his body. If it served no other purpose, this

strange, obsessive search provided moments like this,
moments in which he was delivered to a state of almost childlike happiness.

On the passenger seat next to him was the ragged old
briefcase inherited from his father after four decades of use.
It contained the most significant of the Bridey materials. His
office closet now overflowed with what had to be one of the
largest collections of raw data ever assembled in a search for
a single person, with the possible exception of the Lindbergh
baby. His portable phone, roaming for a nearby cell, protruded from a side pocket of the briefcase, next to a buckled strap
showing the wear and tear of two professional lives. He
reached over and pressed the "off" button. With a quiet beep,
the small green light gave up its frantic search.

South of LaCrescent he veered back into the hills, under
railroad overpasses and past small farms, and then high over
the river valley. Despite nearly a half-century as a resident
of the area, he had no idea that such beauty existed anywhere in the Midwest, let alone two hours from his home. He
rolled through the mountainous landscape, past small picturesque towns in which Barney Fife could have been the
deputy sheriff. When he turned the car radio to an oldies station, a doo-wop group from his boyhood sang, "Over the
Mountain, a Girl Waits for Me." If there was anything to syn-
chronicity—anything to intuition set free from cognition—he
was exactly where a benevolent universe wanted him to be.

Crossing the Iowa border, he wound down out of the hills and
past Luther College in Decorah, then east to the county seat
holding the marriage certificate and other records relating to
Carol Brown Gifford. By the time he pulled into town, it was
after business hours and too late to examine courthouse
records. So he checked into a roadside motel just outside the
city limits.

The evening was passed reviewing grand jury testimony in
a banking case, interrupted by frequent consulting of the TV
schedule to find a good movie. Finally, he abandoned the

grand jury transcript and pulled out the collection of Bridey photos he had assembled throughout the search. Newspaper photos from the day of the O'Banion funeral—one at Sbarbaro's Mortuary (uncovered late in the process from the Chicago Historical Society) and another at the cemetery— had been enhanced, colorized, digitalized, blown up and reproduced so many times that he had at least a dozen copies of each. Even the freckles were now clearly visible on her youthful face. The same was done with a freeze frame from the TV documentary and the two photos found in the St. Agnes archives, one from the joint passport with her father and the other taken at her Confirmation. In the latter she wore a lacey cotton chiffon dress of a beige tint. A tentative smile, with lips slightly parted, enlivened her face. A small cross hung from her neck.

He sat on the motel bed, propped up against three pillows, looking at the photos spread out on the bedspread. The face in the pictures still moved him profoundly. If his reaction was not quite as excited as the first time he gazed upon her image, it was every bit as adoring. And his determination to solve her mystery was stronger than ever.

The specific details of her face as shown by the enhancements, including a light dusting of freckles along the nose and upper cheeks, were as familiar to him as his own. The images had long since yielded all they could in the way of factual leads, but where science had left off, intuition picked up. Nature despises a vacuum, and his always-active imagination had effortlessly filled in details, creating a personalized work of art, his own iconography. From a few snippets of aged film his imagination had woven a tapestry as detailed as any movie backlot. It was art at its most elemental, creative and healing. And it was to that creation, as real to him as any living person, that he was devoted. Not even when it seemed certain that Bridey had succumbed to prostitution and death in 1937, did he abandon the narrative that had provided so much comfort. One didn't have to believe in mysticism to admire the workings of the human mind and spirit and their genius for symbol and metaphor.

As sleep began to overtake him, he sat up and placed a safe-arrival call to Betsy. He treated her to a long speech on the subject he had just been contemplating. She claimed to hold the same general beliefs, but then invoked her favorite psychological adage: "Remember, Riley, neurotics build sand castles; psychotics move into them."

With that caution in mind, he slipped into a deep, restful sleep.


"CAN I HELP YOU WITH SOMETHING?" inquired the middle-aged woman wearing a print dress and a big smile. She stood behind a counter in the neo-Gothic county courthouse perched atop the town's highest hill.

In spite of years of experience with the intricacies of county recording systems, Riley affected his most helpless manner today. A small display of neediness could produce a storehouse of riches in a rural courthouse.

Smiling awkwardly, he pulled a file from his briefcase. "I'm doing some genealogical research, and I think I've picked up the trail of a second or third cousin who once lived in this area. I was hoping you might be able to help me." The cultivation of civil servants, especially ones with the unchallenged power of rural court clerks, was an art he had first mastered when newly out of law school and working as a trial lawyer for the state attorney general's office.

As the most junior lawyer in that office, it fell to him to try eminent domain lawsuits against local landowners in counties far removed from the Twin Cities. Those counties were often comprised of German and Scandinavian Lutherans who were thought to harbor a native distrust for the dark doings at the State Capitol. Crafty old country lawyers—general practitioners with offices between the courthouse and the Masonic Lodge—rarely failed to remind local juries that the young lawyer McReynolds, Irish and non-Lutheran, had been sent from that sinkhole of urban corruption, St. Paul, to cheat some poor farmer out of his land.

But it had never worked. Not once. Those country house-wives, shopkeepers, and farmers looked upon the young lad with the shock of dark hair and twinkling blue eyes more like a mother looks at her own son. And they invariably resented the appeal to their baser instincts. Those good people, fair-minded and unpretentious, were more likely to scoop him up and take him home for a hot meal than they were to succumb to prejudice. That year riding the rural circuit had served to reinforce his unshakable belief in the decency of ordinary people of all backgrounds.

"Is there any chance I could get a look at the probate file for a—" he consulted a schedule in the file, running his finger down a list of names as though not quite sure of who he was after. "—a Dr. Axel Gifford, who, according to the social security death records, died in this county in 1975?" He rotated the paper on the counter so the clerk could see the spelling and date of death. He smiled warmly. "My name, by the way, is Riley McReynolds."

The clerk returned the smile and then lifted a pair of glasses to her face and peered down at the list. She reached for a notepad and copied down the information, saying as she wrote, "1975 was before my time, but I shouldn't have any trouble finding the file in the probate vault." She then turned and walked through a wide doorway and down a row of floor-to-ceiling stacks.

From where he stood on the other side of the counter, Riley could see her looking back and forth between her notes and an eye-level shelf about half-way down the row. Her nimble fingers flicked quickly through the file tabs.

A gray-haired man wearing a short-sleeved shirt and a black clip-on tie emerged from behind the partitions of a workstation adjoining the front counter. Until the man stood up, Riley wasn't aware that anyone had been within hearing distance.

Without looking at Riley, he turned into the file stacks and made his way to the spot where the woman was standing. A brief, muted conversation ensued, after which the man continued down the row and disappeared around the corner. The clerk then rejoined Riley at the front desk.

"I'm sorry," she said, embarrassed, "but that file has been stored off-site because of its age."

Riley suspected that in truth the file was right where she initially expected it to be. But it would be self-defeating to mount a challenge at this point. He knew that, as a public record, they'd have to produce it sooner or later.

The clerk shifted on her feet and stole a look at the workstation from which the bald man had emerged. She then turned back to Riley and said, "I'll put in a requisition for the file, and it should be available tomorrow." She looked up at the old circular clock on the sidewall. "Why don't you come by about 10:30."

Riley nodded and handed her a business card on which he had written down the name of the motel where he was staying. He then turned toward the doorway, but stopped when he heard her whisper, "Mr. McReynolds."

He turned back. After stealing another glance in the direction of the manager's work cubicle, she said, "You might try the public library in the meantime. They have old copies of the newspaper, and you can probably get some information about Dr. Gifford out of them."

At the public library, he was able to pull Axel Gifford's obituary and a file folder containing several articles about him and his family. Taking a seat at a corner table, he paged through the file. Dr. Gifford was a native of the area, a basketball star and class officer in high school, and a graduate of the University of Iowa—college and medical school. His first residency was completed in internal medicine at the St. Louis Women's Hospital, followed by a lengthy second residency in general surgery at the University of Missouri. For thirty years he practiced within the geographical area bounded by the Minnesota border on the north, Decorah on the west, the river on the east, and Dubuque on the south. Several scholarly articles relating to surgical complications associated with diabetes had been authored or co-authored by him, and copies were contained in the file. Though he and his family had maintained a home in Dubuque, the Gifford family property outside of town had remained his principal domicile. A handful of newspaper photos showed him to be a strong and dignified man of ordinary height, with gray hair and a pleasant face that fell just short of handsome. The pictures were taken in the late sixties, more than twenty years after the end of World War II, but it would be hard to believe that the man in these photos had ever looked like Tyrone Power.

The obituary, dated April 30, 1975, noted that he was survived by his wife of twenty-nine years, Carol Brown Gifford, age sixty-seven, and one daughter, Sheila "Stoddie" Gifford, age twenty-four.

Riley did the math. Bridey would have been exactly sixty-seven in 1975.

A search of the newspaper archives produced no hits for "Sheila Gifford" or "Stoddie Gifford." But for the names "Carol Brown" and "Mrs. Axel Gifford" a half-dozen entries appeared since 1946. Four of them were in articles that had no accompanying photographs, and the other two related to church events containing group pictures of the women's auxiliary. In the group photos, the name "Mrs. Axel Gifford" appeared, but always in the "not pictured" section.

Riley made photocopies of all but the medical articles and stuffed them into his briefcase along with a copy of the county map showing the location of the cemetery in which Axel Gifford had been buried. When asked by the librarian what his interest in the Gifford family was, rather than using the standard genealogy pretext (which seemed weak in view of the depth of the research he was conducting), he identified himself as a lawyer and freelance writer doing an article on medical pioneers in the area of diabetes research. These quickly conceived pretexts were the legacy of his time as a private investigator. As at the courthouse, his questions at the library seemed to arouse interest on the part of the staff and a few eavesdropping patrons. In contrast to Chicago, Omaha, or even Leavenworth, small town residents tended to know each other's business, and a snoopy stranger could easily become an object of suspicion.

Of all the leads he had tracked down in the last six weeks, this one had initially seemed to hold the least potential. Had it not been for Tracy Ridgeway's persistence, combined with a scarcity of other leads, he probably wouldn't even be here. But it was now showing considerable promise. It seemed that Tracy's cockeyed speculations might just be correct.

Rather than drawing additional scrutiny by having lunch at the local diner, he grabbed a Milky Way and a Pepsi at a corner gas station and headed for the Waterford Cemetery, high over the river. Traveling along a county highway atop a high ridge, he viewed the lush cropland spreading for miles in all directions, a velvet landscape broken only by an occasional barn or farmhouse. In all likelihood the land was not highly productive, and was doubtless covered by snow half the year, but at this time of the summer it was breathtakingly beautiful. Gliding along the high ridge, with his cellular phone purposely disabled and the Tanzdahl case far from his mind, he luxuriated in the scenery and the soothing taste of the Milky Way. The lightly traveled road rolled and wound with the contours of the landscape, finally dipping between high-walled rock formations that seemed to be standing guard before the rural graveyard which, according to county burial records, contained the mortal remains of Axel Gifford.

Passing under an iron archway into the cemetery grounds, he felt as though he was entering another time, another dimension. The ground rose steeply once again as the internal roadway round its way to a high plateau with a commanding view of the river below. Small gravel stones crunched under the weight of the wheels as Riley's small white Honda slowed to a stop before a stone fountain at the entry to a central walkway.

He got out of the car and headed down the walking path, which it turned out bisected the cemetery's two main sections, one of which had reached full occupancy by the mid fifties. The landscape pulsed restfully to the rhythms of struggles long past, inspiring in Riley a sense of peaceful acquiescence. This was a quiet place. A place of melancholy resignation to forces out beyond human control.

Further along the path the ground took a broad, rolling sweep over a natural elevation and then downward to a point where it seemed unable to resist the pull of the great river a half mile below. Many of the headstones in this, the oldest section, indicated the resting place of Civil War veterans. Union army engravings graced stone markers that were bleached and rounded with age.

Among the modest tombstones of the old section was a single garish intruder, a soaring obelisk held aloft at its base by a host of cement angels. It marked the final resting place of "Lucius Hiram Rohrsbach, PhD: Intellectual, Scholar and Friend to the Deserving Poor." In the world of posthumous self-congratulations, this rural academician seemed to have set some kind of record. *Deserving poor, indeed*, thought Riley.

He chuckled absently as he continued his stroll toward the center of the grounds, where he came upon an engraved tablet describing the history of the surrounding area. The countryside had been settled by some forty families arrived from County Waterford at the height of the Irish potato famine. Of the family names on the tablet, a number were familiar to him, having just seen them on mailboxes lining the county roadway leading into the cemetery grounds. This was obviously a community of uncommon stability.

In accordance with his cemetery-visiting customs, Riley scanned the list of family names for "Reynolds," "McReynolds," and "Carr," they being among the most common of Irish names. There were none, but then he wasn't surprised; this shipload of

297

immigrants had come from County Waterford, and his people, on both sides, were from County Tipperary.

An adjoining map, under the protection of a plastic cover, showed in outline the various sections of the cemetery and the years in which they had been opened. He checked his bearings, and then set off for the section in which four generations of Gifford's lay buried. He easily found a series of modest stone markers, engraved with the names of a half-dozen of them, including Axel's parents. Off to one side of Axel's headstone his eyes came to rest on an undersized marker, its small surface obscured by dirt and overgrown grass.

Riley knelt down on one knee and, with the tip of his car key, began scraping hardened dirt from the grooves of the lettering. He then used his hand to brush away the debris, and put his reading glasses to his eyes. He stared at the exposed lettering: "Reaves Gifford, God's smallest angel."

Suddenly dizzy, he felt as though the ground beneath him had opened. He had just uncovered the last piece in the Bridey mosaic, that tiny piece of evidence that signaled arrival, for good or for ill, at the end point of the search. There could now be no doubt about it. Still on his knee, he leaned toward the other Gifford markers, dreading that he might find one with the name Carol Brown Gifford on it.

At that instant, a large hand landed forcefully on his shoulder. Startled, he whirled around and found himself squinting up at two thick-necked men in sunglasses and dark suits, their features obscured by the sun beating down from behind them. The taller of the two, the one who had grabbed him, wore a blank expression. He said in a firm, commanding tone, "Come with us. We have a car at the end of the road."

Without protest, Riley rose to his feet and walked on hollow legs between his two attendants. For the first time since kindergarten he thought he might lose control of his bladder and pee right in his pants. They walked in formation back down the center lane of the cemetery, and then turned left to a small parking area where a black Lincoln Town Car with an aerial mounted on the trunk sat parked. It looked to be the car he had first noticed in Omaha. A third man sat behind the steering wheel looking straight ahead. The two escorts guided him into the back seat, and then took seats on either side of him.

Attempts to start up a conversation were unsuccessful, in part because he seemed to have lost his voice. It probably didn't matter, though. These guys didn't look like talkers.

When he asked if he could lock his car before they left the cemetery grounds, the driver shook his head, "No."

The ride seemed endless, the feeling made more so by reason of the sphinx-like silence of his abductors. Riley looked over at the dark-haired man seated to his right and smiled weakly. "So, you guys from Chicago?" he asked.

Nothing. Not a sound. Not even a twitch.

Pulse racing and stomach churning, he thought back to the few words these guys had spoken at the cemetery, trying to remember whether anything in their speech patterns suggested organized crime. Though they had not expressly threatened him, the whole business had the feel of a kidnapping. The Milky Way congealed in his stomach as he visualized a barge-mounted crane fishing his white Honda out of the river, muck and aquatic vegetation hanging from its chassis. No sooner had he banished that image than it was replaced by one of him getting compressed like Jimmy Hoffa in a junk-yard auto compactor, his Honda squeezed down to the size of an egg carton.

He tried in vain to impose order on the thoughts cascading through his head. If his body were not found, he reasoned, it would be seven years before Betsy could force the life insurance company to pay off on his policy. But there'd be enough money in the meantime for the family to get by. Good thing he hadn't forfeited his capital account at the firm. He wanted to compose a hurried note to let Betsy know how much he had always loved her. And one to Lizzie about the wonderful life she had ahead of her and how he wasn't mad that she had called him a dictator and a douche bag last year. And one to Teddy to tell him to grow up to be like his mother and his uncles, and not like his father who all his life had gone around looking into things that were none of his business, and finally looked into one too many. A small tear formed on his cheek, a tear borne of regret over the recklessness that brought him to this moment. Another one of his father's maxims repeated itself in his head: "Don't go where you're not invited."

Outside the window, the passing countryside slowly thickened with trees and foliage as the car made its way down a back road, executing a series of left turns and winding its way through steep terrain leading to the river. After a few minutes of gradual descent, the driver picked up a phone mounted on the dashboard and, in a flat monotone, said "West entrance—thirty seconds."

Riley thought of asking what that meant, but the driver didn't seem like the kind of guy to open up. Anyway, he guessed he could wait another thirty seconds to find out whether Betsy was about to become a widow. He was scared. Again the racing thoughts: Why had he intruded into other people's business and given them no choice but to hurt him. But he resolved he wasn't going to cry. He would not give these meat hooks next to him the satisfaction. He would die like a man.

Thirty seconds later, the car emerged from a thick woods and into an open, well-trimmed area, upon which, straight ahead, sat an imposing red brick, five-story structure with an elegant, if somewhat institutional, look to it. The building's façade, dominated by a high portico supported by thick white pillars, was encircled by flowers so thick and sprawling that they brought the whole edifice alive. The driveway on which they were traveling swerved away from the main entrance, taking another left and beginning a slow, curving descent around the building to the south. Extending off the back of the main structure was a three-story wing, before which the car came to a gradual stop. A tall, well-dressed man emerged from the entryway and approached the car. "Please follow me," he said. The man was holding the business card Riley had handed to the clerk at the courthouse that morning.

Riley glanced over at the silent escort seated to his right in the hope that he might offer some advice. The Stockholm Syndrome had already seized him, and he said, "I'd rather stay with you guys." They weren't very nice, but at least they hadn't killed him, not yet anyway.

The abductors maintained their steely silence. The driver looked at him through the rearview mirror and flicked his head in the direction of the tall man waiting outside the car.

Riley took a deep breath and stepped tentatively from the car, tucking his shirt into his pants like a nervous schoolboy. He then fell in behind the tall man, and together they walked through the open double doors into a large, expensively appointed hallway with a floor patterned in black and white rectangles. The large foyer was illuminated by a massive crystal chandelier hanging from a twenty-foot ceiling.

At the end of the long central hallway, an ornate stairway wound its way to the second floor. Riley stood staring at the massive leaded-glass window gracing the stairway landing, when from behind him came a woman's voice, strong and clear, speaking in a tone of subdued celebration, "Hello Riley, we were afraid you wouldn't make it in time."

He whirled around to find himself face-to-face with a woman of average height, looking to be in her early to mid-forties, with dark hair and striking pale-blue eyes. Save only for her age, she was nearly the perfect image of the young Bridey.

Riley's face dropped as he tried to mouth a few words, but his throat caught and his breath seemed to have gone out of him. He could only stare, wide-eyed.

"I'm Stoddie Gifford," she said as she stepped forward and kissed him gently on the cheek. She then put her arm through his and urged him gently in the direction of a side hallway. Smiling up at him as they walked, she whispered, "Mother said you'd be coming, but none of us believed her."

"Mother?" Riley stammered, mind-numbingly confused.

Stoddie guided her bewildered guest down the broad passageway and into a paneled anteroom lined with floor-to-ceiling bookshelves. French doors on the far side of the room opened onto a patio overflowing with flowers. Beyond the patio was a vast expanse of neatly trimmed lawn stretching the length of a football field. Past the lawn he could just make out a high wire fence that seemed to surround the entire estate.

Stoddie sat him down on a couch with deep cushions covered in a thick, earth-tone fabric, near arched windows through which a brilliant afternoon sun streamed, bathing the room with light.

Though Stoddie was old enough to possess the grace and bearing of middle age, she looked much younger. He couldn't take his eyes off this beautiful woman who was the very picture of Bridey Reaves. It was as though Bridey had stepped out of the photographs and kissed him on the cheek. He suddenly felt completely safe. He was not going to die, after all.

The Tyrone Power/Carol Brown lead had been grabbed at in desperation and seemed at first to be a waste of time. But suddenly it had blossomed into the search's fulfillment. He felt sure that the solution to the mystery that had taken over his life—a mystery sealed for seventy-two years—was about to be fully revealed.

Wearing a dark navy suit with the skirt ending just above her shapely knees, Stoddie Gifford was an enchanting vision of familiar beauty. Like the young Bridey, she looked strikingly like Lizzie, confirming the initial visual impressions he had formulated as he sat alone in his Minneapolis den watching the flickering images of the documentary. It was wonderfully eerie.

Stoddie walked across the room, and from a bookshelf next to a large Tudor fireplace, pulled down two thick scrapbooks. Supporting their weight with outstretched arms, she placed them on the coffee table before him and took an adjoining seat. Her eyes glistened as she said, "I think these will answer all your questions, but I'll fill in anything that's not clear." She smiled softly and moved to a seat directly across from him.

Riley's hands came to rest on the cover of the first scrapbook, but his eyes remained glued to Stoddie, fearing that if he looked away she might vanish. Or he might wake up. Stoddie gave a reassuring nod in the direction of the scrapbook.

He finally summoned the poise to lift open the front cover. There in the opening pages were a series of pictures of Bridey, starting with family photos when she was just a child and her parents were still alive. Dion O'Banion was there in the early pages, next to the young Bridey dressed in the uniform of a St. Agnes boarding student; and there was one of Pat Clebourne gazing adoringly upon a radiant Bridey at age twenty-seven, with her dark hair falling across her shoulders. Following that was a solo shot of a tall and toothy Tracy Ridgeway, dressed in checkered skirt and saddle shoes, the Plains Rialto in the near background, the sun glistening off her metal braces. About halfway through the scrapbook, a single page was given over to photos from St. Louis, including a railroad-car diner and a building bearing on its roof a sign identifying it as the St. Louis Women's Hospital. In that photo, a dark-haired woman was looking down at a baby in her arms.

Riley paused to speculate that this must have been the end point of the pregnancy Tracy had suspected, which would mean that the picture was taken within months of Bridey leaving Leavenworth in late 1945. He looked over at Stoddie Gifford, Bridey's daughter. Clearly she was not old enough to have been the newborn child in this picture. Stoddie nodded for him to continue.

The last sections of the first scrapbook contained newspaper clippings relating to Dion O'Banion's death and others dealing with the Clare Turlough murder. When he started reading the clippings, Stoddie interrupted. "There will be plenty of time for that later. Why don't you move on to the second volume."

Riley obeyed, setting aside the first scrapbook and opening the second. On the first page was a yellowing copy of an article that had appeared in the family section of the *Minneapolis Star*, dated July 3, 1952. It was entitled KENWOOD FAMILY PREPARES FOR INDEPENDENCE DAY. Above the article was a picture of the family of John and Maureen McReynolds—mother, father, and all five children. They were decorating scooters, tricycles, and wagons in multicolored crepe paper. Small American flags were taped to the handlebars of the children's bikes. The cut-line identified each family member by name and made special mention of the youngest child, Riley, age six, who was sitting on his mother's lap, enjoying a Milky Way candy bar. Riley was very familiar with that photograph; the original, in glossy black and white, had sat for years in a gold frame on his grandmother's mantelpiece, in a place of honor next to the photo of his uncle Desmond.

Riley looked up from the scrapbook, his face a mask of confusion. Stoddie again nodded for him to continue.

Turning the pages, he found more newspaper clippings, all relating to him in some way, including a sports-page photo of his youth hockey team at the end of an unbeaten season in 1958, and one of him being decked in a youth boxing match. Next to the boxing photo was a note, scribbled in a woman's hand: "No! This is barbarous." It was written in the familiar script of the Palmer Method.

Then came a series of long-distance photos taken with the kind of surveillance lens Riley had used when with the detective agency. The pictures included ones of him and Betsy, ranging from their childhood years through a large color print taken on the steps of Sacred Heart Cathedral on their wedding day. He devoured the pages in rapid succession, failing even to look up when the door opened and a man in a gray suit entered and made his way to a seat behind him in a far corner of the room.

Half way through the scrapbook, the photos became a blend of telephoto shots of him and Betsy and Lizzie and Teddy (skewed toward shots of Lizzie in the last several years), and newspaper clippings tracing Riley's career as a prosecutor. The last entry in the scrapbook was an announcement of his association with Cosgrove & Levi.

In the inside flap of the scrapbook's back cover was an envelope, dried out and brown around the edges. He removed it and unfolded the thick bond stationery, the kind of paper long out of fashion but immediately recognizable to him as the type used by his father.

*October 14, 1954*
*Minneapolis, MN*

*Dear Bridey,*

*I have drafted a great many letters in my lifetime, but this is without exception the most difficult one. I have thought and prayed long and hard over its contents since receiving your call on June 1. Though you will doubtless be bitterly disappointed by my decision, I can only hope that in time you will come to understand my reasons.*

*When you approached me at Desmond's funeral in 1945, with your astonishing tale of flight and tragedy and ongoing danger, I was at a loss to know what to believe. But through my own grief I could see that you were telling the truth, for during his last days at home, before leaving for the European war, Desmond told me of his love for a young woman he had met while at Fort Leavenworth, and of his intention to marry her when he returned. We were like a couple of schoolboys on that last trip to our parents' North Minneapolis home, where we had grown up almost as twins.*

*I couldn't identify you by name or face that sad day in 1945 outside Sacred Heart Cathedral, because my brother had provided me with neither a name nor a photograph. But he described in lovesick detail your smile and your blue eyes. I was not able to see your smile that day, but when you removed the veil from your face and the sunglasses from your eyes, I had no doubt that you were the girl he had fallen in love with. That you were carrying my adored brother's child at that moment made me want to sweep you into my care without any thought to the danger for either you or for my own family.*

*When you told me, almost eight years ago, of your continuing life on the run and your sense of foreboding about your pursuers, we agreed that you could not provide a safe and happy life for the child you and Desmond had conceived—a child who by any measure was a McReynolds. So together we resolved, with the ready agreement of the sainted woman to whom I am married, that Maureen would stage a pregnancy. This she did with convincing skill, including weight gain, maternity clothing, and baby showers.*

*Far easier was the benign deception we practiced upon the St. Louis Women's Hospital, with me in the role of anxious father and you in the role of my wife, delivering a healthy baby boy. The ruse was successful as to all but one person. When we brought the baby home from our "vacation" in St. Louis, my mother—who next to you was the woman in this world Desmond loved most—saw through our artifice the instant she looked into Riley's eyes. She knew this could only be Desmond's child, and she rejoiced just as if her dear son had suddenly returned. You need have no fear of Mother ever betraying the secret. She would die before a word would pass her lips.*

*Maureen and I want you to know, Bridey, that we celebrate with all our hearts your happiness with Dr. Gifford and the birth of your daughter. And while we do not challenge your belief that you are probably now safe from those who would harm you, after long hours of prayerful reflection it is my heartbreaking duty to tell you that we will not release you from the commitment you made on the day of Desmond's funeral. You took a sacred vow that in exchange for our agreement to make Riley our child, you would never seek him out or initiate any contact with him. Those were our conditions, and you subscribed to them. We suspended the operation of that promise only briefly when we allowed you to impersonate a night nurse at St. Mary's Hospital last year when we were told by the doctors that Riley was very likely to die of polio. I knew that seeing him, especially like that, would make your continuing separation all the more painful, but I resolved to take the risk.*

*Now, I have to wonder if it was fair to you to have done so. That encounter seems to have provoked just the kind of plea that I have always feared would come some day. I can now only rely on your sense of honor. As you acknowledged in our tearful phone conversation of two weeks ago, the moral vow you made remains in effect. It cannot be dissolved without our consent—and we do not consent, now or ever.*

*The many considerations favoring the course we agreed upon in 1945—the most prominent being the stability of the family with which he has bonded since birth—are, if anything, more compelling now than they were then. You must understand, Bridey, that Riley is a happy and secure child, thriving in the embrace of a safe and happy family that includes four older siblings whom he adores and who adore him. It would be a wicked thing to even consider removing him from his home and his loved ones, and it would be almost as wicked to inform him that the bond with the only woman he has known as his mother is not one of blood. Experts can argue day and night about such matters, but I know beyond any question that his strength and happiness rests in his belief that he is body and soul a member of this family.*

*It is doubtless within your legal power to work your will upon this matter should you choose to do so, but unless I have sadly misjudged you, you are a person who will faithfully abide by her commitment and leave this much-loved child in the care of those who have warmed and nourished him from the moment the sun first shone upon his face on the front steps of the St. Louis Women's Hospital—those who have changed his diapers, encouraged his first steps, kept vigil day and night during times of illness, and healed every hurt suffered in body and mind for the eight years that have comprised his life.*

*Keeping a child from his mother is an awful responsibility, and I can only pray that I am doing the right thing. With God as my witness, it is my belief that I have taken the right decision. If I am wrong, I will be judged for it. Please forgive me, Bridey.*

*John*

Stunned and speechless, Riley looked up at Stoddie, the sister he didn't know he had. She rose from her seat and made her way to the couch beside him. He reached out and embraced her, the tears on their faces mingling in a warm, salty brew. When they released their hold, he looked into her pale-blue eyes for a moment, and then quietly said, "Where does 'Stoddie' come from?"

She gave a short, gasping laugh as she wiped tears from her eyes with the back of her hand. "I'm Sheila Stoddard Gifford. Stoddard is my grandmother's name on my father's side. I've never been called anything else. It's a good name."

He numbly nodded his agreement. "Yes, it is a good name. One of my best clients goes by that name."

"Yes, I know," she said, pointing to a chair behind the couch. Riley turned to see Ev Pederson, his eyebrows arched high in his forehead as if to say "What's a guy to do?"

Ev rose from the chair and took a seat on the other side of Riley, who by now looked like one of those dumbfounded guests on *This Is Your Life*. The only thing missing was

Ralph Edwards, and it wouldn't have surprised him at all if Ralph were to come sailing through the door, scrapbook in hand.

When Ev got through pumping his hand, Riley said, "I don't know how much of this I can absorb right now, but what the hell's going on?"

Ev looked over at Stoddie the way a junior officer defers to the CEO, which for all practical purposes was what she was. Stoddie signaled for Riley to sit back and get comfortable. She then started in, "I'll give you the broad picture now, and then I'll fill in the details later. And I'll start at the beginning."

She stared at the ceiling for a moment, taking a deep breath. "When Mother's parents—our grandparents—were killed in a car accident in 1922, Dion O'Banion supplied the altar flowers for the funeral. He always did that for poor families—especially Irish immigrants living on the North Side of Chicago. When he laid eyes on Mother, a heartsick fourteen-year-old orphan adrift in a foreign country, he was so smitten that he declared himself her benefactor and protector, including arranging for her room and board at the St. Agnes Convent. He was a dear man to her, and she very quickly came to love him as a surrogate father."

Stoddie bit her lower lip gently. "She didn't know that Mr. O'Banion was one of the biggest gangsters in Chicago . . . in fact, she wouldn't even have known what a gangster was. She only knew that this lovely man, with the sweet face and lilting voice, loved her and watched out for her. To her, he was warmth and candy and new outfits and trips to the amusement park." Stoddie shook her head ironically. "At first she wondered why there were always two large men who accompanied them on their outings, and she once asked Mr. O'Banion why his suit jacket had lumps of steel inside it." She narrowed her eyes and smiled.

Riley smiled back, but his eyes begged her to continue.

"Mr. O'Banion said he had steel braces for his bad leg. It was only when he was murdered in 1924 that Mother learned from the newspapers that he always carried three guns in specially made pockets. Anyway, shortly before he was killed, Mr. O'Banion sat Mother down in a side pew of the convent chapel and handed her a suitcase with straps around it. He said that it contained very valuable pieces of paper that she should keep, and that if anything ever happened to him, she should use the papers to take care of herself. He also told her never to give the suitcase away, and that his partner, Hymie Weiss, would see to it that she was protected."

Riley was brimming with questions and started to interrupt. Stoddie smiled but put up her hand, gently signaling for him to let her finish. She looked over at the clock on the mantelpiece and then back at him. "Well, anyway, Mother looked in the suitcase once after Mr. O'Banion was killed, but she was a sixteen-year-old girl so confused and grief stricken that she had no idea what the strange-looking pieces of paper with a lot of writing and squiggly designs were. She couldn't believe they were valuable.

"Hymie Weiss assigned someone to watch over her at the funeral, but that only made it worse for her. She said that Weiss and his friends stared at Al Capone across the grave as if they intended to kill him, and it scared her half to death. She thought they were all going to start shooting right then and there. Anyway, she stayed at the convent and tried to finish that year of school. Hymie Weiss was true to his word and watched over her with almost fatherly tenderness. But Mother knew from the newspapers that Weiss and Moran had murdered several Capone gang members. In the meantime, Mother had been getting calls at the convent saying that if she didn't turn over the suitcase, she would be killed.

"She seriously considered giving up the suitcase and joining the convent as a novice, but Weiss kept telling her that she had made a promise to Deanie, and that even if she did turn over the suitcase, they would kill her anyway. Terrified, she felt sure Weiss would eventually be killed, too, as indeed he was the next year. So she packed up her few belongings and fled Chicago."

Stoddie exhaled a breath from a face filled with renewed sorrow and admiration for what her mother had gone through at such young age. "I don't know how she kept together, body and soul, but we can be tremendously proud of her. She hopped a bus out of Chicago and by prearrangement headed for a convent in Wisconsin, where she posed as a novice. The Capone people came looking for her at the Chicago convent, and they even broke in one night and ransacked her old room.

"When she turned eighteen, she left the convent in Wisconsin, assumed the name Clare Turlough, after her birthplace, and took a series of waitress jobs, never staying in the same place for more than six months. She finally ended up in Omaha five years later. When Capone went to prison in 1931, she hoped that she'd be safe, but she found out from the mother superior at the Chicago convent that his confederates were still looking for her."

Now up and out of her chair, Stoddie walked to the window and stared out at the rolling grounds. "In 1933, Mother finally let down her guard and fell in love with a police officer, Patrick Clebourne." She turned from the window and nodded, confirming the accuracy of his investigative findings.

Riley hadn't gotten it all right, to be sure. He had no idea, for example, that she had hidden in a Wisconsin convent or that it was years before she got to Omaha. But he had gotten the Clare Turlough part right, and he allowed himself a small glow of self-congratulations.

"How did she and Clebourne know that the Mob was still after her?" Riley asked.

"They didn't know how the Mob found her, but Detective Clebourne thought it was because she had been spotted by some Omaha character once associated with the Chicago Mob, who then sent word back to Frank Nitti, Capone's successor. But whatever the reason, according to Mom, Clebourne came upon what he thought was the perfect ruse: a friendless dead prostitute with physical characteristics close enough to Mother's to pass for her. I don't know if it was a good match or not, and neither did Mother. She only knew that it seemed to have worked, at least for a while."

Riley turned to Ev Pederson and asked whether his car, and his briefcase in the back seat, had been retrieved from the cemetery. Ev nodded affirmatively and said he'd get the briefcase. Moments later, one of the security agents who had abducted him from the cemetery, entered the room and set the briefcase down on the table. On the way out of the room, he winked at Riley.

Riley reached in the briefcase and extracted a file marked "Turlough Crime Photos." Removing the photos from their envelope, he handed Stoddie blow-ups of the dead woman who had gone to her grave as Clare Turlough.

Stoddie reached for a pair of reading glasses and examined the first photo—the most gruesome of the series. She let out a gasp and turned away, her hand covering her mouth. She sat with her eyes closed for several seconds and then looked back at the picture. "Oh, my God, this is awful . . . I can hardly tell this isn't Mother. No wonder they were all fooled. That poor woman," she said, shaking her head. "How did you ever figure out this was somebody else?"

Riley reached back into the briefcase and pulled out the enhancement of the newspaper photo taken at O'Banion's graveside. He placed the two photos side by side on the coffee table, together with a computerized analysis of Bridey's face in outline, crisscrossed by a dozen lines and vectors. "This comparative analysis was done by a forensic artist with the help of computers never dreamed of in 1937. He told me, to a scientific certainty, that these were two different women."

"Amazing," she said, shaking her head with a blend of curiosity and grief, grief for a woman beaten to death and then buried by strangers with a name and identity that she never knew in life. "Patrick Clebourne must have freaked out when this opportunity popped up at just the right time."

312

She looked over at Riley with an expression of exaggerated admiration. "You were very clever about how you picked up the trail. You must have checked hundreds of name combinations before getting to Clare Turlough."

"Clever? I suppose so. But tell me why Patrick Clebourne didn't follow Bridey when she fled Omaha."

"Because that would have given away the ruse. Everyone would have known what had happened. So he stayed where he was, but was in regular phone contact with Mother and intended to join her as soon as it was safe. But the Mob came to suspect what had happened and watched him closely. When he refused to lead them to her, they killed him."

Stoddie watched to see if all this was sinking in, and then continued. "Anyway, you were very clever, as I was saying. But then you had an advantage over the Mob; they wouldn't have had a copy of Bridey's passport from her school file at the convent, like you did. Hit men are not as charming—"

"—How did you know about my visit to the nuns?" he interrupted. "You couldn't have had anyone following me that early in the search." He looked over at Ev Pederson, who maintained a mischievous smile and never took his eyes from Stoddie. Riley elbowed Ev in the ribs. "I never said anything to you about who I was looking for, only that I was trying to solve an old mystery. Don't tell me you got into the files in my office on one of your visits."

Ev playfully blocked Riley's elbow, giggling. "No, I never went in your files. In fact, I didn't know a damn thing about what you were up to until you went to Kansas. I only knew that when the family hired me to run the Trust, I was told that as much business as possible was to be sent to you, and that I could never let you know why."

Riley looked back up at Stoddie. "Well? What about the convent?"

She walked back to the couch and, before resuming her seat, pinched him on the cheek. "How'd you get so stupid all of a sudden? Sister St. Catherine—you know, the one in her nineties—has been placing coded messages in Chicago news-papers since 1926. Whenever she wanted Mother to know something, she just used the code they worked out seventy-one years ago when they roomed together in the novices' wing of the convent. When she sent a message that you were search-ing for Bridey we ordered our security people to keep tabs on you." She laughed. "We didn't remember that you had been a private detective back in law school, so it never occurred to us that you'd 'make' the tail." She smiled and nodded. "In fact, even though you picked off the tail in Omaha, you didn't know you were being monitored while in Kansas."

Riley nodded back and grinned as if to say that he had sus-pected Sister St. Catherine of knowing more than she had shared. He then asked, "How did Bridey end up here?"

Stoddie started to answer, but a groundskeeper on a motorized lawnmower drove past the open French doors, nearly drowning out the sound of their voices. Unable to read her lips, Riley cupped his hand behind his ear and said, "Try that again."

In a voice now much louder than necessary she said, "My father's family, the Giffords, had lived in this area for three generations when Mother met Dad."

"So she came here after Leavenworth and fell in love with your dad?"

She shook her head, "Whoa . . . slow down. Mother had never heard of my father or his family. She believed, wrong-ly I think, that the Mob was still after her when she fled Leavenworth. My father was a medical resident at the St. Louis Women's Hospital when Mother, using the name Maureen McReynolds, delivered you in 1946. Dad said that the man posing as her husband didn't seem to be the real father. It made him wonder what the true story was."

Ev Pederson and Stoddie exchanged looks. Riley turned to him and then back to her. "Yeah, okay, so then what?" he asked, bouncing his knee up and down at a pace akin to Tuffy's tail when he knew he was about to get a treat.

314

Ev pointed in their direction. "Do you two realize that you're both bouncing your knees up and down like a couple of race horses." Riley looked over at Stoddie and, sure enough, she had her knee going, too, but in such a ladylike fashion he had hardly noticed.

"I think we're going to get along great," said Stoddie, laughing out loud. "Anyway, Mother was terribly vulnerable at the time, having given up her baby. When she left the hospital, she stayed in St. Louis from sheer exhaustion. She just couldn't run anymore. With you safe with John and Maureen, I think she half wanted to die anyway, so she just got a job as a waitress at a restaurant that didn't require a social security number. If the Mob caught up with her, that's just the way it would have to be. But Dad had fallen in love with her and just kept pursuing her until she came to trust him. Then she fell for him, and eventually told him the whole story. In 1947, using the name Carol Brown, she went home with the young doctor. I guess she chose that name because of some movie. They were married shortly afterward, and I was born in 1953. In 1954 she lost a baby son, Reaves, our brother, in the sixth month of pregnancy. She then had to have an emergency hysterectomy. According to Dad, she almost didn't survive all that, thinking it was God's punishment for giving you up."

Stoddie's eyes glistened and her voice cracked. "Mother then tried to get your father . . . or I should say your uncle . . . to agree to release her from the promise she had made when she gave you up. He wouldn't do it, and after he died, Maureen wouldn't consent either. To this day Mother has remained faithful to her vow that she would never contact you. But, oh, how she's prayed that you'd somehow find her."

Riley sat dumbfounded, looking like a man whose life had been turned inside out. Did his father do the right thing? Could he have been any happier outside the family in which he had grown up? It was all for the good, he supposed. He suddenly felt a series of small holes in his heart where his brothers and sister, now his cousins, had once filled the space. They knew nothing of any of this, and never would. But it was a loss, nevertheless. And his mother, Maureen— oh, God, his mother. She was the formative presence in his life, and however much Bridey loved and longed for the child she had given up, that longing could not have exceeded the love of the mother he had known his whole life. Were she to find out that he had located his real mother, she might just die of a broken heart. No wonder she had been so upset over this search; she knew that this one was the real thing. He thought of how he could keep her in the dark, of how he could say he had finally given up the search, just the way he had eventually outgrown the Grand Duchess Anastasia and Amelia Earhart and a dozen other surrogates who over the years had occupied the circuits of his unconscious longings. But would it work? Probably not, for Maureen had always been able to read his deepest thoughts, the tiniest creases on his uncomplicated face. In any event, he would think about that later. Now, he would luxuriate in a dream fulfilled—in paradise found.

Stoddie had said nothing during his short meditation, but she now leaned forward and placed a hand on his knee. "Would you like to hear about the money and the Trust?"

He nodded assent.

"Okay," she said. "The papers in the suitcase were stock certificates that formed a portfolio of securities that Dion O'Banion had purchased with the $500,000 Al Capone paid him for the Sieben Brewery just before the prohibition authorities seized it. Beyond the quick scan she had given those documents at age sixteen, Mother never opened the suitcase again until after she married my father. She had no idea what she was carting around. She knew it wasn't cash, so she figured it was unusable for her needs. When she finally, almost casually, showed the suitcase to my father and said it was just a bunch of papers, he almost fainted. He went to his investment adviser, and in one afternoon they figured out all the accrued dividends and stock splits and current valuations and determined the market value of the whole thing. That was in 1950, and the portfolio was worth $67.5 million.

Riley's eyes widened. "$67.5 million in 1950? It must be worth five times that now."

Stoddie stole a sidelong glance at Ev Pederson, who smiled wryly. "Much more than that, I'm afraid. With some of the best legal and accounting advice available anywhere in the country, Dad liquidated most of the portfolio over the next several years and capitalized the real estate development activities of the company he set up, The Stoddard Trust. We don't even know what it's worth on any given day—but even after all the gifts we've made, we estimate it's value at around a half-billion dollars."

Stoddie allowed a moment for the number to sink in. "I'm only half kidding when I say that the best part of your arrival is my being able to hand over responsibility for this darned thing to you. The Trust's operations are deliberately complicated to maintain the secrecy that Mother still feels is necessary. The Mob probably gave up a long time ago, after they murdered Pat Clebourne as a final act of frustrated vengeance, but it wouldn't be a good idea for any of Capone's successors to find out that O'Banion's $500,000 had grown into one of the largest private real estate fortunes in the country."

Riley expelled a deep breath. He looked at Ev and then over to Stoddie. "I've got to call my wife," he said in an effort to impose some order on the emotional avalanche that had befallen him. "And Skeeter, my assistant, was expecting to hear from me by this time, too. She'll wonder where the hell I am."

Pederson nodded and they all stood up. Stoddie reached over for Riley's hand. She then kissed him on the cheek and said, "The Stoddard plane is standing by to pick up your family." She then smiled. "I can't wait to meet Lizzie. I have three sons, no daughters. I want to see this girl who looks so much like Mother and me." She started to walk toward the door, but turned back. "I assume that Skeeter can be trusted with all this? Nothing has changed in regard to the essential secrecy of the enterprise."

"Believe me, Skeeter will be the most trustworthy person in this whole thing." He then turned to Ev, and with a mischievous smile said, "My first official act as the new head of The Stoddard Trust is to appoint Skeeter as the executive vice president in charge of everything that might come my way. Just write up the resolution in her real name, 'Eleanor Swenson'—that'll get her mad."

"I'm looking forward to meeting her too," said Stoddie, as she lifted the phone receiver and punched in a three-digit code. She then held the receiver off to the side, cupping the palm of her hand over the phone. Her expression changed as she looked up at Riley. "Now comes the tough part."

Riley felt a small current travel along his spinal cord. The culmination of his adventure was now upon him. He was going to meet the object of his obsession, the face that had reached out to him through a piece of ancient celluloid in a lonely graveyard so many years before; the woman he had chased through three-quarters of a century as Anna Reaves and Clare Turlough and Suzanne Sheridan and Carol Brown; the woman who had formed him in her body nearly a half century before. And she was also the woman who had come to him in the form of Amelia Earhart and Anastasia and all the others; the woman who represented the fulfillment of a lifetime of longings he had been unable to name.

His legs went rubbery and his knees trembled. It must have shown, for Ev Pederson took hold of his arm in a steadying gesture. The light banter of a moment before had vanished, replaced now by an odd reverence for the reunion about to take place.

Stoddie lifted her palm from the receiver and said into the phone, "May we come now?" She then nodded her head in silent acknowledgment.

She walked over to Riley and put her hand gently on his face. "You have to know something, Riley. Mother is dying."

Riley just stared dumbly at her, nearly paralyzed. He said nothing.

"Her first stroke was eight weeks ago. After a few days she seemed to rally, but for the first time in her life she could no longer care for herself. That's a terrible realization for a gritty survivor like Mother. The doctors confined her to bed, and though her voice and speech had not changed, her ability to retrieve words was impaired. She kept saying that you were coming." Stoddie lowered her eyes. "We all thought she had slipped into some childlike dream world, so we just humored her. The doctor said that that kind of delusion can grip an elderly person facing death. But Mother was irritated at our reaction, shaking her head at me the way she did when I failed to solve some equation in grade school."

There was a quiet knock on the door, followed by a nurse poking her head into the room. She looked over to Stoddie and said, "3B." Stoddie nodded and turned back to Riley, who had not taken his eyes from her.

She looked up at him and said, "Ten days ago she suffered another stroke, this one paralyzing most of her body, including the muscles of the throat that control one's ability to clear the lungs of fluid and, of course, to talk. When that happened, she started to slowly suffocate. The doctors pronounced her beyond recovery and recommended that everything, including water, be withheld so that she could die comfortably. They wanted to administer morphine to shorten her suffering."

Stoddie shifted on her feet and crossed her arms across her chest. She took a deep calming breath. "Every day before the second stroke, she communicated to me, sometimes just by scratchings on a tablet, that you were coming and that she had to stay alive. She made me promise to keep her alive until that time, even if she had passed into unconsciousness. When the second stroke stopped all ordinary communication, I could see in her eyes that she was holding me to that promise. So she's had no morphine for her pain and just stares blankly out the window. We don't know if she's even hearing anything or recognizing us at this point. The doctors don't think so, but I still keep talking to her—and I think she understands me."

Stoddie looked away and bit her lower lip. Then she reached up and threaded her arm through Riley's. "Now let's go see our mother."

He followed her across the room to a large bookcase, which opened to reveal a small private elevator designed to carry six passengers. During their short ascent to the third floor, Stoddie explained that the overall facility they were in had been built by the Stoddard Trust in the mid fifties to care for disabled children. When the Salk Vaccine eradicated infantile paralysis, the building was converted to a nursing home and hospice. The rear wing was added at the time of Axel Gifford's death, and it became Bridey's primary residence.

The slow-moving elevator came to a stop on the third floor. It opened directly into a large elegant foyer. A woman in a traditional nurse's outfit directed them to a short hallway, which in turn opened into what had once been a sitting room but was now outfitted with a hospital bed surrounded by monitoring equipment. A doctor in a business suit was leaning over the bed.

Riley's steps slowed as he caught sight of the figure in the bed, propped up by pillows almost to a sitting position. Stoddie, too, stopped her forward motion and looked over at Riley with a small reassuring smile. She then took his hand and pulled him forward.

Still leaning over the bed before the patient's unmoving eyes, the doctor said, "There's a guest here to see you, my dear."

Stoddie stepped forward, replacing the doctor in Bridey's sight line. As she whispered endearments to her mother, Riley stood transfixed by the sight of the woman he had first seen through the grainy black and white film shot by a newsman seventy-two years before. There was not a shred of doubt that this was the person in the documentary, the young girl from County Clare, the grief stricken ward of Dion O'Banion. Beyond that, she was nearly the perfect image of

the age-enhanced portrait drawn by Norm Pennington, the
forensic artist from Colorado. A lump formed in his throat as
he also recognized her as the night nurse in the polio ward at
St. Mary's Hospital more than forty years before, the one who
seemed always to be there when he awoke in the night. It
crossed his mind that if he had compared the age-progression
drawing of Bridey in her forties with his memory of the night
nurse, he might have arrived here weeks earlier.

As he looked upon the face of his mother, he was filled with
such a torrent of emotions that he could feel his heart slam
against his chest and blood course through his veins.
Through the chaos of those feelings, he mentally verified the
cheekbones, the shape of the mouth, now withered but still
unmistakable, and the hair, white as snow but still soft and
thick, reminding him of the angel hair that decorated the
base of his family's Christmas tree when he was a child. And
those eyes—the eyes that prior to today he had seen only in
his daughter—eyes now staring inertly past her attendants
into the next world.

Stoddie leaned over and kissed Bridey on the forehead.
She then raised herself to a full standing position and, while
looking up at Riley, placed her hand on the small of his back,
gently urging him forward. He looked at her and then back
at Bridey before yielding. Placing his hands palms down on
the bed, he leaned forward, positioning his face directly in
her line of sight.

In an instant, her brow creased and her eyes filled with
tears. An uneven breath escaped through parted lips, accompanied by the smallest noise from deep in her throat. Those
pale-blue eyes, still dazzling in their beauty, focused on his
face. A smile tugged at the corners of her mouth.

Stoddie raised her hands to her face as tears cascaded
down her cheeks. The doctor bowed his head at this small triumph of love over death.

Riley lowered himself onto the side of the bed, pressing up
against the now-emaciated legs that had carried this proud

and beautiful woman through one tragedy after another—
through the loss of parents at a tender age, followed by the
murder of an adoring surrogate father and then, seventeen
years later, the assassination of a police detective whom she
loved. And then, finally, the death of the Army officer to
whom she had surrendered her body and heart.

He studied the creases of her face and wondered which of
the serial tragedies had accounted for which lines. His eyes
left hers only long enough to pick up her hand and place it
against his cheek. He could feel his heart sing with the
rhythm of her thoughts, now expressed at a level too deep to
be seen or heard. Every now and then tears would collect in
the corners of her eyes and spill across her cheeks. Then her
eyes closed and she entered another level of consciousness to
tend to the process of dying.

Riley gently let go of her hand and rose from the bed. He
stared down at her peaceful face for a minute or two, then
turned toward the hallway. Stoddie directed him to a side
alcove where he could place a call to Betsy. As he sat on a
small couch next to the phone, he scanned an adjoining cabinet on which sat the same picture of Desmond kept on his
grandmother's fireplace mantel. Next to it was a World War
II-vintage Victrola and a stack of old records. He reached for
the brittle jacket at the top of the stack and placed it on his
lap. It was "Vera Lynn's Greatest Hits." The first song was
"The White Cliffs of Dover."

Stoddie appeared at the entryway to the alcove. "It was
Mother's favorite song. She said she played it over and over
as she waited and prayed for Desmond's safe return and the
health of the baby she was carrying. After the first stroke,
she made me pull out the old Victrola and play the album for
her. We played it so often and so loudly, I'm surprised you
didn't hear it in Minneapolis."

Riley looked up at her. "I did hear it."

Stoddie left him alone to call home. At the sound of Betsy's
voice, he started to sob so hard he could hardly speak. She must

have thought he had finally, at long last, gone completely mad. Disjointed and fantastic though it was, scattered and over-wrought as he seemed to be, she was able to extract from his halting words an internal logic that soothed a mounting and unfamiliar panic in her. Bridey had been found, he said through quivers and gasps, and she was Lizzie's grandmother. Betsy initially thought he had said she was like Lizzie's grand-mother, and took him to be saying only that he had been right about the striking resemblance. But no, that wasn't what he had said. He had said that she was Lizzie's grandmother and that it would all be explained when she and Lizzie and Teddy went to Holman Field in St. Paul, where The Stoddard Trust private jet would be waiting to fly them to Iowa.

And so Betsy collected Lizzie from a theatre rehearsal and Teddy from a soccer game, and they drove to the airfield where a gleaming white jet with no corporate markings idled outside a private hangar.

Precisely thirty-two minutes from takeoff, the sleek and nearly soundless plane eased its way down onto a landing strip that appeared out of the surrounding cornfields, high above the Mississippi River where the jagged bluffs begin their undulat-ing roll. The passengers were conveyed by Stoddard security officers along the same back road over which Riley had passed only hours before. The car pulled up to the side portico, and the three most important people in his life stepped into the sun-light of a cloudless afternoon. Lizzie and Betsy gave out an audible gasp when they saw Stoddie standing next to Riley.

Riley stepped forward and hugged each in succession.

He then turned to Stoddie, and extending his hand in her direction, said, "I'd like you to meet my sister, Sheila Stod-dard Gifford—Stoddie to you."

Beaming from ear to ear, Stoddie made a beeline directly for Lizzie, locking her in a bear hug that almost took her breath away. When she broke the embrace, she took Lizzie's face in her hands and said, "So that's where all that DNA ended up."

She then turned to Betsy and gave a warm, but more conventional hug, to her weeping sister-in-law.

With Lizzie on one side and Betsy on the other, Stoddie led the group through the entry, down the hallway, and through the library to the hidden elevator. Lizzie was still a little stunned, and Teddy seemed to have blanked out on the whole experience. But Betsy had quickly put all the pieces together.

When they arrived upstairs, Bridey's eyes were unfocused but open and somehow knowing. The nurse had been in to rearrange her bed and straighten the spread that covered her to the waist. Her head faced the afternoon sun at an angle. The room's several chairs were placed on that side of the bed, with Stoddie's chair directly in front of Bridey. The two of them seemed to communicate in the wordless language of mother and daughter. Save only for an occasional twitch of a facial muscle, Bridey showed no outward signs of responsiveness.

Stoddie leaned over the bed and whispered, "Riley has brought some more visitors, Mom."

She then rose from the chair and looked up at Riley, who took a seat and replaced her in Bridey's view. "I brought your grandchildren to be with us," he said. He then gently pulled Teddy by his shirtsleeve to a spot directly in front of him. Teddy's small shoulders were crunched up, and his eyes frozen open, as though he was on his first roller coaster ride. From the wings, Betsy gave him a gentle poke in the arm, and on cue he sputtered the words that had been quickly rehearsed, "I'm Teddy, Grandma."

Though Bridey's expression remained unchanged, a small petal of happiness seemed to open behind her eyes.

Having delivered his only line, Teddy squirmed from Riley's grasp, where he had been held, vise-like, for his short performance. He ran a tight pattern behind Riley's chair and buried his face in Betsy's midsection.

Riley reached up and guided Lizzie onto his lap where, abandoning her normal distaste for any uncool expressions of affection for a parent, she wrapped her arm tightly around her father's neck, just as she did when a little girl. Riley could feel her quickened breathing and racing pulse. She looked over at Bridey but kept a grip on Riley like a drowning child. As Lizzie came into her grandmother's sight line, Bridey's eyes moistened and then teared, and the facial muscles that no longer obeyed conscious commands creased in happiness. She gave a soft purr.

As his own eyes watered over, Riley knew that Bridey was seeing herself as a sixteen-year-old girl, in that brief period in 1924 before gunfire in a State Street floral shop changed her life forever. And she no doubt wondered whether Deanie, whom she expected to see presently, would approve of the many humanitarian uses to which his money had been put. Riley wondered that too. With each kindness bestowed by The Stoddard Trust, perhaps Deanie's debts to the men who had died at his hands were being slowly amortized. By the time of Bridey's arrival on the other side, his sentence might have been fully served, and the many benefactions he dispensed when alive would join with the charitable gifts his money had since made possible in such a way as to expiate his sins. It was a nice thought.

As the afternoon sun receded and shadows began to grow long across the plush carpeting of the room, the whole of Bridey's surviving offspring gathered to keep watch through the night. Stoddie's husband and three sons had arrived from Dubuque, her children falling in ages between Lizzie and Teddy.

The gathered loved ones were overcome with intermittent giddiness of the type that seems always to afflict the sleep-deprived. All that was grim or morbid had been denied entry to the room, as the remarkable woman who had surmounted all of life's heartaches prepared for her departure from this life. In time, her breath became shallow and infrequent and at 3:21 A.M., with her family joining hands around the bed, the woman who against all odds had stayed alive long enough to summon the child she had formed but had never known, inhaled a last short gasp.

"Have a nice trip, Mom," said Stoddie as tears poured down her cheeks.

On the other side of the bed, Betsy wrapped her arms around Riley's waist as he stood staring at the earthly remains of the woman he had been seeking his whole life, the corporeal reality behind Anastasia and Amelia Earhart and all the others to whom he, like the little bird in the children's story, had put the question: Are you my mother? The yawning, ineffable void into which he had poured so many fantasies, was at last filled.

THE SERVICE WAS PRIVATE, for family and close friends only. A local bishop, whose diocese had benefited richly from the generosity of The Stoddard Trust, said the Requiem High Mass at a picturesque river church some distance from Bridey's home parish in order to avoid unwanted crowds. The two security officers dressed in black, now joined by six others, stood along the perimeter of the church grounds, every now and then talking into their cuff links. The scene repeated itself at the cemetery high above the river bluff, where Bridey's mortal remains joined those of Axel and Reaves Gifford and those whose names had graced the passenger manifest of the famine ship from Ireland.

Back at the private airfield, the Stoddard jet sat regally on the east-west runway awaiting the arrival of the Trust's new chief executive officer. Riley's small white Honda was parked at the side of the hangar, awaiting return to Minneapolis by a Stoddard employee.

Ev Pederson said, "I'll meet you in Minneapolis on Wednesday and bring along the Trust's financial officers, but, in the meantime, do you have any instructions?"

Riley veered from the course set by Ev. He walked over to the Honda and opened its back door, signaling for Lizzie and Teddy to come over and climb in. He then looked over at Ev, and said, "Yeah, I've got an instruction. Get rid of the jet."

# 19

——————

D RIVING NORTH ACROSS the Iowa border, the highway
climbed up and through the mountainous formations
protecting the soft valleys and river basin below, and
then flattened as it headed northwest toward Rochester,
finally straightening and leveling for a monotonous approach
to the Twin Cities. In the back seat Teddy was angry that
they were not returning on the totally cool jet, and Lizzie
wondered aloud if, with her father's new job, she would be
able to get a car.

They fed Teddy at a Wendy's in Rochester and, thus anes-
thetized on a wave of sugar and cholesterol, he disappeared
sleepily into the headphones of his CD player.

Lizzie spoke uninhibitedly about whether they would have to
move, about how few good-looking boys she had seen on this
trip, and about how spooky it was to gaze into the eyes of that
pretty woman who looked just like her. She didn't use the word
"aunt" in reference to Stoddie, or "grandmother" in reference to
Bridey, because it was too unnatural. After all, she had an aunt
and a grandmother whom she loved dearly, women who had
fussed over her from the time she was a baby. The notion of dis-
possessing them of those semantic endearments, titles that

they had carried for the full sixteen years of her life, was down-right unsettling. But then the idea of referring to her blood relatives as "Bridey" and "Stoddie" seemed too impersonal to do justice to the bond that had so quickly formed between them. So, for the time being, they remained nameless. It would be some time before Lizzie McReynolds, beneficiary of a double portion of tribal love, would fully integrate the windfall of affection with which she was graced.

As for Riley, the flatlands between Rochester and Minneapolis had taken on a new beauty. Even the mini-warehouses and strip malls appeared stately and elegant. He was rapturously happy, and the whole world was returning his smile. While no memory existed for the few precious hours spent with his mother at the St. Louis Women's Hospital in 1946, surely there had been clues along the way—bits and pieces of overheard conversations by his parents, fragmentary references to his "specialness," references that had been put down to his being the youngest child in the family; and the sensation of being less like his siblings than they were to each other. But those clues had gone unacknowledged or quickly exiled to the unconscious. Just as surely the stored snatches of information had accumulated and broadcast the small, persistent intimations that, when imperfectly translated, sent him chasing after surrogates in the form of a downed aviatrix and a murdered grand duchess

The empty place in his heart, never consciously acknowledged but containing a small throbbing loneliness from the time he was a child, was now filled.

He looked over at Betsy, asleep with her head leaning against the passenger window, and thought that he too might now be able to converse with birds and squirrels and plants. The radical happiness of her life, so nearly within his reach but always incomplete, seemed to be settling in around him.

All his adult life he had resisted the abstruse mysticism of the romantic tradition. But in a crystalline moment in time, when Ellen Tanzdahl's love for her young son intersected with the celluloid images of a 1924 funeral in which a teenage girl looked up into a camera and summoned the child she had yet to conceive, he succumbed to its urgings and set out on a search for completion. Maybe they were right, those who say we exist in a time-space continuum; maybe the events of the last seventy-two years had unfolded simultaneously. Or, more likely, maybe we are equipped deep in our spirits with an instrument so exquisitely sensitive, so finely tuned that it finds its way, against all odds, to its natural moorings. It could be a form of intelligence, obscure and confusing at times, filled with detours and culs-de-sac, but when properly interpreted and obeyed contains a kind of loving infallibility. This was all too strange, too unknowable. He wouldn't even try to express it, not even to Betsy. In fact, he didn't want to think about it too much. It was as fine as tissue and as fleeting as a distant melody; it was an experience to be felt, not reasoned.

IT WAS NEARLY 4:00 P.M. when the Honda and its road-weary passengers pulled into the circular drive in front of the Loretta Heights Senior Residence, the home of Maureen McReynolds. His had been a childhood made nearly perfect by this woman to whom, it turned out, he bore no genetic relationship; this woman who had given of herself with a love so fierce that he had counted himself among the luckiest boys in the world. Luckier even than his sister and three brothers who seemed to attract a smaller measure of her devotion. It was into him that she had poured her love of literature and music and philosophy. It was she who had sat by his bedside around the clock, weeping softly as she kept vigil during periods of illness. And it was she who was cross with him when he neglected his potential or gave in to selfishness or indolence. She had even gracefully given him up to Betsy, whom she eventually came to view as an even greater blessing in his life than she had been.

Riley stopped the car before the front entrance. Betsy got out of the passenger side and opened the back door. She signaled for Lizzie and Teddy to join her so that Riley could park the car and meet them on the back patio. Lizzie groused a little as she pulled herself from the car, turning around to take a swat at Teddy as he pulled on her belt, nearly causing her to lose balance.

Teddy smiled in triumph as he scooted across the back seat and jumped from the car. Betsy gently but firmly pulled the earphones from around his head and tossed them and the CD player back into the car. She then brushed the hair from his eyes and tucked in his shirt.

Teddy looked up at the soaring façade of Loretta Heights and turned up his nose. He whined, "It smells like pee in this place, and everybody's all crunched up. I don't want to go see Grandma."

"She's not even your grandmother, you little dweeb," said Lizzie as she tried to adjust her belt.

"She is too!" snapped Teddy.

"Is not!" said Lizzie, throwing him a goofy, sneering look.

Now upset, Teddy looked back into the car at Riley. "She is too my grandma, isn't she, Dad?"

Riley looked at him sweetly. "Yes, she is your grandma, kiddo, and she always will be."

A soft breeze blew in his face as Riley rounded the corner from the lower parking lot to the ground-level patio of the home's east wing, past the large picture windows of the recreation area in which the crippled and decaying bodies of the oldest residents sat randomly among balloons, flower arrangements, and large colorful wall murals depicting storybook characters and historical figures. Many of these folks, no longer having access to their recent memories, had receded into the distant past and were living out their final months and years as arthritic children. Not so, though, with Maureen McReynolds. Her body had succumbed to more than eight decades of wear and tear but, with the exception

331

of occasional forgetfulness resulting from the small strokes from which she seemed to quickly recover, her mind was working well. Riley wanted her to live forever, this woman who had done so much to form his character. By an act of providence, he had been at the deathbed of one mother—the one he had never known but had loved all his life—and it would take a while to absorb the full implications of that experience before he could bear to lose another.

Maureen must have feared what was happening when she mounted such a determined case against his latest search. And when she lost that battle, and he kept at his dogged pursuit, she must have resigned herself to the outcome. For she alone among the McReynolds survivors knew Bridey's real identity and the fact that she was still alive.

From Bridey's residence in northern Iowa, Betsy had called her mother-in-law and spoken the words that Maureen had hoped she would never hear. Betsy knew how upset and afraid she was and wanted to be the first person Maureen saw on this of all days. She wanted to take a few moments to prepare her for the sight of the son who was no longer hers.

As he made his way up a small flight of outside stairs that rose to the open patio, Riley's hands trembled and his pulse began to race. When he stepped onto the patio, he looked over to the spot where they held their visits on sunny days. There he saw the small, precious collection of humanity, the four people in this world whose love he could not live without. Lizzie and Teddy sat quietly on their grandmother's right side, looking expectantly up at their father as he approached. Her eyes glistening, Betsy stood behind Maureen's wheelchair, her hands upon her mother-in-law's shoulders, forming a tight, supportive grip.

When she caught sight of Riley walking toward her, one of Maureen's hands went up to grasp Betsy's. Her lips began to tremble, and her eyes filled with tears. When Riley was still a few steps away, she raised her eyes to him and began to speak, pleadingly. "Your father made me promise. We didn't want you to know . . . after he was gone, I didn't want to lose you." She looked down at the Kleenex twisting in her hands and gave up a quiet sob. "She gave you to me. She gave you up. We knew all that money would come to you eventually, but I didn't want it to happen while I was still alive . . . I wanted to be your mother as long as I lived, so I held Bridey to her promise."

Teddy sat wide-eyed, confused, a little afraid. Everyone around him was crying. Lizzie, who adored her grandmother, was sobbing into her open hands, her shoulders heaving. Betsy stood gripping Maureen's hand.

Riley went down on one knee before his mother. He took hold of those bony and discolored hands and kissed them. He then turned his tear-stained face to hers, and with gratitude too large to be expressed, he just nodded.

# 20

_____

T HE NEXT DAY, at peak traffic hours, Riley snaked his
     way through residential neighborhoods in order to
     avoid the hundreds of angry drivers forming an ugly
karmic cloud each morning. He would rather be moving in
the wrong direction than standing still in the right one, and
this neighborhood route through town, though sometimes
frustrating, usually yielded new and inventive ways to get
from home to the office. But not today. The city engineers
were getting better at confounding people like him by setting
up one-ways and horseshoe configurations that sent him off
course time after time. But with the new peace that had settled over him, these minor irritations barely registered.

Freed of the surrounding stress—and after a short consul-
tation with a legal ethics professor—the thorny issue of Gus
Tanzdahl's misconduct in the divorce action had been resolved in his mind. In a stretch, Ladge's elaborate rationale
for withholding documents could be made to seem plausible,
and in that seeming plausibility lawyers of a flexible ethical
character might find a safe harbor. But not him. And, in any
case, he could not allow Cosgrove & Levi to sit on the sub-
poenaed documents without himself becoming an accomplice

to a fraud against the court. So, in spite of a career-long aversion to being an instrument of injury to any client, he would do what had to be done.

As he turned right into the parking lot, he noticed a truck backed up to the loading dock. A couple of movers were stacking boxes in its back end. It was 7:30 A.M., a full half hour before the office officially opened for business.

He punched in the code at the front door, passed through the lobby to the receptionist's desk, and grabbed a handful of pink message slips sitting in his slot. Flipping through the messages as he walked down the hall, he occasionally turned to steal a look into an open office where the early-birds could be found on most mornings. A light was on in Sara Hall's office, not unusual considering that she started most days around 6:30 A.M. Knowing his decision would be a blow to her chances for an early partnership, he briefly considered dodging her office. On reflection, though, he decided that he had an obligation to bring her up to date, to tell her of his decision to make full disclosure.

The usual array of high-watt lamps in Sara's small office spilled light out onto the hallway carpet. When he turned into the office, he saw that it had been stripped of everything except a bare desk, credenza, couch, and bookshelf. Gone were the wall paintings of which Sara was so proud and all the personal knickknacks normally spread across her credenza. Where the pictures had once hung were now only ghostly outlines.

He walked behind the desk, pushing the chair out of the way. The drawers of the desk were open, evidence of a hurried departure. A sense of loss washed over him at the realization that Sara was gone, somehow a casualty of the Tanzdahl controversy, probably a scapegoat for Gus's frustrations. He missed her already. They had gotten off to a rocky start, but he had come to admire her skills as a lawyer, to say nothing of her grit and persistence. He felt a little wounded that she had not told him of her plans.

He shifted his briefcase to his other hand and made for the door. As he approached the hallway his eyes fell upon a copy of Ladge Wilkaster's brief sitting on a small end table next to the couch. In the thick ink of the marking pen Sara was fond of using, her distinctive handwriting could be seen on the brief's cover, spelling out the words "Shameless Bullshit." A smile creased his face as he turned to the dog-eared pages at which she had apparently taken the greatest offense, the most prominent being Gus's sworn statement that he had made the handwritten notes on the compliance schedule after the stock transactions had been completed.

Riley stuffed the thick memorandum into his briefcase and continued down the hall to the double doors of the partners' conference room. When he entered the room, instead of the firm's special ethics committee, he found a room filled mostly with strangers, an odd lot of people led by the head of a public relations organization hired by law firms during times of crisis. Spinmeisters of all descriptions were working furiously with the firm's senior litigators in a hysterical damage control initiative. The ornate conference chamber was now a functioning war room.

At the end of the sprawling conference table was a Washington, D.C.-based image consultant who specialized in law firm meltdowns. He had built his reputation during the savings and loan debacle of the late 1980s, when the banking authorities went after several high-visibility law firms.

The centerpiece of his PR strategy in this case—as expensive as it was disorganized—was a series of press releases in which the firm rolled out that most tired of all industry clichés: its "Zero tolerance for misconduct." George Stonequist doubtless approved of its vacuous simplicity, but Riley knew that the public had long since come to view it as the functional equivalent of an admission of guilt, ranking close to an assertion of the Fifth Amendment.

The participants hardly looked up when Riley stepped into the room. He caught the eye of Vic Laslow, one of the senior

partners, who backed away from the conference table and
joined him at the front of the room. Riley looked at him and
asked, "What the hell's going on? Why all the fanfare?"

Vic gave an angry nod. "I can't believe you don't know. Sara
Hall, the loyal team player we assigned to keep an eye on
you, went to Judge Hammergren and reported that she had
uncovered an ongoing insider trading conspiracy involving
Gus Tanzdahl and Stenham Investment Company." He twisted his face in disgust. "She was kind enough to fax us a copy
of her report and the original of her resignation letter, both
of which were also sent to Clint Tarrymore."

Laslow reached into a pile of documents and fished out a
copy of Sara's letter. "You'll see that though she doesn't say
so specifically, between every line is a screaming inference
that the firm actively enabled the scheme at crucial points
and, in the end, tried to cover it up." Moving behind Riley, Vic
reached over and pointed to a paragraph in the letter. "You
can see here that Ladge Wilkaster was singled out as a likely aider and abettor. Can you believe that bitch!"

Riley looked up from the report and stared curiously into
Vic's face. "I didn't expect this, either, but I have no trouble
believing it. She obviously thinks that what she's written
here is true. She's a member of the bar, too, you know, with
her own set of professional obligations."

"Yeah," said Vic, "but as an associate she had the right to
rely on our interpretation of the facts and circumstances.
That brief we cranked up last week was more than sufficient
to cast doubt on the insider trading suspicion. She could have
kept her month shut."

"Only if she considered the firm's assessment to be at least
plausible, and obviously she didn't. Given her beliefs, she did
have to go to the tribunal—to Judge Hammergren." He gave
Laslow a sideways glance and shrugged. "I don't blame her a
bit."

Vic looked confused. "How can you of all people defend her?
She didn't even let you know what she was planning to do."

Riley shook his head resignedly. "She'd have gotten no resistance from me." He then turned and walked from the room.

Back in his office the message light on his phone panel was blinking. He punched the retrieval button and listened to the first two messages, responses from calls he had placed at the end of the previous week. The last of the messages had been recorded at 10:55 P.M. on Saturday, and it was from Sara, who must have assumed he would pick it up before coming in on Monday. Her voice, normally strong and steadfast, broke with emotion as she told of her decision and gave a concise statement of facts and relevant citations to the ethical rules by which she felt bound. Not surprisingly, her analysis of the issues focused heavily on the overly broad relationship between Tanzdahl Industries and Cosgrove & Levi, all of which she thought made this kind of ethical meltdown inevitable.

In Ladge Wilkaster's anxiety to tightly control Gus Tanzdahl and Tanzdahl Industries—for himself as a director and for the firm—he had become the architect of his own doom. A first-year associate would have known that such interlocking roles were like dry timber waiting for a spark. When Cosgrove & Levi took on representation of Tanzdahl in the divorce case, the spark was provided.

But it was less the words themselves than it was the texture of Sara's voice that revealed her true motivations. Almost from the beginning, it turned out, she had suffered over the manifest injustice of the strategy laid down by Ladge and Gus Tanzdahl. Her service of the unapproved change of custody documents on Clint Tarrymore—the ones that led to Ellen Tanzdahl's attack on Riley at the restaurant—had been ordered by Ladge Wilkaster, just as Riley had suspected. She apologized for her part in that deception and for any difficulty he might suffer as a result of her present actions. She closed by saying that she thought he would understand why she had to take the course of action she did.

He smiled and mumbled to himself, "Indeed I do." For all the admiration he had developed for Sara's persistence and legal intelligence, it was as nothing compared to how proud of her he was at that moment. The young woman he had misjudged during the initial stages of the case had turned out to possess a finer moral compass than he ever would have guessed. The feeling now breaking over him was one of protectiveness toward her, for she was sure to be blackballed among a large and influential segment of the legal community as a result of her actions, to say nothing of her prospects of ever again representing a large corporation. The early partnership she had coveted was now thoroughly beyond her reach.

Skeeter, who had arrived just as the message was being broadcast over the speaker phone, looked up from Riley's couch, where she had taken a seat. When the message ended, she winked at him and said, "I knew there was something about that babe I liked."

# Epilogue

---

S EPTEMBER 2, 1996. From the window of the thirty-second floor of the new executive offices of The Stoddard Trust, Riley could see groups of employees leaving the State Capitol in St. Paul. The Judicial Building, housing the Court of Appeals and Supreme Court, was also in full view. Tourists mingled with employees as they strolled in the warmth of a pleasant summer day.

So lost was he in a meditation about the mysteries of life that he didn't hear the new secretary enter his office until she placed an armful of reports in his in-basket. Skeeter, now installed as an executive vice-president in a corner office down the hall, had hired her as Riley's assistant.

He looked over and smiled, nodding self-consciously. When she left the office, he turned again to the view out his window. How different this work environment was from Cosgrove & Levi. At the law firm the air seemed always to crackle with stress and controversy. This space, in contrast, was nearly monastic. Sun streamed through the windows and spread itself across the plush offices and corridors like a blanket of tranquility. What few human sounds could be heard were muted—buffered by white noise. How deceiving it all was, for that small suite housed the decision-making power behind a real estate empire consisting of 73,000,000 square feet of "Class A" commercial space located throughout the United States. The whole operation was overseen by a select group of discrete and highly paid employees, most of who were now housed down the hall, close to Ev Pederson, who continued to run the day-to-day affairs of the Trust. Each property was owned by a separate, seemingly unconnected corporation, which was, in turn, part of a regional holding company. A deliberately twisted maze of intermediate entities ultimately upstreamed its net revenues to The Stoddard Trust, where most of the profits were distributed by the grant-making committee to a host of charitable causes.

Riley chuckled as he considered that Al Capone, no small philanthropist in his own right, might approve of the use to which the money pilfered by Dion O'Banion was being put. Maybe Deanie and Al had even put down their weapons and became pals again on the other side.

It is an axiom in the financial world that medical doctors are singularly inept at business, much as pitchers are assumed to be bad hitters. But in the case of Dr. Axel Gifford, late of northeastern Iowa, the perceived wisdom was gravely in error. Dr. Gifford had made it his life's work to protect and nourish the legacy that had been settled upon Anna McBride Reaves, the woman he loved. The contents of that tattered suitcase, lugged from one hiding place to another by a frightened young woman, contained the stake of what would become one of the most complex and profitable private business concerns in the United States. Axel Gifford—possessed of a first-rate business mind and an unquenchable love for the beautiful girl with the pale-blue eyes—had seen to that.

Riley's one regret was that Nancy Kunz and Tracy Ridgeway, two women he had come to adore, had not accepted his invitation to move to St. Paul and join him in the management of the Trust. Though each had agreed to serve in the grant-making side of the Trust—Nancy in the medical research division, and Tracy in the area of adult literacy—neither wished to come out of retirement and move to Minnesota. They knew nothing of each other, these two exceptional women whose lives had been so enriched by Bridey as she fled her pursuers through the years.

Bridey had fled their presence in 1937 and 1945 respectively, but she had not forgotten them. Trust historical records revealed that each had benefited during a crucial period of her life from gifts secretly initiated by Bridey—Nancy in the form of a fellowship in internal medicine, and Tracy through an educational grant in library science. Neither had known where the money originated.

With Gus Tanzdahl's indictment and imprisonment for insider trading, Tanzdahl Industries dropped its founder and former hero like a bad habit, in the process casting blame onto Cosgrove & Levi, from which the company withdrew all legal work. Under ordinary circumstances that loss would have resulted in the layoffs of roughly thirty lawyers and twice as many support personnel, but with the transfer of essentially all the legal business of The Stoddard Trust to the firm, Cosgrove & Levi actually grew in size and profitability.

Suspecting that Ladge Wilkaster had been less than ethical in his management of the Tanzdahl relationship, the firm's new management committee demanded his resignation along with that of Barney Bost. Ladge was much aggrieved by that decision and initially threatened to sue. His resentment ran especially high considering that he had "unselfishly" become the chief government witness against Gus Tanzdahl, the man to whom he had sworn undying fealty just weeks before. When threatened with indictment, old Ladge sang like a canary. It took two stenographers to get it all down.

Poor Gus never had a chance. The sight of him and Brad Stenham on the six o'clock news, doing the perp walk into the Federal Courthouse, sent scores of Tanzdahl employees into fits of merriment.

The press release announcing Ladge's departure from Cosgrove & Levi said that he was leaving the firm to spend more time with his family, a comically unsuitable explanation given that Ladge had no children and his marriage was being dissolved in a particularly rancorous divorce action.

George Stonequist took his book of business and collection of vintage Speedo swimwear to another firm, where he and his clients were warmly welcomed. Vic Laslow became the general counsel of Tanzdahl Industries and led the company in its decision to dump Cosgrove & Levi as its principal outside law firm. Given his long-standing adoration for Gus, Vic's sudden abandonment of the CEO-turned-jailbird was breathtaking in its audacity.

Ellen Tanzdahl, ably assisted by Clint Tarrymore, pressed ahead with her marriage dissolution with a confidence befitting her new self-image. She ultimately became the holder of one of the largest property awards in the state's history. She was granted nearly sixty percent of the marital assets—some $30,000,000 in overall value—leaving Gus with roughly $20,000,000 with which to pay his insider-trading fines.

Trudi Hansdale, the wealthy socialite to whom he was betrothed prior to his run of bad luck, broke off the engagement the day Gus's indictment was handed down.While behind bars, Gus took up Christian Fundamentalism with a vengeance and, upon his release, became an itinerant, if not altogether ethical, faith healer, drawing the scrutiny of attorneys general in six states.

In the reception area of the Stoddard Trust executive suite hung a large oil portrait by a distinguished Chicago artist. In it, a hauntingly beautiful young woman with dark hair and pale blue eyes stares wistfully out the window of a flower shop. In the background, a man with soft blond hair gazes adoringly at her as he prepares a display of flowers. They are both smiling.

— END —

# Acknowledgements

When an attorney takes up the pen for any purpose other than composing legal documents, it is a very uncertain business. Lawyerly conceit diminishes as the realization sets in that writing fiction is a lot harder than it looks. Those who get past the initial awkward and embarrassing failures are likely to succeed only in proportion to the support they receive from others. In my case, the support has been prodigious.

For the third time in my life, the University of Minnesota threw open its doors in welcome. The debt I owe that wonderful institution is beyond repayment, and the gratitude I feel is beyond words. This time around, it was the University's English and Creative Writing Departments that provided me with a learning environment and the very finest of instruction. There are few places in this world where an aging lawyer with a long-delayed ambition to communicate through fiction could be instructed and encouraged by the likes of Patricia Hampl and Garrison Keillor, to name just two of those who so generously shared their talents.

Also, at crucial times along the way, I received assistance and encouragement from a number of highly accomplished novelists and writers, including Judith Guest, the late Tom Gifford, Vince Flynn, Steve Thayer, Jim Olsen, and Matthew Tarses. I wish to offer special thanks to Jon Hassler for his example and assistance, but even more so for his friendship.

Warm thanks must also go, of course, to the persons outside the literary world who have played an important role in my second career, starting with my wife of thirty-five years, Anne (Tuny) Randolph O'Rourke, who gently pointed out the absurdity of much of what found its way into early drafts of this story and its predecessor. The same can be said of my son and daughters, who, though brimming with useful suggestions, could not bring themselves to critique their father's words with the loving frankness of their mother. And a special thanks to my father-in-law Harrison

Randolph, who since my earliest boyhood has been a shining example of decency, moral courage, and honorable manhood.

Thanks also to my colleagues in the law, with special gratitude to Mary and Paul Anderson, Pat Delaney, Jim Samples, Michael Lindsay, Tim Marrinan, and legal ethics specialist David Sasseville. And to those dear and admired colleagues who left too soon but whose memory accompanied me throughout the writing of this book—David Graven, Diane Moritz, Fred Rosenblatt, and Jerry Newsom. *Requiescat in pace.*

To Dr. John Coe, former chief medical examiner of Hennepin County (Minneapolis), whose service overlapped my time on the bench. To retired FBI agent Mike Goergen, a friend of long standing who enthusiastically and generously advised on both the forensic and investigative aspects of the story. And to Rhonda Gornick, who after years of transcribing dictation of FBI agents, was miraculously able to make sense of my verbal ramblings.

To my lifetime friend Peter Beck. And, in Chicago, a special thanks to my good friends Ron Magers and John Oelerich

And on the 100th anniversary of their birth year, I want to express gratitude to my parents, John Norbert and Mary Kathleen O'Rourke, now settled peacefully next to each other on a high hill overlooking the Minnesota River. Despite considerable evidence to the contrary, they believed their children were fundamentally perfect and blessed with talents that would allow them to do much good in this world. Neither one of them ever knowingly inflicted an unkindness on another human being, and for that I feel sure they are experiencing God's abundant mercy. Every boy should be so lucky.

Michael O'Rourke
Minneapolis, Minnesota
August 2003